Pr... P9-BZF-106

Kris Longknife
AUDACIOUS

" 'I'm a woman of very few words, but lots of action.' So said Mae West, but it might just as well have been Lieutenant Kris Longknife, princess of the one hundred worlds of Wardhaven. Kris can kick, shoot, and punch her way out of any dangerous situation, and she can do it while wearing stilettos and a tight cocktail dress. She's all business, with a Hells Angel handshake and a 'get out of my face' attitude. But her hair always looks good. *Audacious* maintains a crisp pace and lively banter . . . Kris Longknife is funny, and she entertains us." —*Sci Fi Weekly*

"The [fifth] book in this fast-paced, exciting military SF series continues the saga of a strong heroine who knows how to kick serious ass and make an impression on friends and enemies alike. Mike Shepherd has a great ear for dialogue and talent for injecting dry humor into things at just the right moment . . . The characters are engaging, and the plot is full of twists and peppered liberally with sharply described action. I always look forward to installments in the Kris Longknife series because I know I'm guaranteed a good time with plenty of adventure. *Audacious* doesn't disappoint in this regard. Military SF fans are bound to get a kick out of the series as a whole, and fans will be glad to see Kris hasn't lost any of her edge." —*SF Site*

"Mike Shepherd is a fantastic storyteller who excels at writing military science fiction. His protagonist is a strong-willed, independent thinker who does what she thinks is best for humanity . . . There is plenty of action and tension . . . This is a thoroughly enjoyable reading experience for science fiction fans."
—*Midwest Book Review*

continued . . .

Kris Longknife
INTREPID

Mike Shepherd

ACE BOOKS, NEW YORK

THE BERKLEY PUBLISHING GROUP
Published by the Penguin Group
Penguin Group (USA) Inc.
375 Hudson Street, New York, New York 10014, USA
Penguin Group (Canada), 90 Eglinton Avenue East, Suite 700, Toronto, Ontario M4P 2Y3, Canada
(a division of Pearson Penguin Canada Inc.)
Penguin Books Ltd., 80 Strand, London WC2R 0RL, England
Penguin Group Ireland, 25 St. Stephen's Green, Dublin 2, Ireland (a division of Penguin Books Ltd.)
Penguin Group (Australia), 250 Camberwell Road, Camberwell, Victoria 3124, Australia
(a division of Pearson Australia Group Pty. Ltd.)
Penguin Books India Pvt. Ltd., 11 Community Centre, Panchsheel Park, New Delhi—110 017, India
Penguin Group (NZ), 67 Apollo Drive, Rosedale, North Shore 0632, New Zealand
(a division of Pearson New Zealand Ltd.)
Penguin Books (South Africa) (Pty.) Ltd., 24 Sturdee Avenue, Rosebank, Johannesburg 2196,
South Africa

Penguin Books Ltd., Registered Offices: 80 Strand, London WC2R 0RL, England

This is a work of fiction. Names, characters, places, and incidents either are the product of the author's imagination or are used fictitiously, and any resemblance to actual persons, living or dead, business establishments, events, or locales is entirely coincidental. The publisher does not have any control over and does not assume any responsibility for author or third-party websites or their content.

KRIS LONGKNIFE: INTREPID

An Ace Book / published by arrangement with the author

PRINTING HISTORY
Ace mass-market edition / November 2008

Copyright © 2008 by Mike Moscoe.
Cover art by Scott Grimando.
Cover design by Judith Lagerman.
Interior text design by Kristin del Rosario.

ISBN: 978-0-441-01651-8

ACE
Ace Books are published by The Berkley Publishing Group,
a division of Penguin Group (USA) Inc.,
375 Hudson Street, New York, New York 10014.
ACE and the "A" design are trademarks belonging to Penguin Group (USA) Inc.

PRINTED IN THE UNITED STATES OF AMERICA

10 9 8 7 6 5 4 3 2 1

1

Lieutenant Kris Longknife had been looking for a fight for most of the last week. Strange enough, not only had the pirates she was hunting been lying low, but no one in all of human space had offered her the chance to cross swords, cross lasers, cross fire, or even toss a few cross words their way.

This had to be a first.

Kris finished zipping up her shipsuit and turned on Abby, her personal maid. For once, even she was beating a hasty retreat to her own quarters next door to Kris's.

Kris put an end to that. "We need to talk."

Any talk with Abby inevitably entailed cross words, often crossed knives, and, occasionally, cross fire.

Abby stopped in her tracks and, without bending her rigid spine even a fraction of an inch, glanced over her shoulder. "I've never known you to have problems getting a word out. What's been keeping you so quiet?"

"I'm not quiet," Kris shot back in her defense, and realized just as quickly that Abby was, once again, counterattacking before Kris even got her own attack decently under way.

"All while I was dressing you, Your Lieutenantship, Highness, and Longknifehood, you were silent as a statue."

Kris's repost sounded weak even to her. "Lost in thought."

"Well, when you find your way home, I'll be next door helping Cara with her schoolwork."

"She's doing very well," Nelly, Kris's personal computer, chimed in from where she rode on Kris's collar. The idea that Nelly, after her latest upgrades—worth a major chunk of the cost of the ship they were riding in—was spending a hunk of her capacity helping a twelve-year-old girl catch up on her school learning was not what Kris wanted to hear.

"Thank you, Nelly," Abby said.

"No thank you, Nelly. That is what we need to talk about. A warship is no place to raise a twelve-year-old girl."

"The *Wasp* is not a warship," Abby said with a sniff.

"Yes it is," Kris snapped right back, placing her hands on her hips. "The *Wasp* mounts twenty-four-inch pulse lasers and sports Smart Metal™ armor. And we are out here, past the rim of colonized space, trolling for pirates."

"That is no never mind," Abby said, her hands now on her hips. "I am the contracting rep. I initialed the contract and represent Wardhaven aboard the *Wasp*, and I know there is nothing in the contract of this merchant ship that makes it a warship."

"We've got a rump company of Marines."

"And a whole lot of scientists and their equipment on board. This ship is covered with shipping containers."

"We've got to look like a merchant ship if we're going to get a pirate to take a shot at us. Any smart pirate would just sail on by a warship," Kris said, voice rising.

"There you go, talking like one of those Longknifes," Abby snapped. "No wonder Admiral Crossenshield insisted I be his contract rep on the *Wasp*. And you better believe Captain Drago and half the crew breathed a sigh of relief when they found out you wouldn't be in their direct chain of command."

Kris started to point out that they were civilians, and whatever relationship they might have with a Navy lieutenant, it wouldn't be hooked to any chain of command. Certainly not any chain of command that a normal, sane Navy might have.

But Kris heard the creak of the door opening between her cabin and Abby's, and a dark-haired head with the hugest round eyes peeked in.

When Kris had first been introduced to Cara, she'd taken her for maybe eight, nine years old. The ship's food had been kind to the girl, but she still didn't look her full twelve years.

Except for those dark, limpid eyes . . . Eyes that had seen so much and lost so much more. Eyes so young should not have that much old in them.

"Are you arguing about me, Auntie Abby?"

"No, honeybunch. Aunt Abby has these little talks with the princess regularly."

"You're not going to lose your job, are you? We won't have

to leave the ship, will we?" Cara struggled to just say the words, but they trembled at the end.

"My Cara, you don't have to worry about that. Not one bit. The princess here can't fire me. Her momma hired me, and her momma's gonna have to fire me." Abby chuckled wickedly. "And this here princess wants to talk to her momma even less than you ever wanted to talk to Gamma Ganna."

If it was possible for hugest eyes to get bigger . . . they did. "Really?"

"Really. Trust me. Now you run along back and do some more of your schoolwork with Nelly."

"Nelly makes learning fun," Cara said, and closed the door.

"I make learning fun," Nelly said, with more glee than should ever exist in a computer's voice. "Wow."

Kris plopped down in her desk chair. It didn't have quite the effect she wanted. The *Wasp* was under an economical merchant acceleration of .85 gees. She kind of floated into the chair. Abby crossed the room to sit on Kris's narrow bed. Although Kris might be a major stockholder in Nuu Enterprises, the *Wasp* was a warship, and facilities were Spartan. Aboard the ship.

Now, the living conditions for the boffins were another thing. Professor mFumbo had taken it for granted that the containers were his to fill with scientific gadgets, quarters, separate recreation facilities for the fully tenured and the technical support. Same for the health club and spa.

Well, at least the Marines were making good use of the workout facilities. Good thing, with the ship doing a leisurely and muscle-weakening .85-gee cruise.

"Shall we finish this conversation . . . at a dull roar," Abby said, her voice just above a whisper. "I take it that you are not happy with the setup here."

"When Grampa Ray offered me the *Wasp*, it . . . it sounded like just what I'd dreamed of. A ship to explore the stars out beyond the rim of human space. A research team to study what we were looking at. A team of Marines and some twenty-four-inch pulse lasers in case we needed to do something about what we found. What more could a girl ask for?"

Abby chuckled dryly. "It might be nice if we were actually doing that."

Kris tried to chuckle, but the sound came out more as a snort. "Who'd have thought that while Earth and the rest of humanity were arguing over spreading out or hiding from any aliens by staying home, some Rim rats would just take off and do it all by themselves!"

The *Wasp*'s third jump had been into a system with an unreported colony. That had quickly led to the discovery of three more and rumors of a dozen others!

"When do you think that the king or your papa is gonna answer your report?" Abby asked.

Kris just shook her head. Starting up a colony cost money. Lots of it. Someone was making a mountain of unsecured loans to finance these new outposts of humanity. Someone was sponsoring the explorations that found habitable planets. That left a big question of who. And why!

Questions neither King/Grampa Ray nor Kris's father, the Prime Minister of Wardhaven, had answers for. And as if the "Sooners," as they called themselves, weren't enough of a problem, they'd attracted pirates.

Starting a year or two ago, about the time Earth and the Rim gave up on making a go of the Society of Humanity, the tramp merchant ships that made irregular calls among the Sooners started disappearing. Two in just the last three months.

As much as the Sooners did not want to see a uniformed naval officer from Wardhaven . . . and a Longknife to boot . . . they were almost happy to see the *Wasp* and hoped that someone with the authority of the law was finally taking an interest in them.

Kris fidgeted. It was nice finally to be appreciated by someone, even if it was the Sooners, who shouldn't have been where they were. But it left her with a bunch of unhappy scientists whose exploration was on hold. And a crew waiting, waiting, waiting for the pirates to make their move.

"What's eating you, woman?" Abby demanded.

"Nothing," Kris insisted, then noticed that her right foot was tapping out a rapid tattoo. She froze it in place. Now her stomach wanted to spin.

"Don't you go lying to me, boss. I'm Abby. I know you, baby ducks." Her maid eyed Kris sideways. "You got your panties in a twist because those pirates won't come out and play with you."

"No," Kris insisted.

"What's it been, one, two months since someone took a pot-shot at you? Since you blew away some very deserving rats?"

"Something like that," Kris admitted, lamely.

"Kris, I think you're starting to enjoy all that fuss and feathers."

Kris had been warned by those who should know, experienced cops, old Gunny Sergeants, that the rush could become as addictive as any drug. Was she hooked on being not quite killed? On doing the killing? She swallowed hard on the thought.

Abby shook her head. "Woman, get your head on straight. You got nothing to worry about on the *Wasp*. Don't you think we can recognize those silly-ass games your great-grampa plays that he thinks will keep you safe? Yep, he made me COR, but when hell's a popping, Captain Drago's going to be looking your way for orders. 'Cause you'll be there, at his elbow. And me? I'm gonna be under the bed holding Cara safe."

That forced a laugh from Kris. Despite Abby's constant claims to being a twice-baptized and very devout coward, Kris would more than likely be trailing Abby into the shoot-out.

"Now, if you don't mind, I've got to help a little girl catch up on a whole lot of schooling. I don't know what they were doing in those Eden schools, but it wasn't teaching."

"Worse than when you were in those schools?" Kris asked.

Abby just snorted. "And you thank Nelly for me. She's a real good teacher."

I AM A REAL GOOD TEACHER, Nelly chortled in Kris's head.

YES, YOU ARE A REAL GOOD TEACHER, Kris agreed.

AND YOU SHOULD CHILL OUT.

GO TEACH THE LITTLE GIRL. YOU ARE NOT MY SHRINK, Kris snapped. Maybe it was time to quit upgrading Nelly every time something new came along. It seemed that every new addition to Nelly, no matter what it was supposed to do, just gave her more of an attitude.

I HEARD THAT. AND IT'S 'TUDE. THAT IS WHAT CARA CALLS IT.

Oh Lord, now my computer has a real live teenage girl to show her the ropes. What have I done to myself?

Kris headed for the bridge. At least she'd get some respect there.

2

Kris didn't make it halfway to the bridge before Professor mFumbo waylaid her.

"When are we going to do some science?" he demanded in a deep bass voice that almost made the bulkheads vibrate.

"I understand that pirates have this tendency to kill or enslave the crews of the ships they capture," Kris said as matter-of-factly as she could. "Read it in the papers. Grampa Trouble says he even crossed paths with pirates once. Ended up one of their slaves."

"I believe it happened twice," mFumbo said, scratching his chin. "One really must wonder how smart someone is who made that mistake twice," he said, ambiguously, then smiled and moved to clarify his remarks. "I should have thought that any educatable man would learn quickly that Marines do not good slaves make."

Kris allowed a smile only when he finally got around to saying just who was lacking in smarts. "So you can see how I might put a higher priority on killing pirates even if I must leave some of the secrets of the universe to wait a bit longer."

"Regrettable. Very regrettable."

Kris managed to get three paces closer to the bridge, but the professor stayed right in step with her. "Ever wondered why we didn't spot these fuzzy jump points before?"

He raised an eyebrow as Kris came to a halt.

"I have been kind of curious," Kris admitted.

"I have been very curious," Nelly said.

"I should expect you to be, Miss Nelly," mFumbo said, with a slight bow toward Kris's neck where Nelly rode. More of a bow than he'd ever afforded Kris's princess status.

"It seems that it was only five years ago that all our work

with the alien technology on Santa Maria finally paid off with an improved atom laser."

"I hadn't heard that we cracked any of their technology," Kris said.

"We didn't actually. It was something we discovered ourselves while trying to unlock something of theirs. Anyway, we discovered different harmonics in gravity waves and a way to sense them with a tuned atom laser. It should lower the cost of atom lasers in time, but right now, they're horribly expensive."

"But the *Resolute* just happened to have one," Kris said slowly, wondering just who had been jobbing whom out at Chance.

"Yes. Interesting, that," mFumbo said.

"So if we had fired up the *Patton*'s atom laser," Kris said, a smile growing, "we would not have found the fuzzy jump points."

"It was an old Iteeche war-era cruiser," he said, shaking his head. "No, not likely."

SO I WAS WRONG. YOU WERE RIGHT. SUE ME, Nelly shot back to Kris alone. Where had that come from? What had Kris set herself up for when she let one little twelve-year-old slip of a girl on board? That girl had to go.

YOU WILL NOT SHIP HER OFF THE *WASP*. CARA IS MY FRIEND. CARA IS GOING TO STAY HERE AS LONG AS I DO.

And was that a threat? Kris thought, careful to keep it to herself.

But before Kris could say anything, Professor mFumbo apparently mistook the silence between them to mean he was free to go on to a different subject, "We've found out something interesting about these fuzzy jump points."

"Yes," Kris said. "What?" Nelly demanded.

"They don't wander as much as the other ones do. Something about their harmonic nature allows them to stay closer to a single point. Either that, or the fuzziness around them helps us follow them more easily."

"That should cut down on bad jumps," Kris said.

"Very likely."

"So what are we going to find behind these jump points? New territory opened up toward the end of the Three's time," Nelly said pensively, "or the center of their civilization, held together by the latest jump-point technology?"

"A very good question that I can do nothing to answer while the princess here is busy chasing miscreants. Or maybe I can."

"Or maybe you can?" Kris asked, wondering what sort of trap the professor had set for her.

"Since the jump points are more steady, we think we can send an automated probe to do an initial look behind them. You know there is a fuzzy jump point in this system?"

Kris admitted that she did.

"If we could send a remote probe to check out the other system, we could have it waiting here for us when we return and maybe save ourselves some wasted time."

"But merchant ships don't launch probes. If a pirate ship enters a system and sees us and a probe in it, it will be a dead give-away that we aren't what we're trying to appear."

"Yes, but if you held off launching the probe until just before we jump out of this system . . ."

"And since you've already readied the probe?"

"Yes, there is that matter," the professor admitted, his hands open, palms up, in polite supplication to Kris.

"I'll tell Captain Drago that you want to launch a probe," Kris said.

"Thank you very much," Professor mFumbo said, and headed in the opposite direction from Kris.

Kris watched his retreating back. New technologies. Not so much our cracking the secrets of the Three alien cultures that built the jump points, as our discovering this or that on our own as we bounced our heads off the lockbox of their still-unfathomable knowledge.

Well, humans learned many ways.

No, human scientists learned. Others, like pirates, might upgrade their equipment. But the pirates Kris hunted weren't all that different from the cutthroats the Romans put down in the ancient Mediterranean Sea.

"Two minutes to zero gravity," the *Wasp*'s MC-1 announced as Kris entered the bridge.

"Morning, Lieutenant," Captain Drago said.

"Morning, Captain, any unknowns in system?"

"The answer is the same as it's been the last two days. No, ma'am, though of course a hostile could have entered the system from the other jump point an hour ago, but we'll be another half hour finding out."

Kris repeated the old joke. "Captain, you really should do something about that speed-of-light lag time."

Drago gave the same answer. "Isn't that a more proper job for those unemployed boffins of yours rather than this only slightly reformed pirate?" And it was true that the bridge crew of the *Wasp* did look more like pirates than respectable sailors. From the captain's purple coat, gold earring, and white bell bottoms to his navigator in cutoff shorts and tank top, the crew appeared delightfully reprobate.

And the *Wasp* had started life as a pirate ship. She now smelled much better. The crew might be flamboyant, but hygiene was a daily concern. And being the best former sailors Wardhaven's spy master had ever contracted for, they knew their job backward and forward.

Especially the twenty-four-inch pulse lasers the *Wasp* didn't officially have.

"Ah, Professor mFumbo tells me the project is impossible. Something about relativity. Oh, speaking of the good doctor, he has a probe he wants to launch."

"So he told me," the captain said. "I told him if it was okay with you, it was okay with me."

"Hm," Kris said. "I told him about the same thing, but I don't remember him mentioning you."

"He must have been an impossible child to parent," Sulwan Kann muttered from her place at the navigator's station.

"That assumes he had parents, a fact not in evidence," the captain muttered.

"Is there any problem with launching this probe of his just before we jump?" Kris said, trying to stay on topic. Despite the professor's approach to getting their okay, if it was safe, the scientists deserved some research.

Captain Drago nodded. "I've had my crew check out the probe. Separation should be no problem. It won't get under way until we are far from here. We'll do it."

"Weightlessness in ten seconds," Sulwan announced. Kris scrambled for her station to the far left of the captain, where she could keep an eye on offensive weapons and sensors.

At zero, the *Wasp* cut all power and did a flip to put the bridge head on as it drifted to a halt a thousand meters from where the jump point roiled in tortured space. To the naked eye, nothing was apparent, just a small section of space where the stars seemed to shine a bit strangely.

"Sulwan, you got the nav beacon loaded?"

"It's in Drop Bay 3. The scientists' gadget is in 4."

Kris didn't ask about Drop Bays 1 and 2. If Jack was half the Marine she expected him to be, two Marine assault crafts were standing by. Fully manned and ready . . . and armed.

"Launch the beacon," Captain Drago ordered.

There was a slight rumble through the hull, and then the nav buoy came in view on its way to the jump point. Bigger, blockier than a government beacon, this one looked like fifty-year-old technology. Just what a merchant skipper might use to probe a strange jump point and not damage a slim profit margin.

The jump buoy held station off the jump point for a few moments while a few more tests were run, then powered up and disappeared through the jump. Sulwan started a clock. At two minutes she'd take the *Wasp* through after the buoy had announced to anyone listening that they were coming through.

In nearly four hundred years, there had only been one instance of two ships using the same jump point at the same time, coming from opposite directions. The resulting mess had cured humanity of ever wanting to do that again.

Inside human space, every jump point had two buoys assigned to it. Out here, Kris and Captain Drago were improvising as they went along.

"Ten seconds until we jump" Sulwan announced.

And the jump buoy reappeared before them. "A ship will be coming through the jump in fifteen seconds," it announced.

"That wasn't the message I put on the buoy," Sulwan said.

"Nav, reverse thrusters. Maximum power."

"Reverse. Maximum. Captain," Sulwan answered, jamming the reverse thrusters knob all the way back.

"Nav, steer right fifteen degrees, down thirty degrees."

"Right fifteen. Down thirty degrees, aye, Captain."

And Kris's inner ear started doing slow rolls as her gut was slammed hard against the buckle of her seat belt. The *Wasp* shed all forward momentum and took off backward. But even as her body went through the required contortions, Kris kept her eyes on the forward view port. The screen stayed blank for the longest time.

Then a ship twice the size of the *Wasp* materialized as if from out of nowhere to loom over them.

3

"Engineering, give us everything you've got for reverse," Drago said into his commlink. "Nav, keep us backing, but do not reverse ship. I will not give them a shot at my engines."

"Aye sir. Get out of here but protect the engines."

While Captain Drago handled his ship, Kris eyed the other. On-screen, it looked like a medium-size merchant. A bit big for a tramp freighter, doing catch-as-catch-can business between the small ports on the Rim and beyond. Still, its long, central spine was loaded with containers. Forward, it broadened into a bridge and housing arrangement for the crew. Amidships was a disk containing whatever cargo didn't do well in vacuum, and possibly some passengers. That was where the *Wasp* had its twenty-four-inch pulse lasers. Aft were the engineering spaces, a rectangle for the fusion reactor, plumbing for the magnetohydrodynamics generators, and huge bell-shaped plasma engines.

"Sensors, is that a single reactor?" Kris asked Chief Beni, her own man, who was running that station just now.

"Looks that way, ma'am," he muttered, then did something to his board. "But I'm still looking."

Kris slaved her board to his. Beni might be leadership challenged on liberty, but with anything electronic he was a wizard. Just now, he used only passives, listening but making no noise that would tip a pirate's hand that the *Wasp* was anything but a soft, defenseless carrier of wood and drawer of water.

Then again, a pirate would be doing its own best to look as innocent as a lamb . . . and hide the wolf within. At the moment, they were even in the lamb department. Or one might actually be what it claimed.

"Hmm, ain't she a mite bit underpowered with a single

Westinghouse 1500 series reactor?" Chief Beni mused to himself, and jacked up the gain on a couple of his short-range sensors. "Seems like there's a whole lot more neutrinos coming out of that single reactor . . . and they're spread out over a whole lot more space. Those engineering spaces looked a bit luxurious for just one teapot. Skipper, I make two Westinghouse reactors. And expect they're 2200 series at that. You got a wolf trying to fake it in woolies."

"Damn," Captain Drago said.

"Straight," Kris added.

"Your orders, Your Highness."

So King Ray didn't know these people nearly as well as Kris did. And this bunch had no problem following *this* Longknife into the mouth of hell. In a fast countdown to a fight, Drago wasn't looking to Abby, he was asking Kris.

She swallowed the first thing that came to mind . . . *Let's kick some pirate butt.* Instead, Kris muttered a much more sedate, "Let's make sure someone like Helvetia isn't also trolling for pirates. Wouldn't want Grampa Ray faced with a media blitz 'cause two good guys shot each other up."

Someone on the bridge snickered at Kris's familiarity with a man everyone else knew as King Raymond of the United Sentients.

And somewhere on net came a "Damn, one of those Longknifes *can* grow up." It sounded familiar."

"That you, Jack?" Kris asked Captain Jack Montoya of the Royal United Sentient Marine Corps, who now commanded the rump company aboard.

"Not me, ma'am, not a chance. Though I do admit sympathy for the conclusion."

Further discussion was suspended as the ship looming over them opened communication channels. "Hello, stranger, this is *Compton Maru* out of Orama. What ship are you and where you from? Where you bound?"

Captain Drago took the commlink. "This is the *Lucky Seven Horse* out of Hampton, and I'll tell you where I'm bound when you tell me where you been."

That elicited a laugh, much as Kris expected. Profits were razor thin out here and a good way to go broke was to follow in the wake of another ship, trying to sell your cargo in an already satisfied market or buy up cargo that had already been shipped.

Kris might be Navy and Drago . . . whatever he was . . . but they'd spent enough time in bars among merchant captains to learn that much of the trade.

The laughing voice became serious. "You tell me something interesting, then I'll tell you something more interesting."

"Sounds fair," Drago said. "Our last stop was Magda's Hideaway." It really had been. "They took all our agricultural implements and were still hungry. They didn't touch our heavy machinery. Somebody got there first."

"That little burg ain't growing anywhere near as fast as its founding fathers thought it would. If they ain't careful, they're going to get overextended on their loans," the voice from the larger freighter observed.

Kris let them ramble, and took the ship above her apart layer by layer—as much as passive sensors allowed. If the ship had lasers, no capacitors were charged. Dead in space, the ship was no longer running plasma through its engines. Its only power source was a trickle off the racetrack of hot plasma. That kept the ship's main battery charged.

"Could you power a laser directly from the main storage battery?" Kris asked the chief.

"You shouldn't be able to, ma'am," was the answer she expected. "Power cables aren't designed for that surge. However, a small three-incher might dribble something out. Couldn't pierce much ice armor, but then, we're just a thin-skinned merchie," he said, with a wicked grin.

A knife might not be much, but in a fistfight, it could run the table. But a guy pulling a knife in a gunfight was in for a surprise. A big one.

"Where you been?" Captain Drago asked.

"We're just coming back from Xanadu," the other claimed.

"Trying to trade among those crazies?" Drago asked.

They'd already learned about Xanadu, the supposed home of the Abdicators. They were a bunch of nuts who insisted all humanity had to go back to Earth and hide from the coming alien hordes that would wipe us out. They'd been noisy forty years ago, then had gotten kind of few and quiet. Kris now knew why.

By some twisted logic, the leader of the Abdicators had moved all his followers far out beyond the Rim. Supposedly to hide. Considering how insanely crazy their beliefs had been before, Kris was none too sure she wanted to know what they'd become out on their own for half a century.

"They may be crazy, but they have money. They bought everything I had. I'm hauling my containers home empty except for some with wines and proto-pharms they sold me. If you got the range, they're a good place to drop by. Where you headed?"

But whoever was doing the talking over there must have figured he'd done enough babbling to distract the captain of the *Lucky Seven Horse*.

On Kris's board, a capacitor appeared, going from green to yellow to red as it sucked power from the ship's main battery.

"Evade," Kris shouted, but Nelly had already activated a jinks pattern in the helm. The *Wasp* danced left, right, up, down, and a feeble three-inch laser burned empty space.

"What the hell," came from the other ship on an open mike, then it went dead.

A red wash in the engineering spaces showed both reactors on the other ship coming to full life, overpowering whatever cover they had been hiding behind. The pirate ship shot away from the jump point, following a twisting course that danced its engines in and out of a direct shot from the *Wasp*.

A half dozen laser capacitors went from not there to yellow to red as they sucked up a charge.

Then the sensor board got hazy.

"They're trying to jam," Beni observed, did something to his board, and some of the jamming went away.

"Shields," was Kris's next order.

And she hated herself for it.

A slight bulge on the nose of the *Wasp* hid one of her two innovations. On order, Smart Metal™ deployed like a huge umbrella, rotating as it went. It both hid the ship behind it and provided a defense against lasers.

During drills, Kris had first ordered, "Raise. Metal," or "Raise. Defenses." Someone on the back of the bridge had whispered, "Shields. Up," quoting from a long-running space opera. The bridge crew had a good laugh, but from then on, no matter what order Kris gave, the answer from Defensive Systems was always, "Shields. Up."

"Shields. Up," now answered Kris. No one laughed.

"Keep backing ship," Captain Drago ordered. "Guns, let me know when you're fully charged."

That was the *Wasp*'s other secret. For three hundred years fusion reactors had produced the plasma that rocket motors streamed out to move the ship. That plasma, on its way to the engines, passed through magnetohydrodynamic coils that generated electricity for the ship and its weapons.

The *Compton Maru* had gotten under way, exposing its vulnerable engines because otherwise it couldn't charge its lasers.

The *Wasp* backed up, using only its maneuvering engines. By all rights, it couldn't charge its pulse lasers off that dribble of plasma. But on Kris's board, the four laser capacitors were rapidly moving from green to yellow, headed for full red. Thanks to new science and a recent refit, the *Wasp* stripped electricity directly from the plasma flux in the reactor.

The times they were a changing. And this pirate was about to find out.

Then Kris got her own surprise. The *Compton Maru* sprouted a shielding umbrella from its own bow. This one had a leaping tiger on it. Its jaws agape, its claws dripping blood.

"Aggressive type, aren't they," Sulwan observed.

"Let's see if they can walk the walk," Kris said, mashing her commlink. "Ahoy, *Compton Maru*. This is the USS *Wasp*, and I am Lieutenant Longknife, Wardhaven Navy. You just fired upon me. Dump your core and prepare to be boarded."

"You can go to hell," shot back in reply, but in the background there was a startled cry of "Not a Longknife." Followed by "Shut up."

The two ships circled each other. Captain Drago kept the *Wasp* pivoting on its long axis, nose always to the *Compton*. The pirate, for her part, did her best to open the range while keeping her engines covered.

The range was point-blank. Hand grenades in a broom closet.

But the *Wasp* stood between the jump point and the pirate, giving the latter only lousy choices. She could turn and run for the jump point across the system, giving Kris an easy up-the-kilt shot at her reactors. Or charge the *Wasp*, hoping to slip past her into the jump point. Or fight it out.

"The hostile's lasers are fully charged," Chief Beni said.

"Any idea how strong they are?" Captain Drago asked.

"I'd guess five-inchers. And weak for that," the chief said.

"Your Highness, what are your orders?"

Kris thought about that for all of a second. "He's not getting away from us, Captain. If he wants to dance, we dance, but he can't run."

"Yes, ma'am. Weapons are online. They are yours, ma'am."

The exact nature of the *Wasp*'s registry might be subject to debate. What Captain Drago and Kris had quickly agreed upon was her weapons policy. Laying aim and closing the firing circuits would be done by a serving Wardhaven officer. One must respect international law . . . even if it was with a wink and a smile.

Lieutenant Kris Longknife, Wardhaven Navy, aimed Battery 1 for the tiger's mouth. It was about the right distance out from the bow's center to have the bridge behind it. Of course, if they were rotating their ship behind the shield, like Captain Drago was rotating the *Wasp*, burn through on the shield might hit anything—or nothing.

"Pirate ship *Compton*, this is your one and only warning. Dump your reactor, or I will fire on you," Kris said, voice cold with death.

Silence answered her.

"Prepare to change jinks pattern," Kris announced. "All hands, prepare for radical evasion."

On the bridge, people cinched in already tight seat belts. "For what they are about to receive, may we be truly grateful," some wag muttered.

"Pirate ship *Compton*, I will fire on you at the count of three," Kris said into her commlink.

Obscenities were her only reply.

"One," Kris said. NELLY GET READY TO IMPLEMENT RADICAL EVASION ON MY MARK.

READY, KRIS.

"Two." MARK!

The *Wasp* shifted from a soft right climb to a hard left drop that left Kris's stomach somewhere a dozen kilometers away in the cold vacuum of space.

Where it was being fried by three laser beams from the hostile.

"Fire One," Kris said as she closed the firing circuit for the first of *Wasp*'s pulse lasers.

The mouth of the tiger glowed, then fumed, and finally gaped as the *Wasp*'s laser burned through the shield. To the void behind it. Yep, the ship was rotating.

And now it also started to jinks.

NELLY, EVALUATE THE EVASION PATTERN.

IT IS A BASIC ONE. I AM ALREADY FORECASTING IT.

Kris aimed her second laser for opposite the ragged hole in the shield that was already healing itself, blocking out the view of what lay behind it, ship or void.

At the last second, Kris played a hunch, changing her aim to the right paw of the tiger and firing.

The paint boiled off in a nanosecond, leaving the shield to burn and buckle. Thinner now from the loss of metal to Kris's hit and the effort to patch it, burn-through came quicker.

And raked the ship hull behind it before Laser 2 winked out.

"*Compton*, you are hit, and your shields are failing. Dump your reactor, and we will board and offer assistance," Kris said.

"Never," was the one-word reply.

And six lasers reached out for the *Wasp* from the wounded pirate. They were not so strong as Kris's ship's twenty-four-inch pulse lasers, but at this range, a hit by anything could slice the *Wasp* in half.

The ship jinked away from four of them. The fifth one spent itself on the shield, boiling off a few kilos of Smart Metal™.

The sixth one raked *Wasp* aft of amidships but missed engineering. At least the lights did not dim, nor did the reload light on Battery 1 slow its rapid climb from yellow toward red.

"Damage Control," Captain Drago demanded.

"Containers open to space. We're working on them."

Captain Drago turned to Kris. "Can you get this over with? I like my ship the way it is, not holier than thou," he said dryly.

"Firing Three," Kris said. She had Nelly widen the focus of the twenty-four-inch laser, raking a major portion of the shield. Damaged, it was now too thin to do much more than hide the bow of the pirate, providing a fan to cover the bare rear of the bridge.

As 3 winked out, all pretense at a shield vanished. The pirate spun on its long axis in full view. But not giving up.

Its capacitors began to recharge. A thin wisp coalesced to cover the bow. The tiger was back, a raised paw, the middle finger elevated in the universally recognized insolent salute.

"Some folks just don't know when to quit," Kris said.

"Leave us alone," boomed from the commlink. "You get out of here, or a lot of people are going to die."

"You're going to die," Kris pointed out.

"We got the crew of two ships on board. You shoot at us again, and we'll see just how much vacuum they can breathe."

"Oops," Kris and Captain Drago said at the same time.

"Kris," Nelly said, "unless they've changed their rotation, I know where the bridge is."

"Target it." A red pipper began to circle the flimsy shield. Not, to Kris's surprise, focusing on the raised digit but somewhere around its toes.

The longer Kris waited, the more the chance that they might change their rotation. Kris mashed Battery 4's firing circuit.

The laser slashed through the spinning cover. Sections spun off into space. There, revealed for all, was the bridge.

But only for a fraction of a second as the twenty-four-inch laser opened it to space, slagging human flesh, instruments, and gear.

"Surrender now or my next laser will hack your reactors' containment fields to bits," Kris ordered to anyone who might still be listening.

"What about their prisoners?" Sulwan asked.

"We have only their word that they have them," Kris said, keeping hard eyes on their target.

"You're a hard woman," Drago said. "I hope you're right."

So did Kris.

Then the cores of the two reactors dropped out into vacuum, and the *Compton* began to coast along its last vector.

"We surrender. You can board us. We won't fight you," was spoken by a new voice.

"I hope for your sake you don't," Kris answered. "We've got a Marine company that could use a spot of exercise."

That got no reply.

"Captain Montoya," Kris called to Jack.

"Standing by," he answered.

"Prepare to board the pirate as soon as we come alongside and match their speed and vector."

"Aye, aye, ma'am."

"Captain Drago, please place your ship alongside that derelict."

"Yes, ma'am."

"Hot dog. More prize money," came from the wag in the back of the bridge.

4

It took a half hour for the *Wasp* to catch up and come along-side the pirate. Once there, Jack launched two Marine squads in LACs. One team would capture the stern, the other the bow. Most of the Marines would storm the amidships gangway.

At least that was the plan.

As Drago completed a perfect match between midship hatches, Kris kicked off from her station, snagged the hatch, and launched herself aft to join the Marines of the boarding party.

And ran into Abby, towing a full set of combat gear.

"Thought you might need these. Just the things for the well-dressed princess," her maid drawled.

"Isn't there a bed you need to be under?"

"Got bored there by myself."

"Where's Cara?"

"At the computer, playing some silly game."

Kris tried one other tack to duck her mothering maid. "Didn't you hear? They surrendered."

"Yeah, right," Abby said, and blocked Kris's path aft until she did her own surrender and accepted the first armored piece of what constituted full battle rattle.

"You're not very trusting," Kris said, pulling on the bottom.

"Not at all. Unlike some princess I know, I learn from bad experiences." So Kris pulled on full armor while others stretched a tunnel between the *Wasp* and the now-quiet pirate. That could have provided a route for a full assault, but the pirate's main lock refused to open. Kris arrived just as Jack to her, Captain Montoya to his company, concluded his assessment of the situation.

"Strange how nothing much seems to work on the *Compton*. If I weren't such an optimistic guy, I'd think they were setting a trap for us," Jack said. "Gunny, you got an opinion?"

"Pirates are not known for their adherence to preventive maintenance schedules," he growled. "It could be just what you'd expect from scumbags, sir."

"So true. Okay, crew, let's get some of the stress and suspense out of our lives. LACs, I want you to seize positions on the forward and aft parts of the ship while we storm the center. We go in sixty seconds."

"Ah, sir, Staff Sergeant Thu here. Regretfully, LAC One will have to disappoint."

"What's your problem?"

"We've been checking out both the entrance points forward. One was onto the bridge and has a very big hole punched in it by somebody's misaimed laser."

"Careful, Sergeant, said aimer is drifting at my elbow."

"And it was perfectly aimed at the time it was fired," Kris shouted toward Jack's mike.

"Well, sirs, whatever it was then, it's ruining my day just now. 'Course, to be honest, even if the hatch opened, it would only take me onto the bridge, and I could walk in there, hatch or no hatch. It's the lower emergency air lock that is the main problem. The inner door is wedged open. We open it, and we could be blowing out all the air forward."

"So we go to version two of today's orders," Jack said, betraying the informality he'd gained as a Secret Service Agent, trying to protect one Princess Kristine Longknife. "Both LACs will enter by the stern, and we'll take the bow after we secure amidships. LAC Two, what's your situation?"

"We are ready now, sir."

"We start in sixty seconds."

The *Wasp*'s huge amidships cargo bay that Kris and the Marines occupied had already been sealed off. Now a squad of Marines headed into the open tube to take up positions just outside the *Compton*'s hatch. Jack led two more squads down the rabbit hole, but Kris found Gunny and Abby blocking her way.

"I think we ought to wait here, Your Highness. It's getting mighty stuffy in there," Gunny said.

The Marines who had gone with Jack were in fully armored space suits, their faceplates down, breathing tanked air. But Kris had learned not to argue with Gunny. At OCS, an old commander had told the class that the proper spelling of Gunnery Sergeant was *G O D*.

Kris had seen ample proof to support that theology in the last three years. Kris waited.

"We're in," Jack announced over the net.

A moment later a private had been ordered to test the air. "This place stinks," was his only comment.

Kris's previous experience with a pirate ship had stunk of sloppy ship handling, stale cooking, and unwashed crew. But the stink that rapidly worked its way up the passage tube was a whole different blend of filth, sewer, and death.

Kris kicked off from where she hung and headed down the tube, Abby and Gunny right behind.

The stench grew as she approached the *Compton*'s hatch. Once through it, she found herself in a similar cargo bay from the one she left, somewhat the worse for lack of care. Jack and his three squads held there as they searched for booby traps and found nothing. Most had their masks up, saving tanks that might be needed later. A few did not.

"Where's that smell coming from?" Kris asked.

Jack shook his head. "Life support is on minimum. Air circulation is hardly going, but still, this?"

"How are things aft?" Kris asked.

"We took them down," came from a sergeant on net. "Only gentle lambs back here. They have no idea what the bridge crew were doing, they just tended the teakettle."

"We'll see how that holds up in court," Kris said dryly.

Jack looked around, frowned at nothing in particular and the stink in general, and said, "Gunny, take two squads and clear the stern spine from here to Engineering."

"Aye, aye, sir," Gunny said, and organized one of the squads there and the one that had just arrived to deploy aft, covering for each other and moving slowly.

He'd been gone less than a minute when he came up on net. "Sir, Your Highness, you want to see what we just found."

Kris headed aft, gun at the ready, Jack in the lead.

The stench got worse as soon as they left the cargo bay. The central spine of a cargo ship always had stairs for use when the ship was under way. It could be broken up into rooms, but since that cost money, it was often just one long, open space.

The *Compton*'s spine was square and broken into compartments.

The first compartment had the usual pipes and conduits

along the wall and a spiral stairwell offset from the center enough to allow a solid-looking airtight hatch to close off the bottom of the compartment.

The second compartment was where the stink came from.

Men and women blinked up as Kris started down the ladder. They looked like skeletons wrapped in filthy rags. Most were wired to deadeyes welded onto the outer bulkhead. They drifted listlessly as the ship turned slowly, surrounded by a cloud of their own filth. A few were free. They provided whatever care they could to the others.

That care couldn't extend very far. All they had were their own two hands and maybe a gentle voice. There was no visible source for water. One bucket might have served as a latrine. Now its content littered the air of the compartment. A woman glided through space, trying to recapture what had come free.

Kris gagged. "Who did this?" she demanded.

One squad of Marines was on full alert. The other moved around the compartment, cutting prisoners free. A man in what might once have been a merchant service officer's uniform floated toward Kris. He was bent over, trying gingerly to massage his left foot. That was where he'd been tied down, and it looked black and ugly.

"I'm Dan Orizowski. I was second officer of the *Jumping Jill*, a freighter out of Geneva."

"You senior here?" Jack asked.

The begrimed man looked around. "I am off the *Jill*."

"Your senior officers?" Kris asked.

"Killed for resisting."

"Is this all one crew?"

"No." A grizzled old fellow now joined them. "I'm Onally MarTom, chief wiper on the *Outside Straight*. Don't know where we were registered. Our captain surrendered when they asked, but they killed him and all the officers without even blinking."

"Who?" Kris asked, her voice low. She recognized her tone as deadly. Jack's lips were a thin line. He'd give her no guff.

"I don't know their names, ma'am," the old chief wiper said, "but I'll never forget their faces."

"Captain, what say we get this man some faces to look at."

"My thinking exactly," Jack said, and turned to Gunny. "I want the whole company over here. Reduce the admin watch to minimum on the *Wasp*. Full battle rattle and demolition loads."

Kris coordinated with Captain Drago. "I'm stripping my Marines for a rat hunt. Can your sailors keep an eye on the ship to make sure no rats make it off or across to you."

"I'm getting video of what you're seeing, and even with life support on full boost, we're getting some of what you're smelling. I'll have armed sailors looking out for anyone that you miss."

"Could your crew take care of these people?"

"Cookie is preparing oatmeal and got the largest pot of coffee perking. Those that aren't shooters are ready to help distressed mariners. Even some of the boffins are standing in line to help."

"You do the humanity thing. We'll do the other stuff."

"Kick their butts good."

Kris brought Jack up to date. He nodded. "Give me five minutes to get everyone in place. Let them have more time to stew in their own juices. I don't want to face desperate men with anything less than overwhelming odds. I don't care how many of them die. All of them are not worth one of my Marines."

Kris gave him a thumbs-up.

Sailors and boffins arrived to carefully tow out the former prisoners. The Marines aft, told there might be solid work for them forward, quickly cuffed and led up the engineering staff, still protesting their innocence to anyone listening.

No one was.

The LACs were launched again. The *Compton* had life pods. Their present position was a good four-year drift in a pod to an only marginally inhabitable planet. Anyone who tried to escape that way faced a long, slow death. As tempting as it might have been to let them try, the LACs had orders to corral in the life pods and head any pirate in them toward a date with a judge and a noose.

At Jack's orders, the Marines popped the hatch and started their way up the forward spine of the *Compton*.

5

The four-hundred-foot climb up the first forward spine compartment would have been arduous at one gee. In free fall, Kris went hand over hand. Ahead of her, Marines were already fanning out to secure the next compartment, the second of five.

So far no weapons fire. No booby traps. Possibly these pirates had never expected to have to defend their own ship.

The first resistance was in the forward-most compartment. The hatch leading out of it was dogged down and locked from the other side.

"Shall we blow it?" Gunny asked. With a glance, Jack passed the question to Kris.

She mulled it for a moment. Just coming into the space with the Marine rear guard was Chief Beni. Apparently, rage at the pirates' behavior toward their merchant prisoners had overcome his usual desire to be wherever action was not.

She waved him to her. He looked around to see if there might be anyone else but him that she wanted. She shook her head and waved him forward. He came.

"I want to talk to those thugs on the other side of this bulkhead. Jack me into their net," Kris said.

His eyes lit up at the prospect of doing good without any unnecessary risks. A minute later he had spotted a cable conduit, had its cover off, and was rummaging around its innards.

"You're in, Your Highness," he chimed through a grin a moment later.

Kris considered for half a second what she wanted to say and chose a simple "This is Lieutenant Kris Longknife. We have come for you, ladies and gentlemen. You can survive the next few hours or not. It doesn't matter to me and my Marines."

Around Kris, a few Marines pumped air. "Ooo-Rah."

Beni must have put Kris on a hot mike on the other side, or the damage Kris had done made all mikes hot. Her remarks raised a mumble of comments, most of which were obscene and biologically improbable. One was repeated several times. "Why don't you just go away and leave us alone?"

"I've considered leaving you alone," Kris said.

That got a lot of happy noise from the other side.

"But I'd hate to leave this big hulk drifting as a hazard to navigation." There was also the matter of prize money for the *Wasp*'s crew, but that didn't sound like something that would move a pirate to repentance.

"I could just blast the bow off the ship, leave it here, and tow the rest of this hulk to a port."

There was a long silence. Around Kris, Marines followed that option to its obvious conclusion . . . and grinned.

It took those on the other side a bit longer to think it through. "Where would that leave us?" finally came from someone.

"You would be left all alone."

"Until someone picked us up or we died."

"Considering how far out you are," Kris said, thoughtfully, "I suspect you'd be long dead before anyone happened by."

"You're just going to hang us anyway."

That was what Kris wanted to do, but that wasn't the law in human space. "Few planets have capital punishment," Kris pointed out, generating frowns from her Marines.

"You going to take us to one that don't?"

"I will take you to the nearest planet with a recognized court system. Cuzco, I expect."

"Do they have capital punishment?"

"I honestly don't know." NELLY, I DON'T WANT TO KNOW.

YES, KRIS.

The negotiations went on like that for the next hour. In the end, they all surrendered, and no shots were fired.

"You didn't want any of your Marines hurt," Kris pointed out to Jack.

He nodded, then shook his head. "Would have been nice to send a few of them to meet their maker."

"We killed the worst of them. The bridge crew was fifteen strong when the fight started." Only parts of three bodies had been recovered from the wreckage.

Every ship's officer excepting the engineer had taken the

brunt of a twenty-four-inch laser . . . and come up the worse for it.

Which left a certain young Navy lieutenant with what the brass euphemistically called a few "leadership challenges."

She had forty-seven former prisoners that were in pretty bad shape. They needed medical care, and they needed it quickly.

She also had thirty-two new prisoners, all of whom were loudly expounding on their innocence . . . to the no one who was listening . . . from the confines of a hastily expanded brig on the *Wasp*.

And Kris had a very damaged hulk, which turned out to have a very full load of expensive cargo. Leaving her with a lot of questions about how that had come to pass.

Her first two problems said get gone from here. The third left her reluctant to abandon what she'd done. There was also the problem of the *Compton Maru* being the scene of several crimes that were greatly in need of investigation.

Kris was saved from the first problem. The health of the pirates' prisoners improved as Doc did a couple of miracles. The *Wasp*'s corpsman, widely rumored to have been a board-certified MD before his alcoholism cost him dearly, stayed sober and did good. He racked up bushels of good karma as more and more legs passed from likely candidates for amputation to just in need of careful and tender care. Several of the tough old sailors recovered with amazing speed.

Which led to the next challenge that Kris really should have seen coming.

Onally MarTom slipped a meat cleaver from the mess and tried to use it to part the hair of one of the brig's new denizens.

Fortunately, a Marine interrupted him.

Kris was there only a second behind Jack while the Marine was still struggling with a surprisingly strong and very distressed mariner.

"He killed my captain," the man screamed in frustration.

"And he'll pay for it," Jack assured him.

Outnumbered and overpowered, the man broke down in tears, but he still cursed them one and all for standing between him and his captain's murderer.

Gunny arrived to lead him off. "I'll get him drunk on Doc's ignored supplies. That'll at least start the healing. When he sobers up, he'll be glad he's not a killer. He isn't, you know."

"He showed a pretty solid commitment to making a go of it if you ask me," Kris observed, still trying to parse some of the old sailor's curses. And she thought she'd heard them all.

"I'll double the guard," Jack said. "Keep the ones keeping the bad guys in where they are. But I'll add a full team in the next compartment to keep the sightseers and hackers out."

Which left Kris wondering if she ought to do something about the pirates sooner rather than later. King Ray had dragooned a retired Wardhaven judge into joining Kris's crew. Being a hobbyist astronomer, she was delighted to be aboard.

Kris had assumed the *Wasp* might be called on to pass quick and efficient justice on some minor matters. Capital piracy, murder, and slavery went quite a bit beyond Kris's plan.

And there was the requirement that any court chartered in Wardhaven follow the Ordinance of Human Rights that had been the cornerstone of the now-defunct Society of Humanity.

Central to that was the ban on capital punishment.

But not every planet had signed the Ordinance. Kris's father had almost lost his chance to be Wardhaven's prime minister when he'd used every stalling tactic in the politician's handbook to keep Wardhaven's signature off the Ordinance. Not forever, only long enough to hang the kidnappers whose mishandling of Kris's little brother, Eddy, caused his death.

With luck, the nearest planet would also not have signed the Ordinance. Longknifes did not like kidnappers.

So while Doc healed the freed, and Jack kept alive the not yet dead, Kris led a scratch salvage-and-repair team through the wreck of the *Compton Maru*. Most were borrowed from the *Wasp*'s crew, but the boffins supplied their own techs, and the Marines also provided their electronics and engineering specialists.

And Kris donated most of Nelly's time after the computer demanded a go at the mess Kris had made.

Kris's well-aimed twenty-four-inch lasers had made quite a mess of the *Compton*'s bridge. Even when they patched the holes and glued an airtight bubble over the bridge, they also had to set up a string of lights.

Anything that required electrical power was fried, right down to the smallest lightbulb. "Oh, can I have the ship's computer?" Nelly said, as soon as pieces were identified.

"You think you can get something out of this?" Kris said.

"Everyone else on board has a hobby. Jigsaw puzzles are all the rage among the scientists. Pretty lame from my perspective. But that looks like it might be a challenge."

"Take all the pieces we find," Kris ordered, "to the electronics lab. Maybe Nelly or one of mFumbo's experts can make something out of it."

"Maybe a watch that runs slow," Chief Beni muttered, but he gathered the scattered shards and boxed them up for transport.

It was when they got their first look inside the shipping containers that matters got serious again.

They were full.

Since all documentation on them was in the now-defunct computer, that left folks to speculate on why a pirate ship had a full cargo.

"Could they have winched the cargo containers off the ships they boarded?" Sulwan mused.

Jack shook his head. "In zero gee, with only makeshift gear? It would be a whole lot easier to send the cargo off to wherever you were selling the ships."

Captain Drago nodded. "These pirates started off as mutineers. So where are their officers?"

"They were pretty quick to murder the officers of the ships they took," Kris pointed out.

"Someone needs to answer us some questions," Jack said.

But all questions were met with sullen silence. Even the reactor snipes suddenly took to studying their fingernails.

No one objected when Gunny suggested that, what with them in zero gee, and none of the prisoners able to exercise, maybe they'd all be a lot safer if they were cuffed to their bunks. And when ex-pirates suddenly turned space lawyers demanded their rights, Marines overruled then with a few quick butt strokes.

"We need to get this show moving," Kris concluded.

With the *Compton*'s bridge unable to command anything, the techs went looking for a backup. As expected, the first spine compartment forward of amidships had plug-ins for an emergency bridge, but like most merchants, it had no stations. There should have been a few in the spares locker, but, to no one's surprise, there were none. Six were salvaged from the 4.7-inch lasers and reprogrammed as needed. Three more were brought over from the *Wasp*'s spares locker.

In a week, with a mixed crew from the *Wasp* and former hostages, both ships were ready to get under way.

And the time hadn't been a total waste.

Professor mFumbo's techs hadn't launched their probe given all the excitement over the *Compton Maru*'s arrival. Once things calmed down, they modified it for high acceleration and sent it off at two gees.

It ducked through to the next system and reported back six hours later that there were two old jump points in that system and three fuzzy ones. And two planets in the inhabitable zone.

Kris had to quell a budding mutiny among the scientists. "We will get back here," she assured them.

6

A week later, the *Wasp* led the *Compton* toward the space station above Cuzco. "The stationmaster regrets that he only has two docks unoccupied," Captain Drago reported. "One can off-load containers. I told him to put the *Compton* in it. That leaves us with only one place to go."

"Is there a problem?" Kris asked, knowing from the way Drago was drawing this out that she was asking a needless question.

"We'll be across the way from a Greenfeld light cruiser."

"They've got a Greenfeld cruiser in port." Jack grinned. "I hope we're not interrupting anything," did not sound at all like the Marine meant it.

"What ship?" Kris asked.

"The light cruiser *Surprise*," Drago said, with his own tight smile at the appropriateness of the name.

"Does Georg Krätz still command her?" Kris asked.

Sulwan looked up from her board. "Harbormaster's records say he does."

"Good, I've had several fine dances with the man," Kris said, beaming. "He's the father of several girls, all interested in naval careers, just like their father. I suggested that he and they would have far more successful careers in the Wardhaven Navy than they could ever hope to have in anything controlled by Greenfeld. I'm looking forward to continuing our conversations."

Jack rolled his eyes.

Kris sniffed. "If you Marines can think of war as a continuation of politics by other means, why can't a princess continue politics by socializing?"

Next day, Kris got her chance to socialize or politic or maybe fight a very small war.

A handsome—one might say dashing—young Greenfeld lieutenant approached the *Wasp*'s quarterdeck, offered his captain's
compliments, and asked if his captain might have the pleasure of
Princess Kristine Longknife's company at dinner that night.

Kris would have turned down an invitation to the *Surprise*'s
wardroom as too risky, but Krätz was wise enough to choose
the most expensive . . . and neutral . . . restaurant on the space
station. After only a minor argument with Jack, Kris sent her
acceptance down to the JOOD, and the deal was done.

"I'm going with you," Jack muttered.

"I expected you to. Jack, you dance as well as he does."

Kris politely did not hear Jack's answer to that.

"I gonna have to gussy you up all princesslike?" was Abby's
only question.

"Nope," Kris said. "Formal Navy dinner dress. Small medals.
Skip the Wounded Lion. He's seen my ribbons. I've seen his. We
know who we are," Kris said, with a smile.

"I better tell Jack to tone it down," Abby said, and headed off
to do just that. Four hours later, Kris almost regretted going
Navy standard tonight. Surely, there was no uglier evening dress
than what the Navy put its women in. The skirt hung like a
burlap bag. The blouse was uncomfortable.

"You're wishing you were in a nice set of petticoats and
crinolines," Jack whispered beside her.

"Security officers are not authorized to read my mind no matter what the latest new law may say," Kris shot back, and moved
forward. Jack opened the door for her, resplendent in his dress
red and blues. A sword and issue sidearm hung from his belt. No
such allowance was made for the women, so Kris had her automatic hidden in the usual place.

Kris was three steps into the restaurant when she spotted
Captain Krätz standing up from his table. He was accompanied
by a young ensign. She wore formal Greenfeld Navy evening
dress that managed the impossible. She looked worse in it than
Kris did in hers. Clearly the women haters in Greenfeld's military had bested their kin on Wardhaven.

Distracted by the uniform, it took Kris an extra moment to
identify the woman in it.

She almost missed a step.

Beside her, Jack's nostrils flared, but he manfully suppressed
a snort.

Kris took a quick glance around the room. It was early, still well lit, and almost empty. But around the captain's table were four occupied ones. The men at them were in civilian clothes, but there was no mistaking the hard bodies under those clothes, the close haircuts, and the steely look to their eyes.

Were any of them hers? Kris spotted two women Marines she knew only too well from their doing bathroom guard duty for her. Four Wardhaven Marines, four others.

Krätz had observed the niceties.

Kris allowed herself one more second for a glance at the room, not to take in its expensive decor, but rather to note the right-hand corner of the room, where the few other customers were huddled over their food, meticulously not making eye contact with those on the left side.

Very likely, it would be a quiet dinner. No, very likely the fireworks would be reserved for the main table.

Secure that her back was covered, Kris focused her full attention on the main table. Krätz, despite a bit of graying around the temple . . . or maybe because of it . . . was magnificent in his formal blue and whites.

Beside him, somehow made frumpy by Greenfeld formal naval dinner dress, stood Ensign Victoria Peterwald. *Ensign!*

Kris didn't know where to start; she had so many questions.

Krätz started for her, sweeping her a full bow from the waist. When the young woman beside him balked, it took only a slight tap to her elbow to make clear that *She's a princess, you are not, and this is Navy business, and* we *will do it* my *way.*

Vicky chipped off a quick shallow curtsy.

But her captain stayed in his full bow.

With a scowl, Vicky curtsied again. Lower. And did not recover, but went a bit lower. Then some more.

Finally, her head was even with her captain's.

Only then did Kris smile and give them a most regal nod of the royal head. "Thank you, Captain, Ensign, but we are in Cuzco space, and I seriously doubt their government recognizes United Sentients patents of ennoblement."

"But graciousness is recognized throughout human space," the good captain said, rising from his bow. "Your Highness, may I present to you my new junior communications watch officer, Ensign Victoria Smythe-Peterwald."

"I am glad that we are finally formally introduced," Kris

said, forgetting for the moment the several times they had informally tried to kill each other.

"It is good to meet you," came from the ensign, as if each word out of her mouth was a snake or spider out of the fairy tales.

As Jack held Kris's chair for her to sit, the captain did the same for the young woman. She seemed startled by the chivalry.

You have an awful lot to learn, Miss Vicky, Kris thought to herself. *So do I, but at least I know I do.*

Kris decided to open the conversation. "I was rather surprised to see the *Surprise* tied up along the next pier. If it isn't a state secret, can I ask how you come to be here?"

"Some people might consider it just such a state secret," Captain Krätz said, with a chuckle and a glance at the young woman he was escorting. "But a look at the ship you escorted in tells me that both our planets are likely concerned about the same matter. How did that freighter come to be so shot up?"

"I'm afraid that I did it," Kris said, not quite succeeding at looking bashful. That only got her raised eyebrows from both the captain and the ensign.

"It fired on the *Wasp* while we were making like an unarmed merchant," Kris said in formal report mode. "I was on weapons and returned the compliment. I put a twenty-four-inch pulse laser through their bridge, and that was the end of the discussion."

"Just like you did to my brother," Victoria Peterwald shot back.

"Ensign, we talked about that," the captain said, giving warning.

Kris shook her head. "Excuse me, Captain, if you will," Kris said, "Ensign Peterwald and I need to get this out in the open. She may never agree with me, but she needs to hear my side." Kris turned her full attention to Victoria.

"You killed my brother just like you did that freighter crew," Vicky got in first.

"I was involved in your brother's death, but not 'just like' those people on the pirate's bridge."

Vicky's mouth was half-open, a retort already coming, but with a glance at the glower on her captain's face, she bit it off and shut her mouth.

"Your brother had my ship on the ropes. It was his ship and crew or mine. I fired six-inch lasers, aimed for his engines, not bridge. His evasion actions, or maybe it was just dumb luck, put his bridge where we were aiming.

"On his ship, every crewman had a survival pod. We did not find a single one on that pirate ship. When I opened up their bridge, they were all doomed. Most of their bodies were blown out into space.

"On your brother's ship, they all activated their survival pods. With the exception of your brother's, they all worked. His didn't. Consider that."

Kris paused. She studied the beautiful blue eyes across from her. Tried to measure the acceptance, the comprehension in them. It didn't look like much, but there was some.

"There is one more thing I can add, though I doubt if anyone in my government will back me up."

"What is that?" Captain Krätz asked.

"If it's not a state secret, could you tell me what were the series numbers of the survival pods on the *Incredible*?"

"The *Incredible* and the *Surprise* were built at the same time. We all used 68000 series pods."

Kris nodded. "The defective pods on the battleships we fought at Wardhaven all had a 90000 series identifier. Do you know what was the number on Hank's pod?"

Both Krätz and Vicky shook their heads in silence.

"I have a picture of his pod. I could show it to you now, but I won't." Hank's body was still in the pod. That was one picture Kris did not want to show Vicky. There were still pictures from poor Eddy's kidnapping that Kris had never seen. Would never see.

"Do you know Hank's survival pod number?" Vicky asked.

"Ninety-seven thousand, five hundred, and twelve," Kris said.

"Holy Mother of God," Captain Krätz muttered.

"That's impossible," Vicky said.

Kris rolled her hand, palm up on the table. "My computer has all the photos taken on my space station of your brother's pod, both before it was opened and after. Several of them clearly show the pod number. Do you know the pod number on your battle station, Ensign?" Kris asked.

The woman looked at her captain. "Yes I do."

"I also know mine," the captain said. "And it's nowhere near a ninety thousand.

"Why was I never told this?" Vicky demanded.

Now it was her captain's turn to roll his hands open, palms up.

"Do you believe her?" Vicky spat.

The captain was silent for a long minute. "There is talk, late at night, in the back rooms of private clubs," he said slowly. "Some in the Navy wonder. Some in the Navy remember Ralf Baja and Bhutta Saris and wonder why they're not around anymore. The Navy is not that big a place, and you can't have the crews of six super battleships vanish without them being missed. So, yes, ma'am, if you had to pick between the words of a woman who, just as cool as could be, shot out a pirate's bridge, and the babbling of a political officer, whom would you trust?"

A waiter appeared, kept his distance until several sets of guards waved him forward, then took orders from only those at Kris's table. He had been well briefed and left quickly.

"I don't believe you," Vicky whispered, when the waiter was well gone.

"Care to tell me why?" Kris asked.

"Let's say my dad's Navy just tried to pound your planet into rubble. Let's say you were decorated for stopping them. How many friends did you lose?"

"A lot," Kris said evenly.

"And yet, you are sitting here talking to me, my captain here. Eating dinner with us. No. You're lying."

Kris nodded slowly. "How much history have you studied?"

"Quite a bit," Vicky claimed.

"What happens when two evenly matched countries go to war?"

Vicky seemed to puzzle over that one for a while, then glanced at her captain.

"When two nations of nearly equal strength resort to war to resolve their differences, it is usually a disaster for both," the Greenfeld officer said. "The war is long, bitter, and indecisive. Neither side can win, but neither side will give up. Generations may perish in the fight. Nations' treasures may waste away, and nothing is proven. Is that what you are alluding to, Your Highness?"

"That is what the wiser heads in my father's high command tell me when I get angry at the deaths."

"That is what the wiser heads in our command councils say," Captain Krätz said. "So far, they have prevailed."

"Why are you telling her this?" Vicky asked her captain.

"You could just as easily ask her the same."

Vicky turned to Kris, her eyes questioning.

Kris shrugged. "Two plus two is four. A war between ninety planets and a hundred will be a bleeding ulcer. Neither of these facts can be made a state secret. Only a fool would try. I'm not asking your captain how many battleships are building on Green-feld. He's not asking me about Wardhaven or Pitts Hope. He has his guess, I have mine. We probably aren't off by more than two or three. But none of that really is worth the time of day. Let me ask you something I'd really like to know," Kris said, turning to the captain.

"I have four armed security men to my back. I assume you will not ask me to commit treason within their hearing," he said through a broad smile.

"I will assume they have no better sense of humor than my Marine escorts do," Kris said. There were chuckles from both groups of guards.

Kris waited as the salad arrived, unfolded a napkin in defense of her disgusting evening dress, and picked up a fork. The others did likewise, but waited when Kris paused before spearing a bit of her Caesar salad.

"Why are you here?" Kris asked Vicky.

"I was drafted and ordered to the *Surprise*," she grumbled. "Now I go where he goes," she said, with a rueful nod to her captain.

As Kris so often did, Vicky had given her an answer, but only the tip of one. Kris wondered if that was all of the answer Vicky really knew.

"Georg," Kris said, staking a regal right to a familiarity that a junior officer of her rank had no call on. "How many Greenfeld naval officers have as great a love of daughters as you have?"

The captain had started to frown at the familiarity. After all, he was trying to break one trillionaire daughter to junior-officer status and needed Kris to help, not hinder. But now he smiled.

"I don't think there's a captain in the fleet who's resigned himself to enjoying, maybe I should say, surviving, feminine surroundings as much as I have."

"Your oldest," Kris went on. "She should have graduated from college by now. Did she join the Navy?"

Now it was the captain's turn to ruefully shake his head. "Commissioned in the Nursing Corps on her graduation day."

"Is she on the *Surprise*?"

"I would have gladly had her here, but there is a boy."

"Isn't there always?" Kris interjected.

"Sad to say, yes. He comes from a good family, and he is on a battleship. So she asked for orders to that battleship."

"Do you trust him?"

The look Kris got from the captain was a puzzle she could not fathom. He almost smiled as he started again. "I will let you in on a state secret, Longknife girl. In Greenfeld, a loyal wife, be she wealthy or poor, will take nine months to present her husband with a fit little baby. However, blushing brides, in their eagerness, almost always do it in six or seven months. Strange that, no."

The security guards behind the captain relaxed into their seats. Kris had no doubt that had the captain begun to reveal a more technical detail, they would have dragged him away. But from the smirks on their faces, a few of them might well be married and already beneficiaries of that bridal miracle.

"And your daughter?"

"Has been courted for almost six months and is still on active duty."

Kris's confused frown at that brought a dry "Get pregnant, get discharged" from Vicky.

"How medieval," Kris said.

"I mentioned that to my father," Vicky said, her voice desert dry. "Let's say we agreed to disagree. Thank God I know where to get birth control."

"Not on my ship you don't," her captain said.

The ensign wisely filled her mouth with her salad.

Kris stepped in to redirect the conversation. "When I asked why you are here, Vicky, I didn't mean in the Navy. What I was really asking was why you aren't back on Greenfeld. You cost your father a lot when he sent you to Eden, and I doubt your stay in the Navy will be any less expensive." The way Captain Krätz rolled his eyes cut Kris's doubt by half. "But what I really wonder, girl to girl, is why you aren't tending to your knitting quietly back home?"

"I don't knit, and I never do anything quietly," Vicky shot back. "And I could ask you the same question. Why aren't you doing something"—Vicky seemed at a loss for words . . . and settled for—"back on your lovely Wardhaven?"

"Why am I not on my lovely Wardhaven?" Kris said, begin-ning to move rather tasty but probably horribly fattening crou-tons out of her salad and into a row. "I don't want to be any closer to my mother or father than I have to."

That got a snort from Vicky and a thoughtful look from Krätz.

"I'm committed to a naval career and for some strange rea-son, the fleet can't find any job for me near my father, the prime minister." That got a third crouton into rank and a dry chuckle from the ensign.

"I refuse to become involved in politics . . . and every time I get too near Wardhaven, I get sucked into that mess again, and my father gets even madder at me. How am I doing?"

Vicky now needed the napkin to suppress her laughter.

Captain Krätz eyed Jack and got a serious nod of validation. Then he shook his head. "Your file is making better and better sense."

"And if you report all this," Kris said, "do you think it will make better sense to your intelligence analysts?"

"They wouldn't believe a word."

"Then let me add one more bit of wisdom. They shipped me off to Eden because they thought it was the only place in human space where I'd be safe."

"And you might have been if I hadn't been there," Vicky said proudly.

"Hire better assassins next time. I didn't even work up a sweat doing my escape and evade from those bozos."

"I captured your grandmother," Vicky pointed out.

"Major mistake on your part. The Marines took it personal. You never want a Marine company personally mad at you."

"You realize she's critiquing you," Captain Krätz said.

"I thought she was just bragging."

"You might learn a thing or three if you listen to her. Your father or his minions have been trying to take her out for a long time, and she's still wrecking their plans."

"More often than not, the only reason I'm messing with an-other's plans is 'cause someone's messing with me," Kris said, with a sigh. "I wish you'd just leave me alone."

"Is that why you're out here?" Vicky asked.

"I figured if I was out beyond the Rim, I might get some peace and quiet. That why you're out here?"

Vicky turned to her captain and raised an expressive eyebrow.

"Strange, isn't it," the captain said, "when chasing after pirates is safer than being back home."

"Are we chasing pirates," Vicky asked, "or is the *Surprise* just pretending it is?"

Captain Krätz shrugged his shoulders. "How'd you get a shot at a pirate?" he asked Kris.

"Notice how the *Wasp* looks like a simple little merchant ship." They nodded. "They took the first shot. I got the last one."

Their steaks arrived with appropriate trimmings. Kris and the rest paid appropriate homage to them before Kris threw out the next question.

"How bad is it, being a boot ensign in the Greenfeld Navy? My memories of being the junior officer aboard ship are much more fondly memorable as they disappear in the rearview mirror."

"You started as an ensign?" Vicky asked.

"Yes," Kris said, "with a captain who made my life far more miserable than I suspect Captain Krätz is making yours."

Vicky raised her eyebrows as if to doubt that possibility.

"Making ensigns miserable is one of the prime perks of a captain's job," Captain Krätz insisted. "Is that not so, Captain?" he said to Jack.

"We have a thing called the Fifth Amendment, sir, and I'm going to invoke its protection, sir. Otherwise, I might have to apply for a transfer to your Navy."

"We're always looking for a few good men."

"What is it about men?" Vicky exploded. "I get handed this ensign gig. My brother starts out as a commodore. He bosses Captain Krätz around. Me, I get bossed around by just about everybody. It's not fair," she growled at her captain.

He said nothing, just took another bite of his steak, chewed it for a moment, and then waved his empty fork at Kris. "As a lieutenant, two mighty promotions up from a lowly ensign, would you have any advice for my JO here?"

Kris thought the question over for a moment, then shrugged. "As a wise chief once told me, if you don't want to be Navy, get out."

Vicky scowled sidewise at her superior officer. He shook his head. "That is not an option for the moment."

"I see," Kris said. And thought some more. "Your brother started his Navy career as a commodore."

Vicky nodded vigorously at that.

"From where I sat, that was part of what killed him."

"What!" Vicky almost shouted.

"Do you disagree, Captain Krätz?" Kris asked.

The captain patted his mouth with the white linen napkin and put it down. "I can't say that I do."

Vicky studied them for a long moment. Kris let the silence stretch. She was learning that more often than not more was learned in the quiet between words than was ever conveyed by them. Now she waited for the young Peterwald woman to show she was learning . . . or not.

"Explain yourself. I would have thought that a commodore was safer, more powerful." Vicky paused for a moment. "As an ensign I sure don't feel any power. Or very safe."

Kris eyed Krätz. He shook his head. "I can offer only advice. You have walked in her shoes and survived. You can speak to her from experience."

Now Kris put her own napkin down and pushed back from the table. Beside her Jack did the same. Around them, the security people turned their chairs to face out, giving them as much privacy as their station and the risk factor allowed.

"A commodore does seem to have a lot of power . . . if he or she knows how to use it. Captain, did Hank know how to use the power of a commodore?"

The captain shook his head. "Sadly no. He played with the power, but he neither understood it nor knew how to wield it."

"That was my observation, too," Kris said. "Captain, how long have you been preparing to command a cruiser?"

"Ensign to command captain, twenty years," Krätz said, "including two years commanding a destroyer, Your Highness."

"How long had Hank worn the uniform?"

"Four months when he died."

"That, Vicky, is what killed your brother. Power he didn't know how to use. You're an ensign. Do you have any power?"

"Painfully little."

"Are you able to use it properly?"

Now Vicky turned to face her commanding officer. "I am learning to be a very good assistant communication officer."

"You are," he agreed.

Vicky turned back to Kris. "Are you saying that it's better to do a job you know how to do than fake doing a job you can't handle?"

"I think so."

"I paid good money to get a copy of your file. It sure doesn't look like you practice what you preach."

Beside Kris, Jack snorted. "Amen to that."

"Whose side are you on?" Kris asked, elbowing Jack.

"The side of me staying alive," he said.

Kris got serious. "You bought my file. You read it. Did an analyst explain it to you?"

"I just got the file."

"Captain, you might walk her through it. You can explain to her where I was just bleeding lucky and where maybe I had a little help from my friends."

"Would you, sir?" Vicky asked, sounding like a boot ensign talking to her superior officer for the first time that evening.

"My orders are to educate you. To help you stay alive and learn. I think that could be considered part of my job. Though I warn you, your father probably would not consider Kris Longknife a proper role model for his daughter."

"I don't think any father would consider me a good role model," Kris said dryly.

"Certainly not for any of my daughters," Captain Krätz agreed. "But I remind you, Ensign Peterwald, anyone without dumb Longknife luck would have died a dozen times doing what is recorded in that file. And no, none would have occurred while you were paying the piper."

Vicky looked very thoughtful as they finished their dinner.

Done, Captain Krätz stood. But before he turned to leave, he gave Kris an informal bow. "I believe your file says that your first skipper was a Captain Thorpe?"

"Yes," Kris said, avoiding adding anything more.

"He is no longer serving in the Wardhaven Navy."

"I believe not," Kris said, trying not to sound evasive.

"I ran into him recently. He has hired on with a merchant shipping line that is providing irregular service to ports beyond the Rim. Are you aware of these illegal colonies?"

"I've visited a few. Never ran into Captain Thorpe."

"I understand such shipping lines are the main prey of the pirates. I hope nothing happens to your former captain."

"So do I," Kris said, not sure exactly what she was being told or how she felt about it.

Outside the restaurant, Jack leaned close to Kris's ear. "How much you want to bet me you are going to regret helping that young woman stay alive?"

That was a bet Kris was not willing to take.

7

FOUr hours with lawyers experienced in what passed for a modern, up-to-date legal system on Cuzco, and Kris was missing Chance's nice informal approach to the law.

While Kris had blown *Compton*'s bridge and all its watch standards to kingdom come, and with it the ship's papers, what was left of the hulk still told a tale. The reactors had the serial numbers stamped on them by Westinghouse. That company's database said they had been installed on the *Big Bad Bustard*, presently under Lorna Do registry. Its last-known port of call had been Nobel Pride six months ago.

A fast message to the port authority there brought back a ship's bill of lading and, suddenly, the containers were talking, and the cargo was matching up . . . some of it.

Some containers were missing and some new ones had been added. Apparently Nobel Pride had not been the last port of call.

This might have been of minor interest, except the owners had insured the ship and cargo with a consortium of assurance companies. Now they were retaining lawyers. The case of Humanity v. the *Compton Maru* pirates moved into a larger courtroom.

Kris was taken aside by half a dozen pale men in suits and told that there would be a finders' award for her and her crew. Now would the Navy kindly go back to doing whatever it was Navy people did when decent citizens weren't interested in them.

Kris took one look at the quaint sum of the finders' fee and had to leave before she punched out some well-dressed type.

The crew of the *Wasp* had gone through the experience of capturing her from pirates, and well remembered the prize money the Chance court had awarded them when the pirate ship was sold to become the *Wasp*. For the last two weeks there had been little talk among the different tribes aboard the *Wasp* other than how they would spend their portion of the prize money.

The crew of the *Wasp* firmly held that they had the main claim on the prize money. They had fought the *Compton* and captured her fair and square.

The Marines pointed out that they certainly had something to do with the capture of the pirates. So advised, the sailors graciously concluded that the Marines did have a point.

Few people are dumb enough to argue with Marines.

But when the boffins waded in with their claim, things got heated. "Where were you when they were shooting at us?" was a rather strong point in the sailors' and Marines' favor.

"Our necks were as much on the line as yours when that pirate was taking potshots at us." And "It was three of the containers that we were in that got sliced open to space." And "It was our sensors you were using for ship ID and targeting."

That did seem to provide a certain counterbalance to "You was all hiding under your bunks."

The atmosphere on the *Wasp* got downright frosty, and several mixed work details almost came to blows before Kris called a public meeting and let each side choose four speakers to say their piece. Being well aware her crew could implode, Kris took the extra precaution of having Captain Drago and Professor mFumbo included in their four. And met with them beforehand. Some might say the fix was already in.

Both captain and professor let their hotheads have their say, then carefully got the stampede going in a circle. The final conclusion had the advantage of a certain logic.

Clearly, the crew and Marines of the *Wasp* had their necks on the line as the *Compton* attacked. And they fought her until she was dead in space and surrendered. There was also no question the boffins had their necks on the chopping block when the *Compton* started shooting. Not a totally unforeseen event, since they had all signed on to a ship with one of those Longknifes, if not at the helm, then too close to it for any real comfort.

The final agreement split the prize money. The crew and Marines who fought the ship would get a double allotment from those who risked their neck aboard it. With portions being organized in accordance with the old law of the sea.

That left the crew in a happy mood. Gliding back to her

quarters with Abby and Cara, Kris discovered just how far that happy mood went.

"And you will get part of that money, too," Abby told Cara.

"Me!" said the twelve-year-old. "I didn't do nothing."

"Even the cabin boys on those old sailing ships got a portion," Abby assured her.

"I could get some money?" Cara let out a squeal.

"For your college fund," Abby pointed out.

"I'm going to college?"

"Why not. I did," Abby said. Now Kris listened closely. Any new word about Abby's hidden life before she started running Kris's life was always to be treasured.

"But Ganny Ganna said a girl didn't need to know more than she needed to—"

"You ain't with Ganny Ganna, and you saw what her way of living ended up doing to your momma and Ganna."

That left the youngster silent.

"I put myself through college at night," Abby said. "I worked hard to earn the money and learn what I could. You, girl, can go to college like people like the princess do. The right way. And this money will be the start of your nest egg."

Which all sounded great until the assurance people made their offer. Their finders' fee would pay for about five minutes of education for Cara.

"Nelly, does Nuu Enterprises have an office on Cuzco?"

"Yes, Kris."

"Get me in touch with our chief."

The chief shortly referred Kris to the sharpest law firm on Cuzco dealing with maritime issues. Several of the partners had been following the *Compton* situation and were a bit disappointed not to have become involved in the case.

To their delight, Kris ended that.

"Exactly what is your interest in the *Compton*?" the seniormost partner asked Kris when he came on the line.

"I, and the crew of the *Wasp*, captured the pirate ship. Under the traditional law of the sea, the *Compton* and cargo are ours."

"All of it?"

"Until you persuade me otherwise."

"Hmm, I'll need to do some research."

"You do. Be sure to check on the recent decision from Chance. You can contact, ah . . ."

MAYDELL ALLGOOD, Nelly put in.

"Maydell Allgood of the planet Chance High Court for a very recent decision."

"I'm not sure we have them in our legal decisions database."

"Well, you'll want to see the case."

"Very well, now about payment. Are you putting us on retainer or shall we take this on contingency?"

"What kind of contingency?" Kris reminded herself that not all the pirates were in the brig of the *Wasp*.

"Ah, you're Kris Longknife. We've done a lot of work for your offices here. How about one third. If there is no money in it, you don't pay us a dime."

"And if there is, you get a third of it. Just a third, no other expenses, right?"

"Hmm, you drive a hard bargain, but yes."

"Let me talk with the other interested parties," Kris said, and rang off.

"SO, how do we want to do this?" Kris asked after laying the whole thing out to all hands over the PA system. The system exploded with comments that, while they might reflect what Kris felt, were not what a princess should say.

Captain Drago silenced his commlink. "We'll get back to you after we've had some time to talk this out among ourselves." Professor mFumbo, who'd just come on the bridge, agreed.

"We've got about a day to decide," Kris added.

"Sad to learn we can't hang all the pirates," Captain Drago said, looking rather piratical himself, then added, "I'm glad I have both you and the professor here for a moment. Could we duck into my in-port cabin for a moment? Captain, you might want to come along, too," he said, nodding to Jack.

Uh-oh, Kris thought, but said nothing. With Kris and company, which somehow had grown to include Abby, seated around a small conference table, the captain closed his door.

"What do we intend to do next?" he asked. "Will we have to hang around here for all this court business?"

"Not if we hire a legal team," mFumbo put in.

"We really shouldn't be here long, not on official Navy business," Kris agreed.

"So, what do we do next?"

"Explore," mFumbo said, emphatically.

"Yes, yes," Captain Drago said, looking like your average pirate with several loaded cannons up his sleeve. "But where?"

"Something tells me you already have an answer to that question," mFumbo said, looking quite unhappy.

"Well, I've been looking at the fine print on my contract."

"Abby," Kris growled.

"Don't you go looking at me, your high-ship-ness, this is the first I've heard about this."

"I assure all of you, this is the first our honorable COR has heard about this. You see, I met a man in a bar last night."

"If there is a treasure map with X marks the spot in this story," mFumbo said menacingly, "you're a dead man."

"No, no map, I assure you. It's just that a man I talked to is one of the Sooners we've been running into. His problem is that he is here, back on the inside of the Rim, and he, and a cargo he has arranged, need to be there, out beyond the Rim."

"He wants to start up a colony," Kris said slowly. "I don't think I want to encourage that."

"No, no, Your Highness, not start up a colony. His brothers sent him here to gather things they needed for a world that has been theirs since their grandfather staked his claim or snuck a claim or whatever we decide is the legal situation of these folks. Anyway, he swung a ride on a passing ship, but, what with the pirates and all, he hasn't been able to get back."

"With the *Compton* or *Big Bad* and her crew in the dock, different docks," Kris said, "that may change."

"Was the *Compton* the only pirate?" Drago asked.

That got shrugs or "Your guess is as good as mine" looks from around the table.

"Anyway, my contract says that I may offer passage and transport goods for a fee if it does not interfere with my principal duties."

"And who decides that?" Kris asked, wondering just who and how such language had slipped into the captain's contract. Apparently Grampa Ray wasn't the only one trying to twist this voyage of discovery his or her way.

"My COR," Drago said, with a more-piratical-than-usual grin.

"And what's my cut of the take?" Abby asked through a cut-throat grin of her own.

"This is not happening to me and my science team," mFumbo said, standing up in protest.

Kris shook her head. "And what high crimes am I going to be accused of this time? No, Abby. No!"

"But my contract," Drago cried.

"No!" Kris repeated but was surely drowned out by "No, No, No!" from mFumbo.

"Would you at least talk to the man?" Drago pleaded.

"Why?" came from around the table, not just Kris.

"He's been stuck here a very long time and really wants to get back home. And I'd rather he be the one to talk to you about, ah, some of the other aspects of his trip here."

"What aspects?" Kris said.

"He's waiting right outside." Drago wheedled. That had to be a first for a ship captain.

"No, no, no," mFumbo repeated.

"Would you keep a man from his wife and unseen newborn?"

"You're laying it on mighty thick," Jack said.

"He is truly a man in need," Drago insisted.

"No, no, no!" said mFumbo, but he was sitting down now with a resigned air about him.

"I suggest that we have three votes," Abby said, sounding quite reasonable. "First, if we'll see the man. Then a second to see if we take him on as a passenger." Suddenly the maid's grin switched to pure viciousness. "And a third, if Drago loses the second, to decide if we space our beloved captain."

The captain seemed to weigh the option, then nodded. "I'll take those odds. You don't know what I know about our traveler."

As the room mulled that, the captain invited a young man in.

The man was in his twenties, dressed in worker's jeans and flannel shirt, and flashed a smile full of innocence that most kids lose by five. "Hi, I'm Andy Fronour of Pandemonium."

"Pandemonium, what kind of a name is that?" mFumbo asked.

"Grampa always said he didn't want to roll out a welcome mat for just anyone. Thought that would keep down the lay-abouts."

"Has it?"

"Wasn't much more than a couple of dozen families until twenty years ago."

"What changed that?"

"Say you're a kid, eighteen, twenty, and your folks are true believing Abdicators. What do you do if you want off Xanadu?"

"Are you in the same system with Xanadu?"

"No. We're next door to them, one jump over. Grampa came out a different set of jumps. Figured us to be five good long jumps from anyone. But we're only three jumps, if you don't mind a real crazy sermon after the second one."

"How do they feel about you taking their rebels?" Kris said.

"It's working out fine. We weren't interested in the rest of the human race any more than they were. We just didn't mind if you skipped assembly meetings. Didn't have any real assemblies except for square dancing every Saturday night."

"Do they know you're here?"

"No, the ship that dropped by had been to Xanadu and gotten the very cold shoulder. But as they were about to close down their on-planet sales, a couple of dozen immigrants showed up and asked for a ride to Pandemonium.

"A market that close got the skipper's attention, and he was mighty glad for the guiding hand. Anyway, I can't really say we weren't glad for his coming, either. Our population had grown quite a bit, and we needed just about everything he had."

"Which he gave you out of kindness?" Kris said.

"Nope, we don't have that much hayseed in our hair. In the early years, Grampa paid for the start-up using some really strange hydrocarbon strings native to the planet. It had been a while since anyone came by, and we had a lot of them stored up. I'm told that some of them do really nice things with food."

The strange biologies among the stars had provided more than one new spice and cured several diseases. The real question was why a ship captain who had such a source would quit visiting.

"He has fifty containers," Captain Drago put in. "We'd have no problem carrying them."

"So, do we head to Pandemonium direct or via Xanadu?" Kris asked.

"You're in charge," Drago said. Kris snorted at that.

"Why not leave the crazies alone?" mFumbo suggested.

"I don't think either my grampa or my father would like that," Kris said slowly. "You got nutcases who think we all need to crawl back into Mother Earth's womb to hide from some really nasty alien horde they say is coming. And aren't a bit bothered by the thousands of people that would have to die for every one that survived. On top of that, they believe that some kind of good aliens will take them away when they die, and if you died doing what the Guides tell you to do, those selfsame aliens will treat you like kings and queens."

Kris shook her head. "Seems to me that we ought to check in on them every fifty years or so."

"That sounds fairly logical," Jack said, with only a bit of a scowl on his face. "But are you sure it's not just a Longknife thing? Something horribly dangerous needs doing so, of course, you've got to be the one to do it . . . on a shoestring?"

"Could be, but let's just suppose you're a Guide and you hate all things human. Who do you want to be the first human that pries open your Pandora's box of worms, snakes, and worse? Some Joe Blow merchant captain or one of those damn Longknifes?"

The farmer glanced at the captain. "You didn't tell me there was a Longknife involved here."

"I distinctly remember you did not ask."

"All the ships in human space," the young farmer groaned, "and I have to walk onto this one."

"I rest my case," Kris said. What was it with her family!

8

It took three days to get away from Cuzco. Kris found it painfully slow, but Captain Drago assured her they were actually making record time . . . all things considered.

Those "things" included affidavits that everyone involved in the capture of a pirate had to make concerning everything they did to capture said pirate. Luckily, the crew of the *Wasp* managed to account for every pirate.

There was also the matter of loading fifty more containers on a ship that really wasn't intended to load and unload any. When Kris asked how they would unload the containers to a planet with no station, Captain Drago assured her he was leasing two shuttles specifically designed to make easy work of lifting the containers from orbit down to a planet's surface.

That was something Kris wanted to see. Or better yet, actually fly herself.

And the local Nuu Enterprises came up with a dewar holding a hundred pounds of Smart Metal™ to replace what they'd lost in the fight and to reinforce their shields. Even the crew that winched the dewar into place on their bow and programmed the Smart Metal™ to flow smoothly into place called the use they put it to "shields." Kris gave up. Let someone else fight it out with the copyright lawyers.

Kris didn't have a moment to herself until they locked down ship, slipped their mooring cables, and backed out of dock. Only then did she breathe a deep sigh of relief.

Jack caught her doing it. "You spend a couple of days with lawyers, station hands, and cops doing things where all you risk is breaking a nail, and sigh like you're free from the labors of Hercules when we cast off. We're headed for a bunch of crazies armed with who knows what, and you look delighted at the prospects. Woman, you are crazy."

Kris thought about that for a moment, then gave her Marine the best imitation of one of Abby's disapproving sniffs. "Who's the crazy? The nut leading you, or the nut following?"

Jack turned away, muttering to himself.

Abby watched the station recede on the monitors. "I see that the *Surprise* is still docked on the station. What do you think they're up to?"

Kris eyed the planet below and the cruiser above. "Cuzco is a big place, and last I heard it's part of the Iberium Association. Surely they can hold their own against one cruiser."

"It ain't the cruiser that worries me. It's that redheaded harridan on it. Vicky Peterwald."

"You mean Ensign Vicky," Kris said. "Last I noticed she was learning how to stand a comm officer's watch. You keep a boot ensign properly busy, and even Vicky's gonna have trouble scheduling enough free time to sleep *and* conquer the universe."

"Humph" was Abby's conclusion.

Kris let her have the last word. Unless you've been a sleep-deprived boot ensign, it's hard to describe how much trouble you have juggling all the absolutely-must-be-done-now minutiae that seniors dump on those poor, damned JOs.

Kris was on the bridge three days later when they completed their second jump. Initial reports on the system were all negative. "Where's that farmer? Fronour, isn't he?"

Two minutes later he was on the bridge. "Is this Xanadu's system?" Kris asked.

"Are you picking up anything on the radio?"

"Not a thing," Chief Beni reported from Sensors.

"Then I guess it might be. Skipper I rode out with said he wouldn't have believed that a planet could have people on it and be so quiet."

"I guess if you were afraid of the boogeyman, you wouldn't be sending out any 'hellos' either," Jack observed.

"There is one planet in the habitable zone," Sulwan said.

"Let's see what it looks like up close," Captain Drago said.

That would cost them two days, even at 1.5 gees.

As they went into orbit, the planet was still silent as an undiscovered tomb. "They aren't transmitting anything," Chief Beni reported. "Either there is nobody down there, or every one of my sensors has gone bust or"—Beni paused a moment to scowl at those instruments—"somebody has dug a very deep hole in a planet and hid better than my daddy ever thought anybody could."

"Professor mFumbo," Kris said to her commlink, "you've got two orbits to tell us where the inhabitants are hiding on this planet. Let me know when you find them."

"I can tell you that we haven't found them. I'll call you when I have."

"Thank you," Kris said, then turned to the bridge crew. "Shall we start a pool to see how long it takes our boffins to find the Abdicators? I want the full three hours."

"No fair," Jack said, "I wanted that, too."

"Me three," said Drago.

"Oh ye of little faith," Sulwan said, studying her navigational board. "Even if you aren't operating in space, still you need navigational aids to sail the rivers and seas. Roads to carry the freight." She studied her board some more. And then some more. "At least every other planet needs them."

Sulwan looked up from her instruments. "Maybe we *will* be doing well to find any hint of them in three hours."

Three and a half hours later, Professor mFumbo opened his briefing in the captain's in-port cabin with a sigh and an admission. "The Abdicators do not want to be found."

"So we've been led to expect," Captain Drago said. "Does that mean you didn't find them?"

"I didn't say that, but I want you to know that any team less than the superb one I put together would still be hunting."

Captain Drago raised an eyebrow but said nothing. Sulwan had finally found the Abdicators with the aid of the bridge crew and Chief Beni. Kris would prefer not to have her two brain trusts at dagger points.

"How did you find them?" should get the briefing going.

"They can hide, but they cannot make their heat vanish. The laws of thermodynamics apply even to the Great Guides."

That was the Achilles' heel that Sulwan had spotted, too.

"It didn't help them that it is winter in the northern hemisphere, where they are," mFumbo said, activating a screen. "Usually, you spot an inhabited planet by the vast areas of plowed or fallow fields. Not here. No corn, no potatoes, no wheat fields in stubble. I don't know what they are growing, but it's some kind of perennial that they can harvest calories from and leave the roots in place."

"I've heard about that," Kris said. "Some of the drier areas of Wardhaven are planted in that for soil conservation."

"But would you want just bread to eat, meal after meal?" mFumbo asked.

"They could have bioengineered other crops to have similar root systems," Jack said.

"Enough farming," Kris said. "How did you find the farms?"

"The houses are sod, half-buried in the soil. So are the barns and other outbuildings. But the sod houses are heated and showed up on infrared. We also spotted trails where trucks had traveled recently. The grass under the trails also gave back a different signature than the crop areas.

"And right smack in the middle of the hinterlands, just where you'd expect a city to be, was one. All warm and cozy, with a whole lot more of that road grass," mFumbo said, with a proud flourish.

"The buildings here are low, grass-covered knolls. Some bigger, some smaller. And then there's this mountain. Big, with rock pinnacles coming off it like spires. A real eye-catcher. I think we found the Assembly for the Great Guides."

"Any other towns like that one?" Penny, Kris's intelligence chief, asked.

"Everything else is smaller. Oh, they all have a larger hill in the middle, but nothing nearly as grand as this one, and none is more than a quarter its size."

"It has a large river for shuttles to land in," Kris observed. "It looks like you found what we're looking for."

Jack was shaking his head. "They are clearly very security conscious. Would they really put their most important people in the largest target?"

Kris gave Jack a pat on the back. "You are being properly paranoid, my chief of security, but you are not thinking like a top-dog politician. You are the greatest because you have the biggest and most wealthy trappings of power. They may have a bolt-hole somewhere, just in case. But while they are ruling, they must impress the serfs."

"Did you learn that from your daddy?" Abby asked.

"No, from my first nanny," Kris said dryly.

"Do we know enough to make contact?" Penny asked, keeping them on track.

"I think we know about all we're going to know. I'm assuming that if the professor spent all his time talking about the heat signatures, he didn't find any news channels or other broadcasts on the electromagnetic bands."

"We didn't even find the power plants or power lines. Someone is really shielding them."

"Well, let's go see if anyone is on guard channel," Kris said, and tapped her commlink. "Chief Beni, please broadcast this on as many frequencies as possible. 'Greetings, this is the United Sentient ship *Wasp* in orbit over you. I am Princess Kristine Longknife, empowered to make contact with you.'"

Chief Beni did. His message was followed by a long silence.

Kris shrugged and reached for the mike. "Hi, I am—"

"I heard who you were the first time." The speaker sounded like a very cranky young man. "Would you please shut up and go away. We, the chosen, have no desire to have our eyeballs ripped out and fried before our eyes like you the damned will have done to you."

"If they ripped out our eyeballs to fry them, how are we going to see them do it?" Abby asked.

"Shush. Do not debate ideology or theology with zealots."

Kris flicked on her commlink. "I have come to speak with your Assembly of Great Guides."

"They don't waste time with the doubting damned. Go away."

"I am not going away."

"You have been warned. I have spent enough time sending out a radio beacon for the hordes. We are done here."

"I am going to land and march my Marines straight to your Great Guides."

"You don't know where they are."

"I think you are wrong."

"We will wipe you out."

"I doubt you can massacre a full company of Marines armed with the latest in human weapons."

There was a scraping sound, the kind you might get if a very old type of microphone was being removed from one speaker and taken over by another.

"Miss Longknife," came in an older and more thoughtful voice. "Are you one of those Longknifes?"

"I have the honor of having Ray Longknife as my great-grandfather."

"And you're a princess. Is the rest of human space falling back on those old tried and failed ruling tropes?"

"I prefer to think we are trying a new twist on an old way of looking at things."

"Well, I'm sorry our young protector of the peace seems to have lost his peace. He did have a point. We do not disturb the Great Guides for small talk."

"We Longknifes do not go far beyond the accepted rim of human settlement for small talk."

"There is that. We will let you and a proper escort land. You seem very confident that you know where you are going, but we will light a bonfire beacon for you."

"Not a radio beacon."

"If you know us at all, you know we abhor such things."

"Light your beacon. We'll be down next orbit," Kris said, then waited until her commlink button was clearly red. "Chief, are all links closed?" They apparently were closed enough that the chief did not hear the question.

"So," Jack said, "how big is a proper escort, my risk-taking princess? How many Marines should I saddle up?"

"All of them, I think," Kris said.

That got a wide smile from her security honcho.

Sixty-four minutes later, all four shuttles separated from the *Wasp* and began their descent. They held nearly a full company of Marines in full battle rattle. The only Marine not in armor was Jack, in dress red and blues. He had on his spider-silk underwear, as did Kris and Penny, Abby . . . in uniform . . . and Chief Beni with an armful of black boxes.

Cara wanted to come, too. "Isn't meeting new and strange cultures a great way to enlarge my education?" Got a no from Kris, Abby, and Nelly, in that order. The youngster locked herself in her room to pout. Kris sincerely hoped her negotiations with the Great Guides of the Abdicators would go better than her first try with a twelve-year-old.

The big town was indeed the landing site designated by a

huge bonfire now burning on the right shore of its river, the side with the rocky mountain. The first two shuttles were full of Marines, as was the fourth; Kris's team was in the third. Kris left the driving to others as she scanned everything they knew about the Abdicators. That they were noisy about their views and secretive about their plans was known to all.

ANY HINT AS TO WHY THEY IMMIGRATED OUT PAST THE RIM? Kris asked Nelly.

NO HINT IN ANY OF THE MEDIA AT THE TIME. THEY WERE A GENERAL PAIN IN THE NECK, PREACHING DEATH AND DESTRUCTION ON STREET CORNERS ONE MINUTE, THEN GONE. MOST REPORTS REMARK ON THE UNIVERSAL APPROVAL OF THE PEACE AND QUIET.

BUT NO ONE KNEW OR CARED WHERE THEY WENT?

APPARENTLY NOT, KRIS. THE MEDIA HAD THE USUAL NUMBER OF CELEBRITY MURDERS, DRUG USERS, AND ANTICS TO COVER. AND THE DEBATE ON TAXES, BUDGETS, AND EXPANSION.

SHOW ME THE PICTURES OF THE GREAT GUIDES.

Nelly did. A dozen men, all in middle age, all looking very intense, stared back at Kris. None looked at all interested in what she might have to say.

The shuttle landed smoothly and ran itself up on the bank of the river. Jack dismounted first, then offered Kris a hand so she might step from the shuttle to dry land at no risk of falling into the river mud. The Marines in her shuttle trotted past their officers and ran to join the other Marines in formal ranks.

Not everyone stood row on row, making a great target. A dozen qualified snipers roamed a sort of perimeter. They would have kept back any crowd . . . if there had been a crowd. On the streets visible from where Kris stood, a half dozen women walked as if they had someplace to be. And ignored the show.

The one exception was an large open-top car with a driver in front and a man in back. Kris and Jack, Abby and Penny maybe two paces behind, strolled through the break between first and second platoon and up to the car. The man in the back stood.

"I am Princess Kristine," Kris said to him.

"I am Prometheus, who talked with you earlier. My driver is Lucifer, who had the honor to talk with you first."

Who would name a child after the devil? But now that she was closer, other things became clearer. It wasn't just women walking by, but men as well. All hair was long. Both sexes wore the same bedsheet thing as the two men in the car.

MAYBE IT IS A TOGA? Nelly offered.

Toga, Prometheus, Lucifer was all coming up Greek to Kris. But then, that could be one of the reasons they set off on their own, to build a world they wanted. *Get ready for a wild bunch of mixing and matching,* Kris warned herself.

Prometheus opened the door and stepped to the ground. "I brought you a car, not fire. But from the looks of matters, I would have needed a truck convoy, and we really don't have that many trucks to spare. Would you care to ride with me or walk with your, um, friends." He finished with a bit of a smile, though Kris had no idea why.

"Is that where we are going?" Kris said, pointing at the huge mound at the other end of the street where they stood. It was marked by two stone spires. One was white and richly veined in gold. The other was a kind of blue-gray stone with silver running through it. Kris would have bet anything one was for the good aliens, the other for the one that fried your eyeballs.

"Yes," Prometheus said, "that is where our Great Guides assemble to meet with us. They have graciously agreed to meet with you today."

"If it would not inconvenience your Great Guides, I will walk," Kris said. "I've been cooped up in a starship for way too long. I suspect my Marines would enjoy the walk, too."

"Understandable. It will give us more time to gather the full assembly. Your arrival was more than a little surprise."

"Most systems have jump buoys that announce ship arrivals."

"You will understand our reluctance to do that."

Gunny got the company moving in the direction Jack ordered. The snipers deployed as skirmishers, but the others put on a solidly intimidating show of mass and potential firepower.

Kris and her staff fell in between first and second platoon. Prometheus ambled along, never quite falling in step, on Kris's left. Lucifer was sent off to return the car, clearly borrowed just for guests. Kris took a first try at getting Prometheus talking. "Those spires look huge. Are they one huge rock each?"

"One piece, cut from the living rock and pulled here by raw human power," he said proudly. "The Guides thought such a project would bind us together against anything, and it surely did. Not a single person who Bore the Stones has ever left. Lucifer keeps telling me that his generation should be given the chance to Bear the Stones. A different set, maybe for the rear entry. What do you think?"

"Anything that builds community spirit is always good," Kris said. No need to raise the subject of Pandemonium. Then again, the claim that no one who had Borne the Stones had ever left hinted that some who hadn't had indeed walked away.

Just how much trouble was this colony in?

"Would it be too much to ask how you found us?" Prometheus said carefully. "There's nothing at the jump point. When we arrived, we installed a fiber-optic hub. Nothing is sent over the airwaves."

"I came looking for you after we talked to a trader who had been here." Or so the pirate claimed.

"Oh," the local said.

"Once we were in orbit we saw your heat signature and your mounds." Kris hoped she was not condemning the local peasants to heatless winters. Still, she wanted to keep them talking.

"Hmm," Prometheus said. "The last ship here showed us how our power lines were visible to the jump point, so we bought everything he had to make superconducting wire and restrung our power grid . . . underground. I guess we'll have to add an extra meter of earth to our homes and civic buildings to make sure they stay closer to the ambient temperature."

"You really believe some alien horde is coming?" Kris asked.

Prometheus opened his mouth to reply but then closed it and nodded to something ahead of Kris.

The company approached a large crossroad, grassy like the one they walked, unmarked in stone or otherwise. However, there was a large bluish stone, a meter on a side. Standing atop it, a man in only a breechcloth was in full harangue. His back was to the Marine company, so he didn't see why some of his two or three dozen listeners suddenly grew distracted and looked past him.

It didn't matter, he was either in love with his voice or his message . . . or both.

"The unbelievers will be damned, and boiled in their own blood. The Choosers will take them, by the dozens, by the hundreds and serve them up broiled and fried. Poached and minced. Woe to those who ignored the shouts of we who have heard the Angels of Light and did not turn to follow us.

"But joy shall come to those the Choosers pass over. Those who have given themselves over to the Angels of Light will rise up to the ninth heaven, there to be ministered to by the most high angels. Great is the reward of those who have done everything that was asked of them."

The preacher turned then, following the gaze of his listeners to Kris and her Marines. But it was not them he next addressed.

"Woe to you, Prometheus? It is not the warmth of fire or the guidance of light that you bring. Always it is outsiders. The damned, fit only for the demons to eat. Why do you waste your time and our goods on the likes of these with hardened hearts and deaf ears? Smite them down. Give up your life of comfort and plenty and join your brothers who tell only the truth about what is to come."

"Brother Jonah, I do what the Angels of Light tell me, as I know you do what they tell you. Please continue on with your daily lesson. I assure you, I will do all that the Angels put within my reach to open the ears of those I now take to listen to the wisdom of the Great Guides."

That made quite a hit with the crowd. Kris caught the murmured words "the Great Guides" several times.

"May they bless your efforts more than they ever blessed them before," Jonah said, not willing to let Prometheus have the last word.

The Marines marched on. Maybe Jonah did his shouting a bit more softly. His noise fell behind.

"I didn't think your associates believed in God," Kris said when she could whisper it.

"We don't, but thirty years ago, the Great Guides announced that the Aliens of the Light privately called themselves angels and their home solar system Heaven. Some of the more simple-minded like Jonah are easily confused by that and miss the fine points of distinction that the Great Guides highlighted."

"So everyone doesn't see matters the same way?"

"Jonah's son walked away, and he has never forgiven me. My son, Lucifer, preaches among the young the need for another Bearing of the Stones. His son boarded a starship that I had done business with and now is lost to us forever.

"It is a heavy burden for Jonah to bear."

Kris let the rest of the walk pass in silence.

9

Kris had been in huge buildings, both human built and alien. The Assembly of the Great Guides set new standards. From the outside, it looked like a massive grassy knoll . . . maybe hillock would be a better word. Inside was an enormous amphitheater. The ceiling hung low, almost claustrophobic in its oppressiveness. The conflict between the two feelings left Kris confused.

No doubt the effect was intended.

With a will, Kris shook the feelings. *I'm a Longknife. A naval officer. A princess. You may have the ceiling, but I have the Marines.* The thought brought a grim smile to her lips.

But that didn't let her escape one final thought. There was a whole lot of dirt up there. Hopefully, the Great Guides had better engineers than theologians. It would be a very bad day if the roof picked just now to surrender to gravity.

No Marines were out in front of Kris. Either to avoid getting intimidatingly close or to spread out his troops, Jack had Gunny forming the Marines in a line behind the top row of seats. It was just Kris and Jack, Abby and Penny making the long walk toward the central sanctuary, a huge place in its own right.

Chief Beni hung back with the Marines. Kris could already hear his excuse that he could measure anything from back there.

Kris slowed as she reached the bottom of the amphitheater. What appeared to be the sanctuary stood atop a six-foot wall above the floor. There was no visible entrance.

Then suddenly there was. A wide stairwell opened before her. "We are very honored. The Great Guides have deigned that you should approach them," Prometheus said.

Kris felt delighted with that honor . . . and knew she was being manipulated. Just at the edge of her hearing there was music.

Nelly, ask the chief if we're getting "happiness" or "I believe anything" gas.

Chief Beni says there are minor traces of both gases as well as low harmonics reinforcing them.

Kris tapped two skin patches on the inside of her wrist. The antidotes to both gases shot into her bloodstream. To her right, her team did the same. To her left, Prometheus climbed the stairs, a near beatific joy on his face.

A few feet past the stairs, a rail rose from the floor, marking the limit, apparently, of their honor . . . and advance. Kris reached it, stopped, looked around, and saw only a vast expanse of white marble. So she turned to look the place over until whoever was choreographing this show caught up with her.

Thick carpet covered the riser seats, the better for soft bottoms to endure long sermons or harangues. The Marines covered the entire top row, one every five yards. Every fifth Marine faced backward, keeping an eye on what might come up behind them. Gunny and sergeants roamed along their rank, making sure troopers stayed attentive even though nothing seemed to be happening.

"Beni, any little word of advice would come in handy just now."

"I'm not finding any electronic action in this whole anthill. You know there are such things as hydraulics and mechanical motors, Your Highness. I got a feeling these folks have swallowed a really big old-timer's pill."

Which might be true, but was no help to Kris.

A hissing brought Kris back to face front. There was steam in the air above them; the music was louder and more pounding. Kris had been to a few rock concerts in college that were this lame.

Then again, she'd done them drug free, and most of her friends who hadn't had seemed to enjoy them a whole lot more.

Oh well.

A block of ebony marble began to descend from the ceiling. Twelve white thrones followed. Lights flashed through the steam, making the black stone and gleaming thrones sparkle and roil. Kris counted ten people seated on the thrones, two empty. So much for flexibility.

Kris eyed the descending guides. Nelly, please match

THESE GREAT GUIDES AGAINST THE ONES RUNNING THIS SHOW
BEFORE THEY LIT OUT FROM HUMAN SPACE.

THEY DO NOT MATCH. NONE OF THESE TEN WERE AMONG
THOSE TWELVE.

Which leaves two that could match, but Kris wouldn't take a
bet on them. And which set of Guides had decided the good
aliens were angels. How bloody had been the change in revela-
tion.

Kris knew politics could become a blood sport. Her father
had kept it otherwise . . . most of the time. Apparently, when
angels talked directly to you, things could go real bad.

The slab of marble, or at least what looked like one, settled
twenty meters from Kris. The twelve thrones were just about
ready to touch down. The steam dissipated, letting Kris spot the
supporting cables on the slab and chairs. Nelly estimated they
could support no more than 125 kilos except for the overweight
man who sat in the middle. He had double cabling.

They were not quite down when Kris took the lead. "Hi,
folks. I'm glad you could find time in your busy day to meet with
me. I represent King Raymond I, monarch of one hundred and
twelve planets, and I'm here to open relationships with Xanadu."
Kris blessed them with her best princess smile.

Nothing happened while the thrones settled into place behind the fake marble. Nothing happened while the fat man in
the middle studied Kris for a long moment through small beady
eyes.

"You do not speak to us," he growled. "We speak to you, and
you answer only when it is our wish for you."

"You did notice the Marines lining your sacred precinct,
didn't you?" Kris said.

"I could tell them to leave, and they would obey me."

"You might want to double-check that, fellow. Your 'I believe anything' juice is pretty out-of-date."

"You there," he said, waving at Jack. "Leave us."

Jack's right hand went to rest on his holster. He shook his
head. "Sorry, Charley, it ain't gonna happen."

"Let me tell you what is going to happen," Kris said, casually settling to a half-sitting position on their rail. "Humanity is
set to do another spread out. You're only two jumps from
Cuzco, so it's not going to be very long before there's a lot of

traffic through your system. You are soon going to go public in a big way."

"I told them we should have moved farther out," a woman said, three down from the big guy in the middle.

"Cuzco was growing like a weed even before we moved here," said a man on the opposite side.

"They began the migration eighty years ago. It was too late to change," put in another beside him.

"Silence!" said beady eyes.

Kris spoke into the sudden quiet. "You have only two choices. You can profit from the traffic through your jump points in the usual ways, providing reaction mass, food, and cross shipments from a space station you really need to build."

"Or?" he asked.

"Or someone else will build a space station above you and see that trade is properly supported."

"And if we do not want to trade with the rest of you?"

"That really isn't an option," Kris said flatly.

"You demand that we join in your king's hundred-and-twelve-planet association," the woman guide said.

"Oh no, you totally misunderstand me on that," Kris moved quickly to correct. "No planet may join United Sentients that is not acceptable to all the other members. And no planet without a democratic government has been invited in. There's no question about your joining King Raymond's United Sentients. What we cannot allow you to become is either a rogue state or a resource for fitting out piracy to prey on the rest of humanity."

"And if we choose to have nothing to do with your humanity?"

"I really don't see how that can happen."

"I think maybe we should think on this," said the guy who had complained about the eighty-year effort to build Xanadu.

"I'd be glad to leave you for a month," Kris said.

"Then we will have a message for you in a month," the speaker said.

Kris stood, gave him a regal nod, then led her team out. The Marines performed a smooth retrograde, and in only a few minutes Kris was walking down the street she'd just walked up. Somehow, Prometheus detached himself, leaving Kris with more questions than why everyone was running around in bedsheets.

The pirateship *Compton Maru* claimed it had just called on

Xanadu. Had it? Was that the level of outside contact the Guides were maintaining? This visit had answered none of those, and Kris wasn't interested in hanging around.

Hercules shushed the other guides as their thrones disappeared below the sacred precincts. They had learned the hard way about the tiny listening devices that were so popular in human space. If they hadn't gotten a spacer drunk, they would have been taken even more advantage of by the last few starships through. Now, he and the other guides stripped, turned their robes over to security, and washed themselves thoroughly before submitting themselves for scanning by their own electronics experts.

"Oh Great Guide for our Way, no hidden bugs speak to us."

"What about the Assembly hall?"

"We found nothing there."

"I do not like this," said Leonides. "They always use bugs. If we cannot find them, it only means they have again gained an advantage over us."

"But if this Kris did not bother to bug us, how can we persuade you that you are not bugged, foolish husband of mine?" Gorgo said, with a curt shake of her wet hair.

"It does not matter," Hercules said. "Bring me a new robe and bring me Lucifer."

Robed, the ten adjourned to a room where most decisions were made. Here, deep under the mound of the assembly, a warm spring flowed. From a vent in the earth rose the vapors of the future. But today Hercules did not go to smell the vapors or eat the sacred mushroom; instead, he sat on his throne, first among equals.

Lucifer entered and immediately went to one knee before the Guides as they arranged themselves on their thrones. These did not fly through the air and were solid marble, with cushions to soften the seats of all authority over the present and future.

"Young man," Hercules said, "the twelve have a mission for you and your associates."

"We are ready and worthy of it," the youth said.

"It was foretold at your birth you would be the Bringer of Light. I call upon you to bring down the sky on the faithless."

"How will I do that, O Seer of the Future?"

"In four days, once that interloper is out of our system, you and your companions will go far from Xanadu, but when the Angels of Light greet you, it will be as kings and queens."

The young man gulped, but stood. "I will gather my companions. None of those you called will fail you."

And Lucifer turned on his heels and went from them.

"**Shall** we leave a jump buoy?" Captain Drago asked, as they halted in front of the jump between Xanadu and Pandemonium.

"We didn't leave buoys at the jumps from Cuzco," Kris said. She hadn't wanted to make the Great Guides mad before she talked to them. Fat lot of good that had done. "We gave them a month. We can wait. Captain, take us through."

"Aye, aye, Your Highness. Sulwan, make it so."

With a quick shot of maneuvering jets, they were in another system. Drago put on one gee and boosted sunward even before sensors reported back on what the locals had shortened to Panda.

Passive sensors were the first to hint at trouble.

"I'm not getting any chatter on the communication circuits," Chief Beni reported with a frown. "And I'm getting neutrino emissions from what looks like two ships in orbit over Panda."

"We've never had more than one freighter show up a year," Andy Fronour said from the jump seat he occupied on the bridge. "How could there be two now?"

"We'll have to wait until we establish communications," Kris said. "At this distance, there's an hour lag time between us saying anything and them answering back."

Thirty minutes later, the main screen on the bridge opened up with full visuals. Kris knew at first glance things were not good. Staring at her in the impeccable uniform of a merchant captain was Captain William Tacoma Thorpe, former commander of the Patrol Corvette *Typhoon*, and, given a choice between early retirement and a court-martial, formally of the Wardhaven Navy.

"What is he doing here?" was Kris's first question.

Nothing good, had to be the first answer.

"Unidentified freighter, there is no business here for you. Sheer off and do not approach Presley's Pride."

Kris mashed the kill-screen button.

"Presley's Pride?" Fronour said, leaping from his jump seat. "I don't think there's anyone on the planet with that name."

"Apparently there is now," Kris said, and filled them in on who was talking to them.

Captain Drago didn't seem surprised. He did want to make sure he got it right "He was your first skipper in the Navy." Kris agreed that he was. "And he ended up retiring out of the Navy in lieu of a full court-martial." Kris agreed he did.

"Explains why I get such interesting looks at the bar when I admit skippering your ship," Drago said, rubbing his chin.

"Stay on my good side," Kris suggested.

"What happened?" Drago said, very serious now.

"You're not authorized that information," Jack told him.

"But I sure would like to hear the story," Abby put in.

"If she told you, I'd have to kill you," Jack said.

"You and what army?" Abby said, with a toothy smile.

"Me and my Marines."

"Might be interesting to see who'd be the last one standing."

"Folks," Kris cut in, "I think we have a full to-do list for to-day. Could we put a rousing good intramural fight off until we have some free time?"

"We never have any free time," Abby complained.

"Considering what you do with it, is it any wonder I keep you busy?" Kris said.

"Ah, folks, what do we tell this former associate of our princess?" Drago asked. "In about an hour we'll be getting a new message from him, one showing his surprise at once more crossing paths with his well-remembered subordinate."

"You're the captain," Kris noted.

"I feel a sudden case of laryngitis coming on," Drago said.

"Take a pill, quick," Kris said.

The captain shook his head. "Sorry, my princess, but this is not the part I signed on for. I and my crew will support you fully, but this," he said, with an expressive shrug, "is a matter for 'one of those Longknifes.'"

Well, gal, you did want to have all the fun, didn't you, that nagging little voice in the back of Kris's head said.

Yeah, but I was so looking forward to exploring. Who'd have expected Captain Thorpe to be here ahead of me.

Afraid to face your old captain? Scared he'll buffalo you like he did last time? Kris took a deep breath. Yes, he'd run her ragged, but she'd come up for air . . . and then she'd changed everything. She was the one still serving. He was the one out.

Kris unsnapped her station-chair restraint and went to stand squarely in front of the forward screen.

"Chief, how long before something comes back from Thorpe?"

"Five, maybe ten minutes, ma'am."

"Tell me before you put it on-screen."

Captain Thorpe did not keep her waiting. Five minutes later, Chief Beni announced, "A new message is coming in."

Kris squared her back, schooled her face to neutral, and said, "Put it on the main screen." And found herself staring into Captain Thorpe's confident smile.

"Long time no see, Ensign. Ah, so it's lieutenant now. Tell me, what could bring you out here, so far from the nearest debutante ball? Over," he said, signaling he was ready to yield the connection to her.

"I am Princess Kristine Longknife, commanding the exploration task force on the USS *Wasp*. We are exploring matters beyond the Rim, and thought we'd drop by Pandemonium for some fresh vegetables. Over to you, Captain Thorpe."

Kris kept her voice even, allowing no special inflection to either "Captain" or "Thorpe." She'd gone over that very carefully in her mind. Chief Beni cut the commlink.

"What do we do now?" Jack asked.

"Wait to see how he reacts," Kris said. "He said Presley's Pride. We said Pandemonium. With luck, he'll explain the discrepancy. Meanwhile, Mr. Fronour, could you and Chief Beni please connect us with your family? We've got an hour before our next conversation with Thorpe, and I'd like to know something about things dirtside."

"Lieutenant, I'm getting something from one of the ships in orbit," Chief Beni put in.

"What kind of something?"

The chief's round cherubic face looked pained. "Just a bit of backscatter from a very tight beam it's sending down to the planet. Nelly, could you maybe make something of it?" It was the absolute first time he'd ever asked Kris's pet computer for help.

"It is very weak, and very scattered. We are only picking up parts of the message. And it is very encrypted. I will need a lot more of the message to crack it," Nelly said.

"Have at it, girl. It's not like there's a lot to do. But you, Chief, tell me what kind of noise that planet is making."

The chief shook his head. "There is nothing down there. No power plants, no net. Not so much as a ten-watt radio."

"You sound like Xanadu," Kris told Fronour.

"Not us, ma'am. We had dams pumping electricity to lots of homesteads two years ago. There was a full net, voice and video. Where's it gone?" he asked, voice breaking.

"Someone's closed it down," Jack said.

Kris liked the way Jack chose the gentlest option. The place was just closed down. In time, they would turn it back on. And the young man would hold his baby and wife.

"Jack, put your Marines on alert, just in case we need to help folks turn Pandemonium back on."

"Our pleasure, ma'am," Jack said, with a jaunty salute and a quick about-face. "Mr. Fronour, you want to come with me. The pictures from out here are a bit poor. We could use your help in figuring out the layout of the land." The farmer went with Jack, eager to help. With luck, the Marines would keep him busy and his mind off of the many reasons why his home could be so silent.

Kris turned to Captain Drago. "Check out the lasers. I want the capacitors at full as we approach. Sulwan, could you arrange our final approach to orbit so that we're behind Pandemonium's largest moon for as long as possible?"

"I was about to make the same request," Captain Drago said. "Do it, Sulwan."

"And what other approach do you think I'd make to a former corvette captain's unidentified ship?" Sulwan said with a harsh laugh. "Please, you didn't hire any dumb officers."

The chuckles around the bridge sounded relieved at that.

"Now, Chief, talk to me. Tell me stories about the ships ahead of us and the planet they orbit. So far, you've been way too quiet for my tastes," Kris said, as she pulled her station chair over next to Beni's.

"Ma'am, I regret as much as you that there is not all that much to talk about."

And thirty minutes later, when the commlink flashed red, the chief still had said far too little for Kris.

Kris took a moment, as she stood before the main screen, to make sure that her undress whites were properly in place and her gig line was perfectly straight. She would not allow her former captain to pick at her before her command.

Satisfied, she waved at the chief. "Put him on."

Again, Captain Thorpe's face filled the screen. But it was the bridge behind him she studied. It, and the people on it.

Thorpe's Merchant Marine uniform was impeccable. But those behind him wore a thoroughly ununiform mix of civilian clothes. Two were in mismatched khakis; one's hat had a rated officer's emblem on it, the other a chief's.

His bridge looked about as Navy as Kris's did. Was it his reality . . . or only appearance like Kris's? *Good question, gal. Do you see any answers?* Kris didn't.

One thing was apparent. To the right of Thorpe were two stations. Navigation and helm? To his left were two more. Offensive and defensive weapons? No question, there were too many stations on that bridge for an honest, working freighter.

No doubt, Thorpe had done his own check around Kris's bridge and identified too many stations for a simple exploration ship.

"Well, Princess," he said, twisting her princess status into some kind of crime, "as you can see, this is not the Pandemonium you are looking for but a just-started new colony, Presley's Pride, dutifully registered under Iberium regulations on Cuzco.

"You have no business here. If you do not have enough reaction mass to reverse course and boost out of this system, you may divert to the nearest gas giant and refuel.

"If you approach this planet, I will assume that you are hostile and take appropriate actions. Be aware, my ship is not unarmed," he ended, giving Kris a stern, captainly scowl.

Apparently, his sensors had not yet advised him of the size of the lasers Kris was now powering up on the *Wasp*. She would love to see the reaction on his face when they did, but strongly suspected it would fall between their brief talks. From the way Chief Beni was working his boards, he would soon have a report on Thorpe's guns. Kris could wait on that.

NELLY, WHAT ABOUT HIS CLAIM ON PRESLEY'S PRIDE?

ALREADY SEARCHING THE DATA DUMP WE GOT ON CUZCO.
YES, THERE IS A PRESLEY'S PRIDE. HOLD IT! THAT SYSTEM IS
ALL THE WAY OVER ON THE OTHER SIDE OF THE ASSOCIATION.
THEY HAVE NO CLAIM ANYWHERE NEAR HERE.

Nelly opened a small window on the main screen. It showed
where they were, the six planets in the Iberium Association,
and, some fifty light-years from Pandemonium, Presley's Pride.

Kris allowed herself a deep scowl. "Captain Thorpe, not for
the first time, you seem to have a problem telling the truth to
me. Maybe even to the crew you are skippering. Presley's Pride
is a long way the other way from Cuzco."

Kris paused to let that sink in on those who would be listening to it a half hour from now on Thorpe's command.

"The *Wasp* has aboard her the grandson of the founder of
Pandemonium, as well as fifty containers of cargo purchased for
this planet. We are going to make delivery. I suggest you cause
me and my ship no trouble as we go about our lawful business."

With that bombshell, Kris cut the commlink.

The ship's clock said it was noon, and Kris was hungry
enough to be glad of it. "I'm headed for chow. Captain Drago,
call me if we get any more message traffic from my old friend.
Chief Beni, you're eating with me in officer's country."

Putting her best smile on, Kris headed for the wardroom.

11

Captain Drago would have preferred one galley and mess for the *Wasp*. However, Gunnery Sergeants have definite ideas about propriety. Kris did not make the mistake of disagreeing with Gunny when he said, "This ship needs an enlisted mess."

Having lost that argument, she was in no position to disagree when Professor mFumbo insisted his boffins needed their own lounge for professors and pub for technicians.

On the *Wasp*, there were plenty of places to get a hamburger.

Kris settled at an empty table in the wardroom after selecting a light lunch. It didn't stay empty for long.

Captain Drago took a seat across from her. "What do you think is going on down there?"

Kris tested her salad. The lettuce was showing its age. She had not been willing to take anything on board from Xanadu and really was hoping to buy some fresh produce and meat here.

"I could only guess," Kris said. "What say we wait for more to go on before we start shouting 'ready, aim, fire.'"

"That's nice to hear," Drago said. "Rather startling coming from a Longknife, but nice to hear."

"Kris, is this a 'filibuster expedition'?" Nelly asked.

Kris chuckled. "I don't know what one of those things are, so how can I accuse anyone of doing one"?

"I found it in my research," Nelly said. "Back in the nineteenth century on Earth, freebooters and mercenaries would put together an armed expedition in a wealthy country and go off to a poor one and take it over, loot it, and either leave it or keep running it. Could that be what Captain Thorpe and company are doing here?"

"Very good research," Kris said, knowing full well that her computer was going far beyond what usually passed for a computer search . . . and doing it after setting up the search conditions herself. Nelly was a growing girl. And a surprising one.

Did this come from teaching a twelve-year-old?

No way to tell.

"They've got an ex–Navy captain running it," Captain Drago said. "And I'd bet money that tight-beamed message to the deck was to trigger pullers. Sure fits the bill."

Kris nodded as the piece easily fit into the jigsaw puzzle Pandemonium had suddenly become. "And no doubt Chief Beni will have a full report on the armament of Thorpe's command."

"Yes I do," the chief said, setting a hugely loaded tray down at Kris's left elbow.

"He's in zero-gee orbit," Beni started, only after stretching his mouth around a mightily stacked hamburger. "He's only running a trickle off his reactors. Yep, he has two reactors though he's doing his level best to hide one of 'em."

"And guns?" Captain Drago and Kris asked as their patience wore out. "Has he got anything charged?" Kris finished.

"Full capacitors for two pulse lasers and a long popgun, size on either unknown," the chief said.

Drago let out a low whistle. "Your former captain sounds like someone eager to do unto others before they do unto him."

"Something I noticed before," Kris breathed softly.

"Will we have to fight our way into orbit?" Drago asked.

"Too early to tell. Captain, please launch two probes, one for the jump to Xanadu, the other for this system's other jump."

"Load on them a report on what we've found?" Drago asked.

"Yes," Kris answered.

"But there are no buoys for them to pass a message along to on the other side," the chief pointed out.

"Thorpe won't know that, will he?" Kris said.

"Sneaky, just like a Longknife," Drago said, then started muttering into his commlink.

"What's our sneaky Longknife up to?" Jack asked as he joined the table, taking the space at Kris's right elbow. Their passenger, Andy Fronour, took the seat on his right.

Kris quickly brought Jack up to date on Thorpe's armament.

"So he's hot and loaded. Sure you wouldn't like to come back in a few weeks with, say, a half dozen cruisers?"

"Nelly found a word I'd never heard of," Kris said. "What does filibuster mean to you?"

Jack took a bite from his club sandwich and studied the ceiling for a moment. "In politics, that's what the minority party does to slow down your old man. Or, on old Earth, it's a bunch of jolly optimists with too much time and firepower on their hands going down and helping the poor stay poor." Jack swallowed his bite. "Let me guess, the last one applies here."

Drago shook his head. "This Presley's Pride thing. It's off to hell and gone the other side of the Iberium Association. Are they planning on stripping this place and setting up there?"

"The pilgrims who settled in Plymouth, Massachusetts, Earth, thought they were heading for Virginia," Nelly said.

Kris shrugged. "Whether they rechristen Panda to Presley and say 'oops, we took a wrong turn,' or haul everyone over there, it's not going to be very much fun for them."

"What are you going to do?" Fronour asked, not looking all that interested in what little food he'd put on his plate.

"That is something we'll have to think about carefully as we do this approach," Kris said. "Having you here, however, gives us a lot more options when it comes to calling Thorpe's bluff. The real question is, can we do it without getting a lot of people killed in the process?"

"But if you run for help," Fronour said, his voice shaking, "there may not be anyone here when you get back."

"Yes," Jack whispered softly, eyeing Kris.

Kris weighed all she'd learned so far. Then added in all she'd done to complicate her former captain's own tactical situation . . . and decided it was still too soon to make a call.

"What does Panda look like?" Kris asked. "Chief, you have any good planet pictures yet?"

"We're learning more by the moment, but it's only starting to take shape. Nelly, could you show what we have?"

The computer heliographed a map onto the top of the tablecloth, but it left much to be desired. Was that a terrain feature or a drop of soup left behind by a previous diner?

Kris applied her finger to said item and found it soup. Even with that knowledge, it was none too easy to get her spinning gray matter to factor out the blob.

Captain Drago retrieved a roll of plastic flimsy from beside a stack of readers next to the wardroom couch. Unrolled, the meter-by-meter square quickly became a map of the entire planet.

"Where's the populated section?" Kris asked.

Andy pointed, and Nelly zoomed in the map to show a bay off a large ocean in the northern temperate zone and a river running inland. Beyond that, it was hard to tell yet.

Andy began to fill them in. "The place we settled in is covered with what we call 'broom trees.' Tall things, fifty to a hundred meters, with thick bare trunks and all their foliage at the top. It's not much use, trunk is tougher than steel. Can't mill it. And what passes for leaves can't be eaten. We burn them out, as well as the swamp bush on the ground below, and plant it with bramble berries. Nasty stuff the local animals won't touch but the goats love. After a few years of the berries and goats, we've got the beginnings of a human-usable topsoil, and we seed it with microbes and worms and plant it in a base crop not all that different from what you saw on Xanadu."

"Let's see what I can do with that," Nelly said. "All this greenish purple sounds like your broom trees." A huge block of the map leading up to an inland mountain range took on a light crosshatching, and the map zoomed in closer on what was left.

Along the river leading in from the landing bay and its various tributaries, several holes in the crosshatching showed clear, with a surrounding set of short black lines.

"Those are the burned but still-standing trunks of the broom trees," Andy supplied. "It must be late in the day, you can make out their shadows."

Jack nodded, his lips getting tight. "Not the place I'd want to set a lander down."

"The homesteads are in the clearings," Andy said, fingers going over the very centers of the arrangements.

"What about towns?" Kris asked.

"Not many. Landing hasn't grown a lot, 'cause we're mainly moving away from it. Grampa has picked up sticks three times since we first got here, selling out to folks that had more money than patience for building a place. Most of us Fronours are out here," he said, pointing at one of the tributaries that wandered off to the northeast, a low ridge between it and the rest of the slowly growing population of Pandemonium. Its northernmost boundary was marked by a long line of smoke from a fire.

"You still expanding?" Kris asked.

"I'd imagine so. We're not the only ones." Andy's finger roved over the western and southern boundaries, where fires still burned, as well as several large broom-tree areas that had been left behind bordering cleared land. "It's fall, and that's when we burn."

"How long does a fire usually take, from the time you set it until it burns out?" Kris asked.

Beside her, Jack nodded as his fingers traced over the fire line, then searched the terrain features beyond it. They came to rest on a small lake several klicks north of Fronour holdings.

Andy blinked in thought, then spoke slowly. "The broom trees store a lot of water in their trunks. You light the scrub under it for ten or twenty yards wide, say a mile or two long, then see how hot the fire gets. On a normal dry day, the fire catches and spreads for forty or fifty yards before it dies down. Usually, you can get two, maybe three, strips of that before the rains start and the fire goes cold."

"How long between lights?" Kris repeated her question in a different way.

"Three, four days," Andy said, then finally understand what Kris was getting at. "Three or four days ago, things were normal on Pandemonium and people were going about setting fire lines."

"So if we'd gotten here four or five days ago," Captain Drago said slowly, "Captain Thorpe would be the one doing the approach under our guns."

"We still wouldn't know what he was up to," Kris said, "and probably be even less prepared for the first broadside."

"There is that," Drago said.

"So what are you going to do?" Andy pleaded.

"Find out more about this picture," Kris said, turning to the man. "If I turn my Marines loose on your planet, it will quickly become a small vestibule to hell. Let's make sure we're visiting Hades on the people who deserve it."

Andy looked at Jack, then back at Kris, his face draining of color as he took in the cold heat of their meaning. "I meant for you," he said, stumbling, "I mean, I thought you'd help us."

"We will, Mr. Fronour," Kris said. "But you must realize, the help we bring is never cheap."

While the farmer gnawed on just what was coming in answer to his cry of need, Kris decided lunch was over. She folded her napkin and rose. For the questions she had now, the bridge was the place to find the answers.

12

On the bridge, Kris found a happy surprise. While they'd eaten, Sulwan had done another navigational miracle. Pandemonium had a rather large moon. With a bit of adjustment to the *Wasp*'s course, Sulwan sideslipped her approach to Panda so that the moon stayed between them and the bothersome Captain Thorpe.

"It will cover us right up to our final approach."

"That's going to limit my observations," Chief Beni said.

So a recon bird was knocked together and launched a few hours later. It flew about a hundred kilometers off the *Wasp*'s port bow, reporting what it saw of the rapidly growing planet.

Thorpe was rude enough to try jamming, but that was only expected. The scout was a lot closer to the *Wasp* and continued to do its reporting, switching codes at irregular intervals.

Abby provided the codes with only a slight arm twist from Kris. "These are from my private supply," the maid pointed out.

"No doubt," Kris said. "And, what with all the codes up your sleeve, you can rotate these to the bottom of the deck and bring them out sometime when they'll be long forgotten. Give."

Abby gave, grumbled a bit, and said she needed to attend to Cara's education. However, Cara was much more interested in staying underfoot, watching the goings-on of the bridge crew and the approaching moon. Neither the maid nor the twelve-year-old managed to slip out of Kris's peripheral vision.

Soon Kris would have to make some hard decisions.

The planet stayed silent. As the occupied section slipped past evening into solid night, it stayed both radio silent and dark. Not so much as a flickering campfire lit up the bleakness!

Captain Thorpe fell into silence, too, as it became clear that Kris was not about to wear ship from her closing course. He

continued steady in his low orbit. Which left Kris to wonder just
why he was making no reply to her change in approach. The answer to that might be trailing him by fifty kilometers.

"It appears to be an underpowered merchant ship," Chief
Beni said, looking pained that something might actually be just
what it looked to be. "Reactor isn't good for more than .85 gees.
Tanks are too small for more than a couple of jumps."

Kris's brother Honovi had asked her opinion when he got
the assignment in Parliament of writing new safety regs for
Wardhaven's merchant fleet. The less ship and more cargo
that a merchant hull moved, the better the profit margin. Over-
powerful engines and excessive reaction mass ate into that
bottom line.

Grampa Al had led the business interests that pushed for
trimming the standards to allow for ships that had just enough
range to make it from one port of call to another. "Stations sell
mass. Why ship water from one station to another?"

"How quickly people forgot that not all planets out on the
Rim have stations." Kris had tried to make a joke of it.

Grampa Al had roared back, "Don't tell a businessman how
to run his business. Short-range ships for short runs. Long-
range ships for longer runs! We're smart enough to send what
we need to earn a good return." And he'd won the day.

Now Kris found herself looking at a short-range ship far off
the beaten path. It should be Thorpe's problem. But his problem
could become hers in a hurry. Would he load it with trans-
portees from Panda and haul them off to Presley? Or had it
brought in a boatload of thugs to Panda to rechristen it Presley
and remind them who now owned the sweat of their brows?

But whatever bee was in Thorpe's bonnet, it was clear Kris
would have two separate battles on her hands. One on the ground
for her Marines and one in orbit for the *Wasp*.

Question? Which had the strongest call on a Longknife?

And where did she put several dozen scientists and one
twelve-year-old girl? Kris didn't see any easy answers, so she
settled on asking questions. "Sulwan, how should we handle the
final approach?"

"Interesting you should ask," the navigator said, with a
happy grin. "I've got a really nifty idea."

Kris had hardly got "let's see it," out of her mouth before
Sulwan was showing it to Kris on the main screen.

"Assuming your former captain doesn't mess with his orbit any more than he is now, we head in past the moon about the time he heads behind Panda." The screen showed just that.

"Now, we could keep braking like good, predictable fools and end up coming in with our tail to him his entire next time around. That's a temptation it would take a saint to resist shooting at. Your old boss any kind of saint?"

Kris shook her head sourly.

"I kind of thought so. What do you say we go to high-gee stations, slap on 2.24 gees, and put ourselves in orbit around that large and no doubt lovely moon?" The screen showed them doing a swing around the face of the moon toward Panda and heading back on a high elliptical orbit that had the benefit of putting them behind the moon about the time Thorpe came around Panda. He might catch a glimpse, but not much before they disappeared again.

"Now this orbit is hardly one we'll stay in," Sulwan said. "I figure we cut it short with more high gees, and about the time he's headed back behind Panda, we make a dash for Panda ourselves." The screen showed them coming in high and fast, but out of sight of Thorpe before doing more hard maneuvering in orbit to settle themselves sedately down in the same orbit as the old captain, but 180 degrees away from him. As far as night and day was for the planet.

"Do we have to do it all that fast?" Captain Drago asked.

"No," his navigator said.

"Yes," Kris said.

"Okay." The captain sighed. "I take it that Sulwan thinks we could do things as slow as I might want to do. You, my princess, no doubt want to go for the fast track that gives poor Captain Thorpe as little time to adjust as possible."

"And I'd also like to suggest that some of us put our heads down for a nap," she said, looking straight at Jack. "It's nighttime where we're headed on Panda."

"We, Your Highness," the Marine said.

"We," Kris said.

"Oh joy," Captain Drago breathed. "I shall have my ship all to myself this battle."

"Oh, I'll be looking over your shoulder," Kris insisted. "But from the comfort of dirt under my feet."

"Who's going to provide you an intel feed?" Abby asked.

"I'll take Penny dirtside with me. You stay up here and look after Cara. Make sure you and Penny coordinate."

"And me?" Chief Beni asked.

"You stay up here. I'll use the Marines for tech support. You coordinate with Professor mFumbo and his boffins."

Which lost Kris at least a half hour of the nap she wanted.

"What do you mean, taking me and my scientists into a gun-fight?" mFumbo's deep base roared as he barged into Kris's stateroom, not bothering to knock.

Kris had laid herself out carefully for her nap so as not to muss her undress khakis. She suspected that a part of her, the one that refused to be startled and raise the hairs on the back of her head at this noisy arrival, was expecting this.

"You didn't complain all that much about it when we went trolling for pirates," Kris said, doing a crunch with a twist that got her sitting in her bunk, facing the upset boffin.

"I didn't expect a pirate to bite. None of us did. Do you know we had a pool going in science country. Only two were betting you'd get us into a fight. A fight. As in one. Now you're gunning for a second one, and this guy is former Navy, who has lasers hidden aboard his ship."

"Have your techs identified the guns?" Kris asked.

"No, not yet."

"I assume you are working with Chief Beni."

"It's our necks, too."

"I'm glad you see it that way," Kris said, with as small a smile as she could manage.

"But see here, this is totally too much. We've hardly gotten any science done."

"You didn't object when Captain Drago took on cargo."

"He promised to upgrade our quarters with some of his ill-gotten take," mFumbo rumbled, looking for all the world like a three-year-old with his fingers caught in the cookie jar.

Kris again had to swallow a smile. She'd never have thought the imposingly tall, ebony professor could look so embarrassed. She was tempted to let this conversation go on, but she found herself stifling a yawn. She did want a nap.

"Lieutenant, I suggest you and the other technical support staff review the paperwork you filled out before boarding."

mFumbo twisted his face into something not quite ugly but nowhere near submissive. "So I'm 'Lieutenant' now, am I?"

"And your team are ensigns and warrant officers," Kris pointed out, "in Wardhaven's Naval Reserve, entitled to all the obligations, protections, and fun those papers allow. That includes facing my old captain, who loves to ride ensigns."

The professor and, by the commission issued by the Parliament of Wardhaven, officer and gentleman, took in a huge breath and followed it with a deep sigh. "Dr. Rimlin warned me those papers were not pro forma, not with a Longknife aboard, but I ignored her. She will have a few words to say to me over dinner tonight, and I will be reduced to hanging my head and allowing that a sociologist just might be wiser than a xenobiologist. How the world has turned."

"Now, may I take my nap?" Kris asked, carefully laying herself out on her back again.

"Yes, I will withdraw in abject defeat," Professor mFumbo said, turning out the light and opening the door. "But I wonder how well you will sleep. That little girl certainly did not sign herself into any Navy, now, did she?"

And the door closed, leaving Kris in the dark. She was sleepy, but mFumbo's last salvo had hit home.

The situation on the planet they were headed for was full of unknowns. And if Captain Thorpe was involved in cooking it up, it would not be an easy one to figure out or make come out any way but how Thorpe wanted it. Kris should be concentrating on how to gnaw that knot.

But that knot was not her only problem.

The list of dead at Kris's hands was long and never seemed to stop growing. That they'd been the "bad guys" and died so that good might prevail was comfort to Kris.

The list of those who had died in Kris's various commands was much longer than she liked and also seemed destined to grow. The only comfort Kris could take was that they had all volunteered and died so that others might live in freedom.

But Kris was risking a twelve-year-old. And twelve was too young to volunteer for anything.

13

Kris woke with none of her questions any closer to an answer, splashed some water on her face, and headed for the bridge. They were two hours away from inserting themselves into orbit around the moon, something Kris expected would be a surprise for Thorpe and knock him off his game.

Unfortunately, Kris's game plan was not developing all that well, either. "Have we found the population?" Kris asked.

"No, Your Highness," Chief Beni answered. When the chief took to "Your Highness-ing" her, she knew she was in trouble.

"Nothing on the people?"

"Zero, nada, zilch," Jack said. He was standing next to the chief, hunched over the man's sensors, along with Professor mFumbo, who added his own conclusion.

"We've totally struck out."

"Should we launch a better sensor suite?" Kris asked.

"We did, while you were getting your beauty rest," the chief growled. "Please, trust us, me and the prof's crew know our way around sensors."

"Sorry," Kris said. She could never remember a time when the chief had been this grouchy.

"Everyone is hiding," Jack said.

"Can you blame them?" mFumbo added.

Kris nodded as she gnawed at the problem. "They know there's a warship in their sky loaded with sensors. Bad guys on the ground as well. They're hiding from them. So, of course, they're not showing off for us. Am I usually this slow?"

For a long moment, no one answered that.

"No, Your Highness," the chief said, "you're not usually this slow. Me and the crew are usually able to jack up the gain on things and give you more intel feed than the other guys. Only this time, I can't do any better than they are."

"Maybe when we get closer," Jack offered the chief.

"And maybe not," Penny said as she joined them on the bridge. Andy Fronour trailed only a step behind her.

"Yes, my very esteemed intelligence chief," Kris said, "do you come bearing a rare answer?"

"Which I may keep to myself, if all I'm going to get is more maligning."

"My, my," mFumbo said through a shining white grin, "aren't our warriors touchy today?"

"As they should be," Kris said gently, "since they're the ones who will do a drop mission from orbit right into one huge question mark. Please, Penny, what have you found out that the rest of us haven't?"

"What's the kind of soil down there?" Penny asked, clearly unwilling to give up her advantage yet.

"Alluvial," Professor mFumbo said. "Our soil scientist did a full workup. Not that it told us much."

"Oh, it told you something, you just didn't hear it. I only found it myself while debriefing Andy here."

"Alluvial soil," Kris said slowly.

"Is easy to dig in," Nelly answered from Kris's neck.

"On hot summer days, we kids used to dig into mounds, riverbanks, whatever gave us a chance, and make our own cool forts. Grampa had his own cool storage house to keep ice in."

"The dirt came out easy," Penny added, "and given a couple of days' exposure to air, the cave turned as hard as concrete."

"In my databases," Nelly cut in, "there is a story about a war back in the bloody twentieth century in a place called Vietnam, where the resistance fighters dug tunnels to hide in. The soil there was alluvial."

"So Andy's people have literally gone to earth," Kris said.

"That's what I think," Andy said.

"And the bad guys?" Jack left hanging.

"Got a hot message from my good friend Thorpe to do their own vanishing act as soon as he found out I was leading a bunch of hard cases through his very own jump hole."

"Oh joy," Jack grumbled, "a game of blind man's bluff. I can't tell you how much I love my modern instrumentation. Going blind into a battle with a bunch of thugs as smart as my Marines does not make my bunny jump."

Kris let these answers cascade around in her brain for a moment, weighed what they told her, and found that she still didn't know nearly as much as she wanted to before she took strong men and women into armed battle. But she'd asked for this job. And this was what she wanted to do.

"Chief, look for assault vehicles, trucks, cars. Any kind of transportation. Hunt for their tracks if you can't find their bodies getting warm in the noonday sun. Panda's got too much settled area for a strike team to walk very far. They had to bring or steal vehicles. Where you find them, you'll find the guys holding the guns."

"Doing it, Your Highness," the chief said with a grin.

"You can dig a hole and hide on Panda. We've got to accept that. So we don't look for the cat. We look for the tail on the cat that it forgot to pull into the hole. Look, boys and girls, look."

14

The swing that put them in orbit around Panda's one moon was done at 2.55 gees deceleration. Sulwan put pedal to the metal only after Captain Thorpe was hull down behind Panda.

Thorpe might have gotten a brief glimpse of the *Wasp*'s sudden change of course. If he did, it was through the haze of the planet's atmosphere. It told him Kris was up to something, but only enough to leave him scratching his head wondering.

Kris learned a new thing or two. High-gee stations were never intended to cope with full ground battle rattle.

The *Wasp* would be under high-gee maneuvering until a few minutes before Kris took her Marine company into the boats. Thus, Kris found herself pinned by armor and gear weighing two and a half times its normal burden. Kris really wanted to meet the guy who decided it was "normal." Had *he* ever lugged it?

At 2.5 gees, it was just past bearable. And Sulwan was just getting started. Kris gritted her teeth and tried not to moan . . . at least into an open mike.

The forward screen ticked off the critical movements of the *Wasp* and Thorpe's ship. Just now, Thorpe was on the far side of Panda, expecting to come around for a perfect shot up the *Wasp*'s engines as Kris's ship finished its final break into orbit.

Instead, he'd get a look at the front end of the *Wasp* as it vanished into a lunar orbit swinging far out behind the moon. Kris wished she could see Thorpe's face when he found himself with a whole different set of ballistic problems on his hands.

Captain Thorpe held his face a rigid mask as every plan he'd made in the last three days shattered into question marks.

"What the hell does that Longknife girl think she's doing?"

Mr. Whitebred shouted. As one of the financial backers of this expedition, he considered it his right to shout at everyone. The man would benefit much from trading in his three-piece suit for an ensign's commission. Fifteen minutes under Thorpe's command, and he would learn a lot about leadership.

Unfortunately, the man already considered himself a leader. He had the money, didn't that make him a leader? Not for the first time, Thorpe wondered if this was such a good idea.

But it put that Longknife brat in the crosshairs of his eighteen-inch pulse lasers. That made up for a lot.

"We shall see what the Longknife girl is actually doing in a moment," Thorpe said, voice even, controlled. Around the bridge, his crew responded to his voice. His orders. Not the other man's screeching.

"She's been maneuvering at 2.5 gees," his sensor boss reported.

"I am projecting her deceleration and course," his offensive weapons officer announced. On the main screen, the moon took the center view. The pulsing red pip that portrayed that brat's ship slowed its hurtling flight toward Pandemonium, then cut back to skim a mere hundred kilometers above the moon and head out for a long, looping orbit that would take them a major part of the way to the jump point.

"Do you think she has finally done something logical?" Whitebred asked. "Is she headed back out?"

Thorpe shook his head even before the fool civilian got his question out. "Longknifes don't run," he snapped. "Weapons, project a revised course. Assume continued use of as much as three gees of deceleration. Can she cut off that time-wasting soar over the far side of the moon?"

"Working the problem, sir. Wait one," Weapons answered.

"Sensors, have you found what I asked you to look for?" Thorpe demanded, switching concerns. The young woman on weapons was good. Not as well trained as a naval officer, but certainly more trustworthy than a Longknife. She would attend to her course projection and reply when she had something.

"Yes, sir," Sensors replied. "I have the low-level chatter that is the signature of Smart Metal™, sir."

"Very good," Thorpe said, and allowed himself a smile. "Very, very good."

"What do you mean?" Whitebred asked.

"Just a moment, kind benefactor," Thorpe said. Whitebred preened on the title. Most of the crew knew it for what it was, a true warriors' curse for the money that was foolish enough to think gold could motivate a warrior.

"Weapons?" Thorpe said.

"I have a solution coming up, sir. Just a moment . . . I have a solution. Putting it on the screen."

The old high-soaring ballistic curve dissolved, to be replaced by a new one that swung a bit out over the moon before heading back to skim even lower over its surface.

"How close this time?"

"Less than fifty kilometers, sir. If they aren't lucky in their course, they may plow one big hole in an inconvenient mountain." Weapons' grin showed tiger's teeth at her own joke.

Thorpe allowed a grin in return. "That Longknife brat's luck is bound to go sour sooner or later. She uses so much of it. But let's assume her deal with the devil holds for one more orbit. Where does that put her final approach to our guns?"

"That would depend on how hard she's willing to accelerate away from the moon and decelerate into orbit, sir."

"Assume no more than three gees." Thorpe advised.

"And probably no less," Weapons said. Now she was really smiling as she went about her work. She had a dimple on the cheek nearest Thorpe. She was cute, and young, and so optimistic. Thorpe envied her that. And the chance to do well a job that needed doing.

He turned to see what Whitebred was yammering about now. "Are you sure she can't do more than three gees?"

"Honorable men that I know and respect paid a high price to discover that the Kamikaze-class Smart Metal™ ships can't handle more than three gees," Thorpe bit out.

"But didn't I read somewhere that the Peterwalds had solved that problem?" Whitebred fancied himself an expert in military matters because he had read a lot of things "somewhere."

Thorpe curtly shook his head. "That Longknife brat has served on my corvette and those silly fast patrol boats. They are pure Smart Metal™. There are no reports of Nuu Enterprises learning anything from the Peterwalds and producing hybrids. That's a Wardhaven gunboat messing in our affairs. I know Wardhaven gunboats up close and personal."

Whitebred eyed the upper-left-hand corner of the forward

screen. There, the best picture they'd gotten of the incoming ship was on permanent display. Thorpe had told everyone to get familiar with that target. To memorize it.

Whitebred hadn't been able to ignore it. "It does look like a merchant ship," he pointed out. "It's got that long spin between bow and engines in the stern. And it sure looks like those are containers, making the whole thing look boxy."

"Whitebred, walk with me," Thorpe said, teeth clenched.

Whitebred looked like a deer in headlights. Thorpe pointed him toward the captain's underway cabin. Whitebred went.

And once there, shrank as if from the white-hot rage of a maddened devil. "You will *never* question me before my bridge officers." Thorpe slammed the businessman in a voice so low and frigid as to have glacier force. "Never again will you raise a doubt about any order that I issue. Do you understand?"

Whitebred tried to step back but found himself forced to slump down on the captain's bed. Thorpe towered over him. Whitebred tried to stand up again, but failed. "You can't issue orders to me. I'm not one of your sailors," he insisted.

"No, you are not as useful as the cook's junior helper. All the other financiers stayed back where it was safe . . . comfortable. What are you doing out here, Whitebred?"

"Someone had to look after the moneyed interests."

"You think I couldn't? That Colonel Cortez would be cavalier with your money if you weren't here to nursemaid us?"

"No, Captain, no."

Thorpe shook his head, showing no belief in his master's words. "Whitebred, understand me. One more display like the last one, and I will have you locked up in your fine stateroom. Are we clear on this?"

"You can't do that. None of the crew would turn against their paymaster."

Thorpe snorted, and the smile he showed Whitebred was the ancient one. The kind tigers gave their prey just before they tore their throats out. The financier found his hands rising as if to protect his neck.

"Whitebred, these men and women will march with me into hell. They will go because they know I will lead them out again. You are far beyond your comfort zone. People with your soft hands and doughy white bellies should not trifle in the affairs of true warriors. I would hate to report to your associates safe at home that while we were defeating this Kris Longknife brat, regretfully, she killed you. Think about that."

Thorpe turned to go, then turned back again. "And stay off my bridge. I could suffer your idiotic rumblings when I had only unarmed farmers to chivvy. Longknife may be a spoiled brat, but she is no fool. Killing her will be a fight. A real fight is no place for the likes of you. Do we now understand each other?"

Whitebred already suspected that he would never understand the likes of Thorpe. Never wanted to. But even a lifelong civilian could understand when he'd been given an order as blunt and threatening as this one. "Yes," he said. "I understand."

Thorpe opened the door and headed back to the bridge. Whitebred, stood, tried to smooth his suit, and turned aft toward his room.

"How many gees are you going to need to get us into orbit?" Kris asked, or maybe she moaned. Sulwan almost sounded distressed as she gave Kris the answer she pretty much expected.

"If we want to reach orbit exactly opposite where Thorpe's ship is in its orbit, we'll have to maintain 3.5 gees for most of the next hour, Your Highness."

"Do it, Kris said, then tried to turn it into a joke. "Weighing seven hundred pounds for an hour will be a good reminder to watch what I eat and exercise regularly."

"I recorded that, Your Highness," Nelly said from where she was contributing her own three and a half pounds, all but one of them the result of Sulwan's course. "I'm sure if I offered it for licensed use, we could make a small fortune."

Kris didn't have the energy to roll her eyes at Nelly's latest attempt to be a real girl, chasing the almighty dollar. "I'm sure we could, Nelly, but erase that file. I don't know what Grampa Ray's idea of his kingship is, but I kind of doubt it includes his family selling their princess's voice for media commercials."

"Yes, ma'am," Nelly said, her voice a strange blend of contrition and lost financial opportunity.

"Don't you dare erase that, Nelly," came Abby on net. "You hold on to that file. You can never tell when it might come in handy. Who knows what kind of mess it could get us out of."

Around Kris on the bridge, chuckles were breaking out. Small ones, to be sure, since everyone carried three and a half times their normal weight; still, the argument between a princess, her pet computer, and her maid had to at least match the best the comic net had to offer.

"Abby, I do not even want to think what kind of mess those words might get us out of. Nelly, I want that file vanished."

"Yes, ma'am. I am erasing that file," Nelly said.

"Good," Kris said, and started to nod. Then she remembered her present weight and canceled the nod. And on further reflection, she wondered if she should never have said that "good." Nelly erased "that" file. Not "the" file. And certainly no mention of all backup files. There had been a bit of a lag in the whole conversation. Had Nelly been conferring with another young lady, full of all of twelve years of wisdom?

Kris let out a sigh. Not a big one worthy of Tommy's Irish ancestors. Just a small one, like a dog's pant.

She needed one twelve-year-old off her boat!

But first. "Thorpe's ship is behind Panda," Kris said. "He probably got a glance at us as we got of him. Now we see what we can do about putting one princess and Marine company where they want to be."

15

Captain Thorpe was livid. He had all his lasers charged and nothing to shoot full of holes. "Where's my target?"

"There is no ship anywhere in the space between the moon and our orbit. Nothing to target, sir," Weapons reported.

"There's got to be a target," Thorpe snapped, searching the forward screen. "There has to be."

"Sir," Weapons asked, "could she have done another burn and ducked behind the moon again. Or done more than three gees on her approach to orbit?"

"Not possible, or at least not probable," Thorpe said, forcing his mind to adjust to what his eyes told him.

"Sir, Sensors here. I've got a rapidly dissipating trail of reaction mass."

"Show me," Thorpe growled.

A glowing yellow cloud blazed a trail between the moon and Pandemonium on the forward screen.

"Can you estimate the gee forces that reaction mass would generate on a ship the size we saw on approach?"

"Ah, considering that it got them from the moon to orbit without us getting a single peek at them, I'd say they must have pulled at least 3.5 gees. Sir, I'd also say that the ship is heavier than us by a factor of fifty percent."

Someone on the bridge began a soft whistle. Thorpe whipped his head around, and the noise died. "They said they're carrying containers for this lost corner of the boondocks. So they're heavy. Doesn't say a thing about their combat load. We've got two eighteen-inch lasers and a second pair of 4.7-inch long guns. They are an exploration ship. She should have run when she could."

Heads nodded with him.

"Sensors, get me a full updated scan of this planet. Next orbit, one Princess Kris Longknife will be stumbling around down there, looking for a hairdresser. Let's make sure she gets dressed up right."

"Yes, sir."

Kris ached in every muscle of her body. "What a great way to start a fight," she softly muttered to herself as she glided in full battle rattle for the drop bay of the *Wasp*.

Doc, the *Wasp*'s erstwhile medical support, had set up shop just outside the drop bay's hatch. As Kris approached him, he handed her two small pills.

"What are these?" Kris demanded. She'd quit taking anything handed her at twelve . . . and was much the better for it.

"Just a pain reliever. And don't tell me Sulwan's joyride didn't leave you aching in every bone you got, Princess."

Kris took the pills with a swig from her suit's water while she surveyed the organized confusion of her drop bay. In addition to the four LACs, Jack had managed to cram in both of the lighters Drago had leased. Those two held empty transport containers, which Marines were stoically climbing aboard and improvising ways to strap themselves down to.

"You going to fly the lead LAC?" Jack asked her.

"For the northern platoon," Kris said smoothly, not giving Jack any opening to debate again the proper place for a princess in the coming battle.

"I've assigned Gunny to you as well as First Lieutenant Troy. Now, before you change your mind about leading a platoon, please excuse me while I look over my half of this lash-up." Without waiting for a reply, Jack threw her what might pass for a salute and left. Since space armor wasn't really intended for parade and ceremonies, Kris attributed his display to the equipment and not insubordination.

Not that Kris had any right to complain about a little insubordination here and there.

She turned to Gunny. "Let's land the landing force."

"Yes, ma'am," he said, but there was no salute with the words. He reached for Kris's suit and began tightening this, moving that to where it belonged. "Don't you hate the way high gees make a mess of your web gear," he muttered.

Kris stood patiently through his inspection and corrections. Officially she should be doing the same to him. She did do the proper eyeball check, but, as she expected, there wasn't a single item of equipment out of place on Gunny's battle rattle.

It wouldn't dare.

Shipshape to Gunny's high standards, Kris turned to the four-Marine squad that would ride down with her while Gunny turned his mothering eye on the LT. Maybe Gunny had been down them before. Or maybe Sergeant Bruce had acquired Gunny's eagle eye for anything out of place. Kris's inspection yielded nothing.

"Abby know you're dropping with me?" Kris asked the sergeant as she finished up her inspection.

"Now, why would I be worried about what an Army LT, and an intel weenie at that, wanted?" he said. But he said it with a smile.

Lately, the two had spent more than their usual workout time together. Make that three; Cara was usually underfoot. Was this Marine trying on the role of dad in a ready-made family?

Kris found a word of personal concern on her lips. She swallowed it and settled for, "Sergeant, board the troops." Which the Marines did, smartly and by the numbers.

Sergeant Bruce checked his team, then took the last seat. Kris did a double check before taking the pilot's slot on what the Marines optimistically called a Light Assault Craft. Kris thought a racing skiff was the least vehicle for going from orbit through the fire of reentry and landing on a planet.

Then she'd been introduced to a LAC.

The landing craft was the very epitome of "just enough." Just enough wing to slow it down and fly it to the ground. Just enough controls to get it *somewhat* close to where you wanted it. Nothing else. The canopy over the crew made paper look thick. It was only there to confuse radar's searching eye. Oxygen, cooling, water . . . came from the space suits Marines wore.

But Kris had yet to meet a Marine who complained about the accommodations. When Sulwan released the LAC to space, the Marines behind Kris greeted it with a confident "Ooo-Rah."

Kris could only smile. They'd been fully briefed, even if it had been painfully brief. The mission was a search for a needle in a haystack. A needle that didn't want to be found. Oh, and there was a gunboat in orbit ready to blast them from space if it could spot the Marines. And an unknown-size force of trigger-pullers ready to collect anything the gunboat left alive.

The troops had taken their brief with a shrug. One wag seemed to sum it up. "Sure beats hanging around the boat with nothing to do but hit the chow line."

It was good to be back with line beasts, Kris thought.

16

Kris's job was a bit more complicated than the Marines riding behind her. She had to put the LAC into a small lake about fifteen klicks north of the Fronours' latest homestead.

And do it well before Thorpe's ship came over the horizon.

Also, it would be nice to do it without heating up the LAC so much that it just screamed their location to anyone who might want to laser them from space.

Oh, and there might be radars in at least two of the big river towns. Might be. The radars had, like everything on this planet, not shown themselves. But if Kris was running the show, she'd have put at least a platoon in each of those towns and given them radar and antilander rockets.

Some might consider that nasty of her, but she hadn't found herself all that much worse than others who'd chosen her profession.

And definitely no worse than Captain William Tacoma Thorpe.

Kris made her initial approach steep, then went into soft S curves to bleed off excess energy. She did all this while keeping the inland mountain range between her LAC and the potentially deadly towns. Their radars stayed silent until the last moment. Just as Kris was finally able to duck into the shadow of the mountains, she got a beep out of the dime-store radar detector that had been taped to the instrument panel.

So, her sonic boom had gotten someone's attention, at least enough to have them risk their radar. Kris passed the radar information along to Jack. His LAC was farther back and still high. He was also headed for a river closer to those radars.

And his LAC had been modified to carry two antiradiation missiles. The plan called for him to loft them at anything Kris found. It didn't call for him to say anything to her.

She would just have to bite her nails and wait to find out if this bit of their plan worked, failed, or headed for points unknown.

Battles were just so much fun.

Kris skimmed the mountains, balancing height with speed and hoping she was bleeding off the heat buildup that came with reentry. Her butt told her that her seat was cooler than usual; that was the full extent of her instrumentation.

As she caught a thermal crossing the last mountain range, she spotted her lake and put the LAC into a gentle curve for its inviting blue waters. She set the craft down in a shower of spray, then held it nose high as it skimmed over the water, sending cooling waves off the wings and hull and dissipating the heat over a big chunk of the lake. It had been frustrating to be on the losing end of this game of hide-and-seek. Now, she was a player, and her life depended on giving away as little about her whereabouts as the others had given her.

Kris's LAC slowed, so she headed it for the beach. This lake had a sandy edge leading to a wide grass-covered vale. A couple of meters from the shoreline, the LAC ground to a halt.

Kris popped the canopy and sat while the senior tech got out, tested the water and the air, then did a heat scan on the LAC. She shook her head. "Even the top side is a full five degrees warmer than the ambient, Lieutenant."

The LAC was a one-way ride; still Kris would have liked to keep it around. She stepped out, and Sergeant Bruce and a tall woman Marine towed the craft out to chest-high water. Then Bruce slit open one side panel and tipped the craft until it sank.

The tech did a second scan. "This water is a bit warmer than the rest of the lake, but the river it empties into is only a few klicks thataway. With luck, anyone who notices the difference will put it down to sun warming the shallows here."

By now, the second LAC was drifting up to the beach twenty meters from them. The sergeant in charge of that one took in the situation and immediately began sinking his. The lighter with its large cargo container was a bigger problem.

That one was still hot as it approached the beach. Sergeant Bruce shot a line to it when it went dead in the water a couple of hundred meters short. Some Marines came hand over hand along the line, while others attached their own lines to the main one while collecting on the tail of the lighter.

With that weight aft, the nose rose, the tail sank, water poured into the container, and the whole shebang sank. Five minutes later, all the Marines were ashore and accounted for . . . though some looked muddy and waterlogged.

Gunny pulled up the rear with a small team vanishing all evidence of their passing. Kris put the Marines in single file, posted a pair of mine hunters ahead of her, and led off at a jog for the latest burn north of the Fronour place. The speed heated them up, but their battle suits were intended to make that go away. Heat, whether from the machinery or the human inside, collected in a central reservoir, where it powered up dissipation units called "hoppers" by the troops and something else, which no one recalled, by the suits' manufacturers.

The idea was for the hoppers to spread the heat over a wide area when they were jettisoned. However, with her Marines in single file to avoid leaving a lot of footsteps, dropping hoppers would more than likely leave a heat arrow pointing right at Kris.

"Hold your hoppers for when we walk through the fire area," Kris ordered. "Pass it down the line."

What a battle she was headed into. Orders passed by voice. A map with nothing on it. Did these folks have horses? Was she going to end up riding one into battle?

No. Goats were what they used for terraforming. No way was she or a Marine under her command going to ride a goat.

Assuming she could find Andy's people. They had to be around here somewhere. Probably close to their farmstead. Not too close. Not too far either. But how to spot them?

Behind Kris, Sergeant Bruce ordered his tech to check the air, then suggested that Kris might want to put them on local consumables. "Don't know when we'll need the air we brought."

Kris passed the order down the line.

And kept right on gnawing at her main problem. How to make contact with people who didn't much care to say, "Howdy."

They had gone to ground. But even moles needed air. Air was the one weakness of any subterranean existence.

But before Kris could say, "Hi," to anyone, she had to survive the next pass from Thorpe's ship.

This battle was being played out like an old chess game. Kris

had made her move. Now she'd better find a place to shelter up
and wait out Thorpe's move.

The line of march took them along the side of the still-
burning field. "Fire hoppers to the left," Kris ordered, reducing
her heat signature. Ahead was a field dotted with goats. A couple
of evil-looking rams wandered over to inspect these invaders of
their domain.

"Are they dangerous?" Sergeant Bruce asked Kris. The
wrong person. She called for Andy.

"They can be pests," he assured them, kicking one that got
too close. That one retreated, joining the others a comfortable
distance out to crop grass and eye the Marines.

"I think I've found the only thing that smells worse than a
Marine after a week in the field," Bruce concluded.

"They spend all year in the field," Andy said, in defense of
his farm stock. If only a very minimal defense.

"This place looks good," Kris called out to her platoon. "Let's
spread out the netting. It's nap time, crew."

She could see lips but did not actually hear anyone say, "Yes,
Your Highness." They were a good team.

Hopefully, they'd be alive five minutes from now.

"Where is she?" Thorpe demanded as soon as his ship,
the *Golden Hind*, rose above the horizon of the human-settled
area of Pandemonium. "They didn't kill our communication
and observation satellites just to announce they were here. A
Longknife would need to make a big splash, and do it quickly."

"They also took out our radar at Bluebird Landing," Sensors
reported.

"Did they pick up anything first?"

"Something coming in from the northwest, but it was
masked by mountains for all but a second. Colonel Cortez reports they spotted an incoming pair of missiles and went silent.
However it must have been fire-and-forget as well as antiradiation. It went right through the radar emitter."

"Our investors should have provided something better than
that old crap," Thorpe said with a scowl he was sure to turn toward Mr. Whitebred. The man was back on the bridge though
otherwise well behaved.

He was, however, one of those blind optimists among the investors who had been sure they'd be facing nothing but farmers with squirrel rifles. He had the good sense to blush and keep his mouth shut now.

"Well, they wouldn't be throwing missiles at our radars if they weren't bringing in troop transports behind them. Sensors, find their landing sites. I'm sure Colonel Cortez and his gravel crunchers would be most happy if we blasted this nosy princess from orbit. Let's make it happen."

Two minutes later, with only moments before the *Golden Hind* lost any line of fire at a target in the settlement area, Thorpe was ready to pull his hair out.

"They've got to be down there somewhere," he said, glaring at both his sensors and weapons leads.

"Yes, sir. The problem, as it has been with the farmers, is where?"

"We seem not to have surprised them," Thorpe said.

"The ones we have captured don't claim to have been warned. They haven't seen a ship in nearly a year."

"Save this for later. I want Longknife now. Her ships just landed. Where?"

"We've searched every inch of the settlement. They didn't land on any of what they call roads. No landing runs on any fields. They could not have landed in the trees. We'd see wrecks all over the place. Could they have jumped and their landers recovered back aboard their ship?" the young man on sensors said helpfully.

"Colonel Cortez reported no such sonic booms," Weapons interjected. "Booms when they came in. Nothing going out."

"Let's stick to the likely, shall we," Thorpe said. "Longknife likes water landing for her LAC, at least she did when I knew her. What have you got along rivers and lakes?"

"Nothing, sir," reported Sensors. "Those landers should be hotter than two-dollar pistols. We've got nothing on infrared either pulled up on the beach, or floating. Even if they did cool them, we show nothing on visuals. If she landed, the earth has swallowed them up."

"Like it has the rest of these people," Thorpe muttered. He was tired of hearing that line.

"There is one thing, sir," Weapons said.

"What?" Thorpe demanded.

"Well, sir, we know that they have to be carrying a lot of heat from reentry. Nobody, not even a Longknife, can do a reentry and stay calm and cool." She risked a smile at her own joke.

Thorpe allowed a thin one to encourage her. She, at least, was using her head.

"There are two heat anomalies," Weapons began.

"Anomalies is right," Sensors cut in. "Easily explained by natural causes."

"Two," Thorpe said.

"As if she had split her forces, sir, one out on the fringe in a lake, the other closer to the center but spread all over. Maybe a strike force and a reserve?"

"You're setting up a straw enemy to fit nothing but a bit of sun-warmed lake."

"Where?" Thorpe demanded.

The forward screen was replaced with a map of the settled areas. Weapons highlighted a section of the screen. "This river suddenly warms here, but is cool again five klicks downriver. This lake is snowmelt cool, but down here near the river that empties it, it's warmer."

"Less than a tenth of a degree. It could just be sun warming shallow water," Sensors pointed out.

"Radar says that lake is deep, a hundred meters or more. And it rises quickly at the shore," Weapons said softly.

"Who owns this homestead?" Thorpe asked.

"Ah, just a moment, sir," Sensors stuttered. "A Robert Fronour, sir."

"Isn't he the original settler of this planet?" Weapons said, her voice rising. "Didn't that Longknife girl claim to have someone of his family and cargo for him?"

"Yes she did," Thorpe said, making a snap decision with no doubt that it was the one to make. "Weapons, two targets. The Fronour farmhouse. Target with one eighteen-inch laser. Use the other eighteen-incher to hit the warmest part of that lake. Let's see if anyone is trying to hide in the bottom mud."

"I have the target coordinates loaded, sir," Weapons said. Pushing off from his chair, she flew arrow-straight for her station. She snagged her station chair with one hand and made final adjustments to her firing solution with the other. "We will lose our line of fire in five seconds."

"Fire on the count of three," Thorpe ordered. His "One, two, three" was short, but it got the job done.

The lights dimmed as the pulse lasers drew all the power they could into two coherent beams of light and death. Thorpe's only regret was that he'd have to wait over an hour to find out if he'd finally gotten that spoiled brat.

17

Lasers from orbit are not supposed to be effective weapons against ground troops. Crowbars, rocks, all of those, according to The Book, are an effective way that an orbital force can contribute to issues that are in doubt on the surface below. Assuming, of course, that you can get rocks and crowbars to hit what you want when they're coming in at twenty-five thousand klicks per hour.

Kris doubted the smart staff weenie who so casually dismissed lasers from orbit had ever taken a good lasing.

Without warning, the main farmhouse, say ten klicks ahead of them, exploded. It just blew up in a hurricane of wind, light, and destruction, throwing flaming pieces of itself in all directions. Most of the outbuildings crumbled in the maelstrom.

The very air around Kris exploded as well. One of the supposed drawbacks of lasers from orbit was their tendency to heat up the air they passed through. This was supposed to cause the lasing beam to lose its tightly wound coherence.

Maybe it wasn't quite as coherent as when it left Thorpe's ship, but the house sure didn't notice the difference. And the air, oh the air around Kris. Some of it roared out from the beam's path. Other gusts were fighting their way in to fill the hole in the sky. And Kris's ears got battered by gusts both coming and going. Kris got off easy, she had her visor fully up. The woman beside her had only opened hers a crack. The visor crumbled and left her face streaming blood.

Kris thought the farmhouse was the only target until it began to rain: water, dead fish, mud, and really ugly-looking things with no fins.

"I think they put one shot into the lake. Didn't you say that they had two eighteen-inch pulse lasers?" Sergeant Bruce asked.

"That's how the chief called it," Kris agreed.

"Well then, we know where both of them went. I hope the captain is real grateful to us for absorbing all the attention."

"Kris," Nelly said, "Thorpe's ship is below the horizon. We'll have eighty-five minutes before he comes back."

"Let's put it to good use. On your feet, crew."

"Can we shoot back next time, Your Highness?" some wag asked.

"You show me a target in range, and it's all yours," Kris assured anyone still able to hear.

Kris spent her nap time designing a set of drifter nanos. Folks can hide but they *have* to breathe. Somewhere around here air was being sucked underground and blown back up again. Gently, so as not to leave anything visible from orbit. Kris figured she was closer and should have an easier time of it.

That was before someone zapped one farmhouse, its roaring fire now grabbing all the free oxygen available. Gentle drifting nanos would be sucked right into the flames.

This whole show was turning into a bloody lash-up.

Not for the first time since she'd jumped into Panda space, Kris schooled her face to command neutral, let a breath out in a soft sigh . . . and went looking for Plan B. Or G. Or maybe she was already down to Z.

There was one item on the map Nelly displayed on Kris's eyeball that intrigued the Navy lieutenant. The controlled burn had been started in three layers, each of them about twenty meters thick. Most of what was still burning was in the far line.

But one broom tree in the first line still showed up brightly on infrared. Why? Kris trotted for it, Sergeant Bruce and his squad not far behind.

The most noticeable thing about a broom tree was its trunk. Solid and round at the bottom, it looked like it would take three or four people holding hands to circle it. The trunk rose thirty to fifty meters straight up. At the top it was about as big around as it was at the bottom. Only there, a wild concoction of branches sprang out. It looked like someone had planted a bush on top of a stone column.

But it was the bottom of the tree that Kris now stared at.

There, a good half meter from the ground, the tree again branched out into a wild tangle of holes, dirt . . . and surprisingly thin roots.

There the fire was still hot. "I guess that's how you kill a tree that's as hard as iron," Kris muttered.

"I have nothing like this in my database," Nelly said.

Kris edged around the tree, so she was upwind of it from the still-burning settlement. "Nelly, modify some of those nano drifters. Up their power and turn them loose on this tree's roots. Something is keeping it burning. Is air being blown out from underneath it, or is it being sucked down past it?"

"Doing it, Kris. I have launched two. Damn, I lost one of them to the homestead fire."

"Nelly, I will not have my computer cussing. Clean up your language. You work for a princess."

"Yes, ma'am. I am sorry." And she really sounded it. About as much as a computer could.

"You are picking up bad habits, Nelly. Habits I suspect you are getting from the company you keep. If you want me to let you keep hanging around with Cara, you need to watch yourself. And you might let Cara know that she needs to clean up her act. She is, after all, living next door to a princess these days."

With luck, Kris might solve one of her problems. If the computer and the twelve-year-old really wanted to stay together, maybe Kris could at least get some leverage in this kid-adult relationship. Little things like pirates and filibusterers aside, Kris had the odd feeling that all the adults on the *Wasp* were outnumbered by one little girl. Oh, and a computer that was forgetting who wore it around her neck.

"Kris, I will be more decorous. And I will teach Cara to be more proper as well. And one of my nanos has found a vent and is diving into it. The airflow is from belowground. Should I send more nanos in? The vent is just a single path, but it may branch at any time."

Kris was once more back to juggling that which could merely kill her rather than that which really bothered her.

Question for later consideration. Might Nelly be taking lessons from Abby on how to avoid getting talked to?

Kris got down to business.

"Lieutenant Troy, Gunny, I've found evidence that folks are underground." Kris yelled. It felt weird to be shouting her commands for anyone and everyone to hear. Still, it had been good enough for Alexander and Caesar. Why shouldn't it be good enough for one Princess Kris?

"You want us to form on you?" the LT asked.

"No, stay scattered. I'm just following an air vent right now. Don't know where it will lead, but I'm betting it will be closer to the house."

The LT and Gunny began moving the troops, still in scattered formation, but oriented toward the still-burning home.

Now Kris took a good, hard look at the lay of the land before her. It had seemed level. And it certainly was from orbit. But during the walk up from the lake, the land had taken on a rolling character. It wasn't really hilly, but the bottom of one roll might leave you looking up at the feet of a trooper fifty meters away. And the low points were usually cut deeper a half meter or more by some creek or meandering brook.

Good ambush territory.

It had been a while since Kris lugged a gun over such ground. She gritted her teeth and called up a rarely used part of her tactical training. She should have been more on the ball. She couldn't afford to be slow at this business.

"Kris, the nanos are branching off," Nelly reported. "I've set up a communication line so they can use a tight, low-power communication beam. I think one of them is doubling back."

"Where?" Kris snapped.

"It is under that low hillock," Nelly said, sending a small laser pointer at the rise ahead of Kris. "I think it is coming out the other end."

"Andy," Kris shouted. "We may be making contact soon. You might want to be with me when we do."

With a shout, the young man took off running for Kris. In full battle armor, he kind of lumbered along. But there was no question about his enthusiasm to see someone from home.

From the top of the rise, Kris had a good view of the homestead, now pretty much burned-out but still smoking. Nelly's light led her down the hill, halfway to the wash below . . . and right to a low rock that might have offered a couple of proud owners a good view of their holdings if they wanted to sit there on a cooling summer evening. Kris suspected she knew why it had not been dug up and lugged away.

"The nano just slipped out a view slot under the rock." Nelly reported. "There is someone down there on watch."

Kris considered having the tech folks come over and rip the

rock out. She nixed that idea. There'd be the devil's own time covering that up before Thorpe was back in the sky.

So Kris plopped herself belly down on the ground and stared at the situation from that viewpoint.

Clearly, you don't dig up the ground directly under a heavy rock. Not unless you have a very hard head. Kris spotted a clump of weeds to the right of the rock and reached over with both hands. In a second, she had worked them aside.

To find herself facing a very freckled, redheaded young man about her own age.

He was clearly startled to find himself face-to-face with her, but not slow to react. He jammed a long-barreled, slug-throwing rifle in her face.

"Slow down, fellow. I'm one of the good guys," Kris said, less worried about gender issues at the moment. "I've got a friend of yours here with me. Andy! Andy, could you come have a word with a very angry redhead who's got a rifle jammed up my left nostril."

Andy slid to a stop beside Kris. There wasn't much space in front of the view, what with Kris kind of unable to make more room for fear of getting another hole in her nose.

"Jamie, that you. Jamie, it's me, Andy. Are you down there, Jamie?"

"Andy? Are you in cahoots with these bushwhackers? They done captured you?"

"No, Jamie, these aren't bushwhackers. This is Princess Kris Longknife of Wardhaven, and they've come to help us."

Jamie frowned, nothing even close to conviction on his face. "A Longknife, huh. You know what Grampa says about Longknifes."

"But this one is on our side."

"As I heard the stories, they usually were," Jamie said, but the rifle came out of Kris's face, so apparently Grampa Ray had not come off all that bad in this family's stories."

"Jamie, we need to talk to Pa, and Grampa, too. They okay?"

"Yep, and so are Glenda Sue and Gracie Ann."

"Gracie Ann?"

"Yep, the cutest little thing on two pudgy legs. You get over to the cool house, and I'll see that they let you in. Now close this thing back up and quit messing with my lookout."

The man was gone, crawling backward into the dark. Kris

had shivers just thinking about wiggling around in such close quarters. Still, she did her best to put the weeds back and smooth the earth as she got to her feet. The ground cover here was the perennial that seemed to pass for both cover and crop. The grain had recently been harvested, and there was nothing but stubble.

Standing, Kris took a moment to reevaluate her situation. Andy pointed, eager to get on his way, to a low hill about fifty meters from the burned-down house. Cool room. Or cool warehouse. Kris was hardly less eager to be off and find out what wonders lurked in its cool insides.

But there was this matter of a war between her and Thorpe.

"Lieutenant, I'd like two squads to take everyone's store of hoppers and beat a slightly visible track to the south, say in two groups. Try to make it look like more than just eight troops," Kris said.

"Distract the orbital sensors from here," the young lieutenant said.

Kris projected a map of what lay to the south. "But don't give them any real targets. Five minutes before Thorpe pokes his nose above the horizon, go to ground and get hard to find."

"I understand, Your Highness. If you don't mind, I'd like to take this team, ma'am. Once we're down there, we can set up our watch on the road. Let you know if anything comes up it and do something about anything bite-size and chewy."

Kris glanced at Gunny. He had a fatherly smile on his face for the young officer, and a quick nod for Kris.

"Set up some tight-beam repeaters along your path so we can keep in touch," Kris said, and left the youngster to organize his first command. No, second. He'd had half the company dropped in his lap when the last CO nearly bought the farm on a lovely and violent evening back on Eden.

The LT was whistling softly as he went off to do his duty.

Kris turned to Gunny. "It seems there is a magic door to all the glorious treasures under the hill if we but go there," she said, pointing at the hillock.

"I had a good friend who swore by the little people. Or at them, depending on which way he thought they were leaning," Gunny said.

"I had a good friend like that, too, once upon a time," Kris said. "Word is, these people under the hill are our friends. Let's hope they stay that way. See what you can do about getting our troops in there without leaving anything pointing too blatantly at where we went." And with that in mind, Kris signaled Andy to lead the way.

Behind her, Gunny went noisily about the business of getting the platoon in single file and having the engineers sweep down their tracks. Kris would have to tell Grampa Ray about this next time she saw him and they were on speaking terms. The Marine engineers were using brush to sweep away the tracks just like Apache warriors of old Earth. It had worked for them in their desperate battle against the odds. What ain't broke, hardheaded Marines didn't fix but stole from with pride.

As Kris approached the cool room, she had to smile. At least the door into the hill was a solid, respectable rectangle. That lowered Kris's expectations for meeting halflings or elves. On the way, she had removed her helmet and gauntlets. It didn't seem quite friendly to make her first acquaintance with an ally encased in armor.

The first man she saw caused her to double-check that the door wasn't round. The short, round fellow, with bald pate and white whiskers looked like he'd be right at home in some fantasy epic. If the tall, thin woman beside him had offered Kris an apple, she would not have taken a bite out of it. Instead, the woman eyed Kris as if sizing her up for some cauldron and let her pass.

Kris's move on down the rabbit hole was brought to a quick halt as, in a flash of gingham skirts, a young woman raced out the door Kris was obviously being directed toward. With wonderfully golden hair and an improbably pale complexion, the young woman easily met the local role of Snow White.

A second later she hit Andy with all the force of the irresistible object. That had to be painful, and the poor kid was bound to find black-and-blue marks on herself in the morning where tender human flesh met the hard, unyielding tools of war. But Snow White's mouth had found Andy's, and the only sound to escape them was pure yearning.

Kris assumed it was pure. This had to be Andy's wife. Otherwise, matters were going to get very interesting very soon.

"Mommy," came from the door at the end of the cool room as a grandmotherly type, gray hair in a tight bun, carried a handful up what Kris now saw were dirt stairs.

"Mommy. Mommy!" came again as the cutest meter of humanity struggled to escape adult control and then did. Perched on her own two feet in defiance of gray hairs and the law of gravity, the little girl drove her pudgy feet forward, one half-balanced step at a time, to what had to be Mommy.

Kris thought Snow White's hair was the fairest and most golden she'd ever seen, but the small version of her was golden almost to white. The toddler reached her mother's skirts and gave them a puzzled look.

Mom was fully off the ground, her pale legs wrapped around the armored and camouflaged waist of the man holding her and showing no interest in letting go. The tiny tyke studied this image of her mom, a setup of skirts and legs Kris suspected was never seen before by these young eyes. After puffing up her lips into the most determined look ever worn by someone with only six teeth, the girl reached high above her head, grabbed a handful of motherly skirts, and pulled. "Mommy!"

Awareness seemed to dawn on Snow White quite suddenly. Awareness at several levels. First, of her daughter making absolute and personal demands. And secondly of the adults around the room. Kris wondered if she was wearing anything like the silly grin that seemed to have infected every witness to this reunion, which had managed to stop, just barely, short of full conjugal relations.

Suddenly demure, the mother dropped gracefully to her feet. Momentarily, a look flitted across her face that told of legs in hard contact with a sharp and unyielding object . . . and now hurting.

Settled gracefully on her own two feet, she reached down for the child, who . . . levitated . . . into her arms. Clearly, levitation is not a human skill. Of that Kris was sure. Even two-year-olds didn't do that! But that *was* what Kris saw.

It was either time for glasses or a rewrite of the physics books. Or maybe Kris was looking at such short miniatures of the human condition as something nice to have around.

I am too young to have a ticking biological clock, Kris warned herself and forced herself to grit her teeth against the little invader. But around her, several hard-case women Marines were showing soft, round eyes. And even Gunny was grinning like a proud grampa.

The woman held up her little darling. "Andy, may I introduce you to Gracie Ann, the youngest of the Fronour family and your daughter."

"Glenda Sue? No."

"Yep, she's yours. She goes straight for my breasts, just like her dad."

Which brought on a laugh from the locals, so Kris did her best not to blush. They were farmers, and things were done in front of them every day that Kris had been protected from until she was twelve and confronted with the red proof of her womanhood . . . in the quiet privacy of the girls' restroom at school.

At least the principal had been quick to assure Kris that she was not dying of some horrible disease. Mother's only reaction had been to agree that maybe the chauffeur should lay in a supply of female sanitary napkins, what with Kris's age and all.

Thank heavens Henry's wife Lotty had corrected the education Kris got from the girls out behind the gym.

Glenda Sue slipped Gracie Ann into Andy's arms. Maybe it was the armor, but the two-year-old went just as quickly back to mother. But once her well-padded rump was safely held by mom, the toddler began to play with the strange man now in her world.

She yanked on his hair, pulled the mike from his helmet ring, gave it back, and pulled it off again as soon as Andy had reinstalled it. A tech took it this time and, with a smile, draped it over his shoulder out of the reach of pudgy fingers.

"It's getting a mite bit crowded in here," the whitebeard said, joining the group around Andy. "And Grampa wants to have a word with whoever is in charge of our rescuers."

So saying, he led the way through the door and down dirt stairs. Whoever said that dirt here got hard as concrete once it got in contact with the air had it right. Kris was careful with her weight, but the stairs showed no tendency to crumble.

Too bad Kris couldn't be equally careful with her height. Both the floor and ceiling were uneven. Kris divided her time, half watching her step, the other half looking out for her head. As luck would have it, she was watching her head when she stumbled and looking out for her feet when she banged her head.

Surely, there is no justice. At least, not for Longknifes.

Fortunately, they had not far to go. Down one flight of stairs from the cool room, along a short corridor, then down a ladder. At that point, they turned once, then a second time, and finally a third while going only a short way in each direction. That took them to a room with a rough table and a couple of chairs. The wall on both sides had been left with a step up that served a dozen people as seats.

At the end of the table, eyeing Kris, was a man easily Grampa Ray's age. Only his days had been lived in the sun doing hard work, not at any desk. His hands were curled on the table, knuckles large and red. Kris suspected arthritis was finally enforcing a pause on the old workhorse. And he didn't much care for the break. Beside him sat a woman of equal age.

Kris stood, waiting for introductions.

A few more people squeezed into the room, dimly lit by a single electric lantern. When the elder seemed happy with what a glance around told him, his scowl got even deeper.

"So we drew a Longknife. I thought I'd seen the last of your kind when Ray didn't manage to get me killed on Hamdan II."

"You and he seem to have saved humanity," Kris said softly. "We haven't heard from the Iteeche in over eighty years."

The man snorted, but did grin at the praise. "Yeah, we did settle their four-eyed bacon. We sure did, didn't we, Hilda?"

"Those of us that survived the butchers passing themselves off for colonels. Admirals," the old woman said. Her teeth must have been false, for she had a whistle when she spoke. One eye was covered with a cataract or something. Curing things like that was supposed to be minor surgery.

Kris schooled her face to a gentle neutrality and waited to see where this was going.

"We ain't needed your like for sixty years," came from a man sitting against the wall. Around the wall, people nodded and agreed among themselves that he was right.

"You sure haven't," Kris said into their wave of self-affirmation. It died down after a while.

The old man shook his head and actually smiled at Kris. "Nice of you not to point out that we're hiding down here like a bunch of rabbits just now."

"I figured you'd bring it up when you were ready to," Kris said. "If you don't mind my asking. This is quite a setup you have. I kind of doubt you dug it while those raiders were inbound. This well-prepared defense certainly has thrown a wrench into their plans. How'd you come by it?"

The elder's smile deepened. He took the praise for what it

was, a pat on the back, well earned, but "defensive." Around the wall, some congratulated each other as if they had won the war.

"Didn't Andy tell you? Iteeche and Earthmen was a fun game when he was growing up. They'd dig tunnels and underground forts and ambush those 'dirty Iteeches.' "

"I told her about our forts," Andy put in. "I kind of left out the Iteeche stuff. Out there, the four-eyes seem to be pretty well forgotten. At least where I was."

"They are, some places," Kris agreed. "I kind of have my great-grandfathers to remind me how close we all came to being an extinct race that might be the subject of an anthro paper half a million years from now for some four-eyed college student."

"Do they have colleges?" Andy asked.

"I never heard tell they did," the elder answered. "Did the generals know more than us guys down at the gun batteries?"

"Not that I ever heard," Kris said. "We beat them back without ever learning a whole lot about them."

"All we needed to know was how to kill them," the woman said.

"So," Kris said, changing the topic away from the distant past, "when did you start digging?"

"A bit after Andy left," the old man said. "A tub wandered by here, not much trade on it, but a dozen couples got off. They were from a little place I'd heard of, Finny's Rainbow. They'd been hit by a raider. He stole all their ready cargo, a lot of their herds, and for fun, burned out a couple of spreads. The merchant tub had given them a lift out of the kindness of his heart . . . and an IOU signed in blood."

"We took them in, arranged places for them to work," the old woman went on. "I didn't much like the story they told. Told Bobby Joe that times must be getting raw back inside the Rim, its violence was starting to leak out to us. Some folks listened and spent their spare time digging. Others, city slickers, figured they knew better. I hope they're enjoying the hobnailed boots on their backsides." At that, she spat. Was it just coincidence that it went Kris's way?

"You planning on staying down here until they leave?" Gunny asked. He'd come up beside Kris after the talking started.

"You some kind of sergeant?" the elder asked right back.

"I work for my living," Gunny admitted.

"Back in the war, I had some good commanders. Some bad

ones, too. Some men. A few women. This one any good?" the local man asked, nodding toward Kris.

"I've only been with her a couple of months, but I've seen her shoot her way into a few fights. Shoot her way out with most of her own right behind her. She's not half-bad."

Kris tried to show no reaction to the low level of praise Gunny passed her way. But then, laying it on thick would hardly have impressed this crew.

"Not half-bad, you say. Kind of hard to believe that of a Longknife," the old man said.

"Ain't they usually all bad?" the old woman beside him chipped in.

"That depends on what you want them for, ma'am," Gunny fired right back. "I've seen her come to the aid of folks that sure needed it but had no claim for it. Hostages on a pirate ship once, a whole planet another time. I asked what you were planning to do down here. Sit them out?"

"I kind of hoped we could," the elder admitted.

"They brought a boatload of troops in on a ship that don't have much range. I'm no sailor, but the scuttlebutt among them was that nobody brings a short-legged boat to someplace they plan to strip clean. I think your bug infestation is not going away anytime soon. Me and my Marines, we're good at getting rid of unwanted bugs."

"This here woman," Gunny said, with a nod Kris's way, "she knows her stuff. She's just who you want in a mess like this."

The old fellow—Bobby Joe, hadn't the other woman called him—eyed Kris. "I never thought I'd be glad to see a Longknife," he finally said.

"And I can't believe you're glad to see one now," Hilda said. She said not a word more, but gathered up her self and stormed out. There was a quiet in the dimly lit room for a long moment after her exit. Kris listened to the clomping of her booted feet slowly grow softer as she got more distant. No one said a word until her steps were lost in the dark.

"Her husband died on Hamdan II," Bobby Joe said softly. "My sister never remarried. Never forgot or forgave."

"I'm sorry," Kris said, wondering if some of those who died under her command would be remembered so long. So bitterly. Was it an unavoidable legacy of her career choice? If she ever had time, she'd have to think about it.

Bobby Joe shook himself, as if to break loose of a memory that would never let go. "Tell me, young Longknife, what would you have us do? Grab our squirrel rifles and charge that bunch?"

Kris stifled a frown . . . and swallowed a question. *What did my great-grampa do to you?* Instead, she switched her face to the cold, steely battle one, and said, "Let's see what Thorpe does. His ship should be coming over the horizon just about now."

That got a raised eyebrow from Grampa Bobby Joe. And silence from the kibitzers sitting along the walls.

Gunny smiled. Like a tiger catching his first glimpse of his next meal.

18

Captain Thorpe waited a full ten seconds after the *Golden Hind* rose above the horizon of Presley's Pride's settled area. He considered himself the epitome of patience as he gave his subordinates that sufficiency to gather data and analyze it.

No, it wasn't much time, but we won't be in sight of that Longknife brat all that long.

Still, the moment the allotted seconds expired, he turned to them. "What have you got?" he said, honing his voice to smooth, supportive, but eager for the kill.

"Several things," the young sensor lieutenant said.

"Give me your best."

"We hit something when we lased that lake. The steam coming off of it still shows signs of composites and heat shields."

"Good, but I doubt Miss Longknife was planning on using them to withdraw." Then the full implications of the data hit Thorpe. "She sank her ships! Damn, have you passed that along to Colonel Cortez?"

"Yes, sir," Weapons replied. "He had a good laugh."

Thorpe would enjoy a laugh, too, later, when Longknife was finally dead and they had time for drinks. "Tell me more."

"The most solid datum we have is this trail, leading south from that homestead we lased, sir."

"Most solid, huh." Thorpe shook his head. "Ignore it. She put it there to distract you."

"I figured as much, sir. Down here, north of Bluebird Landing, there's a lot of activity. Radar reflections, hot spots that weren't there last orbit. More electronic background noise than ever before. Something is on the move."

Thorpe pursed his lips. "So the natives are finally getting

restless, or . . . or my apprentice has scattered her forces all to hell and gone. I thought she was smarter than that."

Thorpe tapped his commlink. "Hernando, what do you make of this?"

"Your apprentice should have paid more attention when she sat at your feet, William."

"Has she scattered her forces so widely. Or is this all a ruse?" Thorpe asked, thoughtfully.

"No question she landed up north, the smoke from her burned boats tells us that for sure. Hah, she sank her boats. I told you we should have sent off that scow you lugged us out here on. Even some of my staff spend half their time looking over their shoulder, checking to make sure they can still run for it."

"I couldn't send it away because our investors want an immediate return on their money. We're supposed to stuff it full of gold and wine and other good stuff and send it to them."

"Wine! You haven't tasted what passes for beer down here, have you? We ought to send them a boatload of that swill."

"We'll discuss our investors when we have something solidly in our hands," Thorpe said darkly. "What is your situation?"

"Murky, as it has been since we landed. Either she has somehow managed to talk with some of the locals and got them out scrambling our picture, or she's scattered some kind of force between me and where she made her main landing. Maybe a little of both. I've got a company of reinforcements coming upriver from Friendly Landing to reinforce Bluebird Landing. I've already sent off a platoon from Bluebird to do a search-and-destroy sweep along the main road between here and up north.

"Oh, and the local rolling stock. I don't know how they keep those trucks moving, but half of them are broken-down at any one time, and the other half aren't all that lively."

"Get the impression that our financiers' expectation of this place might have been a bit high," Thorpe said, eyeing Whitebred, who was drifting in the bridge's hatchway.

The moneyman didn't enter the bridge but went elsewhere.

"Hernando, you see anything worth wasting a laser on?"

"Not a thing. But that was a brilliant shot you took last time. Gave us our first hard datum that she'd landed."

"Glad you don't need a shot. It would be only low power. In orbit, it takes hours to recharge one eighteen-incher."

"Whoever you face was stupid, not to attack you as soon as you fired."

"Longknife is not stupid," Thorpe growled. "Do not underestimate her."

"Yes, but who is pushing that ship up in orbit, assuming your wandering girl is down here, getting ready to play patty-cake with her uncle Hernando. I know what kind of ship captain I'm working with. How good a one did she hire? How good a one is willing to work with her after what she did to you?"

"Interesting question. And it could just mean he didn't learn about my shot until he got horizon up next orbit."

"I didn't catch any tight-beam chatter from them."

"So we're all reduced to tight-beam or hollering."

"I am, but man, I have the lungs for shouting."

"Enough joking. You know what we can see from up here. I approve of your movement to contact. Take extreme care. We can't be too sure what she actually has in front of you."

"I will take care, *Capitan.* You do the same. And I will bring you the head of Princess Charmer."

"Out," Thorpe said.

He leaned back in his chair and studied the screen and what his sensor team had put up. It was a hazy collection of question marks, maybes, and possibilities. Was this what the ancients called the fog of war?

If you ask me, it's no way for professionals to fight, Thorpe concluded. Still, it was the fight he had. Damn the civilians for digging around like moles. Animals! If it had been up to Thorpe, he would have turned their little hiding holes into their graves. But the investors wanted a return on their money. Whitebred was always whining about that. Thorpe didn't care. Thorpe was a warrior. He wanted a warrior to fight.

This Kris Longknife claimed a warrior's name. And she had certainly shown some talent at it if you believed half of what the media reported.

Thorpe dismissed most of what he heard on the news. The wealthy and powerful owned the airwaves and put on whatever they wanted the rest of humanity to think. If it puffed up the

Longknifes to think they'd spawned another war hero from their weak bloodline, they knew whom to pay to write the stories.

No, Thorpe would enjoy testing this Longknife brat. She'd been a half-decent boot ensign once upon a time. *Let's see how long you survive when I know you are coming.*

19

Kris spent the time Thorpe was overhead going over a map with Grampa Bobby Joe. It was amazing what she could get from someone who'd walked the land with his own boots. There was a lot here that didn't show up from orbit.

For example, which homesteaders were longtime diggers, and who only got started when the ships hove into view. Two ships coming through the same jump point had gotten everyone's attention. It was a good year when two ships dropped by. One following the other into the system did not strike anyone as a business deal coming their way. Some places just started digging. Others only had to put the finishing touches on their work and start moving their families and gear underground.

Kris studied the prepared ones. It would be hard, but not impossible, to get from here to where she wanted to be by going on to the next homestead at eighty-five-minute intervals.

Kris also learned which farms had gunsmiths, or electronic whizzes, chemists, doctors, and others with important skills. These she also marked on her map. In twenty minutes her map was busy.

And she'd probably gathered more information on Panda than Thorpe had now. One or two ships a year not only meant little arriving. It also meant not a lot of data about this place went out. Just an idea, not yet an assumption. But . . . know thine enemy might not be these guys' strong point.

No, Thorpe probably figured all he had to do was intimidate some unarmed farmers out of their livelihood. That starship captain did not know these people.

Kris knew the full extent of her job: hatch a full-fledged rebellion against heavily armed invaders.

Or were they that heavily armed?

"Want to meet the guy you're up against?" the elder asked.

"I know the one in orbit," Kris said.

"I mean the one on the ground."

Over in the corner, behind Kris when she was facing the inquisition, was a small wall monitor. She'd noticed it earlier, but it showed only a blue screen with a small white logo . . . which turned out on close examination to be a grinning skull . . . so she'd ignored it. Now someone called up a picture from memory. It was hazy, and bounced around a bit. It showed a lander on approach, then cut to troops dismounting in businesslike fashion.

"Can you pause that?" Kris asked.

The picture froze. Hazy at first, the monitor cleaned it up crystal clear after three flickers. Kris and Gunny stooped close to get a good look at what it showed.

"Mark V, mod 2 battle suits," Gunny said. "No, mod 3s. They got the codpieces. Good stuff. Somebody had money," Gunny said, turning to the elder.

"Not enough. Look what comes off the next shuttle," the old man said with a sour grin.

The next lander was a standard shuttle, unarmored. The troops who tramped off it held M-6 rifles . . . or good knockoffs . . . but from the soles of their boots to the tops of their white berets, there was not one stitch of armor.

"Looks like somebody filled out his battalion at a bargain basement," Bobby Joe said. "I wonder how good they are."

They formed ranks and marched off the pier. Whoever was in charge didn't know to stay out of step when crossing bridges or other structures that might not withstand the pounding. Sad to say, the pier held together. But if the troops were supposed to instill fear in the observer, they missed their bet with Kris.

"Their heads are bobbing like a bunch of high school girls," Gunny growled, then thought better of it. "If you'll pardon the expression, Your Highness."

"I was thinking the same thing, Gunny," Kris said. "Half of them can't dress, cover, or keep an interval. Kind of makes you wonder how straight they can shoot."

"My thoughts exactly. Old-timer, you called it in one. Somebody unloaded a bunch of half-trained recruits. Cheap they may be, but they're up against a princess who cared enough to send the very best," came from Gunny, with a wolf's grin.

Bobby Joe came to stand beside the Marine. "That's the way

I took it. I figured when it came time for us to take back the daylight, we'd start with this bunch. Still, I have to admit, I'm only too glad to share the honors with you and yours."

"You said I could meet the guy in charge?" Kris said.

"That's coming in a second," the elder said, and a moment later, the picture got knocked around, ended up showing ground and sky and somebody's web gear. The Mark V was serious stuff.

When the picture leveled out, it was focused on one man's face. Olive skin and black eyes gave the camera a hard, measuring look. "You live?" the man demanded.

"Yes sir," came with a stammer and hiccup.

"Then broadcast this to whoever is watching. I am Colonel Hernando Cortez. I and my troops have come to restore order on Presley's Pride. All terrorists who turn in their weapons in the next twenty-four hours will be allowed to live. Anyone seen under arms twenty-four hours and one minute from now will be shot on sight. Further orders will be issued, and their nature will depend on the cooperation we receive. Did you send that?"

"Yes, sir."

"Gimme that." The camera changed hands. And ended up dropped on the ground. The last picture it sent was of a boot about to crush it underfoot.

"Hernando Cortez," Kris said softly.

"A Hernando Cortez," Nelly put in helpfully, "was one of the first conquistadors. He conquered the Aztecs of Mexico."

"Looted their gold and enslaved their people," Bobby Joe added.

"Interesting choice of names for their ground commander," Gunny said.

"Could be just coincidence," Kris said. Then chuckled. "Didn't Cortez burn the ships that brought him in. Wonder how this Cortez took to us sinking ours?" Kris would have to ask him . . . once he was her prisoner.

"Thorpe's under the horizon," Sergeant Bruce announced as he entered the room. "They've got an underground garage, and we've rigged five of their trucks with trailers. About time to saddle up and head south."

"We can borrow your trucks?" Kris asked the elder.

"I suspect Jamie gave your men that understanding," Grampa Bobby Joe said. Jamie was right behind Sergeant Bruce.

"My pa's got the trucks ready to go. And a dozen of our best with the squirrel rifles. I was planning on going."

Andy looked torn. Wanting to go, tired of being gone. Bobby Joe reached for him. "Son, you been gone too long. Not sure the neighbors would recognize you. Let Jamie and his pa, Billy, take this herd out. We need some good shooters at home."

A grin swept Andy's face, and he gave the elder a huge hug.

"We'll be going," Kris said. "You have any suggestions for a place that would give us cover eighty minutes down the road?"

"Try the Polska place. She's got a truck-repair barn that ought to be able to hide you."

And Kris and her team, augmented by thirteen locals, started their trek south, to battle.

Kris was on the road when the *Wasp* came over the horizon. She immediately tight-beamed up a short report giving her present status and what she'd found out from the locals. She ended by asking if they'd heard anything from Jack.

Captain Drago appeared on Kris's eyeball a second later. "Jack's been staying quiet, just as planned. And I'm not picking up a whole lot about him from up here, either."

"Any idea what the other guy is up to?" Kris asked.

"Finally, I can say something about that. Since last orbit these folks, Colonel Cortez, huh," Drago said, "have gotten rather rambunctious."

"Not hiding their movements, huh?"

"Abby figures they are, but things aren't going all their way anymore. Here's a picture of the road north from the first town upriver from Landingburg to town two. Notice all the traffic pulled off to the side of the road. Troopers standing around kicking the tires."

Jamie glanced over from where he was driving . . . and doing a good job of keeping the truck out of holes and away from rocks. "These guys aren't all that careful with our rolling stock."

"You're going to have to explain that to me," Kris said.

His pa leaned his head through the open window between the truck's cab and it's flat bed where he was riding. "Ma'am, we got a lot of old stuff. Some of our rolling stock has been rolling since Grampa got it off the lander. It's old. You might even say cranky. Now if you know how to treat it right, it's fine. But you figure you can just twist the key, pound on the gas, and it'll take you where you want to go, you're in for a whole world of stall, flood, and other nasty stuff.

"Every truck on the farm has its own way of looking at you. Why do you think Jamie's driving this heap? He has the touch for it. Me, I gave up on this one years ago."

"Peggy's not a bad ride, Pa, not if you treat her right."

"So you say," the older man said, and went back to talking with Sergeant Bruce on the flat bed.

Kris passed that intel along to Captain Drago.

"Somebody should have thought ahead about what they'd need," the captain said, shaking his head.

"Why bring what you can steal?" Kris answered. "I think this whole thing was worked out on a very tight budget."

"A tight budget that didn't include a contingency for a Longknife showing up," Drago said dryly.

"Let's not put too much into that," Kris said. "If they were planning on folding the hand they got dealt, they'd have run for the jump point while we were incoming. They've stayed this long. They aren't going anywhere without a fight."

"Don't you just hate it when things are like that."

"Thorpe doing any orbit changes?" Kris asked.

"We've slipped sats into orbit ahead and trailing us. Not so much that he'd see them, but enough so we'd know if he tried anything. So far he's just doing the merry-go-round thing."

Kris thought for a moment. "Keeping them in the dark about Jack is one thing. I don't like it cutting both ways."

"What do you have in mind?"

"How about a wide beam? Broadcast your picture of those broken-down trucks over all of the settlement area. Let everyone know their problems. Also, resend that invasion footage. Jack might as well see that everyone he's facing isn't as hard a case as some. He'll know what to do about that."

Which gave Kris another idea. "And while we're at it, maybe you could patch together some of the conversation I had with Thorpe. Let's let anyone listening on an open channel know that the times, they are a changing."

"Will do. I've got one of mFumbo's techs working on that."

"Time for me to go back to playing the strong, silent type. Kris out."

And Kris returned to watching the path ahead of them, swaying with the rig . . . and weighing what move to take next.

She certainly had knocked over the apple cart with that last set of orders. The folks of Panda had gained time by going silently to ground. It must have stunned Thorpe and Cortez. It certainly had messed up their plans.

But now silence was helping the invaders as much as it harmed them. So long as the resistance knew of nothing going on, it could hardly be a resistance. Not an effective one.

Sooner or later Thorpe would start ferreting out those in hiding. If the resisters did nothing to support each other, they'd go down, one by one. Kris and her Marines were unexpected. The question for Kris was what to do . . . and when?

Part of that was solving itself. As she moved south, Cortez swung his forces north. There would be a meeting engagement somewhere along that line of march. First with Jack and his crew. Then with Kris and all.

The deal was to meet up with Cortez when Jack and Kris's forces were together. Cortez of course, would do his best to avoid that. Kris wanted one thing. Cortez another. That was usually when battles occurred. Or elections. Kris had chosen a profession that did the battle thing. Despite her father's strong opinion on the matter, she still thought she'd chosen the wiser.

Drago made his broadcast just before the *Wasp* sank below the horizon. Strangely, it spurred no reaction from Cortez. She'd figured him for a shoot-from-the-hip man, but he kept silence.

"Nelly, Mark the time of Drago's broadcast."

"Yes, ma'am. May I ask why?"

"'Cause, sooner or later, someone is going to say something about my loud and blunt declaration. It would be interesting to see how long a decision cycle the other side has."

"I see," Nelly said. "I should start timers on things like that. That way, I can answer your questions faster."

Another lesson for the kid/computer around Kris's neck.

The Polska place came into view. The "huge" garage turned out to be dug out of a hill about a klick from the homestead.

"Come winter, you ought to see how the wind blows the snow," Jamie tossed out when Kris looked quizzically at the place. "All the barns are like this. You don't want to freeze the tits off your goats, or fingers off your hands. Makes for cool when it's hot and warm when it's freezing. Oh, and makes for one lousy set of targets when invaded," the kid said with a grin.

And two big strapping Polska boys were out in front of the barn, holding its doors wide and waving the small convoy in. Kris was safely out of view from overhead surveillance a good two minutes before Thorpe's star rose over the horizon.

20

"**And** they broadcast *that* on an open channel! To everyone," Thorpe said, struggling to keep his voice under control.

"Yep," Colonel Cortez replied. "I think she's trying to raise the countryside. Get a real rebellion going. We'll have to slaughter a whole lot of sheep putting it down. You got any problems with me getting the captured townspeople organized into groups of ten? They kill one of my men, I kill ten of theirs."

"No!" came as a scream over the net.

"Who said that?" came from both Thorpe and Cortez.

"I said that, Benjamin T. Whitebred. Those town folks are the artisans, the technical experts. They're worth *money*. A farmer whacks one of your pogues, you whack as many hayseeds as you like, but don't go knocking over people we're going to need to keep this colony earning money."

"Who gave you access to this channel?" Thorpe asked, voice low and cold. Two armed guards and the comm officer kicked off from their bridge positions and headed aft for Mr. Whitebred's stateroom. Thorpe mashed the mute on his commlink. "Don't hurt him, but bring him up here. Now."

Finger off the mute button, Thorpe continued his talk with Cortez. "Did you see the way the pictures had been processed. That original feed from our landing. Rerun it," he said to the 2/c sailor who had taken over the comm slot.

The picture of the white berets marching ashore reappeared. Now there was a commentary block over them. "Note that White Hats have no armor," followed at the end of their scene by "And they can't march straight. Can they shoot straight?"

"That sure looks like an incitement to rebellion to me, Hernando."

"That's what I'm thinking," the colonel said. "It's bad

enough to have half my transports broken-down, but to have them pointed out to the locals, oh man, William. They're either laughing at us for being too dumb to drive . . . or inviting any local kid with a slingshot to go out and hit us. I've got to do something about that."

"I know, Hernando, believe me, I know. That Longknife girl enjoys yanking a warrior's chain. We need to give her a good solid yank ourselves."

"Yeah, like a short noose over a tall tree," gave them both a chuckle.

Which Thorpe swallowed quickly as the guards dragged Whitebred onto the bridge. As they did, they liberally bounced him off of the bulkhead, overhead, and deck. The civilian fought them, yanking on the three-foot tethers, one to his left wrist, the other to his right ankle. The guards must have had plenty of practice at moving resisting sailors in microgee. Each would glide from one handhold to another, give him a yank while they were secure, then take off for the next grip.

Whitebred bounced off of anything that got in his way and never succeeded in getting a purchase anywhere. It was pathetic for a grown man to be so helpless. Hadn't the man spent any time training in microgee? What was he doing in space?

The guards found themselves handholds, one on the deck, the other on the overhead, and maneuvered Whitebred to a position where he gently twisted in the wind. Occasionally he faced Thorpe directly. Any half-trained sailor would have known how to cancel his rotation, face his captain, and take his dressing down like a fighting man.

Not Whitebred.

"What were you doing listening in on my command channel?" Thorpe demanded.

"I represent the money, buster. We listen in on anything we want to," would have been a whole lot more effective comeback if Whitebred hadn't been twisting his head around at all kinds of odd angles as he struggled to keep eye contact with Thorpe. Did the bloody fool have any idea how ridiculous he looked? He must have heard the bridge crew snicker at his empty claims.

As much as Thorpe hated playing to the crew, the civilian was challenging him as captain. This could not be allowed.

"Steady this fish you've landed," Thorpe ordered the guards.

They reeled in their catch, leaving him splayed out like some sacrificial animal, one arm and the opposing leg pulled out straight. From the look on his face, painfully straight.

Thorpe released his seat belt, and carefully maneuvered himself until he was almost nose to nose with Whitebred. "While you are on my ship, you will follow my rules. Do you understand?" he said, sharp, hard, but in a deadly low voice.

"I represent the money that got you this ship," the businessman insisted, but the power in his words was drowned by the tears in his eyes . . . and the blubbering of his mouth.

Thorpe glanced at the two guards. They gave the ropes a painful yank.

Whitebred gave a yowl. "You can't do that to me."

"You are on my ship. You are under my discipline. You and your moneyed interests sent me and my sailors and soldiers here. The assumptions you predicated this investment upon have been shown to be inaccurate. I am, at present, attempting to resolve this conflict of expectations and reality. This is a matter that can only be handled by officers like Cortez and myself. You are interfering with our work."

With a flick of his ankle, Thorpe got his body moving back to his command chair. He settled into it with hardly a twitch. Whitebred floated there, awed at what he'd just witnessed.

"Now then, you will return to your room and stay there. Comm Chief, you will remove any unauthorized communication gear you find there."

"Yes, sir."

"You aren't going to start shooting hostages we need, are you?" Whitebred's voice cracked as he pleaded, not for human beings' lives but for his bottom line.

"Not yet, but not because of you. Because I don't want to. Colonel, have you been listening?"

"Every word."

"You've captured some gommers with mud on their boots."

"Yes, Captain. I've got quite a few."

"Organize the groups of ten, like you said. If you have to shoot, start with the hayseeds. If they have any smarts down there, they'll throw their hand in before you get to anyone that our employers might weep for at his funeral."

"Good thinking, William. Will do."

"Just one of the advantages of being a couple of hundred

klicks above the fray, Hernando. You want me to broadcast a martial-law decree."

"I recorded one my staff worked up. I'll send it to you."

About the time Cortez's martial-law announcement arrived, the Comm Chief returned, several comm stations in his hand, all trailing wires that showed they'd been yanked out with little thought to their reinstallation.

"He still sniveling?"

"No, sir. At the moment, he seems quite happy. I think he convinced himself he had something to do with the outcome."

Thorpe scowled as he shook his head. "How do such fools survive into adulthood?"

"Kind of makes you wonder why he was the only one champing at the bit to go with us," Weapons said.

"Show me Cortez's announcement," Thorpe ordered, and reviewed the video. It would be nice to have something as entertaining as the broken-down trucks or the "shoot the white hats, not the armored troops." Still, Cortez, snarling into the camera threatening to shoot ten of them for any one of his they shot would surely get attention.

Thorpe glanced at the clock. Hardly time before they fell below the horizon. The Longknife announcement had been when they were almost directly above the settled lands. Somehow that brat and her team had produced a better product in less time.

Of course, she didn't have to deal with Whitebred. And once the fighting started, neither would Thorpe.

He shook his head. Let Longknife think she'd won something this time. When the bullets started flying, she'd discover that she couldn't count on a slow decision. Not from Hernando, and not from her old captain.

"Broadcast the video," Thorpe ordered, then settled back in his chair to study the main screen. It showed all that he'd learned from the latest pass. North of Bluebird Landing there was that nebulous cloud of something. His troops would drive into it while he was on the other side of this troublesome planet.

Now there looked to be three clear paths moving south from the lake they'd lased with such interesting results. Three!

Two went along opposite sides of a wildening creek. No, call it a river. The third started off from the farmhouse they'd burned and stopped just short of another homestead.

For a moment, Thorpe considered hitting that one with an

eighteen-inch beam, then dropped it. Whoever was bossing the Longknife ship had let him get away with being empty last time. He would not trust that he could get away with that again.

You had to wonder where the financiers had gotten this ship. Two weak reactors. Two eighteen-inch pulse lasers that took forever to reload. A pair of long popguns that could hardly cause a dust devil two hundred klicks below.

But I took the command. Jumped at it. God, I hate the beach. I'd have chewed my arm off if that was what it took to get back to space.

The settled area dropped below the horizon. Thorpe would have more than an hour to wonder what was going on back here. "Sensors, are those microsatellites still hanging out there?"

"Yes, sir. They juggle their orbit and come into view for a few seconds, then fire a burst and they're gone again. It can't be very easy keeping them in orbit."

"No, it can't," Thorpe agreed. But a rich brat like Kris Longknife would have toys like those around. Thorpe had nothing like that. Nothing he could make into them.

He swore to himself. Still, he kept a confident look on his face for the crew and waited for the next chance to get that Longknife girl.

Kris viewed the martial-law announcement with Gramma Polska, the elder of the Polska clan. The old woman might or might not have had a few years on Gramma Ruth . . . it was hard to tell. The years seemed harder out here.

What Gramma Polska didn't lack was steel in her backbone.

"One of my boys was in Deverton when they landed. We ain't heard from him since. Told him he was a damn fool for going, but there was this girl. He said he'd talk her into moving out here in no time at all. Xanadu girl. You'd have thought she was already used to the idea of moving on."

"Gramma Polska, we didn't come here to start a bloodbath." Kris found it easy to say the half-truth, half lie. It didn't pass muster under those old gray eyes.

"So I heard about you Longknifes. You say you never start a fight, but holy Mother of God, do they find you. You want to tell an old woman what you are planning on doing with the dozen of her boys that are champing at the bit to go along with you and your Marines?"

Kris shook her head. "It's not that I know and won't tell you. Simply put, I really don't know how this thing will go down. It looks like most of their soldiers are headed north. I'm heading south. We're going to meet somewhere in the middle, and a meeting engagement is one of the most slippery things we do in my business."

"And you ain't interested in counting your chickens before any of them takes up playing the harmonica."

"That's what my Gramma Ruth would tell me," Kris agreed.

"Smart woman. She a farm girl?"

"Was before she married a Marine."

"So, you going to use my kids, grandkids as . . . what do you call it? . . . cannon fodder. Yeah, I heard in the Iteeche wars your Grampa Ray used up a lot of cannon fodder."

That wasn't what Kris read in the history books. But Kris had less and less trust in what the learned scholars and newsies reported. She weighed several options and chose the one that seemed the most honest. "Ma'am, I'd like to promise you, but I won't. If it would make you more willing to let them come and do what I order, I guess I could raise my hand and swear any oath you want. But the truth is that what we're headed into won't be easy to do and harder to foretell.

"I sure don't plan on using anyone as cannon fodder. And I kind of suspect my grampa Ray didn't think he was using all that many as you've heard about. Still, how a fighting man says he was used after a battle and what the commander thought he was doing may not come out sounding anything alike."

The old woman snorted. "I've had a few relationships go that way. To hear some guys talk, you wouldn't think we'd been on the same planet, much less in the same bed. I like your honesty, girl. I think I'll trust you with my boys. Oh, and a couple of my girls are good with a gun. You got any problems with them going along?"

"My mother would, but I'm hardly one to talk."

"What you going to do about this martial-law thing?" Gramma Polska asked, changing the topic.

"What would you do?" Kris asked right back.

"I'd tell folks not to kill any of those rascals. Not now. Not until the time comes. They're looking for a fight. Don't get in their way. Sooner or later, they'll find one. Then they'll do enough dying. Maybe enough that they ain't all that interested in killing unarmed folks."

The farm boss woman shook her head. "I know that's not what you wanted to hear, but that's what I'd tell people."

"Nelly, did you record what Gramma Polska just said?" Kris asked, with a quick glance at her neck.

"I have a short-term record, Kris."

"Include that in a tight-beam to the *Wasp* as soon as it comes over the horizon. Add my voice to a picture of Gramma Polska— 'I am Princess Kris Longknife of the Wardhaven Navy, and I strongly advise people to follow Gramma Polska's advice. A time of reckoning is coming, but it is not now. Don't do something that causes these outlaws to hurt your friends.' "

"I will tight-beam it as soon as the *Wasp* is up."

"Good. How long did it take Thorpe to respond to our first broadcast?"

"Ninety-two minutes. He was almost below the horizon when he sent the martial-law decree."

"Let's get our reply to that one up as fast as we can."

"Kris, in a minute Thorpe's ship will be out of line of sight. Shouldn't we be getting back to the trucks?" Nelly said.

"Time flies when you're having fun." Kris sighed.

"Let me come with you," Gramma Polska said. "My family will feel better about going if they see me with you."

So Kris headed out of the huge sod-covered barn with food, full fuel tanks, and two extra trucks. One of them knew just the farmstead to head for, so it took over the lead.

The time with the *Wasp* went quickly. Captain Drago got the message responding to martial law and rebroadcast it in less than a minute. Information continued to be thin. It looked like Jack's scouts had made initial contact with Colonel Cortez's lead troops. At least Cortez's vanguard was no longer charging up the road as fast as they could drive, but had slowed down and now had people walking point and flank guards. That would give Kris more time to get south.

And Cortez more time to bring up his full force.

Every coin has two sides to it.

And, if Kris could read anything out of the cloud of noise around that vanguard, Jack was drawing them in to exactly the ambush they'd planned.

Make that ambushes. Two is always more fun than one.

Kris rode in the back of the truck this time, letting Jamie and his old man share the cab. She studied the rolling terrain, then eyed the troops in the trucks around her.

The Polska truck was in the lead, navigating across the sea of grass by whatever system these folks used. Here and there residual stands of broom trees stood, their land covered with underbrush that the locals avoided driving through. That would give away a lot to overhead observers.

But it was the troops Kris studied. In trucks with mostly Marines in the back, the troops had posted a watch, then flaked out to sleep. If you got time to spare, grab a wink had been the advice of the old sweats since before Caesar.

It was the other trucks that caused Kris to squint hard . . . and worry. The volunteers were up, looking around, fondling their rifles. A few cleaned their weapons. But the smart ones were very few. How would these people handle it when they saw their targets fall? When the man beside them fell, his head half-gone? What could Kris expect from these amateurs? They were fighting for their very lives. It was their freedoms that were on the line. But had they had enough time to realize the stakes? Could they find in their guts what they needed to go on when everything that was natural and human screamed run?

Kris sat down with a new problem to chew on. How do you train civilians into fighters in the short time she had? A very short time, Kris found, when she called up the map. Jack would spring the first trap in a bit more than one and a half orbits.

21

Colonel Cortez did not like the smell of what lay ahead. The ground was low and stank of marsh. Not the honest stench of the marshes humans had known forever . . . and drained on Earth. No, somehow this waterlogged mess had an acridly sweet smell to it. Nothing was right on this godforsaken planet.

If Cortez hadn't already issued orders to put a stop to the bitching about "Why not let the damn locals have the damn place," he would have muttered something like that himself.

He searched what lay before him with his binoculars. As the photomap Thorpe had sent him showed, there was swamp as far as the broom trees let him see. And directly in front of him a grassy mound ran straight and narrow for about three klicks.

It wasn't exactly a road. Like everything on this planet the natives called Pandemonium, it was different. No solid gravel or asphalt road for these folks. No, they'd planted this causeway with one of the perennial grains that the locals harvested. From the stubble, someone had actually come along recently and cut a crop off it. Must not get much traffic.

One of the officers from the psalm singers had a couple of local hostages wading in the ditches on either side of the causeway. They were nearly up to their necks.

"I told you it's deep," one local hollered, loud enough that no one could avoid hearing. "We had to get the dirt for the road from somewhere. We dug it out of the muck beside where we put the road. And we kept a lookout posted with a rifle handy. There's something in this water that likes to nibble on toes."

That last claim Colonel Cortez didn't know how much to credit. But it got a lot of the white berets around him muttering prayers and eyeing the water darkly. You couldn't see six inches into the muddy stuff.

"What do you make of it, sir?" Major Zhukov asked as he climbed aboard Cortez's command vehicle, one of the few army green battle rigs on the planet.

Cortez shook his head. "Here is where *I'd* ambush me, if I had anything like a formal fighting force. Your Guard Fusilier could lurk out there in the water and only surface to shoot this bunch to a bloody pulp. Not so?"

"Just so, sir. Just so," Zhukov said, with an expressive sigh. Zhukov had been sent along on this joyride by the wise fathers of Torun to make sure that the lone company of Guard Fusiliers they rented out was returned in good shape. Some battle experience gained . . . with someone else paying the bills . . . but no real damage to the merchandise.

Cortez had wanted to rent the entire Fusilier battalion, but the penny-pinching fathers of Torun had learned something about defending their planet from that unidentified squadron of battleships that suddenly appeared over Wardhaven while their own fleet was elsewhere. Cortez got one company from them and had to settle for filling out the rest of the battalion from New Jerusalem.

Oh, and the financiers had been glad for the savings.

Colonel Cortez turned to the major. "Do the engineers attached to your Guard company have sensors that would let me see warm bodies in that muddy water or pick up the electrical impulses of a sharpshooter's heart if he's standing half a klick away behind that ironwood tree?"

"Certainly, sir. We have a fully capable company of engineers on Torun," the major said with a bleak smile. " 'But engineers, we don't need no stinking engineers on this pissant planet.' Isn't that what your investors told you and Thorpe when you asked the Council of Torun Elders to rent some to you?"

"Your treasurer set a mighty high price for a platoon of engineers."

Major Zhukov snorted bitterly. "Their expensive engineer toys were bought while he was cashing the checks. He squealed at every penny as it fell through his tight fist. The gear my infantry is wearing is ten, twenty years old. A lot better than anything we've seen on this planet, mind you, but not something our glorious treasurer had to pay for. He let it go 'cheap.' "

"I'm just glad he let it go. I don't know what we're facing, but it's got to be better than these psalm singers."

"Don't knock them. They didn't look too bad on the march up. You got any estimate of what this Longknife kid has?"

"Nope. Thorpe's not telling me a lot about her. Cusses her plenty, but not a lot of hard data behind all the noise."

"I don't have anything on Thorpe and her, but one of the junior officers from the Lord's Ever Victorious Host did confiscate this from one of his soldiers."

Zhukov pulled a plastic flimsy from his shirt pocket and unfolded a large picture of a busty redhead in a white dress that looked only thinly painted on over her many curves.

"That the Longknife girl?"

"Unfortunately not, Colonel. That's Miss Victory something. Originally, the article came with a picture of her and Kris Longknife, but the kid who had this said she was just a thin beanpole. He zoomed up the Peterwald girl and ditched the Longknife kid."

"Rather shortsighted of him."

"At the time, I don't think he ever expected to meet either of those girls, except maybe in his dreams."

Cortez glanced at the story. " 'Guilty of many sins for which both harlots will burn deep within the worst fires of hell.' What kind of rubbish is this?" Cortez began to wad up the flimsy, but Zhukov put his hand out to stop him.

"It's from New Jerusalem, sir. They can't put pictures of near-naked girls from other planets on the covers of their tabloids without assuring the guys reading them that said girls will burn in hell."

"And that matters to me why?"

Zhukov flipped the paper over, ran his finger down the second column quickly, then stopped. "Read that paragraph."

" 'Miss Longknife committed many licentious acts on New Eden, including riding in cars with men she was not related or married to, masquerading as a soldier, violating planetary data censorship rules, associating with hooligans of the worst sort.' Zhukov, this does not leave me quaking in my boots."

"Keep reading, Colonel, the last sentence."

Cortez skipped down a half inch. " 'After a major disturbance of the peace that left thousands dead of gunshot wounds and explosives, Miss Longknife was escorted off New Eden by Wardhaven Marines only moments before she should have faced judgment for her many sins.' "

Colonel Cortez looked up as he finished reading. Zhukov raised an expressive eyebrow. "How many Marines does it take to escort a debutante, and how heavily armed were they? Are they still with her?"

Now Cortez did read the graph, slowly, wringing it out. Not one extra drop of information dripped out for him. "I don't know," he said slowly. "Thorpe showed me pictures of the ship she rode in on. Small freighter."

"What's a Longknife doing on a small merchant ship?"

"What's a Longknife doing interfering with our little rape, pillage, and put-under-new-management scam for this planet?"

Zhukov took off his helmet and wiped at the sweat running down his face. "What is a Longknife doing here?" He put the helmet back on. "So, sir. What are we about to do here?"

"If I run this collection of rattletrap trucks down that mound of dirt, there's going to be no way to turn them around."

"So we walk?"

"And leave our spare ammo, water, and heavy machine guns behind? I think not, Major."

Major Zhukov made no more attempts to answer his own question. He paused, an expectant expression on his face. The one smart junior officers learned early in the Torun Guard.

"We will wait for your Guard Fusiliers to catch up, and for Thorpe to make another pass and see what's changed in front of us. Then, all together, we take the battalion across, with plenty of hostages out front."

"They will think twice about shooting," Major Zhukov said.

"While we're waiting, Major, you might get some of the prayer group down on their knees . . . with knives."

22

Kris wasn't surprised by the picture Captain Drago unloaded to her next orbit. The hostile forces still sat where the road crossed the swamp. This Colonel Cortez could read the ground as well as she. And it spelled ambush in easy-to-read letters.

He was looking things over and giving it a long think.

It also let his rear guard, the only troops he had in armor, catch up. Smart man. So much for Kris's prayer for a brash, dumb one. Nelly had not been able to find out anything about a recently cashiered officer by the name of Cortez.

As further proof he was not dumb, the colonel didn't waste his time. He had some of the white-beret soldiers slowly making their way forward up the causeway on their hands and knees.

Kris zoomed the picture in as much as she could, then studied it carefully. Yes, one of them held something in his hand that glinted in the afternoon sun.

Kris chuckled. So, someone had saved money by skipping mine detectors. Whoever was in charge was using those white hats to fish for mines with their knives.

Jack wasn't under orders *not* to mine the causeway. Of course, that didn't mean he would.

Kris swallowed her chuckle. Ten hostages stood close to the slowest mine hunter. If Jack had put explosives out, things were going to get bloody a bit sooner then they wanted.

These developments were something Kris would like to talk over with her officer and NCOs. However, her LT was busy laying down two alternate tracks for this advance to contact.

And now Gunny and the other sergeants were riding along in rigs with civilians. Talking to them, telling them the bare necessities that might keep them alive. A glance at the trucks around Kris showed that the NCOs had the rapt attention of the listening farmers.

Kris assessed her progress. Measured where she needed to be by first light tomorrow. The two looked to balance.

Dear Lord, but she hated the waiting.

"The situation in front of you has not changed in the last ninety minutes," Thorpe's image observed from the clear air in front of Colonel Cortez. In front of the ground pounder, the map flimsy updated itself. "Quit wasting time and get that show of yours on the road," the starship captain ordered smartly.

Easy for him, his neck wasn't heading into an ambush.

Cortez had worked with Thorpe before. He'd learned to take calls like these in private. That didn't mean he liked them.

"Do you have any information about what kind of Marines Kris Longknife left New Eden with?"

The feed from the ship looked like it froze. Certainly, the face Thorpe showed the colonel did not change. Not so much as a breath of change.

"What kind of Marines . . . ?" he finally said.

"One of our lieutenants came across some information about Kris Longknife getting in trouble on New Eden."

Thorpe interrupted. "That woman is always in trouble."

"Yes, sir," Cortez said, but did not allow his train of thought to be derailed. "Miss Longknife was reportedly escorted off planet one step ahead of the law. The information did not identify how many Marines or if they were fleet Marine force, recon, or embassy Marines. Nor did it say if she still had them with her."

"Thorpe said slowly. Wardhaven Marines."

"Yes, sir."

"What did it say about them?"

"Nothing, sir. It was a gossip column that mentioned the Marines in passing."

"Civilians never care about the troops," Thorpe spat.

"Yes, sir. But Longknife and Marines. Are they still together?"

"Why would Marines waste their time with her? No, Colonel, once the Marines got her out, they got her out of their hair."

"I would certainly think so, sir. However, there is this little matter of what she is doing here. We did not expect her. No source suggested we might encounter her here. But here she is, claiming to command a Wardhaven ship. What's the name of it? *Wasp*? Not exactly the name for a merchant."

"But she is carrying cargo for one of the farmers here. She said that when she refused my order to sheer off."

"There is that, sir. I admit, matters are very confusing."

"The woman could confuse a bronze statue," Thorpe snorted, then eyed Cortez. "Are you going soft on me, Hernando? Has she got you so confused you're chasing your tail? You want to cut and run in front of this . . . this . . . rich brat?"

"No, sir. Not at all," Cortez exploded. Back home in an officers' club, such talk might result in someone being invited outside. And that someone might be on sick call the next day.

That someone would not bear the proud name of Cortez.

Now the colonel swallowed and went on. "However, Captain, my forces are gathering here in front of where I would have arranged an ambush. Before I stick my head into it, I'd like to know as much about the situation as I can. I do not like what I have learned. Do you know anything I should?"

Cortez managed, with effort, to turn that last remark into a question. A question it might be, but it was still good for taking an inch of skin off of William Tacoma Thorpe's proud hide.

The starship driver's face did not turn beet red. Not quite. He heard everything that Cortez had included and intended. He took a long moment to reply.

When it came, his words were deceptively soft. "Colonel, you have your orders. We have good reason to believe that whatever forces Longknife has landed to train and equip the local terrorists are ahead of you. Advance and destroy them."

Cortez saluted. "Yes, sir."

Thorpe returned the salute. "Execute your orders. Let's kick some Longknife butt."

The image in front of Cortez vanished into the air. Cortez had his orders. Now all he needed to do was make them happen.

He shook his head.

23

Colonel Cortez adjusted his body armor as he stepped down from his command vehicle's control center and let the door slam shut. Major Zhukov approached him but did not salute.

That was nice of him.

There were snipers out here; Cortez could feel them on the back of his neck. The young major was restraining himself from sending them a message. "Here's the man you want. Kill him and make me commander here." Cortez wondered if by sundown today he might wish someone had put him out of his misery.

He certainly hoped for a happier ending.

Ten paces off waited the four company commanders; Cortez waved them to him. Captain Afonin was the only one in full battle gear. He led the company of Guard Fusiliers. His record was spotless, lacking only combat experience. If he survived the coming battle, he would be far ahead of his peers in the race for a general's star. The young man's grin showed he knew all that and was eager to begin.

The other captains' white smocks and white berets showed where the gold crosses had been removed from them. The two youngest of them greeted their colonel with scowls as if they wanted to continue the debate about wearing something that glinted so brightly in the sun . . . and made them such targets.

Promotion in the Lord's Ever Victorious Host was as much by theological catechism as by military skills. As far as Colonel Cortez was concerned, these first two had memorized far too much catechism and not spent nearly enough time in the field getting their white smocks dirty.

Cortez watched with more interest the advance of the third captain. Older, passed over twice, Colonel Cortez had insisted that he get to select at least one of the Host's company commanders. He'd placed his bet on Captain Joshua Sawyer and given him Third Company. With luck, the man would soldier on with Cortez long after this little affair was a happy memory.

Then again, officers of the Ever Victorious were notoriously sentimental about their monthly formation in ranks on the parade field before the temple. If Captain Sawyer could not break that habit, he'd probably retire as a captain in forty years.

As the two Ever Victorious captains halted before the colonel, they saluted as smartly as any toy soldier.

"Drop those salutes," Cortez exploded. The two captains paled as they hurriedly got their offending hands down. Captain Sawyer came to a halt, no sign that he had intended to salute. Then again, his timing might just have been lucky.

"Are you trying to get me killed?" Cortez growled in a harsh whisper. If possible, the younger captain turned even whiter, and his brace stiffened to board straight.

The other officer didn't let any starch out of his brace, but his face did show, if for only a moment's flash, an unhealthy curiosity about Cortez's future. Cortez moved fluidly to stand nose to nose with that officer. He pointed to the swamp ahead. "Out there is perfect ambush ground. You see it?"

"Sir, yes, sir," said both captains, the older leading the younger by half a beat. Captain Sawyer blinked as he studied the ground. He nodded ever so slightly.

"There are snipers looking us over even as we talk. Snipers who can put a bullet in your brain from eight hundred meters. Who do you think those snipers most want to brain?"

The two young captains stood speechless. Apparently, this was not part of their catechism.

"Officers," Captain Sawyer observed dryly.

"You go ahead and listen to that man, you boys," came in a soft cackle. A sergeant under arms was leading ten more hostages to the front of the line. One was a gray-haired old lady who seemed to know the basics of field craft. At least more basics than these two captains.

"You listen, and quit making such stupid fool mistakes," she said as she passed them, her gray eyes looking for all the world like an exasperated DI, even with all the lines of age and wear.

Where are these locals from? Cortez asked himself, yet again. But he had a JO to educate and a rage to keep warm.

"Good God in heaven," Cortez went on. The psalm singers had protested the use of that phrase, but Cortez's Spanish-Catholic heritage found nothing blasphemous about one of the few simple declarative sentences that he and the psalm singers could agree on. Now he put a full storm behind it. "If I see another officer saluting or being saluted, the saluter will be shot. If not by some sniper, then likely by me. Do you understand?"

The rote lead-in got the rote answer from all three New Jerusalem officers. "Sir, yes, sir."

"Good. Captain," Cortez began, choosing the one who'd seemed far too interested in identifying Cortez for a sniper. "Quick march your company up to where the minesweeping detail is on the causeway. You are the vanguard. Advance your force, keeping watch for anything in the water beside the road or in the trees of this swamp. Understood?"

"Yes, sir!" the New Jerusalem officer said . . . and just managed to suppress a salute.

When he did nothing further, Cortez gave him a fish eye.

"Ah, yes, sir, ah, you want me to go do it now?" the captain stuttered in his excitement and confusion.

"If I wanted it tomorrow, I'd have told you tomorrow."

"Yes, sir. Yessir." Again, he just barely avoided saluting Cortez before running off for his command.

"You think he'll remember his orders, sir?" Zhukov asked.

"They were simple enough. And I'm sure a good XO will drop by to help him remember, is that not so?"

"Definitely, sir."

"First and Third Companies will be the main force. Mount half your troops in the available trucks. Have them keep their rifles ready and their eyes peeled for anything in the water or along the swamp beside us. Understood."

"Yes, sir," came from both captains.

"Sawyer, your Third Company will advance first. I will keep my command rig with you."

"Yes, sir. My troops will lay down their lives for the command tabernacle," came out sounding catechism rote.

Cortez didn't much care for the defeatist undertones, but he let it go with a wave of his hand. Certainly, he would find more important lessons to teach this man today.

"Captain Afonin, your company will be the rear guard. Keep well back. If there is an ambush out there, I don't want us to make it easy for them to get all of us in it. If they spring an ambush on us, you spread out and take them on the flank. If we get past the ambush and they snap it on you, I will do the same."

Captain Afonin eyed the two New Jerusalem company commanders, seemed to find little weight in the prospects of their coming to his rescue, but let the conclusion pass unstated and just nodded. "Stay spread out, eyes open, and rifles locked and cocked, sir. No problem."

"Good, then let's do it."

The Guard officers turned to go about their duty, as did Captain Sawyer. The youngest captain seemed taken back. "Aren't we going to end in prayer?" he stammered.

"God help the poor fool that tries to take a bite out of us," Major Zhukov said. "That enough for you, 'cause it's about all I got time for." Eyes wide, the young captain hastened to catch up with Captain Sawyer.

His officers sent on their way to do his bidding, Cortez boarded his command rig. Settled comfortably, he studied the lay of the land ahead. After a full two minutes, he decided that the disorganized milling about outside did not meet with his satisfaction. He only had to shout once to get the first psalm-singing company company dogs trotting out to reinforce the mine-clearance team.

Five minutes later, Sawyer's company was ready to move out. The Fusilier corporal driving Cortez's command vehicle slid it easily into the lead of that truck line.

Cortez pulled his helmet down over his eyes and prepared to receive whatever was coming his way.

24

Captain Jack Montoya, only recent to the Royal USMC, sat on a box, and stared into the cool darkness of the cave. The young boy of about ten who showed it to him first had proudly introduced it as his "fort."

Before today, it had protected the kid from nothing worse than the noon sun . . . and his parents' sudden list of midday chores. Its main advantage had been its closeness to a swimming hole. Until this morning, that the tunnel's entrance was well hidden in the root ball of a broom tree had not been a concern.

It was now.

Jack wondered why so much of Panda got dug. Then one of the young men who'd joined him spotted something at his feet and kicked it aside. A local mole or gopher or some such digging critter left such things behind when it dug. The local got kind of coy as to whether it was the sweat of the thing, or its vomit or poop or whatever. Still, if it came in contact with some bacteria in the soil, what came of it all was an ugly, smelly black wad that pharmaceutical companies and perfumeries paid good money for. It financed a major chunk of this colony.

That money source, coupled with the local's laid-back way of farming, was a main reason why folks didn't mind if their kids spent a lot of free time digging. And Jack had to agree; he'd never met a boy who didn't like messing around in dirt.

Jack stared into the darkness to better see the picture being painted on his eyeball. A tiny nano buzzed on the far side of the swamp, its picture relayed by a series of tight-beams that had, at least until now, apparently passed unnoticed by the armed mob halted at the south end of the causeway.

There was no question that Princess Kris of Wardhaven had

many failings, but once again, her inveterate addiction to fancy gadgets was coming in handy. Certainly, it was giving Jack a leg up on whoever it was over there. The hostiles looked to be reduced to the Mark I eyeball and Mark I, mod 0 ear.

Unfortunately, they appeared to be connected to a quite canny version 1.0 human brain. Colonel Cortez had smelled the ambush . . . and called a stop to his advance.

Still, he hadn't done anything, such as lobbing a rocket at Marine sniper nests, mortaring Jack's local reserves, or otherwise reacting to Jack's deployment. Apparently neither Cortez's eyeballs nor Thorpe's overhead sensors had given away Jack's defensive array. Cortez could smell the danger in this place but couldn't put his finger on any specific targets.

And, fortunately for Jack and his troops, Cortez did not appear to have a whole lot of spare ammunition to use blasting away at anyplace that looked like a good target.

Not for the first time, Jack said a silent prayer to whoever sent these folks out to grab what they thought was easy prey. Not that what Jack had seen of the locals gave him any impression that, absent outside help, they would have gone happily along with whatever these Cortez and Thorpe guys were selling.

The farmers and craftsmen Jack had met since landing liked the hand they'd dealt themselves and had been doing a fair job of organizing matters to put things back the way they liked. A few were none too happy to have helpful Marines drop out of the sky.

Jack remembered where he'd parked the landers and intended to march right back onto them just as quickly as he could.

He hoped Kris did not have other plans. Having been thrown, run, or ushered off of a half dozen planets in the last couple of years, she should be used to the idea of helping folks out, then getting out of their way . . . very, very quickly.

Oops, matters are finally getting organized over there.

Jack hadn't really needed those two idiots saluting what had to be the lead officer. The guy hung around the only rig painted green and with enough cubic volume to be a command vehicle. If that wasn't Cortez, it was his evil twin.

Jack had seriously considered changing the battle plan when he concluded he had a solid ID on Colonel Cortez. Still, Kris had been against turning this into a bloodbath if it could be avoided. Jack held to Kris's plan. Colonel Cortez would live to see this evening's sunset. If he didn't fall and break his neck.

Now everyone was running, jogging, or trotting. Jack held his breath and waited to see if Cortez had stayed within the decision box Kris's command group was betting on.

One company-size force moved onto the causeway at double time. They halted where the crude effort at mine clearing had come to an end. More local hostages were pushed ahead of them. Yep, mine clearing would be done the old-fashioned way, human foot by human foot. Gunny had warned about that possibility. So much for the old rules of civilized war.

Jack reached into his jacket pocket and removed the little box with the bright red button. At present, it was safely protected by a plastic cover. Jack left the cover on. It looked to be about an hour before he would need it.

Now trucks started moving. The white berets rode or walked alongside the rigs, eyes and rifles focused mainly on the water beside the road. Some studied the trees. There were no shouts of discovery, only quiet broken by the yells of NCOs snapping at troopers who weren't sufficiently attentive.

Jack ignored the troops and eyed the civilian trucks loaded with machine guns and troopers. He saw a dozen different makes or models. No three looked alike. Maintenance would be a bear for that collection of clattering spare parts. And spare parts were what they would need in about half an hour.

Waiting for nearly fifteen minutes before pulling up the rear were a dozen trucks of uniformly green and thoroughly military demeanor. Jack zoomed in. These troops were fully armored and loaded for bear. If Jack's command of Marines and a whole lot of eager civilians had to shoot it out with that company of hard cases, matters would get ugly in a hurry.

Jack measured the distance from hunched-over hostages in the vanguard to the last green rig only just pulling onto the causeway. About a klick.

Jack was glad nothing in Kris's plan involved his force trying to swallow that bunch down whole. Cortez knew he was going into country that just begged for an ambush. He was offering anyone stupid enough to take a swing at him what would look to any amateur like such a perfect chance.

Jack's Marines had intercepted two groups of such eager,

untrained locals. Half a squad of his Marines were tied down keeping dozens of them quiet not a klick from Jack's "fort."

On the causeway, the hostages crossed the midpoint of the swamp. They looked beat. The sun was now past noon. The humidity, heat, and bugs looked to have about done them in.

Jack watched as the white berets crossed the midpoint. Then he flipped the cover off his red button and pushed it.

25

"I'm getting radio static," the tech in the backseat of Colonel Cortez's rig shouted.

Cortez jumped to his feet, holding on to the truck's windshield to steady himself as the driver slammed on the brakes.

"Don't stop, man. Floor it," Cortez shouted. He was leading Third Company, so he'd have the hundred meters between its nose and Second Company's tail to maneuver in.

Tires spun, the truck lurched ahead for a second, but then Cortez waved to the driver and shouted, "Halt."

The reason for the static was clearly visible up ahead.

There'd been a popping noise, not even as loud as sleepy darts on lowest power. Small clots of dirty white smoke now drifted on the light wind. And about half of Second Company was struggling in the throes of a tangle net.

The sticky-covered web had a life of its own. Even as Cortez shouted, "Get away from that stuff," a couple of white berets tried to help their trapped comrades-in-prayer. They didn't have a prayer, but were immediately sucked into the trap.

Cortez leapt from his rig, whipping out his automatic. "Get back, you idiots. The next man that gets tangled in that mess I will personally shoot. Get back, damn it."

Whether it was the waving gun . . . or the foul language . . . or the look on Cortez's face, the psalm singers backed away from their entangled buddies.

Cortez mashed his commlink. "Zhukov, please tell me your engineers have a few spray cans of Goo-Off."

"Why should we do that, sir?" the major said in the calm, calculating voice of the financial backers . . . and proceeded to quote them word for word. "In a mere six hours, that stuff will harden and fall off. Besides, we're not taking any. Why would you need to protect against it?"

Cortez didn't know whom he wanted to shoot most. Zhukov for reminding him how much they'd let a bunch of spineless civilians call the shots for them . . . or the spineless civilians.

He turned away from the writhing mass that would be Second Company for the next six hours and let his eyes rove the swamp. He detested the thought of spending the rest of the day standing on the causeway, a bleating target for anything out there.

And a shot rang out.

Not the usual, high-pitched scream of a military-issue M-6 dart. No, this shot had the deep-throated, windy roar of a major-caliber round. Maybe forty or fifty calibers on the old scale. You could follow its passage as it pushed the air aside and the hole collapsed behind it.

It would fly straight for quite a while. But it was slow.

Cortez collapsed at the knees. He just might be able to fall far enough for it to miss him.

The colonel was just landing on the grassy roadway when he realized he wasn't the target. Behind him came the sharp gnashing of metal on metal, punctuated by an explosion of steam. The colonel rolled over on his belly. The air sighed out of him as he surveyed the destruction of that round.

The steel louvers that guarded his rig's radiator were opened hardly more than twenty millimeters. The round that had swooped by his head must have been at least 10mm, possibly more. Some sharpshooter had aimed it between the louvers and hit his target. Once past the armor, the round had sliced through his radiator, bounced off the engine block . . . and taken another bite out of the radiator on its way to find a louver to bounce off of, and then ripped another hole. Colonel Cortez's command rig was not going anywhere until its radiator was switched out.

To his right, left, more deep-throated rounds filled the air, and other rigs down the line exploded in steam that sent troopers fleeing lest it touched them with its hot breath.

The colonel shot to his feet. "Get in front of those radiators, you idiots. Get your worthless bodies in front of the rigs. They won't dare shoot you."

The men in the trucks looked at each other, as if they might find a translation of Cortez's strange orders in their mates' eyes.

Some of the men walking beside the trucks started to move in obedience to the colonel's orders, but it hardly seemed to matter. In ones and twos, fours and fives, hardly seconds apart, the front ends of the trucks exploded in hissing, steaming mists.

Angry and frustrated, Cortez let himself blow up at the uselessness of his patched-together command. He threw down his automatic, grabbed the nearest quaking private, and shoved him down the line. "Go find a working radiator and put your empty head in front of it."

Colonel Cortez struggled to recover his temper. He did stoop to pick up his weapon. A high-pitched round of an M-6 rang out, followed by a fusillade.

"No, no, no," Cortez growled as he stood up. "You don't shoot the heart out of my motor transport so carefully that I don't have an excuse to execute one damn hostage, then start killing my boys. You can't be that stupid after being that brilliant," he said as he looked around.

His command rig was rocking as first one tire, then another, then a third was punctured. Down the line, other trucks went down faster as their tires went flat in pairs or trios.

Soldiers, ordered only a moment ago to put their bodies in front of steaming engine blocks, moved to kneel in front of tires. But whoever was calling the shots wanted the tires dead faster.

Colonel Cortez whipped around. More fire, rapid fire, must mean more shooters closer in. "Look for shooters. Look for targets," he ordered. But even as the words roared out of his mouth, he knew they would be failures. Order, counterorder, disorder.

Cortez had learned that long ago at East Point. As a junior officer he'd watched as flag-and-field grad officers had foolishly reproven the adage. Now it was his turn.

Troopers sliding to a stop or hunkering down in front of tires . . . most of them going flat . . . needed a second to turn their concentration elsewhere.

That second was enough.

The fusillade ended.

The silence was incredibly pure, just the wind through the trees and bush and the drip, drip of water from the nearest radiator. No moan of wounded, no scream for medic. Just mesmerizing silence.

"Shoot, damn it!" Cortez screamed into the hardening quiet.

"At what, sir?" someone dared to call back.

"Out there," Cortez shouted, waving his pistol over the dark, muddy waters. "Out there, they're escaping. Shoot. Shoot anything that moves, or looks to be moving or might move."

The first shots were sporadic. Then, as soldiers came to prone or kneeling or standing positions, the fire grew into a deafening roar. Clips were emptied and replaced. The mad minute lengthened into two. Trees and shrubs trembled, then came all to pieces. Water here and there was whipped to a white froth.

Cortez studied the effects downrange. Maybe they hit something. Maybe rounds caught someone as they withdrew. Maybe some dart addressed "To whom it may concern" had ripped into someone, spreading blood into the water.

Maybe . . . but Cortez saw no blood, no flesh, no effect at all. He raised his hand, and shouted, "Cease fire."

It took a moment for other officers to see his raised hand, to make out his order . . . and to carry it out. A full minute expended itself before the last shooter was shouted to silence.

Now the silence truly was deafening. He ignored his ears and stared to the right of the causeway, then the left. Here or there, a tree, too shot up to resist gravity, tottered and fell.

Cortez looked for any sign of movement. To his left, a bird squawked and paddled madly in circles, its right wing red with gore. "Kill it," he ordered.

A single shot dispatched the creature.

Now the silence was total. The wavelets from its circling dissipated. The water of the swamp grew glassy except where the wind rolled newly downed trees.

If there had been shooters out there a moment ago, there was no sign of them now. No sign of their dead. No sign of their wounded. No sign of nothing.

"Ah, could someone help us out of this mess?" It was the voice of Second Company's captain. He, like most of his company, had spent the last few minutes cringing in the grip of the tangle net, trying to make themselves small and somehow avoid getting hit by either incoming or outgoing.

Cortez turned back to his initial problem of so long ago . . . maybe five minutes before. The colonel's latest survey of them showed nothing that his first glance hadn't told him. "In six hours the stuff will fall off of you. Until then, I suggest you avoid moving."

"Can we breathe?" came from one private.

"Only if you must, and then I would suggest as little as possible," Cortez said, and turned away to survey the wreckage.

SO Cortez was a mad-minute kind of guy. And Kris owed Jack five bucks. Kris had assumed someone at the end of a long supply line and stripped of all his transports would do the logical thing and conserve ammo.

Jack had bet that anyone dumb enough to take this job would have a temper. Also, a name like Cortez just didn't seem likely to think rationally once his ox had been gored good and tight.

It had been a friendly bet. As friendly as any a Longknife could have about a live-fire exercise.

So Jack made sure his sharpshooters were ready to go to ground once their job was done. Last shot fired, not one had begun a withdrawal. Each had a hidey-hole handy, the bole of a broom tree, an islet an inch or two above the water. They'd dug to improve their positions, just enough, but not enough to give themselves away.

Then they'd waited.

The wait had been worthwhile.

And despite Colonel Cortez's deafening response, Jack saw no evidence that the score between them was other than zero to zero.

Except Jack had reduced Cortez to walking, and the Marines still had local transport. Oh, and half of one of Cortez's companies was all tangled up, blocking the road, and would be blocking that road the rest of the day. Jack had allowed two hours for his troops to withdraw from contact and expected to be well to the north before he made camp.

With any luck, he and Kris would be in a position tonight to have a little talk of their own. And Drago would be in position, every ninety minutes or so, to tell them how Cortez was doing.

Would the guy use this opportunity to cut and run? Head south, pile into his landers, and get out of Dodge? Neither Kris nor Jack would put a dime down on that bet.

Both, in their heart of hearts, would love to see the backside of this bunch. But hoping for something is not a strategy. If the guy turned south, it was more likely to go on the defensive and invite Kris to try the tactical offensive.

Jack shook his head. He'd been loving the job Kris gave him. Exercise an offensive strategy by being on the tactical defensive. Let Cortez chase them until they had him exactly where they wanted him. It had worked this time. Would he be kind enough to let Kris and Jack do it a second time?

Time to get started. He mashed his commlink but limited it to the landline net. "Sergeant Thu."

"Yes, sir," came back a fraction of a second slower than it would have on milnet.

"You can untie your locals from the trees they're hitched to."

"They be glad to hear that."

"Tell them they can go home now or they can help us. We need holes dug. If they're willing to dig, we'd love to keep them, and they may be in on the final shoot-out."

There was a bit of silence. "They say if they'll get a chance to shoot up these robbers, they'll do some digging first."

"Good. You have them start digging. You see the other group of locals coming in from the west?"

"I got them marked, sir."

"Leave your corporal to look after this crew, and you ride over to them and invite them to the fun. Same rules. Dig holes alongside the main road. Then shoot if it comes to that. But dig first."

"Sir, I don't think these farmers understand how much a light infantry man loves his shovel."

"Can't think of a better man to teach a man to lust after his shovel than a Marine sergeant."

On the causeway, an occasional shot rattled the silence and sent winged things back into flight. Jack doubted they were hitting anything, but he couldn't be sure. He should have everyone's vitals showing up on his battle board. Not today.

Today, he'd have to wait and see who showed up at the rally point. What a way to make war. That this had been the norm for most of the history of warfare did not make Jack feel one bit better.

He took a last look at the scene across the water from his borrowed "fort," then unplugged himself from the temporary net and headed for the back of the cave. A newly dug exit put him on the surface among a lot of broom trees and brush. He had a two-mile walk for a truck.

He enjoyed it.

26

Cortez wanted to get the first word in when Thorpe came over the horizon, but "What are you doing parked on that causeway?" came before the colonel could get to his slumping command van. He took the call in the open with his staff around him.

Cortez went through several choice retorts, *enjoying the view* being his first unconsidered answer. But the colonel swallowed them all down and said, "Waiting for the tangle net to dry on the half of Second Company that you might notice is down and blocking my advance."

"Don't you have any untangle spray?"

"Not in the budget." That drew a snarl of responses from Major Zhukov and Captain Afonin of the Guard Fusiliers. "You might want to take that up with that Whitebred fellow. I know I would if he was within my reach."

Thorpe took that under consideration for a moment, or maybe he was distracted by other matters. His next comment was, "I'm getting strange readouts from your transportation."

"Yeah, I know. We've been attacked."

"Casualties?"

Cortez failed to suppress a snort this time. "You don't see any hostage bodies lying around do you? Not a single casualty."

"I also don't see any dead attackers' bodies."

"I suspect you're right, though I don't have the fine sensors you have. As I recall, I don't have any sensors."

"But you must have seen something. You were attacked."

"Yep, sniper rounds whizzing by for all of two minutes."

"So, they didn't kill any of you, and you didn't get any of them?" Thorpe sounded incredulous.

"Well, it wasn't as if nothing got hit. Those strange readings you're getting are from my transport."

"Yeah."

"Every truck, every combat rig is dead."

"Dead?"

"Not a radiator in one of them isn't shot out. Most tires are flat. There are two reasons we're sitting here. Half a company is listening to their tangle net dry. The rest of us have nothing but our boots to take us anywhere."

"And you're throwing in the towel because of that!"

Colonel Cortez so wished he'd gotten out of general view before Thorpe started talking. Surrounded as he was by Zhukov and Afonin and a few others from Torun Guard Fusiliers, his options for throwing a fit were limited. It had been a rough forty minutes since the firefight. Now the great Navy father in the sky was accusing him and his command of cowardice. Oh, how Cortez wanted to scream at someone.

Cortez held on to his temper with his fingernails, and asked through gritted teeth, "What makes you think I'd do that?"

Captain Thorpe must have sensed he was only millimeters away from crossing a line that should never be crossed among warriors. He had the good sense to say nothing more explicit than "Ah . . ." Then added, "You haven't suggested anything."

"Then let me suggest that we hold a council of war between my officers, you, and the representative of our financiers. Is Mr. Whitebred within hearing?"

"I'll get him. Wait one."

There was a long silence. Maybe the mess they were in was sinking in on Thorpe. Maybe it wasn't.

Then Whitebred squeaked, "Yes, you wanted to talk to me?"

Cortez quickly outlined what had happened to his command since they checked in last orbit. The space side of the conversation did not interrupt, even for clarification.

"That sounds bad," Mr. Whitebred said at the end.

Was the man so dumb that he lacked any idea just what an understatement that was? "Our situation is not hopeless, but it could be a lot better," Cortez answered.

"What would you suggest?" Whitebred asked.

Not for the first time Cortez wished this conversation was taking place on visual. It would be interesting to see how Thorpe looked as he swallowed his silence.

"My options are rather clear, Mr. Whitebred. I can continue to advance. To seek out and engage the forces under this Longknife girl. So far, they have gone out of their way to avoid serious contact and any casualties."

"They didn't take out a single one of your troopers while they were shooting up your trucks?" Thorpe still couldn't seem to address that fact without his words drowning in incredulity.

"No one was even nicked. I have fifty hostages and was prepared to shoot ten for every one killed. With not even one trooper wounded, I seemed as much bound to do nothing as our published order bound me to do something if she did hit someone."

"Should we change that order, Captain Thorpe?" Whitebred asked.

"It doesn't seem like we'd gain anything by doing that just now. All our mobile assets are down. By the way, Colonel Cortez, I checked back with the troops you left guarding your landers. They do not appear to be under any threat. In fact, no civilians are in view of either of the landing beaches. The locals seem to be making a big thing of ignoring them."

"Could any of them get their hands on a few trucks. Maybe bring us up a load of radiators?"

"Radiators? Ha!" someone spat. Cortez turned to see a sunburned old fellow sitting in a ring of ten hostages. "We don't keep no supply of radiators like that waiting around." He spat again. "You done put all of us on foot, man."

"Did you hear that?" Cortez asked his orbital listeners.

"Yeah. You've been down there awhile. You see anything that looks like a big supply of spare parts?"

"Not in any town we passed through. Farms seem to keep their old stuff around. For spare parts I'd guess, but if we sent a couple of rigs around to collect stuff, I suspect we'd end up with more holed radiators than spares."

The hostage just grinned at Cortez and nodded.

"I'm wide open to suggestions," Cortez finally bit out.

"If you try to fall back, you'll have to do it on foot." Captain Thorpe stated the obvious.

"If I try to advance," Cortez pointed out, "I'll also be doing that on foot."

"But you have to be close to contact," Whitebred put in from his deep well of military ignorance.

"That is true," Thorpe agreed. "You've come so far, Colonel, to walk away from your attackers."

"And could he?" Whitebred put in. "Walk away, I mean. What are the chances this Longknife girl has gotten her hands on some transport? Couldn't they use any borrowed trucks to whip around your—what do you call them?—flanks, and be in front of you no matter which direction you go in?"

"It does seem like Colonel Cortez will be attacking, whatever direction he chooses to head," Thorpe pointed out.

"But in one I'll be getting closer to my base. In the other direction, I'll be going farther." Cortez wanted to say, *You idiots, pull me back to our bases. There's a chance we just might hold in the major cities if I have enough troops to garrison. Wandering around out here, I'm just the latest in a long line of generals looking to have my command wiped out.*

And if he said that, he'd be immediately labeled a defeatist, coward, and loser. That was what Thorpe wanted to do. Label him. Relieve him and turn his command over to Major Zhukov. Cortez threw the man from Torun a hard glance.

Major Zhukov shook his head and took a step back. He waved both his hands and mouthed, *Not me. I don't want this mess.*

Cortez would have preferred a stronger vote of confidence, but a look around the causeway showed no reason for confidence.

"I think he should keep going," Whitebred said. "There's not much more inhabited space north of where he is. He does outnumber the Wardhaven interlopers three or four to one. Maybe five to one. It seems to me that you've got all of them right there. Why shouldn't he just keep on attacking them?"

"That sounds like a good call to me," Captain Thorpe said.

It would, you damn swabby. You're up there, not down here, Cortez thought. But Whitebred had a point. It might work.

And on the way up here, Cortez had driven his troops through plenty of places for a good ambush. If Longknife and her Marines had trucks, they'd be there waiting for them.

Sooner or later, Longknife would strip him of his hostages, and the gloves would come off. Cortez projected a map on the ground in front of him. The distance to the northernmost settlement was barely a quarter of that back to City Two.

If he could just find this Longknife and fix her in place, his four companies should be able to kick the living stuffings out of her. "We will continue to advance, sir, in pursuance of your orders," Cortez said.

"Very good, Colonel," Thorpe replied. "We will talk to you again on the next orbit."

Cortez made sure his commlink was thoroughly off before he said a word. "So we toss the dice. Who knows, we might win."

"Yes, sir," Zhukov said, "but what do we do about all our spare ammo and food, sir? Our men can't carry it. My Fusiliers are maxed out with just our weapons load and armor."

That question hung unanswered by Cortez's staff.

"Ain't you guys ever used hand trucks or wagons?" the hostage that had put in his own thoughts asked.

"And you are?" Cortez asked.

"Abe, sir," the old-timer said, getting to his feet. "Abe Lincoln Corminski if you want all my folks saddled me with. Abe does fine for most."

Another of the hostages, a woman about his age, kicked him. "Abe dearest, you always did talk too much. You quit doing the thinking for these no-good layabouts."

"But, honey, I figure if I get these folks up north quicker, they'll run into whoever is hunting them and this thing will get settled one way or the other, and I can get you back home."

The woman kicked him again, and grumbled something under her breath that sounded like "thickheaded old fool."

Cortez motioned the man to him . . . and out of kicking range of the woman he would bet money was his wife.

"And just what kind of hand wagons or trucks are you talking about?" he asked, as the man came to him. He had yellow teeth and bad breath. On further consideration, Cortez took a step back.

"Well, if you take one of the axles off of these trucks—the ones that go straight through, not two-piece ones—and you put a flat bed on it and a shank out with handles or something and you pull it, a man can haul a lot if it's rolling along on a couple of wheels," the guy said, folding his arms and preening himself on his expertise on hauling things.

Cortez glanced at his lieutenant commanding the Fusiliers' engineering platoon. He'd stooped down to eye the undercarriage of the combat rigs the Guard had been riding in.

He stood and shook his head. "Can't use any axles from

those rigs. Each wheel has its own suspension." He didn't point out that practically all of the six- and eight-wheeled rigs had flat tires as well.

"Not those fancy, duded-up things. You need a simple rig that will do a hard day's work. Like those." Abe pointed up the causeway to where the First and Third Companies' transport lay gathering dust and heat from the day.

The last truck in line looked to have two axles that went all the way through, from one flat tire to the other equally flat one. Cortez turned and led his staff up the kilometer or so to where the truck line started. Yep, most of the local trucks had one straight-through axle holding up the rear.

They also had a lot of flat tires.

"Just how do you propose getting the axles off?" the engineering officer asked. "And then how are we going to put together wagon beds to carry our gear?"

"You got some tools don't you?" Abe said dryly, giving the young officer a sidewise look. "They said you were an engineering officer, I seem to remember."

The lieutenant turned beet red and looked ready to say something that would not go over well.

Cortez stepped in. "Let's say that knocking together a handcart was not one of the requirements for him to graduate from his college, shall we?"

The local made a sour face and shook his head. "Not much of a school," he muttered.

That didn't put oil on the rapidly troubling waters. Cortez cleared his throat to stop the rumblings among his staff. "Lieutenant, go get your team and tools. Abe, why don't you go see if any of the hostages are willing to join you in showing us how to knock together these handcarts."

Abe didn't move. "Just out of the kindness of their hearts, you say. Knock together what some folks risked their lives to knock silly." The farmer folded his arms and didn't move.

Captain Afonin flipped the cover off his automatic's holster. Colonel Cortez gave his head a quick shake and leaned over to put an arm around Abe. His breath did stink. "Let's say that you and your local friends are able to help us with our wheel problem. I say that you can tell them that I'll let them start walking back the way you came. That sound good?"

"Very good, sir. Now, if the man of the house helps you,

what you say to the poor woman of the house also walking south?"

Cortez's eyebrows rose. The guy was wheedling him!

"You really want that harpy turned loose. I should think you'd want us to shoot her."

"She's a mite bit noisy at times, but a guy can get used to that. Kind of come to expect it."

Cortez held his breath and leaned closer. "What say you start getting your farmer friends together now, and I don't shoot your shrew of a wife right now?" Done, Cortez shoved the man at the nearest knot of hostages.

Abe went without a backward glance. That was good, 'cause Cortez might otherwise have shot him. Here and there, a hostage stood. Most stayed seated and gave the standing ones a lot of lip. One woman sat back down.

"Captain Afonin," Cortez said.

The company commander whipped out his automatic and fired a round in the air. Talk stopped. Captain Afonin got the standing ones headed for a truck, then followed Abe as he headed for other clumps of hostages for his little talk.

It went quicker after that.

Most of the trucks had lumber on their beds, either as the bed itself or to protect the metal below. Between the locals and the engineers, they got several long chunks of board into a tripod-and-pulley arrangement good enough to lift some trucks off their axles. Getting the axles out was not an easy task; most tires were determinedly not round.

The process was not without its mishaps. One engineer had his leg crushed when a tripod collapsed and a truck came down early. Several arms were broken. Grim thoughts that Cortez was starting to have about sabotage hung like a deadly cloud over the process as the casualty count grew higher. But that count stayed about even between those in green and the locals. In the end it was dead even at five each, and he resnapped the cover to his sidearm.

Tires proved to be the limiting factor. None of the axles they recovered could take a tire from a Guard rig. Most of the local rigs had been shot up pretty well, even the spare tires. The final tally came in at eight single-axle carts.

The sun was edging below the horizon about the time both the tangle net started to crack and fall off its victims and the wagons were loaded with as much food, ammunition, and water as they would carry. A squad was delegated to protecting the rest.

Cortez got his command to the north end of the causeway and then set his troops to digging fighting holes to sleep in. Ten freed hostages started their way south. The remaining forty were cuffed sitting up to the wagons they would pull in the morning.

The night guards got a serious talking-to. "If anything moves in your line of fire, kill it." Grim faced, they took in their orders.

The night was broken regularly by gunfire. Winged and four-legged critters that caught a guard's attention died without firing a shot in retaliation. Sleep was not all that plentiful, but as dawn came up the next morning, the camp was secure.

27

Kris finally got a chance to talk to Jack around sunset. He risked rigging a tight-beam to the *Wasp*, which immediately passed it along to Kris.

"How'd Short Stop One go?" was Kris's first question.

"Surprisingly close to plan," Jack answered happily. "In one wild minute my fifty Marines pretty much took down every truck they had. They're all afoot now."

"They get anyone?"

"Winged a private who didn't get his butt down low enough when Cortez rewarded us with one of the noisiest mad minutes I ever hope to encounter. I thought these broom trees were tough, but they shot several of them up so badly they kind of came sliding down into the mud low and slow. 'Twas sad to see such giants laid low."

"Just so long as none of us got laid low."

"As I said, one bun shot. How's your recruiting job gone?" Jack asked back.

"I've got quite a procession spread out around me, say eight hundred locals along. My Marines are busy training them."

"They any good?"

"We won't know that until the shooting starts. Speaking of good, what's your call of the invaders? They up to Marine standards?"

"Don't let Gunny hear you even thinking that question. From what I saw of them, there's about a company of heavily armed and armored. I figure them to be nearly as good as ours. Then there are three companies of guys running around in uniforms but no armor. And just a rifle and bayonet. They haven't impressed me. One walked into the tangle web and let it make them into a bunch of fools. Those that missed the fun with tangle net didn't duck all that fast when we shot up the trucks. Give Gunny two or three months with your local recruits, and I bet he'd have them in better shape than these white coats."

"We don't have two or three months. Gunny and his NCOs are doing everything they can with the locals, but a day or two isn't two or three months."

"You getting cold feet?"

"I'm worrying about Short Stop Two."

The pause wasn't all that long before Jack came back. "It's bothering me, too. Looks kind of obvious on the map, and I don't trust this Colonel Cortez with obvious. Not after what we did to him in the last *obvious* ambush ground."

Short Stop Two was a neck on the road north where the ridgeline to the west reached almost down to the swamp on the east. Because of the high water table, the gophers and their droppings had been forced to the surface. Someone had dug up the area, leaving behind what looked like shallow trenches. Now overgrown with bushes and young trees, it had looked, from orbit, like a perfect place to set up a second ambush.

Now maybe it didn't.

Kris gave Jack her present assessment. "He's going to be looking for us there. If we take up positions in the dug-out area and he deploys to flank us, we'll be stuck in place. They haven't shown us any artillery, but even a couple of small mortars could pound that area, and we'd be stuck taking it. These green locals would break and be mowed down as they ran."

Kris could almost hear Jack nodding along with her as she finished. "So, if we skip that, where do we hit him next?" he asked, as soon as she fell silent.

"Don't laugh until I get this all out, okay?" Kris said, maybe a bit defensively. "I've been collecting goats. Goats and pigs, Jack. I'm thinking of staking them out in the diggings, covering them enough so that Thorpe can't get a clear visual on them from orbit but can get a heat signature. I'll bet you dollars to dough- nuts that our Colonel Thorpe and his stalwart hands will look pretty silly after launching a full-scale flanking attack on our barnyard leavings."

Jack chuckled. "Oh, that *would* be embarrassing. And if we did a little battlefield preparation here and there, he might have a casualty or two to show for his effort."

"I'd rather not use explosives," Kris said. She wasn't ready for the affair to get deadly. Not yet.

"Don't worry, I've got another tangle web. Oh, and some of the farmers I've recruited are out digging holes here and there in the sod. Not too wide and not too deep, but if someone isn't looking and steps in one, they are going to have a sprained ankle or busted leg.

"When Cortez heads north in the morning, I expect he'll end up with a couple of those to slow him down.

"I'm looking for Short Stop Three," Kris said. "There are a couple of options. We can talk more when we join up tomorrow."

"Sleep tight. See you tomorrow. Hard to believe that this time we're following a plan that's actually working."

Kris signed off as well, with Jack's words still fresh in her ears. A plan that works. Amazing! But further back in her head was an old commander's warning from OCS. "No battle plan survives contact with the enemy."

This time hers had. So far.

Was that good? Or did it just mean that when everything fell apart, it would be all the bigger mess?

Now Kris had so many volunteers and Marines that she had to spread them out among three homesteads. For most of the day it had taken two or more farms to hide them in whenever Captain Thorpe came over.

Tonight, this dispersion meant that she couldn't talk to most of her recruits. Their morale and skill set would be a great unknown for her tomorrow. She did not like that.

The good news was that tomorrow morning, Jack and Lieutenant Troy would rejoin her. She'd have her command together for the first time since they dropped.

The bad news was that she'd have them all together, and that would make hiding them all the harder. Well, at least she'd get a good look at them. Thorpe had been very quiet since he first fired his big lasers at the Fronour farmhouse. Now that she was concentrating her troops, would he risk another shot?

New battle, but the same old worries. Kris rolled over, tightened her bedroll around her, and went to sleep. There would be plenty of time for worrying in the morning.

28

Colonel Cortez mopped his brow; his handkerchief came away sopping wet. He glanced at the sky. It was still two or more hours until noon. Good Lord, but this place was hot.

"Man down. Medic!" came the shout from his right flank. For the fifth time this morning, Cortez signaled the column to a halt. Major Zhukov pointed at one of the pull carts and aimed them off the road and to where a clump of psalm singers gathered around one of their own who was baying like a stuck pig.

"Watch your step," Zhukov ordered. "Bust your leg, and we'll just leave you." The hostage pullers went at a slow walk, eyes fixed on the ground. One did a hop and skip that caused the cart to slow. Maybe it was a snare, maybe not. No way to tell.

Major Zhukov turned to Colonel Cortez. "This is not working. We're just reacting to *them*, sir," he added.

"Tell me something I don't know," Cortez snapped. He glanced at his deployment; it was standard. First Company was scattered widely in a van a klick ahead. Second was to his left, across half a klick of recently cut cropland. Third covered his right, spread out halfway to where the stinking swamp lay . . . but never more than a half klick out. The Guard was strung out behind him, with the hostages and handcarts mingled in. Half of the carts now carried a trooper moaning his splinted leg.

Casualties kept adding up for a battle not yet started. Cortez didn't know much about the Longknife girl, but from what he saw, she was very good at driving good officers crazy.

Cortez squatted in the shadow of a handcart and projected a map of the road ahead of them. Major Zhukov, still standing, edged the toe of his boot in to highlight a section.

"Yeah," Cortez grunted in agreement. "Yeah, I would probably set up an ambush there, too."

The photo showed the road twisting around a ridge close to a heavily dug-up area between the road and the swamp. If that batch of ground was as hard as most of this planet's worked-over ground was, those dugouts were ready-made fighting holes.

The place must have been dug up a while back. New trees, shrubs, and ferns covered the ground pretty well. It would be easy to hide people in those ditches. "I'll have Thorpe give us thermal images of this area every pass."

"His thermal images haven't done us a lot of good so far," Zhukov pointed out. "No hint as to where that Longknife girl is up north. No nothing about that swamp we got ambushed in. I swear, I could have done better with a blind man's cane."

"Maybe he'll get lucky. Maybe we'll get lucky," Cortez said, staring off at the distant trees. And thinking.

Fact, we got ambushed but good. Fact, highly accurate fire. Rapid fire. But come to think about it, not a lot of automatic fire. No, what had let the air out of his trucks' tires had been single shots. Rock and roll would have shredded the rubber and put holes all around the trucks' fenders. It also would have put holes in troops standing nearby.

No excess holes in the trucks. None in the troops.

Very good shooting.

And no thermal heat sources for Thorpe to spot from orbit.

Who could shoot that fast, that straight, and had battle suits that didn't give off a heat signature?

"God . . ." Cortez started, then noticed the look the wounded psalm singer gave him. For peace in his command he swallowed what he'd intended to say and finished with, "bless."

"Amen," the member of the Lord's Ever Victorious Host appended.

Major Zhukov pursed his lips. "U.S. Marines," he whispered.

"With thermal battle suits," Cortez finished.

"Damn," said the wounded psalm singer.

29

Kris was glad to see Jack's rig being waved in by her scout troop. They motored up and down the breaks that were the prelude to the hills ahead. At the bottom of many of the low, rolling hills were small streams, fed by the distant mountains. The sun had been up for only an hour, but it was already hot.

Jack reported with a salute and a smile. "Good to see you again, Princess. You've got quite a following," the Marine captain said, taking in the lines of trucks behind her.

Kris returned the salute. "Where are your troops?"

Jack glanced over his shoulder at only three trucks. "I didn't see much use in bringing them back and forth. They're out ahead of you, digging holes in the croplands. It's not going to be a lot of fun walking in their footsteps."

Kris gave over to her captain any doubts she still had. He might be a short-timer in the Corps, but he'd been a long time looking after her hide.

"Oh, I passed that zoo you sent forward. Lot of unhappy campers. And not just the pigs and goats," he chuckled.

Kris shook her head. "They're all just looking for a fight. And not a second's thought for the butcher bill."

"The butcher's bill is never in the vids," Jack said.

"And if these young fools don't pay it a bit of mind, they're going to run when the first penny comes due," Kris said. Just once she'd like to lead a real command with trained troops.

No, she had done that finally, and they'd all been just as eager for the first shot. But none had run at the first casualty. Marines wouldn't think of doing that. The locals she had strung out behind her might be another matter entirely.

"The *Wasp's* about due over the horizon. Let's see what Drago has to show us," Kris said, changing the topic.

Captain Drago greeted them cheerfully, as someone might who'd slept in his own bed and eaten in his own wardroom. Kris tried not to grumble; her quarters for the night had been a hayloft in a barn. Her breakfast, a canteen of water and a half loaf of the hard bread they made from the roughly ground grain of the perennial grass they were driving over.

There was a reason she had joined the Navy.

It took Chief Beni a moment to organize his sensor feeds into a coherent picture and download it to Kris. "Colonel Cortez appears to have spent the night at the end of that causeway and is just now moving north."

Jack ran his fingers over the orbital image. "He's deploying his light infantry for flankers and a van. His heavy infantry is holding his center with these carts. Looks like he's using his hostages for mules. And has them in front."

"You booby-trapping the road?" Kris asked.

"Nope, but plenty of holes around it. Should be rough on the van and the flankers." An update of the image came through. The picture Nelly projected on the back wall of the truck they rode in wavered and settled down.

"Oh, look at that," Jack chortled, pointing at the far right of the van troops. "Looks like someone's down and drawing a crowd. I think we just broke a leg."

They paused, waiting for the next refresh. It showed the same small clump . . . and a pull cart being rushed down the road to them. The rest of the formations were holding in place.

"Doesn't look like Colonel Cortez is racing north," Jack said, with a grin. "We may be slowed digging those holes, but he'll be stopped every time one of his boys fills one."

Kris nodded, satisfied that a certain colonel was having a very bad day, then moved her attention farther north.

It was easy to spot the dugouts. Jack's teams were also easily found, even though they were spread off the road and across a greater depth than Kris had expected.

"I've got them in three lines. One's digging holes. The second is farther down the road selecting where to dig more holes. The third is finishing up on their holes, and getting ready to fall back to another line. With lasers overhead every ninety minutes or so, I can't make anyone too good a target."

"You using local homesteads when Thorpe's overhead?"

"Just spreading out. After that first shoot, Thorpe and Cortez know we're here. Your volunteers are the unknown."

Kris nodded. Jack looked like he wanted to say something, but it wasn't coming out. "You got a problem, Captain?"

Jack gnawed at his lower lip for a second, then glanced at the scores of trucks moving along in rough lines. "You got quite a following here." Kris nodded. "What have you paid for it?"

"Paid?"

"Hell has no fury like a noncombatant. I remember hearing that someplace. These kids are carrying rifles, but none ever fired a shot at another human being." Kris wasn't at all sure where this was going and was rapidly getting tired of waiting.

"Some of my locals are gleefully talking about the coming massacre. They want no surrenders. No quarter given."

Gunny had reported similar talk among some of his locals. Kris hadn't heard it. At least not from the clan elders she'd talked to while raising her volunteers. "You've explained to them that's not the way we fight? Slaughtering prisoners is not only stupid, it's against the laws of war."

"Yeah, but I'm not sure anyone is listening. They don't want to go through this again. They figure wiping out this bunch will send a message. Don't mess with us."

Kris shook her head. "Don't they know most of these troops are rented? We set the home folks rioting, screaming about the 'savages' out on the Rim, and what started as a cheap little excursion by some get-rich-quick entrepreneurs will turn into a bloody vendetta to retrieve a planet's lost honor."

"I know that, and you know that, Kris, but how do we make them know that? I'm assuming you're trying to maneuver this into a well-managed surrender, with the less blood the better."

"I admit the thought is rather attractive," Kris said, glancing over her shoulder. Her truck's load was half Marines, half locals. The Marines looked grim. The locals' faces ranged from puzzled to downright unhappy. So, she would have a problem on her hands even before she got to fighting a battle.

One thing at a time.

"I've ordered the zoo to take cover every time Thorpe is overhead. I figure they'll be to the dugouts about noon. One of the locals mentioned that they've got a spider kind of thing that really raises a welt on a man when it bites him. It can lead to fever and all kinds of bad stuff. We've been collecting them to send along with the zoo."

"Oh my," Jack said, through a smile.

"We won't actually rig explosives, though a settlement we stopped at last night makes fireworks for local use."

"Fireworks!"

"Yep, firecrackers, rockets, those sorts of things. Battlefields are usually known for being noisy. What do you think the odds are that if we make a field noisy, someone might turn it into a battlefield."

"Don't you just hate blue-on-blue casualties," Jack said, growing a grin. "Thorpe is really going to regret the day he didn't load his ground pounders back aboard ship and run for a jump point when you wandered into this system."

"What do you think the chances are that he will do just that?" Kris asked.

Jack took in a deep breath and let it out slowly. "That's not something I'd give you a bet on. Not at any odds."

"Yeah, that's what I kind of figured."

30

Thorpe got Cortez on the commlink as soon as the *Golden Hind*'s sensors located his column. "Colonel, what's taking you so long? You're barely covered two miles since I was overhead."

"And I'm doing well to have made that," the colonel shot back.

"You need to plant a boot up the asses of some of your men?"

"I need them to look carefully where they plant their own boots," Cortez answered, and filled the space side of the operation in on what the ground side was facing.

"The locals are digging those holes. Start shooting hostages," Thorpe said with all the moral involvement of a man selecting between two kinds of beer.

"I can't. I haven't actually seen any local digging the holes, and the hostages insist those ferret things, whose droppings were the first thing we confiscated, dig just these kinds of holes."

Thorpe scowled at Whitebred. He'd taken to summoning the businessman to the bridge whenever he talked to Cortez.

"Those pharmaceutical precursors could still bail us out," Whitebred said. "We have four years of harvesting already on board. They'd pay our costs even if we made nothing else."

"I don't care about that," Thorpe snapped. "I want to know if those beasties dig holes that are causing problems for our infantry. Do they dig holes people step in?"

"How should I know?" the representative of the expedition's financiers said with a shrug. "We buy what comes to market. We don't care how it came there. What it looks like in the field. The smelly stuff is repulsive enough."

For another uncountable time, Thorpe noted how different

businessmen and warriors looked at things. And how poorly prepared the intelligence was for this operation. Next time he did something like this . . .

But before next time, Thorpe had to finish this time. He pounded on his commlink. "Mr. Whitebred once again is a glowing fount of ignorance. We'll search our telemetry to see if we can spot anyone digging the holes that are troubling you."

"I've been looking at what you show ahead."

"It doesn't look like much," the spaceship commander said. There was a long pause before he got a reply from Cortez.

"Someone's in the hills overlooking us. I assume that's a scout reporting our progress. I also see you've got some heat signatures under bushes and trees ahead of us along the road."

"But they're too spread out to be worth an eighteen-inch laser shot," Thorpe pointed out.

"I bet," Whitebred offered helpfully, "that as soon as we aren't overhead, they start digging your holes."

"You know that for sure, sir," Colonel Cortez said. His "sir" was gauged to flail half the skin off Whitebred.

"No, no, I don't know anything for sure," came in a crest-fallen voice.

"Thank you, sir, but I don't need any half-baked guesses from orbit," Cortez said.

"There is a group of people on the south side of the river," Cortez said slowly. "They've been moving along slowly, showing up every pass, and growing larger. But they haven't crossed the river. They keep the swamp between them and me."

"When they get to the causeway, they can either cut your line of communications or move to attack your rear." Thorpe knew he was saying the obvious, but he needed to measure the morale of his ground contingent. Officers who lost the fighting spirit started looking over their shoulders for ghosts in their rear.

"Not a problem. My supplies are in my carts. Once I destroy the main force, I can sweep that one up on my way back."

"Assuming the main force is ahead of us and not that one over there," someone on the ground added.

"There is that, Major Zhukov, there is that," Cortez said. "Well, Captain Thorpe, if you don't have anything else, my latest broken leg is now sedated and we are ready to move. I assume everything is quiet in orbit."

"They now have nanosatellites in orbit ahead of us and

behind. They slip above our horizon every once in a while and check us out. I can do nothing without them immediately sounding an alarm. That gunboat could be right on my tail or just over the horizon ahead of me."

"We all must bear our little crosses," Cortez said, and cut the commlink.

"Imagine that man whining about his little problems," Colonel Cortez growled as soon as he was sure his commlink was silenced. And Thorpe's cavalier attitude to shooting hostages!

This whole operation was balanced on the sharp edge of a very long knife, indeed. Killing hostages would contribute nothing to winning this battle. And if matters did not go as well as Thorpe was so sure they would, one colonel might find himself trying very hard to remind this Lieutenant Longknife that the laws of war said POWs were to be respected. No, it would not be pretty to argue that if he was standing there with his hands dripping with the blood of innocent hostages.

The informal contract between them was clear. If they killed one of his troopers, he could kill ten of them. So far the Longknife girl had gone out of her way to leave his troops alive. Cortez would not be the one to change their tacit agreement. Not now. Not when things were, if anything, going more her way than his.

Major Zhukov brought Cortez back from those unexpected thoughts. "And him insulting us, asking us if we're worried about that other group getting in our rear. He who hasn't offered us a kopeck of proof that there is anything ahead of us but a screen," the major spat. "For all we know, his pretty little Kris Longknife could be laughing up her sleeve as she passes us on the other side of the swamp and takes off for our landing boats after leaving a few guns to hold the causeway."

"Be careful what you say, Major," Cortez said behind his hand. "You don't want the psalm singers to think that we don't know what we're doing."

Zhukov glanced around, saw troops in white coats carefully looking away from the command unit . . . but not closing their ears. "But we *don't*," he said softly.

"I know that. You know that, but we must not have anyone else even thinking that. Put on your game face," the colonel said, glancing at the sky. The midafternoon sun glared down at him. He eyed the map, then stabbed his finger at what he saw.

"There. There is heat. See, Zhukov. See. Troops have occupied the ditches."

The officer came to peer over his commander's shoulder. "No visuals of anything but bushes and trees," he pointed out.

"As there is here," Cortez said, waving at the screen well ahead of him. "But there weren't any heat signatures in the trenches before. Now there are."

"Do we attack them this afternoon?"

Cortez measured the distance, both across country and along the winding road, then shook his head.

"No, too far to go, and our troops are tired. Beside, the faster we push them, the more step into these so-called ferret holes. No, let's plan to camp here, a good four miles away from them tonight. We can walk the psalm singers in early and fight in the cool of the morning."

Zhukov preened. "And we can get the Guard to bed early. They will have no problem with a little walk in the dark, no matter how wet it is. It's time we started telling the drummer what the dance will be."

31

As Kris spread her troops over three farmsteads for the night, she had two problems. How to get the most out of tomorrow's misfire at the dugouts was something she'd enjoy batting around with Jack and Gunny. The quality of her volunteers and their exact behavior in a real firefight tomorrow wasn't likely to be resolved tonight. Still, tonight was all the time she had to patch something together.

She started with a small meeting of her best. She'd hardly mentioned how much she wanted some human control over how the dugout "battle" played out before Sergeant Bruce stepped forward.

"If Nelly would be kind enough to give me some nanos, I think I can make things happen just the way you want it, Your Highness. Nothing special, Nelly, just make them wag their tails when they see something."

"Computers have no tails to wag, Sergeant," the computer made clear in a rather schoolmarmish voice. But in the next second Nelly had switched to the voice of a twelve-year-old, tickled that the game was afoot. "But I can rig a couple of nanos to squeak so that only someone listening for the precise squeak could tell it isn't just part of the background noise. What kind of nanos do you want?"

Jack failed to hide a grin. Kris just shook her head. Nelly was developing so many different personalities . . . and trotting them out so fast . . . that even Kris never knew what to expect when she talked to her computer. It could be all fun and games, but could Nelly become unreliable?

Kris had to make time to talk to Auntie Tru about her favorite pet computer.

But Sergeant Bruce was having no problem. "Motion sensors, both for air and water. At least, if I was attacking the dugouts, I'd have that heavy infantry walk in from the wet side. Oh, and some nanos to set the fireworks off in a cascading daisy chain. If I understand your intent, Captain, Your Highness, the object is to make the colonel the laughingstock of his troops. Any casualties are kind of icing on the cake."

Jack eyed Kris, who found herself grinning happily.

"Yes, Sergeant," Jack said, "I think you read your commander's intentions perfectly."

"Nelly, how long to forge the nanos?" Kris asked.

"I've been done it seems like just way foreverrrrr," Nelly said, sounding far too much like that certain twelve-year-old girl who now infested Kris's ship.

For a moment, Kris wondered how Cara was making out, with her teacher groundside. She'd probably spent the time wrapping Professor mFumbo and his helpless boffins around her little finger. The girl did not belong on a warship. Kris would have to do something about that.

Just as soon as she got some invaders to leave this planet. And did something about the mess on Xanadu. She had come out here to resolve that problem. Couldn't forget that bunch of nuts. Hopefully, Cara wouldn't have to wait too long, but Xanadu did come ahead of her. Just as this bunch of uniformed bandits had somehow gotten ahead of Xanadu.

Kris doubted the Guides of Xanadu could get into much mischief while she was stuck in the mud here.

"Sergeant Bruce, could you hold out your personal computer?" Nelly didn't quite order. The Marine did.

"I've transmitted subroutines and the nanos to your machine. You *must* talk to Kris about a computer a bit more capable."

"Nelly!" Kris snapped.

"Yes, Kris. But you really should. At least for the noncoms who you use a lot."

"As you were," Kris growled.

"I am not in the Navy. You can't order me around."

"Don't bet on that to last forever," Jack said, giving Kris an evil grin. "If she takes a mind to it, Kris might draft you right into *her* Navy. She drafted me out of the Secret Service."

"Computers have our rights." Nelly stormed on. "Civil rights. Human rights. Oh," she said and paused for a long second, which, for a computer, must have lasted beyond forever. "Jack has human rights, and you drafted him. If I had rights, you could still draft me. I need to think about that."

The last was spoken in the standard computer voice, the one Nelly only used when she was devoting a major part of her power to something a mere human would likely find beyond complicated.

"Nelly, my dear," Gunny said, "you do know that you're a major part of our team and all of us, Marines and Navy, respect what you do for us."

"You do?" was still in that standard computer voice.

"We do that, my dear. Now, does Sergeant Bruce need any more help with his nanos?"

At OCS, Kris learned that senior NCOs were more like unto God than, well, most humans thought God was. And that NCOs made it a point to look out first and foremost for their troops. Gunny was often more hands-on than any recent apparition of the traditional Divine Being. Though his attention was usually to the surprise and dismay of said subordinates.

Just now, Kris watched Gunny in full transcendent concern for not only Sergeant Bruce but all his trigger-pullers.

"No, Sergeant Bruce is good to go," Nelly said, starting to sound more normal.

Sergeant Bruce nodded. "I think I've got them under my control. I've had my computer cycle them through a series of tests, and everything is working. The range looks to be limited, but I think it will do."

Which left Kris with only one more problem to handle this evening. The one that couldn't be solved.

As Sergeant Bruce marched off on the first leg of his journey to the dugouts, Kris glanced around the large barn she expected to spend the night in. Like most other barns she'd seen on Panda, it was dug out and sod covered. So far, Thorpe hadn't paid any attention to them.

One of the last trucks to arrive that night had disgorged Penny, with old man Fronour and Gramma Polska. Kris couldn't name the other gray heads that dismounted, but she suspected someone had called a meeting of the senior farming clans and forgotten to cc her on the matter.

Bales of hay were being arranged into a kind of forum. Gray heads were settling into seats. Kris had foresworn the political life of her father . . . but she wasn't blind to its trappings.

Penny joined Kris. "Sorry this got out of hand."

"It had to be faced," Kris said, and led them to where a speaker's rostrum would be if the forum were more formal.

Kris stood at parade rest . . . and let her eyes rove the elders before her. Slowly, the babble settled to silence.

Kris cleared her throat, and asked. "Do you have any questions for me?"

The silence gave way to murmurs as heads turned to the people next to them. No one among them moved to stand, to take the lead. Had Kris moved before they were ready, or had the different views failed so far to coalesce?

Pandemonium had no planetary government. Kris had been surprised to hear from Andy Fronour on the trip out just how minimal the town governance was, a council, no mayor. He'd been proud of just how little government they got along with.

Kris hoped she wasn't going to have to teach a whole lot of reluctant souls How to Decide Things 101.

"I hear there's going to be a fight tomorrow up the road a ways," Bobby Joe Fronour said. "What are we doing all the way back here?"

"There will be a battle up the road at what I've come to call the dugout," Kris said, "but we aren't going to be there."

"Don't it take two to have a battle?" The man who stood up held his rifle at the ready, as if he might find an enemy sitting beside him. He was one of the youngest in the barn, hair still flaming red.

Kris gave the question a nod. "If you want to go down in the history books as a great conqueror, it does help if some opposition shows up to fight and get their butts kicked."

A momentary pause got the laughter Kris hoped for. "Us showing up serves no one's benefit except Colonel Cortez's. His launching a smashing assault on a host of barnyard animals should make him the laughingstock of his entire command, as well as human space once the story gets out, don't you think?"

That got a good laugh from the gathered elders, but the red-head just scowled. "You can't win a battle unless you fight one," he said when the laughter died down.

"No, and depending on how fast Cortez recovers from our little joke, he should be in that battle late tomorrow or early the next day," Kris said.

Now she had everyone's attention.

"Where we gonna kill those bastards?" Red demanded.

Kris did not like the question. It presumed a lot. That they would be *able* to kill said bastards, and that they would *want* to kill the same.

Red seemed to have no doubt about either.

Kris could not say the same.

Kris commanded a lot of rifles. Say half again more than Cortez. Kris suspected that the colonel had some doubts about the white coats that made up so much of his ranks. No question Kris had doubts about the civilians that made up most of hers.

Like most civilians, Kris finished college "knowing" the military's whole idea of trained automatons was to turn their troops into zombies who did exactly what they were told.

It hadn't taken her long to unlearn that.

Soldiers and Marines had to be able to do their jobs without thought for one simple reason. They had to load and aim and fire without thought when their brains were too numb or shocked or horrified by what they saw. They had to keep doing it until by doing it, they'd brought themselves out of the hell that made thinking impossible and trained action their only hope.

These civilians had rifles. They had their homes to defend. They had little or no training. They'd probably be good for their first shot. Maybe their second. Possibly a third.

But sooner or later, they'd turn. They'd want to run. In the noise and blood and screams, they'd forget why they came, forget everything but their desire to be somewhere else.

Maybe not all. Maybe a few would find what it took. How many? Victory would go to whichever side held on for a second longer than the other.

Kris eyed the redhead, so sure he knew what tomorrow would bring. So ignorant of it. And she took a deep breath.

"We'll fight Cortez among the rice paddies and hills of the Tzu farm," she said.

"So that's where we massacre them," Red said.

Kris chose not to hear that comment. "I'll have the Marines take down most of the light infantry with sleepy darts. The gopher rifles the local volunteers carry should knock the heavy infantry silly."

"But our guns won't get past their armor." Red jumped in right where Kris expected. She ignored him for a moment to study the reaction around the barn. Red had plenty of folks who agreed with him. About half. The other half looked more puzzled than on Kris's side.

"From painful personal experience," Kris said with a reinforcing wince, "I can tell you that bullets, even those that don't get through armor, can leave you black-and-blue underneath and quite disoriented. That is what I want. The light infantry snoring for a couple of hours and the heavy infantry very much aware that they've been hit, hit hard, and having a tough time finding something to shoot at.

"Five minutes of that, and Colonel Cortez should be ready to listen to an offer for his surrender."

"But I want them dead. All of them!" Red shouted.

"Yes."

"We don't want them SOBs coming back here."

"Panda's ours. Why not kill 'em for trying to steal it?"

Kris said nothing for a long minute while the war party blew itself out. She found Bobby Joe Fronour and Gramma Polska in the crowd. They both looked puzzled, but not ready to join Red in his shout for blood. Finally, old Bobby Joe stood up, and the room fell quickly into silence.

"When we were fighting the Iteeche, there weren't a lot of prisoner taking. Not by us. Not by them. So I'm kind of curious about this idea you got, Miss Longknife. It seemed like your old man was only happy with a dead Iteeche."

Kris nodded. "Maybe in that war there wasn't much room for anything but a lot of dead bodies. God knows, we all came close to being nothing but dead." Even some of the hotheads nodded along with Kris on that.

Red just scowled.

"Since long before we left old Earth, smart generals knew the easiest way to get an enemy off your land was to threaten their line of retreat. Threaten to make it impossible for them to go home. So a really smart general, when he fought, was careful to leave a hole somewhere that the enemy could run away through. Frequently it was all it took to get them running."

"So that's it." Red hardly looked able to get his words out past his rage. "They've ripped up our lands, wrecked our property. Killed God only knows how many of us. You're just going to let them walk away?"

Kris curtly shook her head. "Of course not. My intention is to have Colonel Cortez surrender to us. To have his men lay down their arms and become our prisoners. That is what the laws of war require of me."

"Of you?" This was Bobby Joe's question.

"I am a serving officer of the Wardhaven Navy. Despite being rented mercenaries, these men are in the uniform of their respective planets. To date, in this situation, they have followed the laws of war. As such, they deserve the honors of war and prisoner of war status from me. I would think you would want to offer them the same."

"I want them dead," Red said.

"How high a price are you willing to pay for that butcher bill?" Kris asked softly.

"We kill 'em. That's the end of them," Red snorted.

"Are you sure?" Kris asked.

"What do you mean? Dead is dead." But Red wasn't sounding so sure anymore.

"What do you know that we don't?" Bobby Joe asked.

"Actually, it's what we both don't know," Kris replied. "What do you know about the latest alliances among the city-states of New Jerusalem?"

"I didn't even know they had city-states," said Gramma Polska. "What kind of alliances do they have?"

"Ever-shifting ones," Kris put in quickly. "I'm not sure Lieutenant Pasley is all that up to date on who's switched to whom and who's trying to gain power or afraid of losing it. That alone would be a full-time job."

Penny rolled her eyes to heaven. Around the barn a lot more people frowned at each other. Faced with the idea that even a Longknife might not know everything, it began to dawn on them that they might not know it all either.

And what they didn't know just might hurt them.

"But here's the deal, folks. Let's say that a story comes back to Jerusalem, that a bunch of Godless barbarian hicks on this out-of-the-way planet just slaughtered most of a battalion of the Lord's Ever Victorious Host," Kris started.

To be interrupted by, "We're God-fearing Christians, here."

"Ah," Kris said, raising a finger to make the point. "But are you the right kind of believer? Or is your kind of Christian just as much an infidel as the prays-five-times-a-day Turk?" Murmurs slipped around the barn as the situation on Jerusalem was hashed over, and everyone came to terms with a whole different take on reality.

"What do you think might happen to us if we used the blood and bones of these invaders to manure our crops?" Bobby Joe asked.

"Maybe nothing," Kris said. "Only a fool tells you she knows exactly what anyone is going to do. And a planet with a billion people?" Kris threw up her arms. "After all, look what someone told Cortez about how easy it would be to take down Panda. 'They're *only* farmers.'"

The barn got real quiet.

Kris spoke her next words softly. Folks leaned forward to better hear her. "If you look at old Earth's bloodiest periods, there are several patterns that repeat. One is missionaries come. Missionaries get killed. Army comes. Houses and crops get burned. Natives get killed. And the flag comes last. Suddenly a whole lot of local folks find themselves with an empress or kaiser or president they never voted for.

"Oh, and your women. I got some of them toting guns along with the rest of your troops. That's a no-no. Can't work outside the home, and the same no-no with their clothes. A dress. A long dress, covering them from neck to toe. Oh, and a scarf or something on the head. Always."

The barn didn't stay quiet after that. Kris turned back to her team to let the farmers talk it out among themselves.

"How much of that did you make up?" Jack asked from behind a hand over his mouth.

"None, I think," Kris said. "In high school I did a paper on New Jerusalem." Kris shivered. "I couldn't believe anyone would choose to live like that. I felt like I had to write it out to try to understand it."

"You understand it?" Gunny asked.

"Nope," Kris said.

The barn slowly settled down to a dull roar. It stayed that way until Bobby Joe Fronour stood. He got silence.

"Folks, forty years ago, I started this here planet. I didn't much like folks telling me what to do, and I've lived to see it fill up with folks like me. I set it up figuring on certain things," he said, looking around at the people gathered in the barn, and clearly proud of what he saw.

"I figured if anything I couldn't handle came along, we to-gether could handle it. Well, it looks like something bigger than that has come our way, and I want you to know that I'm mighty glad to have the help of this young Longknife whelp."

Kris had been called many things. This was a first time for *whelp*. Kris wasn't all that sure it was meant to be endearing. Quite a few listeners laughed.

Bobby Joe turned to Kris. "Mind you, I'm none too sure you'll mosey on your way when you're done here or that you and I will see eye to eye about when that golden moment may be."

Kris did her best at a dramatic sigh. "So I'll be adding an-other to the list of planets where I've been thanked but told not to come back."

"Yes," he said, deadly serious. "I imagine that's a hard way to live. But you're the one doing it, not me."

For a moment, Kris tasted the loneliness of what her life would be like for someone so rooted to the fields and dirt.

For a moment, Kris felt the emptiness of her life.

She shook her head, willed away the emotions. People de-pended on her. That was enough.

"Okay, young Longknife, tell us what you would have us do." And with those words, the old farmer sat back down.

The barn held its collective breath.

Kris took a moment to let all that she'd heard and felt soak through her . . . and out of her. Done, she squared her shoul-ders, and said, "I want all of you to accept the surrender of any-one willing to throw down his rifle and put his hands up. I want you to respect any white flag, handkerchief, call of camaradine, quarter, or 'for God's sake, I quit.'"

Red was back on his feet. "And what do we do with 'em. Wrap them up with a pretty bow?"

"No." Kris snapped. "Hell no," she added for emphasis, 'cause this crowd needed all the emphasis she could muster.

"Then what *do* we do?" Bobby Joe asked, climbing to his feet.

Red already had his mouth open to cross more words with Kris. Only old man Fronour could have gotten him to shut his yap, but he shut it and sat back down.

"They owe us, young lady. They owe us," Bobby Joe re-peated as he took his seat again.

Kris wanted to fire something back. Quick. Effective. She found she didn't have any words even close to the tip of her tongue. Thoroughly unusual, that.

"Those guys present a real problem," came from behind Kris in Gunny's deep voice. "If I and my crew find ourselves in a bad place, even if we surrender, our ties to Wardhaven can't be broken. Anyone who accepts our surrender knows that and knows they have Wardhaven to deal with about us.

"But these folks, they still wear the uniform of someone, but they've clearly been rented out to someone else. Gives an old enlisted swine like myself a painful headache."

Kris turned back to face the old Marine. He gave her a twinkling wink. "Seems like something new that an officer might enjoy thinking through."

"Gee thanks, Gunny," she whispered. But he'd bought her time to think and defined some limits. Kris turned back to the farmers feeling almost confident that she did have a good idea.

"One of the things I keep hearing is that start-ups need labor. Lots of people to do the work. Panda any exception?"

"Nope," Bobby Joe said, to be echoed through the barn.

"Now, it seems to me that anyone that's been rented out to carry a gun doesn't owe a lot to those who did it to him."

"I wouldn't," Gunny growled. "Not after seeing a few of my buddies get wounded, killed."

"So I don't see any reason why you shouldn't feel free to offer these fine strapping men a job. Any of them that sign on with you, you can take. Any that want to go home, do."

"With their guns!" Red was back on his feet.

"With the clothes on his or her back," Kris interjected. She had it going her way. She didn't want to lose them now. "Their military equipment is yours. You can sell it if you want. If I was in your shoes, I'd use it to equip a National Guard."

The babble in the room sounded like it might be nearing an agreement.

"What about the officers? The apes that have been giving orders," Red shouted, as soon as the background roar let him. "We going to let them get off with just some hard work?"

Kris had hoped that this question might get overlooked in the interest of getting a few things settled. She could really get to hate Red.

"No," Kris said, already reading which way the room was blowing. Blast it, if she wanted to live by the polls like her father, she would have run for office. But there were reasons why her father did his best to follow the will of the people. They had elected him, and, as often as not, they were right.

Kris let her political instincts loose. "These officers have committed crimes against humanity, all humanity, by their raising arms against a peaceful people. As my prisoners, I would see that they face such charges and pay for them."

"If you can do it, why not us?" was Red's comeback.

"Because they planned their crimes inside the Rim. Inside the belly of civilization. People like them, who might be contemplating such crimes, need to see this, and think long and hard the next time the idea comes up. Justice systems inside the Rim failed to halt this crime. They need a wake-up call. That's not to say you don't have the right to try them yourselves. I'm just asking which better serves justice and the future."

"That sounds more like a political solution than a legal one," Red pointed out.

"Maybe 'cause it's part of a political problem," Bobby Joe pointed out before Kris said anything. Having half risen out of his chair to speak those words, Bobby Joe stood up.

"My boy told me that Earth done given up on its Society of Humanity. Earth and some of its cronies are going their way. The rest of us are going our own way. I hear your great-grandpa done come out of retirement to be a king or something."

"Or something is more like it," Kris said. "Lot of different folks going a lot of different ways. Turns out a lot of folks don't like being told what to do."

That actually got a chuckle out of the barn.

"But it gets kind of lonely out here on your own," Bobby Joe said. "I guess I'm finding out that if you work like hell to make a good place, well, you better be ready to protect it, or somebody's like to come along and steal it out from under you."

The proud old farmer looked around, saw a sad kind of agreement in the eyes of folks looking back at him. He nodded before going on. "What's this United Sentients doing, and what does it cost to join it?"

"They aren't charging a membership fee," Kris said, and immediately knew she'd missed the point.

"Everything has a price. We're learning our freedom has a

price, and we ain't been paying our dues. Now we'll pay full price tomorrow. What's your old fart asking?"

Kris took a second to scratch her ear. Think. Then she shrugged and gave her usual answer. "Representatives from a hundred and twenty planets, maybe thirty by now, are meeting at Pitts Hope. I don't know what they'll decide. If you're interested, I suggest you get some reps there to listen up, say a few words. Decide for yourself what you'll give up and hold on to."

"That may be what we have to do," Bobby Joe said.

It was Gunny who stepped forward. "Ladies, gentlemen, who's going to win tomorrow and who's going to be surrendering isn't something we can figure out tonight. But if we don't get some sleep, it sure ain't gonna help us."

"Spoken like a true topkick," Bobby Joe said, and followed Gunny in heading for someplace to bed down for the night.

"You find your roll, too, if I may say, Your Highness," Gunny whispered as his mouth passed close to her ear. "Tomorrow will come soon enough."

Kris must have been getting too experienced with times like these. She actually did sleep.

32

Cortez waited until the ever-seeing eye in the sky had passed below his horizon before he formed his troops. He'd woken them before the ship came over but left them in their bedrolls, showing the ship warm bodies just where they belonged.

As the troops made their way out of camp, the dozen stay-behinds began feeding wood into the campfires. They and the busted-ankle detail, along with the hostages, would keep the fires burning. Maybe that Longknife girl wouldn't get any warning that Cortez's little army was on the move until it was too late.

It would be nice to have luck break his way for a change.

But luck and hope couldn't pass for a strategy.

Cortez assigned Major Zhukov command of the reinforced company of Guard Fusiliers from Torun. They'd take the wet road and come out of the swamps at the rear of the ditches. Their sudden appearance would be a major surprise for those hayseeds.

The psalm singers would take a more direct route, but they'd have to keep to cover and spread out. No matter how much Cortez pushed them, he doubted he could have them ready to assault the ditches before the next orbit. No, he'd have to spread out, stay cool in the morning dark, and do his best to be out of sight.

Nobody had ever told Colonel Cortez that soldiering was easy. He doubted he'd have taken the job if they had.

No, he had a tough leadership challenge and, to tell the truth, he was enjoying it. That Longknife brat had been calling the shots for too long. Now he'd name a few tunes and see how she liked dancing to his music.

Sergeant Bruce found the island he'd picked out for his observation post. It was little more than a tree and a couple of bushes holding on to a scrap of dirt to keep their trunks above water. But it would do.

The water flowed fast and deep around his little island OP, giving him a good place to retreat to if he needed to hide out awhile. And it gave him a bit of a view if he was reduced to using the old Mark I eyeball for intelligence gathering.

For the moment, what with the range and endurance limit on Nelly's nanos, he chose to use the eyeball. Unless he saw something exciting, he'd keep the nanos huddled around his computer, conserving energy.

It would be nice if Nelly talked Kris into getting the Marines some decent personal computers. Not that the one on his wrist didn't do all the Corps expected. But what the Corps expected and one princess demanded were not even close.

But wish in one hand and spit in the other, and see which you get the most out of. Bruce did not ration himself a laugh at his own joke. He was busy studying what lay before him in the light of a quarter moon. Panda's only moon was a bit bigger than Wardhaven's, so the light was fine. And he could smell and hear.

What he heard were small animals making nice if not familiar noises. They had fallen silent at his arrival; now they were back to full volume. The smell was something all its own, no hint of man or his things. Bruce kind of liked that.

What he saw was marsh grass, mirror-flat water, unbroken by wind. No, something just flopped into the shallow water. There was some thrashing about before silence returned. Some small hunter had gotten breakfast.

Bruce smiled grimly. Some much larger hunters would be making a whole lot more noise real soon now.

Flat on his back, under a bush, ready to push his face mask down and himself silently into the water at the first sign of business, the Marine sergeant lay like some primal beast at the water's edge. A Marine was patient.

Matters would get lively soon enough. The Marine waited.

Kris roused her task force and had them mounted up and rolling as soon as Captain Thorpe dropped below the horizon. Outside, it was still night, but ahead of them was one last pair of farms that would hide them from Thorpe.

Ninety more minutes to keep up the game of "not here." After that, they'd be in the open, and the cat would be out of the bag.

Kris had to shake her head as she watched her task force form up along both sides of her in three loose rows. Farmers nodded at the wheels. Even with their lights on, trucks had a hard time keeping properly in their place.

Maybe not all the drivers were awake.

A freckled gal with a pair of pigtails almost sideswiped the rig next to her. The catcalls she collected were no worse, nor any better, than the ones got by a guy who bumped the rig next to him. Maybe all the shouting put an end to sleepy driving. The task force spread out, and the bumper-car competition ended.

A few minutes later, the *Wasp* raced into the sky above them and Kris mashed her comm. "What's it look like, Captain Drago?"

"Like someone's trying to play with our sensor suite. They got the fires jacked up at the camp. If I didn't know better, I'd say the cooks were planning on burning the coffee."

"Or burning your sensors."

"They'd have better luck with the coffee, my boys are on the job. Anyway, some of the bedrolls are occupied warm, others are cooling warm, and a whole lot of them are way below warm."

The captain paused before going on. "You know, if I didn't know that Your Highness's opposition were all lazy bums, I'd suspect that they'd broken camp and were out causing mischief on this fine morning."

"Those good boys would never do that," Kris said, letting sarcasm flood her answer. "Can you tell me where they are?"

There was a long pause at that question. "I'm not sure I can," Drago finally said. "We've got a bit of heat on the trail to the dugouts, but I'm not sure if I hadn't drawn a line between their camp and them that I'd notice it. They've figured out a good way to go to ground. Good way."

"Dig a hole, put a cool cover over it, and you'd be hard to see, too," Kris said.

"Ah, there you go using words no self-respecting sailor would ever use. Dig a hole. Hide in the dirt. No. No. Not our way. Not at all."

Kris suppressed a chuckle at the weird looks her starship captain was getting from dirt farmers. "Well, how about this. Things are going to get decisive in the not-too-distant future. I want you to creep up on Thorpe's orbit. Get in a position so in a minute or two you could come over his horizon."

"I pop into his gun sights all suddenlike and he might take a shot at me. Not with any malice, you know. Just kind of accidental-like."

"I didn't think you'd want us down here to have all the fun," Kris chided him.

"What gave you that idea? Oh, no, you go right on and have it all," Drago offered.

"I've already computed a course," Navigator Sulwan Kann put in over the comm. "Do you want us coming up his tail or dropping back from ahead of him?"

"Let's allow for the tail chase," Kris said.

"Yes," Captain Drago said, now deadly serious. "Yes. Let's position us for a long tail chase."

"Let me know if you pick up anything at all while you're overhead."

"We will. Bye for now."

And Kris found herself once more alone in the dark night driving into a day that had not yet begun to dawn. But before the sun set, all the questions before her now would be answered.

Colonel Cortez spat out the dirt he'd nearly eaten and tossed aside the thermal blanket as soon as the sensor tech called "Sky Clear."

"Everyone up. Get moving. You're wasting daylight," he shouted. Someone pointed out . . . in a whisper . . . that it was pitch-dark. Like a smart colonel, he ignored the wag.

"Don't wad up that thermal blanket," Cortez shouted at a psalm-singing private who had begun to do just that. Colonel Cortez was well aware that colonels do not correct privates. However, three sergeants in their white beanies were standing around doing nothing as at least one private destroyed his ability to hide from orbital spotting.

"Sergeants," Captain Sawyer said, climbing out of a hole behind the colonel. "See that the men secure their property properly. This may not be the last hole we need to skulk in."

"Yes, sir," the sergeants answered, and began moving among their troops, turning wadded balls into squared-away packages.

"I'm sorry, Colonel," Sawyer said. "The men had been

briefed on the thermal blankets but not since we landed."
Which was a polite way of reminding the colonel that sometime in his copious spare time, he should have issued just such
a reminder.

He hadn't. Nothing could be done about that.

"Captain, your Third Company is the center. I want you to
hit those ditches fast and hard. First and Second Companies will
come in from your flanks," Cortez said, glancing around. If they
were not exactly milling about, they certainly weren't moving
toward the enemy. "What do you say Third challenges First and
Second to a race to the ditches?"

The captain grinned. "Yes, sir. Sergeants, form the men.
Form on me." And with only the briefest of pauses: "Follow
me," Captain Sawyer said, pulling out his compass and taking a
reading. He altered course slightly to the right.

Colonel Cortez trotted off to the right and found the young
captain commanding First Company. "Third Company says
they intend to beat you to the ditches."

The Ever Victorious officer glanced up from where he and a
sergeant were warming tea, from the smell of it. "In Joshua's
dreams," he said. The semiwarmed water went into the grass,
and the sergeant dashed off, shouting to his subordinates. In a
moment they were formed and trotting off after Third.

Except for two troopers. One had stepped into a hole. The
second stayed behind to render aid. Cortez paid little attention
to them. He was already trotting for Second Company.

Someone had his eyes open. The youngest captain had mus-
tered his troops and was already jogging after the other two.

Colonel Cortez swung himself around and followed in the
tracks of Third Company. It was good to get this bunch moving
toward contact. It would be very bad if they just kept running
until they ran right into the fool farmers. Captain Sawyer probably had the smarts to halt his men at the last tree line on their
side of the ditches. Probably.

Cortez would be a lot happier if he was there to make sure.

Sergeant Bruce waited an extra ten minutes after the
Wasp was out of the sky before releasing Nelly's nanos. The
wind was coming from behind him and toward the dugouts. It
should add extra range to the computer's handiwork.

Nelly had also programmed the nanos to look for something to rest on. Some of the ones intended to cover the swamp and its approaches settled onto saw grass, reeds, and swamp scum. They reported their presence to the display on the sergeant's eyepiece, then went silent. It showed good coverage.

A dozen or more nanos rode the wind, reaching out for the distant tree line. If he could get them caught near the top of a few broom trees, he'd have a good view of all the approaches.

For a good part of an hour, the Marine watched nothing happen. Then his wrist unit reminded him that the hostile spaceship would be overhead soon. Bruce closed his visor and pushed himself back into the water. He found a log, pinned a whip antenna on it, and slipped himself under it.

Something was already there, under the log. Something sharp and strong worried the Marine's boot for a second. Bruce pulled his foot out and smashed out with it. That settled the argument. Unless it returned with its big brother or five, Bruce figured he had the log for the duration.

"Hernando, things are going well." Thorpe was glad to see.

"We should have them whipped before you get back next orbit," the ground pounder said.

"Colonel, you sound out of breath."

"I am running. My command is running, William."

"Just so long as it's toward the enemy," Mr. Whitebred said, smiling. Thorpe wondered if the idiot had any idea of the insult he'd just given to the ground half of the operation.

Hopefully, Colonel Cortez hadn't heard him.

If he had, the colonel showed no interest in it. "Have you got anything better on those other hostile groups?" he asked.

"Nothing. One on the other side of the river. One or two north of you. I'm not sure if they haven't all gathered at that area you call the ditches. Hard to tell from orbit to orbit and at night. But there's no activity south of you. Wipe out these terrorists, and the rest will follow like sheep."

"I'm glad you think so," Cortez said.

The colonel's age was beginning to show. He did sound winded.

"Since I have nothing more to report, I'll click off and be

waiting for your count of killed and captured. By the way, if you can capture that Longknife girl, I hear some people are willing to pay a pretty penny for her. More alive than dead, but whatever," he said diffidently.

"We will count what we have to count," Cortez said, and the commlink went dead.

Kris took a drink from the bucket of freshwater hanging in front of the barn door. The sensor tech looked up from his gear.

"Hostile is out of our sky, ma'am."

"Mount the troops, Gunny."

Others beside Gunny moved to obey. A gray-haired woman in a long wool dress of many colors walked quickly among the farmhands, a rifle held comfortably in the crook of her elbow. "We're wasting daylight," she said in a firm voice.

"I don't see no daylight," some wag, a guy, shot back.

"Jacob, don't be more stupid than you usually are," put an end to that.

Drivers were more awake this time. The rigs rolled out of the barn, garage, and other outbuildings and quickly re-formed in the three lines that had become the norm. Inside of ten minutes, the wing from the other ranch formed on Kris's right.

The east was starting to show color. The assault on the dugouts wouldn't be long now. If Kris was in charge of that attack, she'd try to get at least part of the way across the killing ground before good light turned matters deadly.

That was the right way to do it . . . and despite the miserable choices she'd given Cortez so far, he done as well as he could with them.

33

Colonel Cortez raised his hand and signaled a halt.

Officers and noncoms of the Third Company passed the halt signal along. Through the trees, Cortez watched the other two companies go to ground. He'd been half-afraid that some idiot would keep running, wanting to be first at the ditches. At least no one in his rented command was that stupid.

The colonel surveyed his target through night gear. The moon had set, taking most of the light with it. That left him studying the ditches only by starlight. But the farmers were not likely to have any night-vision gear. They'd be hurting.

Unless that Longknife girl had Marines on his front.

Cortez shook off the thought and studied his target. No one stood guard, paced rounds, did anything for security. There were not pickets or outposts anywhere in the thousand meters of flat ground between this tree line and the ditches. Unbelievable. If this was the Longknife girl's idea of security, how had she lived so long?

In the ditches there were one, maybe two heads. From the looks, they were totally devoted to snoring. The wind blew from the trenches, bringing with it a whiff of open latrines. Had they fouled their fighting positions? Cortez shook his head.

Then caught himself. Thorpe had underestimated that girl, and look where he was. Cortez would not make the same mistake.

He checked his watch, and the color of the sky just starting to brighten behind the ditches. His troops would have the shadows with them for another five minutes or so.

Best to make good use of the time.

The colonel pulled out his commlink, switched it on, and immediately switched it off.

Major Zhukov answered with two clicks. The proud Guard Fusiliers were ready.

"Captain Sawyer, advance your company at a low crawl, by platoons," Colonel Cortez whispered. "Signal to First and Second Companies to do the same. Keep low and quiet."

Cortez gave Major Zhukov a single click on his commlink. Around him, a long thin line, first platoon, First Company, advanced at a bent walk for twenty meters, then went to ground in the field. No one had cut this field, and the crop came to a standing man's waist. At a low walk, there was little to see.

Captain Sawyer signaled the second platoon to advance with him and led them twenty meters past the first platoon. When the long line of third platoon started its bound, Colonel Cortez went with them . . . and led them forty meters past second platoon.

So it went, about every minute, the last platoon back would rise to a low walk and bound up to and past the forward-most platoon. When Cortez wasn't moving forward with his platoon, he studied the trenches.

No movement. No action. No nothing.

They could as well be empty as far as he could see.

They were at about midfield, and Cortez was beginning to think he'd be able to get everyone up to the three hundred-meter mark before a shot was fired when things began to happen.

Somewhere in the ditches, there was an explosion. Had one of the Guard Fusiliers tossed a grenade?

For a second there was dead silence as even those around Cortez held their breath. Then some kind of a bomb with a sputtering fuse arched up out of the trenches toward the psalm singers, to explode among them.

Now there was rapid fire coming from the ditches. Cortez couldn't make out the weapon from its sound, but there was lots of it. Above him, shots whizzed through the air. Most of them high, but one man screamed as he was hit.

"Medic! Medic!" echoed up and down the line.

To Cortez's left and right, troopers returned fire enthusiastically, if with no evidence of something to shoot at. The colonel studied the ditches for targets, but bright flashes of light caused back flares on his night gear.

It was time for third platoon to bound forward. Its platoon leader and sergeant were not shouting anything. That platoon wasn't going anywhere.

Cortez stood. "Third platoon, follow me." Running low, he advanced, waving his arm to encourage others to follow. Most did. The trooper next to Cortez went down with a bullet through his jaw. The colonel made sure he ran the full forty yards before going to ground.

Once third was in firing positions and ready to give good cover fire, Cortez turned his attention to first platoon.

They weren't moving from their place in the rear.

Cortez stood up. "First platoon. Advance. Come on, there's only a bunch of farmers up here. They can't shoot."

Troops were up. Their lieutenant was leading them, calling for others to follow him. He got about four paces forward when he clutched at his leg and went down. But the sergeant was up, and he kept them moving under the colonel's watchful eye.

As they passed the lead platoon, the colonel fell in line with them, hustling them forward and kicking the first ones who tried to go to ground before covering the full forty meters.

Colonel Cortez turned as soon as first went to ground, ready to do whatever it took to get second platoon moving, but Captain Sawyer was already up, already moving that platoon out under the watchful eye of its lieutenant and sergeant.

Cortez flipped him a thumbs-up and stooped to take a knee and survey his situation.

There were still flashes of light sparking up and down the ditches, though the first two lines seemed quiet. As he watched, a couple of those bombs lofted up and out, to explode among the psalm singers or the Guard. As far as Cortez could tell, the bomb didn't seem to produce any casualties, but rounds were whizzing over his head. Lots of high shots.

Not all; one that sounded like a military dart whizzed past his ear. That left him wondering exactly where Zhukov's Guard company was. What Cortez would give for a standard battle board, but that required knowing where you were, and a full GPS was way beyond the budget of this lash-up.

Once more, he advanced his companies by lines of platoons. The two wing companies weren't under his immediate supervision, and they weren't advancing as far with each bound. Either he'd have to go over and personally supervise their doing an extra set of bounds, or they'd have a lot more distance to run when he ordered the full attack.

Colonel Cortez scowled and decided he'd funnel them into

the trenches as reserves to support Second Company. Or if the farmers broke and tried to run, maybe the two lagging companies would be in a better position to pursue.

Around the colonel, troops fired and advanced, did their duty as they were trained. He looked at it, found it was good . . . and smiled.

And as he smiled, he realized, it was time.

The lead platoon was only two hundred meters from the first trench. The trailing platoon was about to start its bound. The middle platoon was Captain Sawyer. This would work out fine.

Cortez mashed his commlink. "Zhukov, I'm about to order a general assault. You get ready to receive those that break and run for the swamp. On a five count, check your fire unless you have a clear target."

"You drive 'em to us. We'll bag 'em, sir."

Now Colonel Cortez stood and signaled to third platoon. "Up and at 'em." A bullet whizzed by his ear, but no soldiers dropped as they obeyed his orders.

"Second platoon, prepare to advance as first platoon comes in line with you. Prepare to advance," he shouted, as the trailing platoon came even with the middle one's firing line.

"Advance," he shouted.

"Come on. You heard the man," Captain Sawyer shouted, "Last man to the trenches gets to clean up this mess."

With a shout, second platoon was on its feet and moving at a trot forward.

"Third platoon," Cortez shouted, running ahead of first and second, "prepare to advance,"

"Don't get up yet," a sergeant shouted. "You don't want to get so far out front we shoot you in the back."

Enthusiasm was quickly curbed.

But in a moment, the three platoons were even, and all were on their feet. Some paused to fire. Others shot from the hip.

Here and there, a trooper went down. Most of them were on the far right and left. If they had bullets in their backs from the tardy First and Second Companies, Cortez was going to dock some officers' pay.

But the Second Company was now shouting as it ran for the gun pits. Something in the pits blew up, almost blinding Cortez. The noise was deafening, even though the Guard was now holding its fire. Men fired, shouted, ran.

And Cortez was leading them.

He reached the first trench. As he did, he scanned right and left in the dim light of the dawning day.

And saw nothing.

He fired at the next trench and raced for it.

This one, he jumped into. There were sandbag coverings to his right and left. He fired at one, heard a scream, and whirled to find something monstrously large and dark charging him. He couldn't make out what it was in the shadowed light of the trench; he just fired at it.

His target screamed in rage . . . and redoubled its speed. Cortez pulled the trigger down hard and held it. His pistol went to full automatic.

He hit his target; he didn't miss. But the huge shadow kept right on coming at him.

Then, with a roar, it collapsed at his feet, white tusks gleaming in the dark.

"What in the devil's name is that?" a psalm singer asked.

"That is the biggest porker I ever did see," came from the trooper behind him, "And my daddy raised some prizewinning hams, he did, I tell you."

"Look out, Colonel!"

Came too late to keep the colonel from being slammed in the butt and knocked forward onto the hog. He went down, only too aware those tusks were millimeters from his unarmored groin. He dodged the dead pig's revenge and rolled into the mud beside it.

His hand with the automatic being the hand supporting him, it got a mud bath.

Rolling onto his smarting butt, Cortez faced something with two twisting and sharp horns, long whiskers . . . and bad breath.

That looked eager to butt those horns up his nose.

Cortez pulled his mud-caked automatic out and put two rounds between the eyes of the thing.

Its head exploded with a most satisfactory "thack."

And Cortez noticed, as he wiped off the horned thing's gore, that matters had quieted down.

The battlefield wasn't silent. No, not by a long shot.

Cortez started to struggle to his feet . . . and was grateful to one of the white-shirted ones for offering him a hand . . . even if it did get his whites all muddy.

Out of the ditch, the colonel took a second to survey the [s]uation. There was no more fire. No explosions.

A dense cloud of acrid smoke hung over the battlefiel[d] was heavy with sulfur, not the usual smell of a well-used range, more like after the fireworks on Landing Day.

A glance in the ditch showed him, next to the body of [the] white thing he'd shot, a long string of firecrackers. Cortez [saw] the troopers beside him and realized they were probably g[oing] through the same assessment he was doing.

No dead enemy. No fleeing enemy.

He turned to the farm kid who'd identified the porker. "W[hat] kind of animal is that?"

"It looks like a goat, sir. I don't know what kind. Da[d] didn't raise none. Said they were the devil's own critter."

"I would certainly agree," Cortez said. "Captain Sawyer[.]"

"Sir," the man said, and this time saluted.

Cortez returned the salute. These troops needed to be stea[died] by routines, by rendered honor. They needed to be distracte[d] and fast . . . from their brilliant assault on a barnyard. It [was] damn sure that no enemy was anywhere around.

Cortez knew he'd been had. Could he prevent these troo[ps] from knowing it, too? What a command challenge. To kee[p his] troops from feeling like he did.

"Our fleeing terrorists have been kind enough to leave [be]hind some fine livestock," Cortez said. "Let's see what we [can] do about having a good barbecue."

Captain Sawyer was quick on the uptake; he promptly be[gan] issuing orders. "Sergeant, bring up the wagons. You there," [he] said, pointing at a corporal and his squad. "We'll need a do[zen] or more good fire pits. Start digging them."

First and Second Companies arrived. First was poste[d as] guards and ordered to set up outposts. Second drew the ass[ign]ment of getting wood or anything else that would burn.

While Captain Sawyer saw to the details of a barbecue, [Col]onel Cortez brought Major Zhukov up to date. "So there w[ere] no soldiers here, only dinner on the hoof, huh?"

"No," Cortez snapped. "Not even some brilliant Longk[nife] could time the fuses on those rockets and noisemakers f[rom] hours ago. There is someone out there observing us. I want [you] to find him. Track him down. I want his guts for kite string."

"Yes, my colonel," Zhukov said, and was gone.

Colonel Cortez turned back to the preparation for the morning feast, careful to keep a smile on his lips. Careful to make it look like everything was going just as he planned.

Several of the New Jerusalem troopers were experienced in slaughtering and cooking food on the hoof. They butchered the available lunch, hacking it into chunks that could be cooked quickly. What they did with familiar panache left many of their city-bred comrades looking green.

Most of the hostages dove right in, sharing duties with the knowing troops. In a little over an hour, the goats were sufficiently cooked to eat. The hogs took a bit longer.

Zhukov led a small squad of very wet Guards in about the time the pork was declared done. He dropped a length of wire in front of his colonel.

"He hid under a log, used that for an antenna, and was long gone by the time we stumbled on that out-of-place strand."

Colonel Cortez scowled, tossed a goat leg he'd stripped of all its edible flesh into the nearest fire, and stood.

In a low voice, so only the major and the veterans of his wild-goose chase could hear, he said. "That makes twice that Longknife girl has played me as a joker." He glanced around as his command. "Twice that girl has crossed swords with me and settled for nothing but a touch."

Cortez shook his head. "She will not make a fool out of me a third time. You scouts, get some chow. Zhukov, this hog is amazingly delicious, considering there was no time for us to smoke it. Get something in your stomach. It's been a lousy morning. At noon we march.

"I assure you, the afternoon will be more to our liking."

34

Lieutenant Kris Longknife stood at the top of the hill
and surveyed the work going on below. She, Jack, Gunny, and
Peter Tzu had come up here to get a better feel for the terrain.
For Kris, this was a first look.

For Peter Tzu, it was unnecessary. He'd built everything
within sight by his own sweat, or that of his family.

The head of the Tzu clan fidgeted. His pride in ownership
was now replaced by shades of fear. "This battle of yours. It's
not going to destroy *everything*, is it?"

Gunny looked at the farmer with honest sadness. Jack
glanced away. It was left to Kris to admit. "I don't know. No
battle plan survives contact with the enemy. Only a fool will tell
you in the morning how a battle will go that afternoon."

The farmer shrugged. "Well, at least you're honest."

Kris took a long moment to survey what her people were up
to. The hill where she stood rose gently a hundred meters or so
from the narrow flats that cut a small ribbon between the swamp
and the beginning of the rolling hills behind Kris. The road sliced
through the middle of that bit of flatland, separating the Tzu farm
buildings from their rice paddies.

Most locals were quite happy to grow the hybridized
grass/grain crop planted once and harvested as often as they
came in season. Acres of it covered the hills behind Kris. However, Mr. Tzu, a short man whose face still reflected that his family hailed from old Earth's Asian continent, liked rice.

He'd claimed a holding close to the swamp and laid out
some rice paddies. And found a market for a break from the
usual. As his clan grew, the paddies expanded along the road
and into the swamp. Today, the dikes between the paddies offered Kris some interesting options. Most everyone loved the

gophers and the their valuable droppings; Tzu and his clan hated the little rats.

The four-legged beggars loved rice.

A pack of them could eat a rice paddy empty, root and stem, in a day. To keep them under control, the Tzu clan had been forced to dig caves through the centers of their paddy dikes.

The gophers could come tunneling along and burrow right into the caves. There, they'd meet up with the other Tzu import. Mongooses from old Earth prowled both above- and below-ground.

The gophers could be mean when cornered. The mongooses seemed to love cornering them. The gophers usually lost.

But for Kris, it meant that she had a whole lot of rice-paddy dikes within easy rifle range of the road just begging to be pierced with loopholes.

Which work parties were now doing with sledgehammers and rods. Others were expanding the cool room under the hill Kris stood on. In an hour, two at the most, they expected to have firing positions popping out of this hill.

Anyone who marched up that road would walk right into a cross fire. And the flats left them with little or no cover.

It would be murder.

"If they walk into it," Jack said, reading Kris's mind.

"You think he's had enough of walking into things?"

"You done a good job of teaching him that lesson, Your Highness," Gunny said.

Kris snorted. "I've got more trigger-pullers than this Colonel Cortez, but, except for the Marines, I can't trust any of them to maneuver under fire. If I deploy them in the paddy dikes, in the hill, they can just sit there, firing when I tell them to."

"I don't remember anyone telling you battles were supposed to be easy on anyone," Jack said.

"If you put our people in the paddy caves," Peter Tzu observed slowly, "they won't be able to get away if things go wrong. What are those things . . . hand grenades . . . ? If they throw a few of them in the caves . . ." He ran out of words.

Kris had to put an end to that thought. "The paddies are at angles to each other." She put her hands together to form a ninety-degree angle. "The rifles on the right keep the enemy off of the dike to the left, and left protects the right. See."

"I guess so," the farmer said dubiously.

"The Marines will be a mobile reserve," Kris said. "Th
move to meet what we're not expecting."

"And just what are you expecting?" Tzu asked.

"That they are not going to march up that road in a nice
line, ready to be shot up." Kris glanced at Jack and Gunny.
were nodding agreement. "No, he's not going to do any
the easy way anymore. He's going to be looking for us u
every rock and crack. We'll need to cover our tracks real g

As if to confirm Kris's guess, Captain Drago came o
The *Wasp* was overhead early, working its way up behind Th

"It looks like Cortez has finished his morning tea party
reported. "They are breaking camp at the dugouts and ge
back on the road."

"What does their travel array look like?" Kris asked.

"Similar to yesterday's. He's got his light infantry out c
ing his flank and forming a vanguard. His wagons and heav
fantry make up his main body. Oh, and now they have so
the light infantry riding herd on some of the animals. They d
eat all of them."

"It would be hard to eat all we left there," Jack said. "
does their invalid detail look like? Can you see how many o
main body are hobbling, or riding in the carts?"

"Wait one" was followed in less than a minute with
fifty-seven to sixty-one of them are wounded. That's a
double what he had last night. Looks like he caught modera
sualties taking those dugouts." Drago laughed. Gunny and
joined in.

Kris grimaced at the lay of the land beneath her. "Our
bush has a cross fire to it."

"Yes, Your Highness," Gunny agreed, "but our folks wi
under cover, not be out in the open when the shooting start

Peter Tzu just looked more worried by the minute.

"Captain Drago, could you send us a picture of Cor
troop layout." He did.

"Nelly, could you overlay his troop array on the groun
fore us."

In a moment, a heliograph appeared in front of them, sho
troops in white smocks scattered over the hill in front of
and the rice paddies. Coming up behind them was a main col
of armored infantry and wagons. Trailing them were several

guards wielding long poles as they tried to keep farm stock together. Still, they had rifles slung over their shoulders.

"Do you think they'll stay as spread out? I can't see someone choosing to wade through a rice paddy when he can walk along the dikes."

"But how do people *in* the dikes shoot at people *on* the dikes," the farmer asked.

Kris again formed her hands into a right angle. Tzu nodded but still didn't seem convinced.

"We'll need to put rifles in the second, third, and fourth lines of dikes," Jack said. Gunny nodded.

"But those hand grenades," Tzu repeated.

"If we stack bales of hay or grain at the ends of the tunnels . . ." Gunny said.

"They'll catch fire," Tzu said.

"But if they absorb the explosion and fragments . . ." Kris said.

"It should cut down on the casualties," Jack said.

Kris also wanted to examine options for deploying her Marines, but having a civilian in her war council was not going as well as she had hoped. They started down the hill to do what needed doing. She'd talk about the Marines later.

How many battles had she gotten herself into since she joined the Navy?

Too many, a small voice said.

And none went anything like the battles she read about in the history books. Would some professor, from the safety of his dusty ivory tower, match this battle up against historical precedent and make its conclusion look easy and foregone?

Of course, he'd know what Kris and her troops had done. And what had worked. And what hadn't work.

Matters weren't that easy under a hot sun with dust rising from digging shovels. Hindsight was easy. Foresight wasn't.

And the two of them were separated by an agony of distance.

CORTEZ had come to hate these little talks with the starship captain who rode so comfortably above it all. The colonel had cut Thorpe off in midresponse when he passed over after they

took the ditches. Thorpe hadn't even bothered to call down
next two passes as the troops ate the fruits of their victory.

But now Cortez was moving to what had to be contact. O
after he asked Thorpe for coverage of the next likely amb
point did the starship send down the photos and map.

And Cortez hadn't gotten around to mentioning that
Longknife ship was passing over sooner and sooner a
Thorpe's ship. Let him and his ship sensors find out for hims

Cortez examined the strange arrangement in the swar
ahead of him. Captain Sawyer had identified them as rice p
dies.

"People could lurk under the water and come up out of i
shoot at us as we go by," Major Zhukov observed.

"And shoot at us from this hill," Cortez added.

"It's obviously a good place for an ambush," the ma
agreed, "but will this Longknife girl do something that ob
ous? Will her Marine leaders let her?"

"All good questions," Cortez agreed. "That first ambush
an obvious one . . . and she got away with it. Our breakfast s
was obvious . . . and she passed on it. She's got to engage
sooner or later. Have you spotted any good ground up ahead

Zhukov shook his head. Sawyer shrugged.

"So," Cortez concluded, "she either gives up the last g
ambush site, or she doesn't. Either way, I intend to walk into
damn fox trap loaded for bear."

Cortez studied his map. "We'll take a break here, a g
mile shy of their ambush." He thought for a moment. "Saw
your company has handled the vanguard position fine, b
think I want to replace you there with another bunch."

"Who?"

Cortez knew his grin was pure evil, but he loved it at the r
ment. "The gift they gave us. What else?"

Kris licked her dry lips. It was hot . . . and she was nerv
She'd done all she could. Now she was just waiting for Cor
to show up.

The Marines had added several refinements to her plan.
sticky net was laid out, ready to take down a chunk of the v
A half dozen of the fastest Marine sharpshooters had been
tributed to leaven the local riflemen and -women. They w

stationed close to the road and loaded with sleepy darts. Their orders were to concentrate on the light infantry.

The rest of the Marines were held in three reserves. She'd use them to counter whatever surprises Cortez came up with. She expected some good ones from him. That still left her nervously licking her lips. Was she making a mistake—trying to fight this thing to a surrender? Only time would tell.

Kris's commlink clicked, then clicked again. Sergeant Bruce had come in shortly after noon from his job observing the fun and games at the dugouts. He'd gotten a laugh and a new tough assignment. He and a couple of locals were spread out in observation posts well in front of Kris's ambush.

Two clicks meant he wanted to talk. Kris clicked once.

"They're about a mile out. Looks like someone called a break. The officers are circulating among the men giving final reminders. My bet is we've been spotted."

No surprise. Kris would have no surprise in this fight.

Kris gave a single click, and the commlink went silent.

That was the problem with fighting smart people. What looked good to you looked good to them. When she'd met Thorpe, he hadn't been dumb, just driven. She had no reason to think he'd have a dumb ground pounder working with him.

Kris turned to the folks around her observation post/command center. "Pass the word. They're a mile out and have stopped for a coffee break. We can expect them anytime."

Civilians and Marines scuttled off to pass the word. The waiting was over.

35

Kris stood in her command post, its viewing port hidd
among the roots of a pecan tree and some berry bushes arou
it. Quite a few clumpings like these, or even orchards, had grov
up in and around the fields planted with the grass/grain hybr
They helped keep the water from running off too fast.

Now they hid Kris and, in other places, shooters.

Cortez marched up the road . . . and around Kris, peop
laughed. His vanguard was a herd of goats and pigs!

At a nod from Kris, the tech disabled the sticky net. No u
tying up a bunch of dumb animals. With luck, Kris would rea
tivate it and still collect some good troops.

Or not.

The pigs and goats stomped or pranced or did whatever th
natural inclination was, over a net that had not been design
with hoof traffic in mind. Pigs' hooves sank deep into the n
cut this, connected that. Before the herd was halfway over it, t
net was sticking to hooves and being pulled up and out.

One of the goats tried to eat it. That one complained loud
as the net stuck to its mouth, and then it made no noise at
when the net stuck its upper and lower jaw together.

Herders, white-shirted soldiers with long poles in the
hands and their rifles slung over their shoulders, kept pushi
the back of the herd into the net. At least they did for a whi
Soon they were too busy laughing to pay much attention to t
animals . . . or their own situation.

Several of the animals were now stuck together. Hogs did
like being stuck to hogs. They definitely didn't like being ti
up with goats. Matters started going badly for the goats.

The herders laughed harder. Two rolled on the ground.

Beside Kris, Peter Tzu shook his head. "What a waste of good animals. And to let them suffer." He glanced around. "They will know something is wrong."

"Why?" Kris asked.

"Any good farmhand would be out there taking care of those poor animals." So there went Kris's last hope for surprise.

Down on the flats, a sergeant trotted up to join the herders. The laughter stopped.

The sergeant pulled up the bullhorn hung around his neck and put it to use. "You in the farmhouse. Come out with your hands up, and there will be no problem."

The sergeant only waited a quick five count before he reslung the bullhorn and unslung his rifle. Beside him, the Bo Peeps tossed aside their crooks and unslung their rifles, too. At a signal from the sergeant, they advanced on the homestead.

Several took guard positions, covering all directions. Others dashed into the house. In a moment, the sergeant was standing at an open upstairs window. "No one here," he reported, using the bullhorn.

That was one way to communicate, Kris thought, and where he was only announcing what the opposition knew, it wasn't a bad idea. Beside her, the commtech said, "I'm getting action on comm frequencies. I can't crack the codes."

"Nelly?"

"I could in half an hour, maybe longer. Assuming they don't change codes every fifteen minutes."

Which wouldn't be such a problem in a battle not likely to last an hour. "Jam all frequencies," Kris ordered.

"Done, ma'am."

Which meant Kris would not talk to her people on the radio net, either. But being on the defensive on ground of her choosing, Kris had prepared for that.

"A call coming in from Gunny," the commtech said.

Kris accepted the landline phone. It had two buttons on it; one was flashing. "Yes, Gunny."

"We've got action in the draw behind your hill. Two squads of heavy infantry. Hold it. They're breaking up, one squad heading up my hill, the other up yours."

Gunny's was supposed to be a reserve position, the next hill over dug in along its crest. The shooting should have started

before anyone coming up that hill got too close to them. K
had firing positions on both sides of her hill. The second lig
on the phone lit. "Just a second, Gunny; Jack's calling."

A glance out Kris's observation post told her why. Light i
fantry was spreading out over the first two or three paddy dik
So far none had spotted a firing position.

Kris checked the main road. A platoon or two were movi
in bounds up the road, one platoon doing overwatch while t
other leapfrogged the line of prone troopers. Cortez had co
mitted less than half of his troops.

Damn, when Kris gave the orders to shoot, everyone she h
would start shooting. Cortez would see exactly what she had.

"Jack, wait one," Kris said, then turned to the commtec
"Can you stop the jamming just long enough for me to make
all-hands announcement."

"No, ma'am, they started jamming us as soon as I start
jamming them." Of course they would.

"Jack, when I give the order, take down the troops on t
dikes. Try to get the word to the farmers not to shoot. Let's
not to give away all we have."

"All I got is runners, and I hope you're about ready to gi
the word."

"Send them running. Let me talk to Gunny," she said, a
punched the buttons. "Gunny, give yourself a slow five cou
then take down the heavies on your front."

Kris didn't need to tell him he would not be using slee
darts. The force it took to punch through armor made even
sleepy dart deadly.

"Roger, ma'am. Starting one—"

Kris punched back to Jack. "Prepare to fire on Gunny
shot."

Then Kris turned to Penny. "Tell everyone in this hill not
fire."

"Don't fire." And she was off.

The word passed from gallery to gallery. Kris doubted
would get to everyone, but it should keep the fire down a notc
Maybe she'd have some surprises left for the next assault.

A single shot rang out.

And the valley before Kris erupted with fire.

The small viewing port deflected the full shock and bla
from Kris, but its impact was immediately visible.

Men dropped.

The platoon moving forward had their guns at the ready. At the first sound of shooting, they let go on full automatic.

Kris didn't see any targets, but they sprayed the area before them liberally. The complaining farm animals took most of the brunt of their fire. But only for a moment.

Under the hammering of fully automatic fire, Kris could just make out the pop, pop, pop of M-6s firing single shots, low powered for sleepy darts. Men went down in ragged rows. Some twitched. A few managed to get an arm under their heads like they probably did at bedtime. However they did it, they went down.

Out on the rice-paddy dikes, others were going down, too.

Some were hit and going down. A couple looked like they were just dropping. Maybe Jack's Marines weren't getting all of them, but it was hard to tell who was hit and down and who was faking. Maybe the fakers would play it smart and just stay down.

Yeah, right.

The platoon on overwatch was giving as good as it could but couldn't find anything to aim at. Their rapid-fire volleys To Whom It May Concern didn't hit anywhere Kris had stationed gunners. Still, the leaves were flying from the tree and bushes in front of Kris's position, and a noisy round shot into her command post to bury itself in the ceiling.

"Fire enough, and you're bound to hit something," Kris mused to the senior clan members sharing the command center with her, then hardened her voice for Red. "Put the gun down. Don't even think of firing from here. I don't want this hill firing this attack, and I sure don't want us showing where we are."

Gamma Polska put out a hand, rested it on Red's rifle. The barrel sank to the floor. "Seems like a chicken way to fight a war," he growled.

"Colonel Cortez is just feeling for us," Kris said. "I doubt he expected to lose everything he sent in this time, but this is not his main attack."

The rapid fire from the white-shirted troopers quieted as they went to sleep, or, in the case of those hit by the farmers, screamed for help. Now Kris could make out the shriek of M-6s on full power. The shots were carefully spaced, and though Kris could not risk a run to one of the gun ports that opened on the

other side of her hill, she was willing to bet money that Gunny
team was taking down each of the heavy infantry in that gull
Probably one shot, one target.

"Comm, raise Gunny," Kris said.

"I'm flashing him, but he's not answering" told Kris th
Gunny was indeed busy. On Kris's front matters got active.

One of the white-clad soldiers who'd fallen off the dike ha
been faking it. Down, he spotted a firing port.

Yanking a grenade from his belt, he pulled the pin, leapt u
and tossed it at the opening in the dike. Then he dashed over th
dike to escape his own grenade's blowback.

Five rapid pops stopped him. Even before his grenade e:
ploded, he was falling, headfirst, onto the other side of the dil
wall. From what Kris could see, legs up, body down, th
grenadier was very likely head down in muddy water.

Sleepy darts weren't intended to be lethal. However, if yo
went to sleep facedown in two feet of water, the darts did not
ing to help you breathe.

This was battle. People died.

Through the phone, Gunny's voice came. "The heavy ii
fantry on your and my hills are down," was all he said.

The guy drowning in front of Kris wasn't the only fello
whose name would be on the butcher's bill for today.

No, maybe not.

Across the paddies from Kris, one of the white coats came
his feet. He had no gun, and his hands were held out in the un
versal sign for surrender. He climbed up onto the dike and hasti
made his way to where his comrade lay, feet down.

Kris held her breath as the man pulled his buddy from th
water, arranged him so that his mouth drained water, then gav
him one or two breaths of artificial respiration. When the hal
drowned man began to cough up water, the rescuer smiled.

A single pop, and the man looked down. Someone had put
sleepy dart right in the middle of the guy's chest.

And the guy lay down and went to sleep.

"Ha," Kris said into the phone, but for all to hear. "Let's se
how Colonel Cortez takes to our way of fighting."

36

CORTEZ scowled. He'd watched that loving tableau of battlefield mercy through his binoculars. A moment earlier he'd watched as half a Guard platoon had been wiped out by hidden fire. Thus ended Cortez's planned envelopment of what he'd mistaken as a limited position.

"This is not a small force," Cortez muttered to himself.

"It must be at least battalion size," Major Zhukov said. "Maybe bigger."

"But how many of them are those damn Marines?" Cortez asked, chewing his lower lip.

"If we can trust this scandal mag," Captain Sawyer said, unfolding the cheap newspaper he'd confiscated from a trooper, "all the Longknife girl has is what's left of an embassy Marine company that she didn't get killed in her last escapade."

"She's had time to return to Wardhaven, to be reinforced," Zhukov pointed out.

"Enough!" Cortez snapped. "We're here to boot her out. Quit talking and start booting. She's spread shooters wide to cover this whole front. She can't be strong everywhere. And if most of her firepower is these damn farmers, I'll bet you my eagles she can't get them to move an Earth inch under fire."

Cortez gauged the reaction of his subordinates. Sawyer's face was a wolf's grin. And a hungry one at that. Zhukov's eyes had narrowed. He was holding his judgment. A good XO.

"Sawyer, your company is nearly full strength. Take it wide around the swamp side. Stay low on the far side of the farthest-out dike. Zhukov, send along a squad of the Guard."

"It will be done, sir," Zhukov said, sprouting a tiger grin.

"You there," Cortez said, signaling to the youngest captain from the psalm singers. "Take what's left of your company and

climb those hills on our right. I want you to set up fire lar
down both valleys, the one where our Guard squads got hit a
the next one over. Don't let them come around our flank. Do
let her move troops from one hill to the other without knocki
some daylight into them. You understand?"

"Yes, Colonel."

"And don't just sit on your hands. Probe those two hills
don't want you launching a full-fledged assault, but don't
them ignore you, either. Probe for firing positions. Are they is
lated spider holes or connected by tunnels? If they are co
nected, send me a runner and carefully, boy, carefully wo
at getting some of your shooters into their tunnels. I would
mind at all if you broke them. Not at all."

"Yes, Colonel." The kid looked scared and excited. Cor
would keep an eye on his left flank. He didn't intend for him
do much more than hold Longknife's troops there in place, l
the kid might surprise him.

Good surprise or bad surprise?

"Zhukov, you go with Sawyer. I'll take the rest of the Gua
and psalm singers and advance in the center. Not too far. N
too fast." Cortez eyed the ground before him. The trees alo
the edge of the swamp were the only solid cover he had to a
proach the farmstead. The hilly side showed some cover, ev
an orchard here and there, but nothing solid.

He turned to the Guard captain. "Afonin, advance wha
haven't given away of your Guard to that orchard. Looks li
peaches. Set up fire lanes to cover that first hill. I'll take the l
of the Jerusalem Rifles and set them up in the woods beside
swamp. Our job is to keep enough fire on the hill that they do
dare reinforce whatever they've got in those rice paddies.
think the dikes are hollow. Not sure how much they've g
there. Zhukov, Sawyer, you will clean them out of the rice pa
dies and close on the hill. We'll roll them up from right to lef
Cortez finished. That was the way to go. Roll them up a piece
a time. He had all the time he needed.

As soon as Longknife tried to maneuver a bunch of farmhan
under fire, they'd break and run. Yes, this would do the trick.

"Any questions?" he asked.

There were none.

                    *   *   *

Kris got a call up to the *Wasp* while things stayed quiet.

"I see you and them are at each other's throats," Drago said when he came on. The tight-beam aimed straight up cut through the jamming. The *Wasp* was now trailing right behind Thorpe. Drago came on no more than a minute after the other passed below the horizon. "Do you need anything from me?" he asked.

"Not now. Thorpe doesn't dare fire at us while we're this close. Can you tell us anything about what they're doing?"

"I can show you where his troops are for the next minute or so. I don't have any idea what he's up to."

True to his word, Drago and his magic eyes above did give Kris a good view of what was happening in the woods two miles from where she huddled underground. Cortez wasn't running. No, he was clearly ordering his men for another attack, adjusting his forces, sending some to her left to take another go at Jack, another group to her right to have a go at Gunny's crew.

And there were plenty left to move up the middle.

An attack all along the line?

Cortez wasn't that dumb.

The force headed for Gunny's hill looked to be the smallest. Was that a feint?

But if they were the best he had, that could be his main thrust. If Gunny lost the back door, things could come unhinged in a hurry. Kris shook her head; this was the problem with overhead imagery. It let you count noses. What those noses were attached to, how good they were, and what they intended didn't show in a picture from nearly three hundred klicks up.

Kris picked up the phone. "Jack, Gunny, did you get the pictures from the *Wasp*?" They had. "You see a need to change anything around?"

"Sure looks like he's coming for us," Jack said. "Not sure which of us he's after first."

"Me neither," Gunny said.

"Then I suggest we see what we can do with what we've got," Kris said. "I think I'll take a walk."

Leaving Penny to send a runner if anything interesting started to develop, Kris ambled off to review her troops.

Close to her OP, volunteers had gotten the word not to shoot. They were none too happy to have missed out on the first volley, but they liked what they saw. Plenty of white shirts lay in the dust. A few called for help; most just snored.

"Could we send someone out to help their wounded?" older woman asked. Kris saw in her eyes a grandma who'd w ried many a young'un through a tough situation. Kris allow that she and a couple of other volunteer women could.

Kris followed them down to the cold room, the large stor area that got the digging started on this hill. They even had left over from last winter. They might be pioneers, but that di mean they expected to rough it. Three women with buckets water and ladles led the way out the cold room's thick door.

And got shot at from the homestead.

They ducked back. Kris found a broom, a white rag, and tr it again. "You got wounded lying out in the sun," she shouted. " got water and bandages. You gonna let us take care of them?"

"No guns," the sergeant shouted on his bullhorn. "And go back in the door you came out. One of my men *thinks* yo making a break, and you'll get a bullet for it."

"Can we bring your wounded in out of the sun?" the g hair shouted over Kris's shoulder.

Hmm, not a bad idea, Kris thought. If they got a wounded under the hill, troops might be more careful about t ing grenades into holes. Which must have been apparent to sergeant. There was plenty of time for an argument before shouted. "Okay, but only the bleeding. Leave sleepers there."

Which meant that as soon as one of them woke up, he expected to join in the shooting. Maybe Kris hadn't been smart as she thought. Sleepy bullets had only recently co into the inventory and data was scarce on long, drawn-out t tles with the stuff.

NELLY, NEXT TIME THE FIRING STARTS, REMIND ME TO DER SOME MARINES TO REDART THE GUYS WHO ARE DOWN.

YES, MA'AM. I'M SEARCHING THE SOURCE MATERIAL. THER NOTHING IN THE GENERALLY AVAILABLE LITERATURE ABO HOW MANY SHOTS A PERSON CAN TAKE, ONE AFTER THE OTHE

Which wasn't to say that the tests hadn't been made, o that the results had been kept out of the public records. *Sometin you just couldn't do a good deed for all your trying.*

The six women slipped out and started their work. No took a shot at them. A second group, this time including a cou of strapping young boys, and two equally big girls, slipped ou lug the bleeding into the cool room.

No one objected from down the road where the main hos

camp was. Apparently, while they redeployed into their next attack, there was room for humanitarian care.

Or maybe they were just too busy to notice.

Five went into the valley between the hills to help wounded troops in armor. From these Guard Fusiliers there was gratitude for water, and help bandaging wounds, but no takers on being evacuated. They clutched their rifles and lay ready to do what their orders called for once the shooting started again.

NELLY, REMIND ME TO PASS THAT ALONG TO GUNNY.

YES, MA'AM. HARD CASES FOR HARD CASES, judged the computer.

The judgment struck Kris as obvious. That her computer felt compelled to make it, and did, struck Kris as another reason to talk to Auntie Tru.

Once the rescue operations had the bugs worked out, Kris continued her walk back inside the caves. Here and there, fifty-pound bags of rice half blocked or provided cover in the tunnels. Someone was thinking ahead for when the cave openings got breached. Kris shivered in the cool dark. If it came to fighting in here, the blood would be ankle deep. But if it came to fighting in here, would she throw in the sponge?

A woman came along with a wheelbarrow, pushing one of the fifty-pound rice bags. She seemed to know the caves very well. After looking around for a minute to get her bearings, she upended the barrow and dumped the sack. "That ought to cover that entire end of the cave. No religious nut is going to tell my daughter what she can be. If Amy wants to be a doctor or a dancer, she's gonna be what she wants to be."

Kris nodded. There wasn't much room for compromise here. Maybe she didn't need to worry so much about these folks running.

Still, the worst bloodbaths happened when neither side saw any reason to retreat.

Princess, you better come up with some good reason for Cortez to throw in the towel. It doesn't look like these folks even want a towel handy.

A skinny redheaded gal galloped up to Kris. "Penny says stuff's happening you want to see." Kris followed her at a fast jog back to HQ. A glance out told her it was time.

"Get me Gunny and Jack on the line," Kris ordered.

37

Jack stood clear as a hulking farm boy wielded the five-kilo sledgehammer. His girlfriend held the rod in place. The guy was very careful. The first two swings had not done much more than chip the hardened dirt.

The third swing drove the iron rod down as far as it would go. The kid dropped the sledge and, with the girl's help, worked the rod around in widening circles, creating more room for a rifle without widening the fire port. When they pulled the rod out, Jack shoved his rifle into place and nodded.

"It fits fine," he told his eager hands.

The boy hefted the hammer, the girl the bar, and they headed a couple of meters down the narrow cave, ready to do it again.

Jack put his eye to the notch and studied the swamp in the distance. Close in, a small kid was sweeping into the muddy water the dirt the rod had driven out of the firing hole.

It wouldn't do to make it any easier for Cortez's shooters to spot where the fire was coming from. So a ten-year-old kid was hanging out there. Sooner or later, Cortez would get his act together, and his troops would move up. Jack did not want to find that out by having that kid shot off the dike.

Jack headed down the cave, bent over but moving at a trot. Tommy Tzu told him they had only recently dug out this dike. "We figured we had enough space between the house and the new paddies, but the little beggars ran all the way out here and ate an entire field clean in one night. So we dug."

"Glad you did," was all Jack could say.

He stood up as he entered a cross cave with more headroom. A freckled gal attentively watched his commline. "Nothing from Lieutenant Longknife, Captain," she reported.

"You keep listening. I'm going outside."

"I'll tell you what I told my brother. Keep your head down, or Mama's gonna be real mad. You do have a mama, don't you?"

"Despite what my men may tell you," Jack said, eyeing a young Marine who had attached himself to the phone . . . or the girl at the phone, "I was not hatched. I have a mama."

"I told you," the girl said, sticking her tongue out.

"You gonna take his word or mine?" the private shot back.

"Why don't you follow me, Marine," Jack said.

None too happy to be distanced from the comm girl, the Marine followed. They'd cut an exit from the tunnel and covered it with a reed mat. Jack rolled through it and landed, feet-first, in muddy water. Rifle in hand, he waded a couple of meters before raising his helmeted head.

When the Marine did the same, Jack snapped, "Get your head down." The Marine did.

Jack brought binoculars up to study the tree line across glass-smooth, brown water. Not a breath of wind disturbed the water or cooled the sweat popping out on him as the sun warmed his armor.

Sergeant Bruce, who led the squad Jack had at that end of the dikes, low walked up to him, then settled into two feet of water, his back to the dike.

"Anything over there?" Jack asked, still moving his glasses slowly up and down the tree line.

"I'm willing to bet they're there, but I ain't seen them. You'd think I'd catch sight of a white shirt in all those trees."

"Unless someone dunked them in the first mud hole they came to," the private said.

Jack raised an eyebrow. Low rank didn't mean low smarts.

Turning, Jack surveyed the deployment here. About half of the sergeant's squad was strung out along the dike, keeping their heads down and rifles out of the water. Along with them were over a dozen farmers. Jack wanted these folks out of the dike caves just in case he needed fire put on someplace not covered by one of the loopholes that the couple were knocking.

Whoever ran that last assault had assumed Kris lacked the troops to cover a wide front. They wouldn't make that mistake again. Sergeant Bruce had watched some half-decent heavy infantry surface from an underwater approach march when they attacked the dugouts this morning.

Jack had a tall youngster from the farmers wade out to see

how deep the water was here. It was a good kilometer before he found any kind of channel. Between here and those trees, the water was mostly knee deep. Whoever assaulted the position would come through shallow water.

Jack blinked. A moment ago there had been nothing in the tree line. Now a line of men, a few in full armor, a whole lot more in filthy shirts and pants, were wading into the water not a half klick from Jack. They moved like silent brown ghosts. The more of that muddy water they covered before they were noticed, the better off they were.

Jack dropped his binoculars and reached for his rifle.

"Oh boy." Sergeant Bruce grinned and stood, signaling for his troops to do likewise.

"For what they are about to receive, may they be truly grateful," Jack's private said as he sighted his rifle in.

"Sleepy darts or live ammo, sir?" Bruce asked.

"Sleepy darts, but use a double dollop of propellant," Jack said. "There may be no wind, but that's a long half klick."

Selectors clicked along the line.

"Sir," the freckled comm runner said, sticking her cute nose through the mat. "Your lady friend wants to talk to you."

"This ought to tell her all she needs to know," Jack said, and fired the first shot of what had to be Panda's last battle.

AS Kris waited for her flank commanders to come to the phone, she watched things get interesting on her front. Armored infantry pushed several two-wheeled carts ahead of them as they slowly advanced on the peach orchard some four hundred meters in front of her. And there was also movement in the trees bordering the swamp.

"Lieutenant," said Gunny, "I've got a thin foam of light infantry spread along my front. No one too close to anyone, but they are coming down your ridge, mine, and one behind me."

"Then I think we better tell them to stop," Kris said. "The longer it takes them to get here under fire, the more of them ought to be laid out somewhere on the grass."

"My opinion exactly. How's the captain's front?"

"I don't know. I'm still waiting for him to come online" was answered by a volley of M-6s popping off sleepy darts and hunting rifles doing their thing.

"That says it all," Kris said. "Shoot 'em if you got 'em," Kris shouted, both for the phone and the rifles around her.

The hill came alive with fire.

Out beyond the peach orchard, a couple of the armored infantry stumbled and fell as they took hit after hit. Still, most of them picked themselves up and ran to catch up with the carts that were now being pushed at a run. Hunting ammunition didn't do a lot against serious military-grade armor.

Kris commanded here, but she also had one of the few M-6s in her hill. She frowned to herself, deciding between just watching, like the book said a good commander did, or doing something about those folks galloping her way with bloody intent.

Kris hefted her M-6. Trotting a couple of galleries down, she found four riflemen who were holding their fire.

"No use wasting shot and powder on hide that thick at this distance," the elder one told her, as if she might disagree.

"You might pass that message along to the folks up and down here," she said, and got a smile from him. He sent two of his younger charges trotting out with that word from the Longknife, but stayed to watch as Kris unlimbered her military-issue rifle.

Kris got a good range readout, fed it into the sight, then clicked the ammo selector to seriously deadly and flipped the propellant selector to its highest setting.

"You're gonna feel that kick tomorrow," the old fellow said.

Reminded, Kris fitted the rifle solidly into her shoulder, then squinted into the sights. Out in the sun, a sergeant was shouting orders to those pushing a couple of carts.

Kris breathed out, timed her pulse, then gently squeezed off a round between beats.

The sergeant took the hit square in the back. He flew a good three meters before going down in a long slide that left a track of dust in the air.

"Good Lord," the old man whispered.

"Help us," his younger sidekick finished. And struggled with his ears. "You could have warned us about the noise."

"Would you believe I've never actually fired this thing on full power," Kris said, and jiggled her own ear.

"Think you could get that barrel a tad more out of here?" the younger one asked.

"But not too far," the oldster suggested. "If they spot the barrel, we'll have every rifle out there aimed at us."

"I'd just move on to another firing position," Kris said, with an impish grin.

"And we would, too," the youngster said, grinning right back.

While they joked, Kris settled into a more forward firing position. Three shots later, and two targets down, she noticed their little crack in the hill was taking serious fire. After the second bullet made it through the port, Kris headed elsewhere. The older fellow followed her, leaving the younger to keep an eye on their hole from well back.

Kris dropped two more of the armored infantry before they made it to the peach orchard. There, they did a good job of disappearing among the trees, behind upended wagons, or by digging in. They also laid down a serious base of fire on Kris's hill.

As Kris trotted along the main cave, she saw shooters in gallery after gallery stuff rocks into their fire ports. Kris tapped the elder who'd been walking with her since she started. "We've got to keep up our own base of fire. If we go all silent, they'll charge us."

"I hear you," the old man said, "but you got to understand, we only have so much ammunition. It's not like we fight a war every year or so. Brass is hard to come by. It's easy to reload." The guy flinched. He must have just realized reloading was not an option at the moment.

Kris kicked herself; she hadn't taken an inventory of how much ammo her shooters had brought to this fight. The old guy had a good point. But if they didn't keep up their side of the shoot, Cortez and his boys would walk right in and start shooting them up close and personal.

Note to self, next fight bring a logistician.

"Tell everyone to conserve their ammo," Kris said, "but we have to keep up our base of fire. That's all that's keeping them out there and not in here."

The elder nodded and headed back up the main cave.

Back at her observation post, even with no shots coming from her little hole in the mountain, there was so much lead flying that no one was getting too close to the lookout.

"They are seriously pissed at us," Red said.

"We ain't exactly been kind to them," Gamma Polska agreed.

"You invade folks' home planet," Penny said, "you can't expect to win a popularity contest."

"Are we good?" the leader of the Polska clan asked Kris.

"That depends on how much ammo they brought," Kris said. "If they shoot themselves dry, they are in a world of hurt. Then, of course, we could shoot ourselves dry first."

"I was wondering when someone might think of that," Red said, maybe just now realizing what he'd never thought of before. Supplies matter in a fight.

Kris considered her options. She could hunker down and wait to see who ran out of ammo first, or . . . Actually she didn't have any other option. This was a battle she hadn't planned on, against a colonel who never expected her to show. It would be decided by who had the last round in the magazine.

Unless . . .

Kris needed to change her thinking. Elevate her thinking.

Oh. Right. That might do it.

Then again, Captain Drago and the *Wasp*'s crew might not appreciate her dropping this hot potato into their laps. Well, they'd signed on with her. They couldn't expect it to be boring.

NELLY, WHEN DOES THE *WASP* COME OVER?

THORPE IS OVER US JUST NOW. THE *WASP* SHOULD BE ALONG RIGHT AFTER HIM.

"Comm, I'll need you to punch me a link through to the *Wasp* just as soon as you can."

"Yes, ma'am."

38

Colonel Cortez did not like the way this battle was going.

Too many of the Guard's heavily armored men lay in the dust on the near side of the peach orchard. Their forty-year-old armor hadn't done so well against the newest mod of the old M-6.

The fire from the peach orchard hadn't started out nearly as strong as he'd expected, and it was already tapering off. Cortez considered sending out a runner to jack up Captain Afonin, but thought better of it. That damn hill was firing back plenty.

Only a half dozen sharpshooters were firing among the psalm singers here in the trees. Zhukov had done a check of ammo during the break. Several of the boxes everyone thought were full of ammo had turned out to have proselytizing pamphlets in them. Just the ammunition a Christian soldier needed.

Zhukov sent a runner. He'd come under fire a full half klick from the dikes. A long stretch of muddy water lay between them and the folks shooting at them. No cover, no protection. The troops were no go.

Colonel Cortez was not a happy man . . . but he was a methodical thinker. Checked on his right. Going nowhere in the center. What did that leave him? He glanced to his left, where a few psalm singers were dug in on the hill, not doing much. "Wonder what the kid is doing on the other side of the hill."

"Sir," said the older captain.

Cortez decided on a different throw of the dice. "Captain, I want half of your command."

"For what, sir?" The fellow seemed more startled by the order than questioning it.

"I'm pulling them back."

"Where do you want me to take them, sir?"

"They're coming with me. You keep the sharpshooters

making noise here." Cortez looked around, spotted a sergeant who seemed more worldly than the rest, and motioned to him. "Pick half the company that know how to shoot, move fast, and will follow my orders without question. Make sure they have a full ammo load, and follow me."

"Yes, sir," the sergeant said, with a happy grin.

While the sergeant collected the team, Colonel Cortez went down the list of things he would need to do the next fifteen or thirty minutes . . . assuming he guessed right.

His eyes lit on some Guards who hadn't been sent one place or the other. Right! Engineers! Just what the colonel ordered.

Now Cortez grinned. Those farmers could dig themselves in as deep as they wanted. It didn't matter.

All they were doing was digging their own graves.

"Sorry it took me so long to punch through to the *Wasp*, ma'am. They're jamming us real bad."

The *Wasp* was almost overhead before the comm tech passed Captain Drago through to Kris with a worried look and apology.

Kris gave her a quick nod and concentrated on Drago.

"Your battle's still going," was his first comment.

"Yeah, I'm in one whale of a gunfight, and I have no idea how much ammo these volunteers brought with them."

"Oh my, that can't be making your bunny jump."

"Not even a little bit. Captain, I need you to settle this, or it may not go down nearly as well as my reputation calls for."

"That bad, huh? Well, you're far too close for me to singe their behinds with my lasers. Even the five-inchers."

"Hey, I've been through that once this week. I am not interested in doing it again."

Kris could almost hear the frown growing on Drago's face. "I know I'm going to regret asking this, but what do you want?"

A small voice from somewhere on Drago's bridge could be heard saying, "Then don't ask that dame."

Kris ignored both. "I need you to get Thorpe out of my sky. I don't care if you scare him out or chase him out or blow him out. But I need to tell Cortez that his ride is gone."

Kris paused to glance out her observer port. The firefight hadn't slackened while she talked. "Bret, a whole lot of good people are going to die if we let this firefight go the full count. I can't think of anyone else but you to stop it."

"How I hate it when you tell me I'm the only one that can save your bacon." Drago sighed. "But then I should have known you hadn't gotten my ship riding his exhaust for nothing."

Actually, Kris had done that long before she thought of this way out. She thought. Well, maybe she wasn't totally innocent of planning ahead for the worst case.

"Thanks, Bret, and thank the whole crew. There are a lot of people down here who are going to owe you their lives."

"Kris, only heroes respond to that kind of talk. Remember, we're just in it for the money."

"Yeah, right," was all Kris could say to that.

"Now if you'll excuse me, me and my pirate crew have a bit of finagling to do. You said you wouldn't mind if we just scare Thorpe out of your sky? I did hear you right?"

"Anything that makes him not available to give Cortez and his troublemakers a ride home."

"Hmmm. Let me talk to my dirty-trick brain trust. I'll get back to you next orbit."

39

Cortez led his last reserves up the hill at the fastest trot he could push them. At the end of the line, his grinning sergeant collected stragglers, peeled off a corporal when they grew to a wad of ten, and let them follow at a slower pace.

Cortez let the squads of stragglers grow. He needed to reach the captain with what he could today, not get there with everyone tomorrow.

Cortez had chosen to fall back a full two klicks before he started across the field and up the first hill. He knew he was in plain sight of any OP on the hill, but at least he was well out of gunshot. Cortez had brought no artillery. Not even a mortar. But then, the Longknife girl and her farmers hadn't so much as rigged a slingshot to hurl anything explosive.

Not for the first time did the colonel shake his head. The idiots who put this thing together were so sure this planet was a cakewalk. Just march in, intimidate the civilians, and start raking in the cash.

Cortez wished the poor troopers he was hustling along were the financiers of this screwup. No, no he didn't. Those pukes would have dropped of a collective heart attack long ago.

Cortez reached the top of the first ridge. Turning the lead of the column over to a corporal, he pointed the man downhill, and told him, "Keep up the pace." Then, raising his binoculars, Cortez studied the situation.

Off to his right, Zhukov and his team plunked away at the troops behind the dikes. There didn't seem to be that many rifles there, not compared to the rattle of fire from that flank. Cortez knew he was facing fire from dug-in positions on the hill he now stood atop. Certainly the hostiles had dug themselves into those dikes. There was a lot more there than met the eye.

The colonel eyed the hill beneath him. Here and there an orchard or a tree with clumps of bushes around it broke up his field of vision, but from this angle it was hard to miss the glint off a gun barrel or the spit of flame when a rifle fired.

He chuckled. These farmers must make their own powder. Smokeless it wasn't. Not as good as the ammo used by his troops. That told him a lot. With the load being variable in both amount and strength, these folks wouldn't be hitting what they aimed at. Not at any kind of range.

Of course, up close, it wouldn't matter. So keep back for now, let them shoot. Who had the worst ammo problem?

"How long do these caves run?" Cortez asked aloud. He didn't see a door into the mountain. Were all the firing positions connected? That was a thought. If he blew his way into any one of the caves, would he be loose among them all? Would his troops in the cave be shooting fish in a barrel?

Now that was a nice thought.

Cortez moved his focus to the next hill. Most of the fire came from a series of slit trenches along its military crest. The end of them zigzagged over the crest toward what was probably a firing position on the other side.

The work looked hasty, but professionally camouflaged from an observer in the valley. The first Guards to march into the valley below them must not have done a very careful look when they were up here. Then again, Cortez's original command post hadn't given him a very good look at those slit trenches, either.

He searched the hill carefully but saw nothing that looked like a fire pit or cave outlet on that ridge. All the fire came from those well-concealed positions along the crest.

The colonel put away his binoculars and started jogging beside his men down the hill. He had a lot to think about.

Kris had run out of things to worry about. She didn't like the feel of that. Not at all.

Drago had his sailing orders. It would be next orbit, ninety minutes, at least, before she'd learn anything about how Thorpe took to the nudge. If it took two or three orbits for matters to develop, it would be getting close to dark.

Come dark, the question would be whose army ran first.

Kris eyed the swamp that separated Jack from the attack on his rice paddies. The assault there seemed stalled. So long as Jack had ammunition, no one looked inclined to try splashing their way across that killing field.

In front of Kris it didn't look any better for Cortez. His fire was steady, but no one looked inclined to risk the open space. One tank could have made mincemeat of Kris's position. A couple of howitzers could have dug her troops out quick.

How long had it been since there was a fair, stand-up fight, just infantry against infantry? She'd have to ask Grampa Trouble next time she was on speaking terms with the old coot.

That left Kris's right. She edged as far over as she could to the left of the viewing port and squinted. Not a lot to see.

That wasn't a good development.

A girl, maybe ten years old, galloped into the HQ. She smiled at Gramma Polska, then turned to Kris. "My momma says you ought to come quick. She says she can see something that you can't see, and you need to see it" came out in a rush that showed no lack of breath.

Kris wasn't seeing anything interesting out of her port, so maybe a different view was called for.

"Keep an eye out here," Kris told Penny. "Let me know as soon as you hear anything from the *Wasp*." Then she followed the little girl into the dark.

Unlike most adults, who had electric lamps, the girl had no trouble seeing in the dim lights stuck into the walls. Kris followed her for a while, risking her steps. Then called a halt and ducked into a cross corridor to borrow a lamp from three riflemen. They didn't fire a shot the whole time Kris was negotiating the loan. As she rejoined the girl, someone fired.

Kris was glad she'd borrowed the lamp, because she quickly entered a new section of tunnel with very little light in it. Still, the girl picked her way along it, bent over but trailing hands on both sides of the wall. Kris found herself once more regretting that last growth spurt in her first year of high school. Clearly, this section of cave was meant for dwarfs, midgets, and ten-year-olds.

Then the girl's bottom went right and Kris found herself following her into all kinds of daylight. Blinking hard, Kris switched off the lamp and looked around.

The afternoon sun slanted into the cave, filtered by green

leaves. To the left dangled the roots of a tree. Over all was the smell of fresh, clean dirt. Kris doubted the rifle standing against the wall had been fired even once.

The girl was getting a hug from her mother and, in an avalanche of words, reporting how she'd brought the princess just like she was told. The mother, an attractive woman in her late thirties, saw Kris's glance at the rifle and seemed to harden a bit. "I haven't seen anything that I thought needed shooting at, not with the slugs that thing shoots."

"I doubt if the armored infantry that came down that gully a while back would have noticed if you'd hit them."

The woman brightened. "My thinking exactly. But I'm going to be needing it real soon. Come see what's happening."

Kris looked, and didn't see much. Across the narrow valley, say a thousand meters, was the ridge Gunny defended, but not all that much of it was visible through the tunnel opening.

"You need to stick your head out to see anything," the woman said, and did. No helmet, no armor, the mother didn't seem to realize she risked a stray bullet. Or maybe she did.

Kris tapped the woman on the shoulder, pulled her back in, and took her place. The tree and bushes provided some cover but little protection. And if anyone got serious about shooting up this little grove, even that would be gone in one heavy volley.

Off to Kris's right, Gunny and his platoon were dug in near the crest of the next hill. The grove of trees they were behind now stood bare, denuded of leaves and most branches.

In the valley, another orchard provided some protection to the survivors of Cortez's heavy infantry probe. No fire came from them; they seemed pretty suppressed.

Kris turned and looked up the valley.

And felt a sudden chill.

A good two klicks out, a loose column of soldiers moved in single file. These were the white-smocked ones; even their hats were white. Not good camouflage. Their outfits must mean something really important to them. Kris corralled her brain and concentrated. Some troops were already slogging their way up the next ridge, so their objective might be farther over.

Or maybe not. If they were going to sweep this valley, they'd want to stretch from here to there, wouldn't they?

Kris turned back to Gunny's disposition. Then stuck her

head out a bit more and looked at what she could see of whatever defense this ridge offered.

The word "broadside" came to mind. Sailing ships with all their guns pointed to the left or right. Starboard or port, wasn't it? If you got across their bow . . .

Kris shook her head and ducked back in. "Is this the farthest-out OP we've got?" she asked the woman.

She nodded silently.

Kris stuck her head out again. Gunny had been adding to his position, digging more zigzags down from the crest position. He'd be able to bring guns from those to bear up the valley, but he'd be taking fire from the orchard . . . assuming those people had any fire left in them.

That was not a bet Kris would take.

Blast it. Drago might well have Thorpe driven out of the sky in another hour, hour and a half. What were the odds this attack would still be developing come Drago's next pass?

Kris risked another look up valley.

The lead troopers had reached the top of the next ridge. They stopped there.

The whole line came to a halt.

Down in the valley, someone not in the line, so likely an officer, stepped forward. Binoculars came up. Yep, an officer.

Kris pulled out her own glasses and studied the man.

Armor. Good armor. Only weapon was a pistol that he wore at his belt. Old-fashioned. Maybe.

He looked right at her. The two of them studied each other for a long moment. Was she looking at Colonel Cortez?

If she was, she was looking at a man drawing up his last reserves for a final throw of the dice.

What was he after?

Kris hardly had to ask. The answer was all around her. This observation post was also an entrance to her subterranean defenses. Colonel Cortez stood a good two kilometers farther up the valley. Scattered riflemen had advanced to about two, three hundred meters from where Kris stood. Gunny and his platoon were a good four hundred meters farther down the valley.

Could his riflemen keep those light infantry out of her mountain? Did Gunny know he needed to?

Kris ducked back inside, took the rifle from where it leaned against the wall, and handed it to the woman. "You are standing on the most valuable piece of real estate on this planet."

"I kind of thought so."

"I'm going to get you reinforcements. Until they get here, you have got to keep all comers out of this place."

"I know."

"Can I take your daughter?"

"Please. She knows caves. I've never seen her get lost."

"I'm counting on her to get me back to the main caves, then to get reinforcements up to replace you. You hear me? As soon as the Marines get here, you get out."

"I'll be back and running."

"Momma, are you going to be all right?"

The woman knelt to be eye to eye with her daughter. "Honey-pot, I'll be fine. You show the princess back to the main caves. She's going to introduce you to some big men with guns. You bring them back up here, then you and Momma are going to run far away from here. Okay, baby girl?"

"I'm a big girl, Momma," the kid said.

Her momma tousled her hair. "Now run, big girl."

The kid backed slowly away from her mother. Kris stooped and headed into the tight opening, moving as fast as she could. Before too long, she heard soft footsteps behind her.

Not long after that came, "That's the wrong way, follow me."

Kris backed out of what sure looked like the right turn and followed the kid for what seemed like an hour but likely wasn't more than a minute or two before the cave opened up to an area that allowed Kris to almost stand.

Now jogging just behind the girl, Kris followed until she heard an M-6 shoot from one of the side galleries. She went on a bit longer, then came to a halt.

"Squad sergeants, report yourselves," she shouted.

Hardly a breath later, a head ducked out of a gallery ten meters farther on and to the left. A second head appeared ten meters farther to the right.

"You bellow, Your Highness?" the closer one asked.

"We got problems," Kris said.

"Not here?" the nearest said in mock horror.

"But it's been going so well," said the farthest.

Kris rested her hands on her hips. "I thought we brought

Marines to this shindig. All I see are stand-up comics who'd never make it if they didn't have day jobs."

They came to her, guns at the ready, their faces all serious. "What's the problem, ma'am?"

Kris filled them in. They didn't need to be told twice.

"That's just flat unkind of them," one sergeant said.

"Don't worry, ma'am, Junior here will take care of them."

"Right, Pa," said the other Marine, who couldn't have been more than a few months the younger. "I'll do the running around, so you won't get your wheelchair stuck."

"We got two fire teams in spitting distance, ma'am. Junior will get them moving up the cave. How we gonna know the place?"

"This little girl is your guide," Kris said.

"I'm a big girl. I'll be nine come June." Kris didn't have a local calendar handy, but she was willing to bet June was seven, nine months away. Oh, to be in such a hurry to grow up.

"Her mom's holding your objective with a squirrel rifle. Relieve her and let her and the kid get out of there. One fire team will hold the OP. There's a fifty-pound bag of rice blocking this cave about halfway to the OP. That's your backstop, Sergeant. If they get past that rice, they'll be shooting our farmer friends in the backs. Understood?"

"Yes, ma'am. One team will hold the OP. No retreat. The second team holds the blocking position. Again, no retreat."

Kris knew she'd just sentenced eight men to victory or death. She hated that.

But there was no other way.

"I'll try to get more rice bags sent up here. See if we can give you a couple of fallback positions."

"Don't worry, ma'am," the junior sergeant said. "We'll hold here. Tad, Debbie, Mary, Steve," he shouted. "It's 'Go Tell the Spartans' time, and you get to be the three hundred."

A blond head appeared at a cave not five meters behind Kris. "You say we're going to have three hundred."

Heads appeared at other holes in the hill. "I said eight Marines are going to do what three hundred Spartans didn't. We gonna hold the line," the junior sergeant announced.

"Ooo-Rah," greeted his chipper order.

The Marines took a moment more to recover extra rounds and rifle juice from their former position, then followed the anxious little big girl up the line at a trot.

"Sergeant," Kris started, but the squad leader waved her to silence.

"I know, ma'am. If they get past Junior's fire teams, they gonna have to fight past every one of mine. The threat axis just done whipped ninety degrees around."

"But don't ignore the other hot spots," Kris added.

"Why do you think we sergeants have eyes in the backs of our heads, Your Highness? Any chance we could get some of third squad up here?"

Kris's platoon here in the center was supposed to be the reserve. Third squad was Kris's very last hole card.

"Sorry, Sergeant, but I'm taking them out of the mountain to see just how far up the valley we can get."

"Well, support, even off axis, ma'am, is fine by me."

And with that, the sergeant set about redeploying his troops, and Kris jogged for her headquarters cave.

40

Is that the famous Princess Longknife? Cortez asked himself as he looked at someone in Marine armor sticking her head out of his objective. Her battle dress was dirty, her face smudged by mud and powder. No rifle was evident, but clearly she'd used one today. On high power from the looks of it. Thorpe dismissed the woman as nothing but a debutante, looking for her next ball.

The powder on her face today was from honest ammunition.

"She's fought a damn good battle," Cortez whispered. And if she was popping her head out of his next target, that didn't speak well for his taking any more time than he had to to start the assault on that hole in the ground.

Cortez raised his hand as the woman's head disappeared from view. "Forward, you men of the Lord's Ever Victorious Host. Forward to Victory or Death."

"Victory or Death," ran up and down the battle line.

Cortez stepped out in front of the line.

"Victory or Death," he shouted again, wondering what kind of nutcases got off on such a shout.

"Victory or Death," came in waves from his unarmored troops.

"Follow me," Cortez yelled into a break in the "Victory or Death" shout, and led the men forward at a walk. Every one of them followed him. Cortez unholstered his automatic: a gift from his first command, pearl handled, match quality. He waved it.

Men behind him yelled, "Victory or Death," and waved their rifles in the air.

Colonel Cortez tried not to grin. This was like something out of the ancient histories. Men with rifles walking into battle. He was two, two and a half klicks out from the riflemen posted on the crest of the left ridge. The right ridge seemed to have all its rifles aimed into the valley, none up the valley.

That was something Cortez strongly suspected one Lieutenant Kris Longknife, Wardhaven Navy, was busy correcting. But Cortez had troops in the farmhouse and the orchard at the foot of that valley. Lieutenant Longknife would find that getting anyone out here to face Colonel Cortez and his merry, shouting band of nuts was not going to be easy.

"Forward," Cortez shouted, and picked up the pace to a fast walk. No need to tarry here, out of range. They'd be running soon enough when the bullets came whizzing around their ears.

"Comm tech, raise me Gunny," Kris shouted without preamble as she strode into the HQ.

"I can't. His line hasn't answered for a good half hour."

"Jack?" Kris countered, taking care to keep her game face on. No one in the room must see the fear growing like a ball of snakes in her gut. *I command here.*

"I can raise a girl that's doing duty as his comm runner, but she says he's busy. If you really want him, she'll give him a shout, but it ain't safe to do much moving around out there."

Which left Kris commanding exactly what she could lay her own two hands on.

"Okay, folks, listen up. We've held Cortez along most of the line." That brought a small cheer from the elders milling around her. Penny didn't join in it, but eyed Kris.

"But he's not calling it quits." That ended the cheer.

"I think he's headed down the valley behind us, looking to force one of our firing ports or observation posts. He wants to get his troops inside the caves."

"Oh God," "No," and "We can't let that happen" seemed to sum up the popular assessments of that.

Kris didn't have time to wait until things quieted. "I'm taking the last Marines we have out to stop the attack. Mrs. Polska, will you see that the fire from this hill stays steady? We can't go quiet here and have them come up our backside."

"I will see to that."

"Red, you want to come with me?" Kris asked.

"You don't want to let me out of your sight, huh, girl?" the guy said with not quite a leer.

"No, I figured you might like to use that gun you're so fond of," Kris shot back. Then she looked around until she spotted the next clan elder she needed.

"Mr. Tzu, the gunners in your house are a problem. We'll have to assault it. How hard and thick are the walls?"

"Wood," the man said, stepping forward. "Good knotty pine, three centimeters thick. We built it about five years back. To get us out of the old sod cabin."

"Could you collect some of your family?" Kris said. "You know all the nooks and crannies people can hide in. We need all the trigger-pullers in that house either dead or surrendered."

"I understand. Give me a moment," and he rushed out.

"Penny, let me know as soon as the *Wasp* comes online. If Thorpe is running, I want to stop this gunning." Penny nodded.

As Kris turned to leave, old man Fronour stepped up beside her. "You mind if I send along a couple of my boys. I can't let Red have all the bragging rights."

"You're welcome to the walk," Kris said. More than one political dynasty was based on being in the right place for the right shoot-out. Longknife, to name just one.

In the cold room, Kris found Staff Sergeant O'Mally, who'd been honchoing second platoon since its lieutenant didn't survive Kris's last donnybrook. She quickly filled him in on her problem. They consulted a map for half a minute and agreed the house had to be taken first.

"You take a good look at that orchard," Kris ordered. "Give me two Marines, and we'll take the house."

"Ma'am, you get yourself killed, and the captain's gonna have my guts for fiddle strings."

"Don't worry, Sergeant, I promise not to get suddenly dead. You take care yourself," Kris said, trotting for the door, where Red and several of the Fronour men and women waited.

Kris slipped out the heavy cool-room door and dashed for a shed packed with twenty-five-kilo bags of rice. The first shot wasn't fired until the next Marine was halfway through his run. The second Marine after Kris had a ricochet off his armor.

Kris waved the unarmored volunteers back.

Clicking her rifle's safety to sleepy darts and power selector

to low, she popped off three shots at the upstairs window where
the fire was coming from. Someone got hit; a rifle dropped from
the window and slid across the veranda roof to clatter on the
dusty ground below.

Kris and the two Marines quickly put to sleep anyone visible. In the silence, a couple of farmers, led by Peter Tzu, made
a run for the rice shed. Someone in the house held a rifle to the
window and let it spray on full rock and roll. The last volunteer
got hit in the leg and finished in hops.

Kris clicked her rifle to deadly and full power, then put three
shots into the wall beside the window.

The shooter went down screaming.

Kris turned to the home owner. "Me and the Marines are going to put a deliberate fire into that house. You cross the yard
one or two at a time. Once you've got a half dozen or more, you
signal me and we'll cease fire and let you storm the house."

"Begging the lieutenant's pardon, ma'am," a Marine with
corporal stripes on his armor said, "but how about I trot over
there and toss a few grenades in before they charge?"

Kris considered the alternative. "Peter?" she asked the home
owner.

"There goes my wife's china, but I *think* she'd rather lose it
than me."

"You could be right, Dad" didn't sound all that sure . . . but
it was accompanied by a grin.

Kris sighted on the house. "Here goes," she said, and started
punching holes low on the first floor. Somebody screamed. The
Marines beside her opened up and chips flew all over the house.
Tzu led his son across, followed a moment later by Red and two
of his boys. The Fronour crew added four to the side porch
when one of them dropped, clutching at his leg.

Kris couldn't spot any action from the house. "Sergeant,"
she shouted, "I think we're taking fire from that orchard."

"Yes, ma'am. You heard what the lady said." And any further
words were drowned out by a barrage of fire off to Kris's left.

She turned to the corporal, but he was already up and running. He hit the porch, let his rifle loose to dangle around his
neck, and in a second had two grenades in his hands.

"Fire in the hole, folks," he said, butted the door open, tossed
in his grenades, then dove for the floor, taking Red and two other
volunteers down with him.

For a slow three count, nothing happened, except Red complaining about a dumb Marine lying on top of him. Then the house exploded. One of the grenades was fragmentary, the other flash bang. Good choice.

In seconds, the Marine and the volunteers were up and charging in over the blown-out door. There were shouts that mainly seemed to say, "Reach for that gun and die."

There were no shots fired.

Kris tapped the other Marine to follow her, and they headed to the next shed, full of drying hay bales, to see what the staff sergeant had laid out for them.

"Captain, we got company," Sensors reported.

"You got a visual?" demanded Captain Thorpe of the good ship *Golden Hind*.

"On main screen, sir."

Thorpe only saw a disk. "Zoom in," he ordered.

The image grew and centered on the screen. It certainly was a silver disk. With a striped tiger bounding toward him, growing to cover more and more of the disk, its mouth, full of teeth, roaring silently.

"What the . . . ?" said his XO.

"Someone has a sense of humor," Thorpe said dryly. "Sensors, tell me what you can about that ship."

"Not a lot, sir. It's jamming us now. But it has two large, 2200 series reactors. Sir, I'm not getting any readout from a trickle track."

Ships under boost generated electricity by running the superheated plasma headed for their engine through coils. That not only got them reaction mass but electricity for the ship and its lasers. In port or orbit, ships kept a small trickle of plasma running around a small track to generate the juice they needed.

It had taken Thorpe forever to reload his eighteen-inch lasers after firing them at the landing because he'd only had the track-generated electricity to draw on.

What kind of a ship would have no track?

Thorpe studied this ship charging his lasers. Ship or disk?

"Correct me if I'm wrong, XO, but aren't there ships now that use Smart Metal™ for a protective umbrella in front of them?"

"You know very well there are, sir. You tried to get the

consortium to rent us one for this balls-up." The XO scowled at
Mr. Whitebred. "They said we didn't need anything so expensive."

"What's that?" Thorpe asked no one. He pulled a tiny laser
pointer from his command chair. "Is that a notch in the shield,
or a mark?"

There was something at one point on the edge of the disk. It
revolved around it rapidly. Thorpe counted slowly . . . and didn't
get past three. "That disk is revolving at twenty revolutions per
minute."

The financier's rep looked at Thorpe blankly. It meant nothing to him. The XO blanched.

"Warships with ice armor rotate themselves at twenty rpms
to keep a laser hit from burning through," Thorpe told Whitebred.

"That's armor," the XO breathed softly.

Now Thorpe scowled at the moneyman. "And whoever sent
Princess Longknife out here with a company of Marines and
top-of-the-line Smart Metal™ for her ship's defense, do you
think they'd scrimp on her gun power? Do you think so, Whitebred?"

"N-n-no," the man stuttered.

"Sensors, can you tell me anything about the capacitors on
that ship? Anything?"

"Not a thing, sir. We are well and truly jammed."

"So, they're just sitting there, waiting for us to take a swing
at their kitty cat with our popguns before they swat us like a fly
with two, no, four twenty-four-inch pulse lasers. Right, XO?"

"The ship we wanted to rent had four twenty-four-inch pulse
lasers and a pair of five-inch long guns. And it had Smart
Metal™ armor. There was only one ship in the yard, just fitting
out, but they'd built a half dozen like it and sold them all, sir."

Thorpe breathed in an angry breath and let it out like fire. He
wanted that girl. She'd taken one ship away from him. Now
this. Two choices gaped before him. One meant death for him
and his ship. The other . . . To run away from that Longknife
girl. Would that be anything less than death? Long. Slow. Without honor.

If it was up to Thorpe, he knew which he'd take. But his
crew had not signed on for suicide.

The words scalded as he spoke them. "Helm, get us out of

sight of that ship. Hard break from orbit. Skim the atmosphere as close as you have to without burning us up. Get us out of here, then set a course for the nearest jump point. I don't care which one. Just jump us out of this system."

Too many emotions were battling in Thorpe's gut. "XO, you have the conn. I'll be in my cabin if you need me."

Thorpe pounded the release buckle for his chair restraints hard enough to half knock the air out of himself. He launched for the bridge hatch and would have bashed his brains out on the passageway wall if he hadn't expertly caught himself and redirected his passage.

Again, the Longknife brat had ruined his plans. Twice.

It would not happen a third time. Next time, he'd kill that woman.

41

Lieutenant Kris Longknife did not like what she saw. In the far distance, white-clad figures in a well-spread-out line moved down the valley, stopping here and there for a moment to shoot, then hurrying to keep up with the flow.

On her left, the line hurried faster, aiming itself at the painfully vulnerable hole into the hill.

Higher up the hill, a couple of those two-wheeled carts were also being pushed toward the obvious target.

Cortez had spotted the chink in her armor and was aiming everything he had left at it. Kris was tempted to start shooting from where she lay now, but it was a good six or seven hundred meters. Nearly two hundred yards closer lay what was left of a clump of trees.

And the surviving enemy riflemen.

Staff Sergeant O'Mally pointed at his enemy. "We've got 'em lying down, acting very dead, but I don't trust 'em any more than I'd trust a Marine in that situation."

Kris eyed the lumps of intermingled dirt, bodies, and fallen branches in what once had been a lovely orchard. No way of telling now what had grown there. Up the valley, the white shirts were now running. Some fell to the fire from Gunny's position on the ridge above. Not nearly enough.

"We got to go. Now, Sergeant."

"My thoughts exactly. Okay, Marines, living forever is way overrated. Up and at 'em. Fire and move."

As the sergeant stood, he just happened to kick Kris's knee out from under her. She found herself falling flat.

"You come along later, Your Highness," he said, and was gone, moving deliberately, firing single shots as he spotted something worth a round. On either side of him, eleven troopers moved in perfectly trained reflections of their sergeant.

Kris pulled herself back up, level with a hay bale. Ahead of her troopers someone tossed aside a gun. Still lying flat, though now faceup, he held his hands to the sky.

One of the Marines went down, blood glistening on the chest of her armor. In the orchard, what had looked to be a clump of dirt exploded in blood and brains.

With a suddenness that was a kick in the gut, this little corner of the battlefield fell silent. The Marines still advanced, studying the wreckage before them over their rifles' sights, fingers tight on the triggers, but nothing moved.

Nothing so much as twitched.

Volunteers now ran ahead of the Marines, moving among the lumps on the ground, throwing bodies over on their backs. Finding here and there one that still had strength to raise its hands. Struggling to get "I surrender" out past parched lips.

One of the farmers went down from a shot to the leg, but it didn't come from those in the orchard. No. Bullets were flying from the running battle line.

"Down, down, get down," Kris shouted as she raced up to the battle-raped orchard. "Your targets are up the valley. You've got to stop them from getting into the hill."

The Marines took to ground, in some cases rolling in front of them the dead armored bodies of the previous occupants of this bit of earth. Looking more than a bit dismayed, the farmers also took their places, prone behind what protection they could find. Quickly, the sound of deliberate rifle fire filled the air.

Five, six hundred meters up the valley, men in white smocks began to fall.

Above the mangled tree that now marked the observation post, two carts rolled down the hill in front of several armored and unarmored men. Kris took them under fire.

The range was long. With the afternoon, a breeze grew. It wafted up the valley in fits and bursts that made aimed fire far too inaccurate for Kris's need of the moment. Still, she carefully aimed her shots and hit some, missed too many.

From the observation port, an armored head ducked out, saw this danger, and crawled forward. That Marine dropped one, then another, then a third of those huddling behind the carts, which rolled ever closer.

A grenade flew over one cart to drop onto the flat in front of the port. The Marine grabbed for it. The grenade blew as he touched it.

Kris had to stop the attack. She could only guess at what was in the carts . . . and all her guesses came up horrible. She aimed for the auto tires of the carts. She hit . . . they went flat . . . but now gravity was on the enemy's side.

Tires flat or no, they kept on moving.

A Marine rolled from the observation post. On her back, she fired so fast it sounded like slow automatic.

Up the hill, troopers in white and armor went down, but an arm came up in one of the wagons, hurling a satchel.

For a moment it looked like the satchel would fly too far.

Then it hit the battered tree stump and bounced back.

The Marine made a grab for it.

The explosion was blinding. Kris felt the blood drain from her face, but she could not lie there holding her breath while she waited for the smoke and dirt to clear. There were still targets, some up the hill, where the carts were only half-shrouded by smoke, others downhill, where white coats, now screaming the charge, lurched toward the smoke.

Kris selected a target. Fired. Selected a new target. Fired. Beside her, Marines and volunteers did the same.

"I'm empty," came in a voice Kris ignored. The second or third time, she knew a commander was called for, not the shooter she'd become.

She glanced around. Several Marines sourly glared at their silent M-6s.

Kris reached for the bandoleer she'd swung around her neck before they left the *Wasp*. She tossed it to the empty Marine closest to her. Kris hadn't been doing a riflemen's job as much as they had.

As Kris turned back to pick out another target, Marines tore into clips of killing darts, cartridges of propellant. In a moment, the fire from the bedraggled orchard again was hellish.

The smoke had cleared from the observation port. Now a huge hole gaped.

Three white coats stormed the mouth of the cave.

Only to be blown backward by shots from within.

Kris yelled. All around her at the mouth of the valley, there rose a yell.

And fire. Fire that made hell seem calm.

White coats fell in windrows within ten, twenty, thirty meters of that smoking gash in the earth. Still, let one get close to it, stand in the mouth of it, and a shot from inside drove him down.

Down and back and bleeding.

A Marine still lived, and that Marine defended that hole in the ground like the mouth of hell.

In the fields along the hills and valley, more white-coated men went to earth. Men dropped into the cut grass of the fields and looked for leadership. Brave men looked to the dead around them, ahead of them . . . and put their faces to the dirt.

The assault had stalled.

White-coated men put their rifles down in the dirt before them and fired no more.

The assault had failed.

Around Kris, rifles fell silent. Above Kris, Gunny's voice could be heard calling, "Check fire. Check fire. Save it until we need it."

The valley grew quiet. Over the ridge, rifle fire was still sporadic, but here, a bird could be heard calling.

Her rifle before her at the ready, Kris drew a breath. She'd lived. She was still alive.

And Cortez's army had been stopped.

The battle wasn't over. It could still be lost. But for now, Kris was alive, and Cortez was stopped.

42

Kris barely had time to catch her breath, celebrate that she could still draw one . . . when she spotted movement out of the corner of her eye. Glancing back, she watched as a Marine made her way forward at a crouch.

She had no weapon!

For a moment, anger flared. What was a Marine doing on this battlefield without her weapon?

It took Kris's numb brain a moment to recognize the comm tech. Why was she out here?

Then Kris knew her brain was mush. There was only one reason for the comm tech to risk her neck out here. And it had nothing to do with the use of a rifle.

Indeed, maybe it was because she didn't have a rifle that no one took a shot at her. For a very long moment, the comm tech was the only thing moving on the quiet, murdered field.

Then she slid down not too far from Kris, only slightly out of breath, and explained the grin on her face.

"Captain Drago sends his regards and respects and reports that Captain Thorpe and company have left orbit, running for all they are worth."

If Kris hadn't been hearing it from so reputable a source, she never would have believed it. Thorpe was running!

This was a tale she wanted to hear from Drago himself.

But that would have to wait.

Kris reached for the largest branch around and looked at it sourly. It was hit in several places and tended to bend in many of those; still, when she held it up high, it stood tall.

"Now all we need is something white. Anyone got a bed-sheet?" No one did.

"Big bandage? Handkerchief? Anything white, please?" she finally said, as all her questions drew blank stares.

One of the Fronour girls said, "I'm wearing white panties."

Kris doubted the mentioned unmentionables would be all that large, but they were white.

"I'll take them, please." Kris said.

The young woman reached around under the calf-length dress she wore and, in a moment, produced the offered garment.

"I been trying to get into your panties for months," one of Red's boys said. "All she does is ask, and you give them to her."

"She said 'please,' " the woman shot back, and tossed Kris the necessary white for her banner.

Sergeant O'Mally offered plastic-cuffs to fix the makeshift flag in place, and Kris got up on her knees.

Sergeant O'Mally only got as far as clearing his voice. But the comm tech already rested her hand on Kris's flag.

"Ma'am, it's my job to come up with protocols that allow dissimilar systems to communicate with each other." She glanced around the battered and bleeding field. "This is my job."

Kris wasn't sure the battered staff would survive a tug-of-war.

Peter Tzu settled the matter. "I took this out of the dead hand of a man in my house," he said, producing the bullhorn that the sergeant had used to blast his demand for their surrender. Peter handed it to the comm tech.

She took it, and the flag, as Kris released her hold on the staff. Kris would let this dangerous job of matching dissimilar systems fall to the woman who demanded it.

The sergeant smiled.

Kris found it hard to believe that, after this battle, a sergeant could smile contentedly over winning such a minor thing as a battle of wills with one princess.

Then, Kris didn't have to report to Jack . . . too often.

Lying flat on her back, the comm tech waved the white flag several times. No one took a shot at her.

"So far, so good," she whispered, and stood, still waving the flag with its tiny bit of white. Still, no shots.

She began the slow process of walking forward. Kris listened to the crunch of her footfalls and the calling of two birds. Maybe more. Still, no shots.

The comm tech stopped after covering about two hundred meters or a third of the way to where the white coats had gone to ground. Raising the bullhorn, she called. "My commander requests a parley with your commander on this field of valor."

Nice words. Kris wondered at her choice. Valor seemed far too clean and neat for what lay around her.

A white coat came to his feet. "Maybe my commander will spare your commander the time for a few words if the subject is your surrender," he called back.

"It is not for junior hirelings like you and me to bandy words when matters of import wait upon our masters' bidding."

Kris had to suppress a giggle. She knew those lines. What was the book? The media event had been a mere ghost, cut down to fit in two hours and robbed of so many of the book's good parts.

SARACEN BLADE, Nelly supplied.

Right, that was the delightful fantasy. And romance. Kris had loved it. Up and down the line, the women Marines were grinning proudly. The guys were making as if to throw up.

What gave Kris pause was the kid from Jerusalem. He'd gotten his lines word for word right. Had that book sold there, too? Or had he played the straight man with no coaching?

Kris waited to see what the comeback would be, but an older man was standing now, dusting off his camouflaged armor and holstering his pistol.

He looked like the man Kris had watched before the attack began.

"As you were, Lieutenant," the man said in a voice that needed no bullhorn to carry over the stilled valley.

And the white coat flinched and went to stand beside the speaker. That man took off his gun belt and said something to the younger. The man stood to attention, shouted, "Yes, sir," and saluted. Then he ran off to find someone.

And the senior began walking toward Kris's comm tech.

Leaving her rifle where it lay, Kris stood. She unbelted her holster and dropped it beside Sergeant O'Mally and began her own long walk to the parley field.

As Kris passed even with Gunny's ridgetop position, she could hear the murmurs of the drugged wounded. As she approached her opposite, she came in hearing of his wounded. Many had yet to receive any care.

"Princess Kristine Longknife, I presume," said a soldier with salt-and-pepper hair escaping from his helmet. The exhaustion that slowed his movements didn't show up in a bent back or bowed shoulders.

"Colonel Henry Cortez," Kris said, and offered her hand.

He shook it firmly. "I go by Hernando. Should I call you Princess?"

"Not unless you want to start another war," Kris risked. "I go by Kris."

"And we are stalling," the colonel said with a bit of a scowl. "You sent forward the flag. Say what you have to say?"

"Before I start," Kris said, "nothing I'm planning on saying would require us to start shooting at each other for thirty minutes or an hour. You have many wounded on the field. Would you like to tend to them?"

The colonel turned around, his frown growing deeper as he surveyed the butcher bill. "I'd like to remove them, but in truth, I don't have all that much gear to tend them with. You may recall where my transport is stuck."

"I have Marine medics and some of my civilian volunteers are doctors and nurses."

"You have more medical supplies than you need?" he said, giving her a questioning glance.

Kris had no idea, but now was no time to stint. She wanted . . . needed . . . to get this proud man comfortable with the idea that he was the supplicant and she the one dispensing benefits.

"Yes. We've been defending. Keeping our heads down."

"If we'd gotten down among you—" Cortez started.

Kris cut him off. "But you didn't."

"But we didn't," he echoed. "Yes, I agree to a cease-fire for two hours. Does that satisfy you?"

"For this valley, or the swamp side of the ridge as well?" Kris asked. The quiet here was still broken by the sound of gunfire from the other side of the ridge.

"Just how low are your farmers on ammunition?"

"Low on ammunition?" Kris echoed back a doubting question. The prime minister would have been so proud of his daughter's skill at lying with a straight face.

Colonel Cortez snorted. "So be it. A cease-fire between all my forces and all those under your command. Can you guarantee the behavior of your irregulars, Lieutenant Longknife?"

"They've followed my orders so far. Corporal, take this flag of truce to the other side of the hill. Tell them what has been agreed upon here. And tell any of our volunteers that they are free to render medical aid to anyone who will accept it."

"Yes, ma'am," the comm tech said. She saluted, then paused. "Are you comfortable without this parley flag, Your Highness?"

Kris glanced at the colonel.

"I'll roast the eyes of any of those psalm singers who toss a shot our way. But don't worry. I doubt any of them could hit a barn door at this range."

Kris was tempted to commiserate with him. Certainly, her farmers shot no better. Instead, she said, "Now who is stalling?"

The colonel nodded. "And you came out here to tell me . . ."

"Have you talked with Captain Thorpe recently?" Kris began.

"No. I've been kind of busy of late, and we weren't exactly on the best of terms after what you did to us this morning."

"I'd say I was sorry about that, but I don't really feel that way," Kris admitted.

"So what about old Captain Bligh?"

Kris thought only the junior officers called him that. "He's no longer in orbit," she said softly.

Cortez shook his head. "Thorpe would never run from a fight. He'd never desert us," the colonel snapped, but his eyes had gone to the sky.

"I have it on good report that rather than fight the *Wasp*, he broke out of orbit and is running for the nearest jump point." That last was a guess, but if Thorpe really was running, why head for the farthest?

"You've talked with your captain?"

"No, my comm tech did."

"And you just sent her off on an errand. I'd love to see her tell that lie to my face."

"What did Thorpe's ship have? A pair of eighteen-inchers? I saw those lasers fired. They couldn't have been larger."

"Yeah, that's all our moneymen would go for." The colonel looked like he'd gladly throttle those men, but it was clear, he was slowly being beaten down by the thought that he'd been deserted, left holding the hot potato for this whole affair.

"My *Wasp* sports four twenty-four-inch pulse lasers, standard Navy issue. It has Smart Metal™ shields. Do you really think Thorpe would have stood a chance in a fight?"

Cortez started to say something, then swallowed it. What he got out was "You know, I'll have to wait until Thorpe is due over again before I will even consider surrendering."

Kris nodded. "He should be overhead before the cease-fire is done. But I suspect my *Wasp* will be here first." And alone.

A couple of Marines trotted by, equipped only with packs and bags marked with red crosses, stars, and crescents. Kris and the colonel watched civilian men and women bustle by, some carrying the small bags that have ever marked doctors, others carrying baskets of linens torn into bandages.

"I don't know how you're feeling about now," the colonel finally said. "But if I don't sit down, there's a good chance I'll fall down. And I don't think that would look good to any of those watching us over rifle barrels."

Kris easily folded her legs beneath her. "I'm glad you offered. I was only a second away from saying the same."

They sat there, in the torn and blasted grass, for a long minute, watching as white coats, Marines, and civilians rendered what aid they could to the wounded. From the other side of the hill blessed silence finally came.

After five minutes of quiet, and a sigh that sounded more Irish than Spanish, Cortez said, "Why don't you tell me your terms? I doubt I could get this command to defend itself against an angry troop of Girl Guides, much less a serious attack."

Kris had no trouble remembering the terms she and several elders had talked about last night. "You will surrender your weapons, munitions, and all equipment brought by you to this planet. All material seized by you will be returned to the civilians from which it came. Upon doing so, you will be treated and protected as prisoners of war. All enlisted ranks will be offered transportation to their planet of origin and returned there."

"That's pretty nice of you," Colonel Cortez said. "Is there a catch I'm missing?"

"All enlisted personnel will be made available to Panda employers and hiring centers who may offer them jobs at the going rate. Those that choose to accept employment will be treated as full citizens of Pandemonium."

The colonel raised an eyebrow at that. "Not a bad offer. By the way, will these employers and employment bosses care for my wounded and pay them while they recover?"

That caught Kris. Her pause went a bit long.

"You and the elders were talking about this last night, huh?" Kris nodded. The colonel's eyes actually sparkled for a second. "You didn't give much thought to what our two armies might look like today, did you?"

"I think that did kind of get overlooked," Kris admitted.

"You say that's for my other ranks. What about my officers?"

"They will have the option of local jobs," Kris said, then went on. "If they don't take it, or are not offered one, they are my prisoners, and I will deliver them to a mature justice system off Panda to try them for crimes against humanity."

"Oh, invading someone else's planet is a crime against humanity now?"

"It's either that or let some local hotheads just string them up."

"But we are your prisoners."

"And I said I would not permit it."

"Thank you, Lieutenant," he said, and seemed to mean it. For a moment he meditated on the terms. Then asked. "Am I included with the officers?"

"No, sir," Kris said. "You are my prisoner. You will face a court."

"I think I saw that coming. You need at least one hanging to discourage the others."

"Preying on small unaffiliated planets can't become a habit, sir. You must understand that."

The colonel rubbed his throat. "You can understand that I might see it differently from where I sit."

"I guess so." At the moment, Kris was seeing matters quite a bit differently from the way they had looked last night.

The colonel glanced around. Many of his troops were being carried to the rear. "You know, I always thought you Longknifes were all horse. No charge. You know what I mean?"

"Yes," Kris whispered.

"So it's my luck to run into a young one that's got a backbone and a good eye and knows how to use them."

"Your Captain Thorpe always seemed to look at me and see my father, Billy Longknife, the politician. Never my great-grandfather, Ray Longknife, the . . ." Kris paused.

"The legend," Cortez finished for her.

"Something like that. I'm still trying to figure out just what."

Cortez chuckled. "If you ever do, for God's sakes, young woman, don't tell a newzie."

"Kris," Nelly said. "The *Wasp* should be above the horizon anytime now. If they stopped the jamming, I might be able to pick him up."

"Right," Cortez muttered. "Don't need that anymore." He managed to get to his feet, faced his side, and shouted, "Turn off the jammers, Captain."

A man stood, and shouted up the hill, "Turn off the jammers, Sergeant." And the message passed up the hill and into the next valley. Kris made the same call back to her line, and a runner took off for the cave.

"So you ran Thorpe out of our sky," the colonel said. Kris nodded. "If I'd known what I was up against, I might have marched my battalion back aboard our transports and taken off, too. Ain't hindsight wonderful?"

"Did you think about doing that?"

"Hell no, woman. Run my battalion away from a few farmers! Even if they did have a Marine company behind them. No way I could run. Of course, that was the situation then. Now . . ." He paused. "But then hindsight is always a whole lot better than what you got going in."

A few moments of silence passed before Nelly announced, "I have the *Wasp*'s signal. Here is Captain Drago."

"Hey, things look a whole lot quieter down there, Kris. What you doing?" He sounded abysmally chipper.

"I'm having a little chat with Colonel Cortez. Whether we keep chatting or go back to shooting depends on what you say."

"Like Thorpe is hot to trotting out of here."

"Did you two shoot it out?" Cortez asked.

"Nope. I showed him my Smart Metal™ armor, and he folded without calling to see what I had under it. Flat folded and started running."

"The young lady down here told me you had twenty-four-inch lasers.

"Four of them."

Cortez's lips formed a bitter frown. "Being abandoned as I am, I have no choice but to accept your terms, Princess Longknife."

Kris held out her hand. The colonel took it. "If I had my pistol with me, I'd offer it to you."

"That pearl-handled automatic looks like a personal possession."

"It is."

"So long as you don't violate your parole and attempt to escape, feel free to keep it," Kris said.

"I'd have to be suicidal to run," he said, eyeing Kris's volunteers, who only now, at the sight of the handshake, were standing up from their firing positions.

Across the field, white coats stood, too. The battle was over. For some, it was lost. For some, it was won.

The wounded pleaded for succor. The dead asked only why.

43

Someone had once said that the only sight worse than a battle won . . . was a battle lost. Kris found that she and Cortez shared the burden of both.

Cortez organized his troops to gather most of the wounded at the upper end of the valley, close to where they fell. Kris spent a hurried hour sending all the Marine medical personnel who could be spared to them, then hunted up all the free local medics, medicine, and bandages, and sent them, too. Only then did she take a moment to begin organizing a camp for her troops.

At Peter Tzu's suggestion, that was also in this valley.

"Put yourself too close to the swamp, and the skeeters will eat you alive. There's an evening breeze off the hills that the little devils can't fly against."

So Kris's camp ended up not too far from the colonel's camp.

Kris almost didn't post guards around her prisoners. After all, where could they run, and her Marines were exhausted. Later that night, when a couple of drunken locals, grief maddened by the loss of one's girlfriend, the other's sister, tried to take it out on the unarmed troops, Kris was glad she had.

Next pass, Captain Drago dropped a shuttle full of all the medical supplies he had, and three of mFumbo's docs, who were actually doctors. That was good, because few of the locally trained medics were prepared for the destructive power of modern weapons. For so many of the wounded they were doing their best, but it was heartbreakingly far from enough.

Sergeant Bruce organized himself a convoy and took off at full speed with a dozen volunteers and a sergeant from the Jerusalem Rifles to contact those left to guard the trucks. They loaded the medical supplies left behind, then added any food available, and were back before supper. The medical gear was much appreciated; the three docs had just about exhausted what they'd brought down. All through the afternoon and evening, they lost patients. Now, with morphine, at least no one died screaming.

While the medics fought their private battles with death, most of the rest of the volunteers were overflowing with joy or exhaustion . . . or both. The animals that had died that noon provided the beginnings of a victory feast. Trucks headed out to nearby farms to get greens, fruit, and other trimmings. They returned with whiskey and beer as well, and the celebration got down and serious.

They had a lot to celebrate. The volunteers' casualties had been amazingly light. Twenty-six dead and eighty-four wounded. Three Marines died holding the observation post. The two that held it to the end were severely wounded and the first on the table when the three docs set up shop. Gunny lost two dead and a dozen wounded holding his ridge. Jack's platoon in the rice paddies retrieved three dead and sent another dozen to sick bay. Kris's middle platoon added a half dozen wounded to those lost at the OP.

Kris's rump company just kept getting smaller.

Come suppertime, Kris was grabbed by Bobby Joe Fronour and Gramma Polska and steered to a long table set up a bit away from the cook fires. "We need to talk," was all they said.

"What are we supposed to do with that mound of rifles and armor?" Gramma Polska asked. "We own it now, but there's not one living soul on this planet that knows what to do with it."

"You've got the right to recruit anyone you want, except Colonel Cortez," Kris said, noticing that he'd also been "invited" to the senior table.

"You could do a lot worse than hiring Major Zhukov," he said. "Ivanovich knows the gear and how to train soldiers in its use. Him, a few junior officers, and senior NCOs, and you'll have the start of an army."

"If we can trust this major of yours," Red said. Clearly, anything Cortez said was the last thing he'd ever do.

"It's your call," Kris said. "But you can't count on me being around the next time two ships show up."

That got the entire table talking. Most of the folks at their dinner couldn't agree on anything. That they'd better do something was a solid consensus.

When the table talk was down to a dull roar, Bobby Joe turned to Kris. "What's this United Sentients confederation your great-grampa Ray is setting up?"

Kris gave a quick explanation, careful to point out that exactly what it was—an alliance, a confederation, or a federal authority—was yet to be determined. "The planets with reps on Pitts Hope right now are the ones who will decide it all."

"Like we ought to be there right now," Red said, and spat.

"Yes, like we ought to," Gramma Polska said. "We certainly should be."

"You'll need a planetary government," Kris pointed out.

"We'll need a planetary government to control our own defenses," Bobby Joe said. "All that armor and rifles won't be worth nothing if we don't set up some sort of militia."

"I'm willing to command it," Red offered, and ducked as all at the table, except Kris and Cortez, tossed food his way.

"How long you going to be here?" Bobby Joe asked.

"I have cargo your son bought that needs to get down here. As soon as I can do that, I've got to get back to Xanadu."

"You opening up that can of snakes?" Gramma Polska asked.

"Have to. Human space is expanding. They're sitting on a major set of jump points. They can't stay a Hermit Kingdom."

Bobby Joe raised his mug of beer. "Good luck on that one."

The table joined in the sentiment.

The *Wasp* was under way five days later at one gee. The *Feathered Serpent* had a prize crew on board, was fueled and in need of a new name. Because of its weaker engines, it boosted for the same jump point at only half a gee. Kris intended to declare the empty troop transport forfeit as soon as they got back to Cuzco; the money would go to Panda.

Aboard the *Wasp* was only a single prisoner—Cortez. All his survivors, including Major Zhukov, had been offered jobs on Panda. Many had three to choose from. None turned them down.

And yes, Zhukov and several other officers and NCOs were training a National Guard for Panda . . . under the close watch of Gramma Polska and Red. They'd be reporting to the federal government on Panda . . . just as soon as Panda agreed what that government would look like and be allowed to do.

Aboard the *Serpent* were representatives of most of the major clans on Panda, empowered to look into membership in United Sentients. The sale of the *Serpent* would buy them tickets to Pitts Hope. They had no other source of funds; Thorpe had taken off with everything of value they had that wasn't too heavy to lift.

But first Kris had to see how the hornet's nest she'd knocked over on Xanadu was coming along.

Not eager to think about that, and knowing she had some serious fence-mending to do with the boffins, Kris spent most of her breakfasts, lunches, and dinners with them for the first two days. "Yes," she promised, "just as soon as we drop off everything at Cuzco, we'll head out, and I do mean *way out* beyond the Rim."

Which wasn't believed at all by the scientists, who took turns telling Kris just how important their bit of research was. Kris did a lot of listening. She didn't understand a lot . . . but she listened.

So it was just before the jump to Xanadu that she had her first meal in the wardroom.

And found Cortez at the head of the table.

"Why aren't you in the brig?" Kris demanded.

Cortez looked to Jack, and the Marine captain stood up. "Ah, Kris, we'd just be serving him the same food. And—" Now Jack glanced around the room, and Kris did, too.

The mess was full. Captain Drago was at the main table; most of his bridge staff was scattered around the room. The young Marine lieutenant who'd done such a good job in decoy duty on Panda was at the foot of the table, along with Gunny and most of the Marine NCOs. Penny and Abby were sitting close to the colonel. And Cara was next to his elbow!

"And?" Kris said, giving Jack the frown she'd learned from her father, right after she was found with her pudgy three-year-old hand in the cookie jar.

"And," the Marine captain continued, after taking a deep breath, "we're having the . . . ah, well, some really interesting and informative discussions. I feel like I'm getting Command and Staff College courses delivered through a fire hose."

"Your prisoner is quite an interesting military historian," Captain Drago added.

"And it's not like he can go anywhere we aren't going," Penny pointed out.

"And he's a lot more fun to listen to than some old vid lecture," Cara added.

The colonel took a sip from his coffee cup, then said, "I do sleep in the brig. Having slept on the ground with no blanket, I assure you, your brig is quite comfortable."

Kris headed for the steam table, drew herself a tray and plate, and started down the line, filling it. "And what is the topic for tonight?"

"*Bocage*, Your Highness. Or hedgerows if you prefer. In the last great European Civil War, midtwentieth-century Earth, the subsequent victors landed on the French coast in an area with thousand-year-old hedgerows. Age and substance had made them just as impenetrable as that mountain you dug into. The attacking side had an impossible time advancing through these hedges and thought they'd made a terrible mistake. What they failed to see was that the hedges had two sides. The subsequent losers wanted to launch their own counterattack and throw them back into the sea. The hedgerows did not let them do that."

"And that helped them how?" Kris said, and knew she was hooked. To make matters worse, they reserved a seat at Colonel Cortez's elbow for her, and before long, Cara was sitting at Kris's feet, resting her head on Kris's knee.

One old colonel and one twelve-year-old were worming their way into Kris's heart. Well, maybe it might work for the girl, but just as soon as Kris had someone to turn Cortez over to, he'd leave the *Wasp* in handcuffs.

But for now, he was interesting to listen to.

A few hours later, they jumped into Xanadu space . . . and Kris found herself with a whole lot of nothing to listen to. The planet had gone even quieter than before. And now, it refused to answer their hails, even to tell them to shut up.

"Captain Drago, 1.5 gees, please," Kris said. "Chief Beni, put together a team of sensor magicians and crack that silence. I want to know something before I stick my head into whatever noose they've woven for me while we were gone."

"They've dug themselves a cave and pulled the hole in after them," Chief Beni reported for the sensor team that had

grown to include every boffin on board who might have something to add to the findings. The null findings.

"We aren't even finding the heat we found before," he added.

Kris thanked them for their effort, then let them leave before
she turned to her command team, which, at the moment, included one prisoner, Colonel Cortez. "So, any suggestions on
what we do now?" she asked.

Jack shook his head. "If there's no threat to our shuttles, I
suggest we land the Marines and have a look around," he said.

Cortez frowned.

"You have a problem with that?" Kris said.

"No, ma'am. It seems that you must do what you must do.
However, I am reminded that both Cortez and Pizarro marched
deep into the two empires they approached. It was a trap. The
natives intended to kill them. That both of them got out of it
alive and as conquerors was never the intent of the locals."

That left everyone with cheery thoughts.

From orbit they could not find the warm houses from before.
"It's winter down there, isn't it?" Kris noted.

Chief Beni nodded agreement. "Better put on your woollies,
Your Highness, when you go down there."

"Put on yours, too. You're coming with me. I want an immediate report on any noise, squeak, or peep."

"But I can work better up here," the chief pointed out.

"We'll be covered from here. You are going with me. Think
of it as an adventure."

The chief just shook his head, dolefully. "Adventures may
be fun for you, but I can do without them. People get killed on
your kind of adventures."

It was an honest thought, but not one Kris wanted to dwell
on, so she kicked herself off and headed for her stateroom and
Abby to get prepared for this newest of adventures.

It only took three shuttles to carry the troops down this time.
Sick bay was still full of Marines recuperating from their jaunt
down to Panda. Today's approach to Xanadu was well spread
out. Jack insisted the first shuttle be down and its Marines already deployed before the third shuttle came in with Kris.

Kris didn't much care for that, but, per his authority over her,
he could and did order it, and she had no choice but to follow her
security chief. Again, Kris was reminded how much she did not
like Grampa Trouble and Grampa Ray messing with her life.

By the time Kris finally rejoined the chief of her security detail, he had a whole lot of nothing to report.

"There's not one active electronic device, one beating heart within a klick, maybe two," Beni reported. He pulled an item from the top pocket of his battle armor, swung it around his head several times, then examined it. "No woodsmoke. I don't think there's so much as a candle burning in this town."

Kris looked up the street to where the temple towered over the lower buildings. If she was going to find anything, it would be there. She was about to give that order when Beni spoke.

"Hold it; I got a heartbeat. It's in that building," he said, pointing to a two-story building that, like everything in sight, had a garden growing on its roof.

Kris held back on the order; now might be a good time to let things develop. A figure climbed the stairs out of the building's basement. Like the people Kris had seen on their last stop, this one wore a kind of toga. Only as he made his way carefully toward Kris could she make out that he was a man. A man looking often back over his shoulder.

About halfway to Kris's perimeter, he started to jog as poorly as anyone middle-aged and out of practice. Kris, Jack, and Penny headed for him. Gunny came along with a squad of Marines.

As they approached him, he shouted in a harsh, out-of-breath voice, "You have to get out of here. And take me with you. Please, take me with you."

"What's going on here?" Kris demanded.

"No time to explain now. You must leave."

"I'm getting heartbeats, a couple of them," Beni shouted. "About half a klick farther out."

"You have to leave. They'll kill you. Kill me," the fellow shouted as he joined them.

Now Kris recognized the man. "Prometheus? Aren't you the official who was our first contact last time we were here?"

"Yes, yes I was. Now please, get back aboard your shuttles and go. And take me with you. Do it now, before they kill all of you."

"Kill us?" Kris echoed. "I don't think you understand the power we have."

"They will kill you. And me, now."

To add emphasis, a rifle spoke. The wind from its bullet buzzed by Kris's cheek.

"Guard detail," Gunny shouted, and a dozen Marines formed a shield wall in front of Kris with their armored bodies.

Three more rifle shots came in fast succession. A Marine went down, cursing, only to stand up and remove a large rifle slug from his shoulder armor.

"Snipers," was all Jack said.

Four M-6s snapped off single rounds. It was too far to hear the results, but there were no more rifle shots. None.

"Back to the shuttles. I think we need to talk to this man before we try to talk to anyone else here," Jack ordered.

"Assuming we do any talking here," Penny added.

The retrograde movement was handled smartly by the Marines. Kris and her new best friend ended up strapped into the first shuttle off. The *Wasp* dropped the fourth shuttle, loaded for bear with bombs and guns, to cover the liftoff of the last launch, but it wasn't needed. Once Kris and Prometheus were gone, the city went back to making a tomb seem like party time.

44

Kris let Chief Beni start the interrogation while their shuttle was still taxiing downriver to find a good takeoff run.

"How did you hide your heartbeat? How did those snipers keep themselves hidden?" he demanded.

"We may be crazy, but we are not stupid," the man snapped back. "We spent forty years seeking ways to make ourselves invisible to the coming alien hordes. Don't you think we can handle a few minor things like our heartbeats? We have electromagnetic blockers the rest of you haven't dreamed of."

The chief didn't look like he believed that, but with the evidence so recently rubbed in his face, he fell silent.

"Why do we have to take you with us?" Kris asked.

"Isn't that obvious?" the man sneered. "I am a rogue, worse than a nonbeliever. I have talked to you, whom the Guides have placed under interdict. My life is forfeit in the worst and slowest way possible. However, rather than let me escape or talk to you, they would let me die quickly, a bullet in the brain."

"And what is it that you are not supposed to tell us?"

The man did not snap a quick reply to that question. He hunched down, seemed almost to shrink in his seat. When he finally spoke, it was hardly a whisper. "I really don't know."

When he made no effort to expand on that, Kris relaxed into her own seat. The shuttle went to full boost, discouraging conversation. Kris let it ride.

Xanadu was a puzzle. It had been so to start with. It was only getting worse as they got deeper into it.

It took two orbits to get all the teams back aboard. Prometheus sat huddled in on himself in her staff room, guards at the exits. He'd emptied his stomach on the way up; never in microgee before, it did not go well with him. Kris had a boffin doc look in on him. He prescribed a pill. The man took it, and a cup of water, but turned down food and drink.

Kris settled into her chair, as Jack and Gunny glided in last. Abby, Penny, and Captain Drago had been there first, followed quickly by Professor mFumbo, who made a point of reminding Kris that research had been promised the number-one priority next.

Kris had no time for squabbles. She was busy replaying the previous visit to Xanadu, trying to figure out this change. Yes, she'd played her cards heavy-handedly in the face of obstinate rejection from the Guides. That would account for the general reaction. But why was this man here? What had changed for him?

"When we last stopped," Kris started slowly, "you and your son were our original contacts. Where is he?" Kris said, a guess. Maybe a shot in the dark.

"My son is gone," the man whispered.

"Gone where?" Kris asked.

Now the man looked up at her, eyes misting. "I do not know. He's gone. Not just out of town. He's left Xanadu!"

"We found people from Xanadu on Pandemonium," Penny said.

The man just shook his head. "You don't understand. Lucifer didn't run away. He left Xanadu with the Blessings of the Guides. That doesn't happen. He left with three dozen young men and women. Together. All with Blessings. Never have the Guides done that. And they took their burial shrouds with them. Shrouds and a handful of dirt from our family garden. They will not come back alive." Now he raised his eyes to Kris's.

"Not unless you can do something to save my son. Will you? Please don't tell me that I've thrown away everything I hold dear to save my son, and you won't help me."

The temptation to give a snap, "Yes, of course," was hard on Kris's lips. But throwaway words would be a travesty in the face of this father's begging. He'd given up everything he believed in for his own flesh and blood. If Kris made him a promise, she'd better be willing to redeem it with the same coin.

Kris looked around. While Prometheus had been talking, Colonel Cortez drifted in and pulled himself down into a chair near the door. He took in the man's grief with sad eyes.

Jack, however, showed what she saw on most faces. This man was a nutcase. He might have just walked away from a can of nuts, but just why was much open to doubt and not worth anyone's blood.

That was it. The Marines had just paid a high price for a planet's freedom. This man would have to trump that if he wanted them to take a bullet for him.

Kris measured her next words with a laser range finder. "Mr. Prometheus, let me see if I understand you." The man locked eyes with her. Kris had often held people's attention at political rallies, command meetings. She'd never held anyone's attention as tightly as she did this man's.

"Your son has left Xanadu. Something that never happens."

He nodded.

"He did so with a few dozen other youths on a mission for the Guides. A mission that they all believe will be suicidal."

Again, the man in the toga nodded.

"But you have no idea what that mission is."

Prometheus leaned back in his chair, took a deep breath, and let it out slowly. "Correct," he said, then added, "except that my son told me that they'd set the nonbelievers to such a war among themselves that the aliens would hardly find a dozen eyes to boil when they got here. He mentioned that once, then got quiet." The man's eyes lit up. "Could that help you?"

Jack shook his head. "Sir, human space has a hundred powder kegs just waiting to explode. Kris here has personally yanked a half dozen sputtering fuses out of as many kegs."

The light went out of the eyes of the father.

"But," Kris put in, "we are in the habit of chasing fuses and pissing on them. Hasn't made us a lot of friends," she said to a general chuckle around the room. "If your son has just become a fuse, or a set of tracks that will lead us to one of those fuses, I think you can count on us looking into this."

"Can you save my son's life?"

Kris reflected on the trail of death and gore she'd left over the four years of her Navy career. That sent a shiver down her spine. "I can try, sir, but I can't promise anything."

She glanced around her table. None would tell this father that he'd come to the right person to plead for someone's life. People died around Kris. Friends, enemies, Kris was an equal-opportunity totem of death. She hadn't set out to be that, but there was something about the name she bore. Longknife.

People who got too close to a Longknife got dead.

"Captain Drago, set course for Cuzco," Kris said. "It's big. Maybe they can tell us the latest in rumors."

"And we can find out about our prize money," the ever-piratical captain added.

45

The *Wasp* docked at High Cuzco station just in time for a late supper. That was perfect, since the principal partner in Cut, Throat, and Hack insisted on doing his talking to "Her Highness," over dinner, not in his office.

"Why should we tie ourselves to the salt mines? That's for the lesser people." The man, likely older than her father, gave off strong hints they might make an evening of it.

Kris took an immediate dislike to the fellow. Not yet an intense dislike, but she suspected the night was yet young.

"You're not going without a security detail!" Jack insisted.

"I'm going on a date with my lawyer. Why should I need a security detail for a date on a safe station like High Cuzco?"

"Little lady, you weren't safe on a date on New Eden, the gun-control capital of human space," Jack pointed out.

Kris refused to laugh at his joke. "Krätz and the *Surprise* aren't alongside, are they?"

"No, so Miss Vicky Peterwald is probably elsewhere plotting murders we know nothing about."

"And which need not concern us. No, Jack. This Morley Preston wants some private words with me. I want to hear them. I do not want him surrounded by my henchmen. Understood?"

Jack growled, "I hear you."

"Good." Kris surveyed herself in the full-length mirror; Abby had outdone herself. Kris almost looked beautiful . . . to her own eye. The nose was still too large. But the padded push-up bra made good use of what little Kris had, using it to catch the male eye, then switching to padding for what wasn't on full display. And none was explosive; Kris had double-checked that.

Cinched at the waist, the blue ensemble flared out to sway

nicely when she walked and give her plenty of space if she needed to run. It also hid her automatic very nicely.

Kris wasn't totally stupid.

Captain Drago appeared at the door of her stateroom. "There's a Morley Preston, Esquire, waiting on the quarterdeck for you. He says he's your date for tonight."

"Those words," Jack spat.

"I'm quoting," the captain insisted.

"Kris, this is a bad idea."

"Now, Jack," Kris said, "if he gets out of hand, I'll break both his arms and one leg and walk home, okay?"

"What's wrong with shooting him?" Jack asked.

"And leave that mess for the waiters to clean up, Jack? People talk about me enough. I simply will not add anything unnecessary to all the rumors." So saying, Kris gave Jack a peck on the cheek . . . and got a whiff of him. All man. Why hadn't he invited her out for the evening? Now *that* would be a date.

Abby handed Kris a wrap that was gossamer thin.

"Gosh, Princess, you look beautiful," came from a certain twelve-year-old peeking from behind Captain Drago.

"Abby, you've got to teach that girl a proper appreciation for classical beauty. And that flattery will get her nothing around me."

"Well, baby ducks, you may not think yourself a beauty, but what I done with you sure qualifies for beau-dacious."

Kris couldn't argue with that.

Jack did not follow Kris to the quarterdeck. Caption Drago did only long enough to remind her . . . again . . . to look into the matter of prize money for the pirate ship they'd captured. And to report that the *Serpent* had just jumped into the Cuzco system.

"With you running us at 1.25 gees and them keeping to an economical .5 gees, I'm amazed they aren't farther behind."

"I'll also look into selling that ship," Kris said.

"I hope the Cuzco legal system doesn't tie the *Serpent* up in legal limbo," the captain said.

"I hadn't thought of that." And she'd better, or whoever tried to steal Panda might get by with paying even less for the lost gamble.

Morley Preston was not exactly waiting for her on the quarterdeck. He was talking to someone on net, talking quite forcefully. "Stand up to them, George. They're robbing us blind. You'll never make partner giving away our clients' lifeblood." His pacing took a turn at that point that brought Kris into view. "Now, I'm having dinner with a very attractive young lady. Talk to me in the morning. And bring me good news."

He blinked, which may have been his way of cutting the connection, and with the blink took on a totally different persona. The angry man was gone; a gracious host took his place. The man's bio said he had five years on Kris's father. If so, then his years had been much more kind. There was no gray in his black hair. His belly would fit comfortably on a Marine, though Kris suspected they earned the flat quite differently.

And he smiled, a toothy affair that involved most of his face. Kris should have felt warmth.

She didn't.

Maybe it was the quick change from anger to smile. Or how lightly the smile fit, like it might blow away at any moment.

Kris offered him a wholehearted smile, teeth flashing, and took his offered hand.

"There are so many quality restaurants to choose from," he said. "We have a reputation across half of space for fine food."

"It's your station," Kris said lightly. "Point me where you want to go."

"Well, I'm a simple man at heart. Meat and potatoes. What do you say to a little place that treats a steak so well that steers are lining up at the back door to get in the meat locker."

Having once stocked a meat locker for a restaurant, Kris found the exaggeration almost funny. She suppressed the laugh, and said, "Lead on."

The steak was as good as promised. Smothered in mushrooms and peppers and a sauce that did not overpower the beef but brought out its flavor and expanded on it, Kris ate it with a fork. Mr. Preston dominated the table conversation. He knew business. He and Grandfather Al would have enjoyed the time. Kris enjoyed the steak.

When Morley did invite Kris to carry the conversational ball, she talked about what the boffins wanted to do in the coming voyage of discovery. Kris hadn't realized she'd captured so much of what the scientists told her until she realized what she was saying was boring her dinner partner if not to tears, at least into changing the conversation.

Mr. Morley Preston enjoyed talking about Mr. Morley Preston and he knew his topic endlessly. But among all the dross he threw her way, there was an occasional gold nugget.

"You're not really planning on jumping to Birridas, are you?"

"Is there a problem? It has a half dozen jump points and the shortest one to a nebula that most fascinates my boffins."

"You might want to take a detour. It just joined the Greenfeld Alliance. A rather sudden arrangement. Poor fools placed a contract for a full space-defense system before the breakup. A half dozen firms on Cuzco formed a consortium to bid on it, too, but Peterwald undercut us." He almost spat that.

"Turns out there was more riding on the contract than just money. The defense system started late and stayed behind schedule. So there was nothing to present a counterargument when a Greenfeld battle squadron showed up last month and suggested they join the Alliance."

"That's a story we hear a lot," Kris said, thinking *detour*.

"Strange thing is, I understand Henry Peterwald was very excited about the new addition to his empire. There's the red-striped hornlizard that roams South Continent. A real nasty beastie. Henry's already off to hunt it. I hope they get that planetary defense up before he gets there."

Kris didn't give much thought to the space-defense system. If a battle fleet took it, it was likely still in orbit. But a new planet, just occupied and not fully broken to its slavery? And a fast, deadly monster to hunt? How many ways can a man die?

And if you threw in a few dozen young kids on a suicide mission from their Guides . . . ?

Kris swallowed a bite of steak and let her lawyer talk of anything he wanted to. She'd learned early on to ignore mere noise. Now, sharp edges, bullets, and lasers. They were real. Those she did not ignore.

Somehow that flat stomach of his didn't require him to pass up dessert. While he enjoyed a magnificent confection of chocolate and nuts, Kris paid tentative honor to a fruit dish.

And got down to business.

"I assume you recall the matter of the pirate ship we brought in under prize crew last time we visited?" brought a chuckle and "I've done little else but deal with it since last you were here. Do you have any idea how old the admiralty rules of prize are? They've never been applied to space."

"I believe they were applied a bit ago. By a court on Chance if my memory is right."

"Yes, yes, I know about that. My clerk had the devil's own time looking up that case. Chance is not the center of the law. Or center of anything. Their case law hardly sets precedent. Now, don't get me wrong, I'm not saying that to you. I'm just telling you what the lawyers of a half a dozen involved parties are telling me." And he proceeded to exhaust a quarter hour telling her all the things that she did not want to hear.

"So when do you think this will be settled?" she finally got in edgewise.

"I have no idea, though a trial balloon is being floated about. What with so many interested parties, maybe the best thing would be to sell the ship and distribute even portions from that sale to all the parties," he said with a brilliant smile.

For the next ten minutes he expounded about the splendor of this idea. One that, if Kris was right about the price of ships and the cost of lawyers, would probably yield enough to pay off all the lawyers' bills and not much more.

Kris spent the time reviewing her options and modifying her action plans. The *Feathered Serpent* must not present its papers to the port master of High Cuzco. Between Abby and Drago, they ought to be able to reflag that ship over the next day or so.

The papers needn't be perfect, just good enough to get the ship a load of fuel and on course for Wardhaven territory.

Colonel Cortez was another problem. She'd planned to turn him and his legal problem over to the fine fathers of Cuzco. When Morley finally ran down, she tentatively asked his advice.

"Oh, you crossed swords with a filibusterer. And lived to sit here in such a lovely dress and tell me about it. You must have some brilliant Marines to handle your dirty work for you, Your Highness. Absolutely brilliant."

Kris saw no reason to claim that she'd gotten her own lovely hands dirty. Abby had said many bad words as she'd spent much of the trip back restoring what she called Kris's "princess skin."

"Your Highness, I've heard about these things. Never drawn up a contract for such an expedition, though I must say a contract to hold up among thieves would be truly a work of art."

Kris was willing to bet money, good Wardhaven dollars, that the original boilerplate contract for this kind of thing had been done by Morley Preston, Esquire, himself.

Kris cut through the jungle of verbiage with a simple question. "Do you think the ground leader of such an expedition could get a fair trial here on Cuzco?"

The man didn't even bat an eye. "Oh my, of course, Your Highness. He would get the fairest of trials. I'd even take him on pro bono, assuming he agreed to sign a contract to let us agent him once we've got him off with parole and community service. I suspect many people would pay well for his advice on what to do . . . and not do in a matter like that. The successful ones say so little. He'd be quite a moneymaking profit center."

Kris stood. Dinner was over. Indeed, if she didn't get this snake out of her sight, her dinner was likely to end up all over the front of him . . . a not-unpleasant thought at the moment.

Morley stood. "But I was hoping that you and I might enjoy the evening. You've been so long aboard ship, and I understand that as captain, you can't, you know, enjoy some of the more pleasant aspects of adult life."

Kris was examining just how she'd break two arms and a leg. But she'd spotted Jack in civvies holding down a table with a woman Marine. Gunny stood only a second after Kris did.

The good guys had not let her out of their sight. And knowing them, they'd probably feel obliged to help clean up her mess. No, she'd keep her dinner down . . . and put this maggot behind her. NELLY, MAKE A NOTE. I WILL NEVER DO BUSINESS WITH ANY FIRM INVOLVING MORLEY PRESTON AGAIN.

NOTE TAKEN. I AM ADVISING NUU ENTERPRISES OF YOUR DECISION.

Turning her back on the lawyer, she marched for the door. Quickly, her security detail formed on her. Only when she was out of the restaurant, and far from the air sullied by that man, did she slow down.

Jack came up on one side of her, Gunny the other. She took both their arms. "I am so glad to see you two."

"That bad," Gunny said.

"I am so glad I'm sharing my life with a bunch of heartbreakers and hard cases the likes of you," she said. She would have loved to rest her head on Jack's shoulder, but there was a limit to what an officer could do, even away from the ship. Even when she was dressed up for a night on the town and so was he.

There was a lot to hate about what she did. The terror. The blood. The killing. The dying.

But there was a lot to like about it, too. Sometimes she got to stop some of the really bad stuff from happening, like Panda. And she got to do it with the likes of men and women like those around her.

She'd put up with a lot of long cruises for that.

46

Back at the *Wasp*, there was no rest for the wicked. Late as it was, Kris roused her staff and went immediately to work.

Abby showed up in a wrap and fuzzy slippers. "Cara likes them," was all she said. Colonel Cortez was halfway through a yawn when he caught sight of Kris's outfit. It is possible for a grown man's eyes to bug out.

"We've got problems, ladies and gentlemen," Kris said by way of preamble, "and several of them need action now." She filled them in on the legal mess revolving around their prize money.

Captain Drago muttered a curse when Kris finished.

"Can't sell the *Feathered Serpent* here," Penny said.

"My opinion exactly," Kris said. "We have to refuel her here, but we need to get her to United space ASAP."

"I'll start forging her new papers," Abby said. "If they only have to stand up to a couple of port calls, that shouldn't be too big a problem. Once they drop the reps off at Pitts Hope, the crew can take the *Serpent* to Chance, get her declared forfeit, and we'll have an ironbound set of papers for her."

"Now there's the problem of Birridas," Kris said.

"Birridas?" Professor mFumbo echoed. He'd just come in. Dressed in a red smoker's jacket, complete with a never-lit pipe, he looked quite debonair. And suddenly very worried. "Your Highness, Birridas is the shortest way to the Ferret's Head nebula. I do remind you that you promised that research would be the next priority. And would be for at least two full months."

"Yes, Professor, and I will not renege," Kris said. "But there's a problem on Birridas." Kris quickly filled them in.

"I see," Professor mFumbo said. "I agree on the detour. It may add a few days to our run, but what must be must be."

Around the table, that seemed to represent a universal consensus.

"Excuse me," Kris said, "but you misunderstand me. We *are* going to Birridas."

The room exploded into dead silence.

"Kris, are you crazy?" Jack asked.

"No more than usual," Kris said.

"Yes, this is more than usual," Jack snapped. "Kris, this man has been trying to kill you since, well, forever. He probably paid the kidnappers of your brother Eddy."

"I know," Kris said, with a shiver.

"Kris, those were his battleships at Wardhaven," Penny whispered softly.

"I know," Kris repeated.

"And besides, Kris," Jack continued, talking slowly as to a stubborn child, "if Henry Smythe-Peterwald XII does finally get himself killed, we don't want a Longknife within fifty light-years. You do not want to go to Birridas."

"I don't," Kris said, "but answer me this. Where do you think Prometheus's kid and the Xanadu nuts are headed?"

"Most likely Birridas," Jack agreed. "I know you'd love to pull out a miracle for that poor man, but Kris, you got to make tracks away from this one."

"I can't, Jack, because my fingerprints are already all over the future death of Henry Peterwald, twelfth of that name."

That brought blank stares from the table. All but one. Penny's eyes lit up. "Oh . . . I see."

"You tell them, Penny."

All eyes were on her. She spoke slowly. "Whether one of the kids actually kills Mr. Peterwald, or not, doesn't matter. They're bound to be swept up in the dragnet before his body is cold. That creates a line back to Xanadu, and Kris has been on Xanadu twice in the last month."

There was a long pause when Penny finished. As the mess they were in dawned around the table, heads began to shake slowly. "We are so screwed," Captain Drago muttered for all.

"Couldn't you just send a warning?" Professor mFumbo asked.

Kris shook her head. "Even if we did, it could be taken as us just trying to cover our tracks. At best, they might credit us with having gotten cold feet on an op after we turned it loose, and we're trying to help them close it down. Either way, it's us killing Peterwald in the end. *I* have to go."

Jack was still shaking his head. "Oh Lord, Kris. You expect to come racing in, shouting that there's a plot to kill Henry Peterwald, and be believed?"

"I have to try.

"I can have the ship under way in thirty minutes, Your Highness," Drago said, rising from his chair.

"Make it so, Captain." He left to do just that.

"Let's see what other loose ends I have," Kris said, and turned to Colonel Cortez. "Prisoner, I had planned to turn you over to Cuzco justice." He stuck his hands out for the cuffs.

"You're going to be staying aboard for a while," got a frown from the colonel. "It seems my shyster is confident he can get you off with a wrist slap. He's already gleefully planning your career as a consultant to future filibustering expeditions. With a fifteen percent take for him."

"I was expecting as much," Cortez said.

"So I'm not letting you off my ship. Not here, at least."

"Thank you, ma'am."

"Thank me?" Kris said, surprised by the man.

"Yes. I made a mistake, getting involved with that mess. I'd hate to be trapped in it for the rest of my life."

Kris didn't know whether to believe him or not. Still, she had a prisoner on her hands, one with skills she was using.

"Penny, correct me if I'm wrong, but aren't POWs who work supposed to be paid for that work?"

"I believe that is required," the kid of a cop answered.

"Abby, after you repaper the *Serpent*, work up a contract hiring the colonel as a consultant in military affairs."

"What kind of pay scale?" the maid/intel weenie asked.

"Something appropriate for a colonel."

Cortez chuckled. "Make it a short-term temporary appointment," he said. "I'm sure the princess will find some judge to take my case. Maybe at this Chance place, where you're sending my troop transport."

"We'd never send you to Chance," Penny said.

The colonel's smile was replaced by puzzlement.

"You see, Colonel," Jack said, "the last time Kris was there, the Peterwalds tried to take over Chance. The folks there really objected to that."

"I see," the colonel said.

"Not really, you don't," Penny added. "It came to a fight, and in that fight, Mr. Peterwald's son was killed."

"Oh my," Cortez said, then a light seemed to dawn. "The son of the man your princess is hell-bent on saving?"

"The very same," Abby said. "Now you see how big a bucket of horse pucky we are in."

"Holy Mother of God," the old soldier said.

"All hands, set getting-under-way details," said the MC1.

47

The trip to Birridas was uneventful. As it turned out, the *Serpent* had none of the necessary gear to forge ship's papers. The *Wasp*, of course, had two sets, one in Abby's cabin, the other in Captain Drago's stateroom. Why was Kris not surprised?

The only important decision that had to be made involved the ship's acceleration. Kris ordered 1.5 gees. She expected complaints from the boffins, but wound up facing Gunny instead.

"Ma'am, I assume you want as many Marines ready for duty as possible when we get there."

"You got that right, Gunny."

"Well, we've got almost a score of shooters in sick bay, ma'am. They need to start physical therapy, Doc tells me, and he was hoping we could cut their weight down to .85 gees."

Kris coordinated with Captain Drago. Twice a day, the ship reduced acceleration. Three times a day, at every meal, Sulwan Kann, the ship's navigator, told Kris just how much trouble it was reworking her course around it.

But the Marines got their therapy. Kris wanted every available trigger-puller up and running when they hit Birridas.

As soon as they jumped into Birridas space, they were hailed and told to go away. "This space is closed to any ship not a Greenfeld warship."

Captain Drago once more proved himself the biggest teller of tall tales in human space. They got permission to dock for emergency repairs. But no one would be permitted to disembark. No one. And there would be guards posted at their gangway.

No one got off.

Of course, Drago didn't mention that Kris Longknife, putative killer of Peterwald scions, was on board. Kris figured once that word got out, guards assigned to keep folks on the *Wasp* would have a new assignment. Storming the *Wasp*.

Kris was strapped into a seat on the bridge as Drago oversaw his ship's final approach to High Birridas. A view of the station showed almost finished laser emplacements, but few of them had the actual lasers installed. Kris suspected none were up and calibrated. Somewhere, a lot of people were working long hours finishing that delayed job.

The station's piers clearly showed the effect of the recent changeover. Every dock had a Greenfeld ship tied up.

Kris spotted only two empty slots, and watched as Drago maneuvered the *Wasp* toward one of them.

KRIS, YOU HAVE A CALL COMING IN.

FROM WHOM? Kris thought her presence here was still their little secret.

HE ASKED ME NOT TO TELL YOU. TRUST ME, YOU WANTS TO TALK TO HIM.

More proof that Auntie Tru needed to spend some quality time wandering around Nelly's bursting innards.

PUT HIM THROUGH, Kris thought with a sigh.

HI, KRIS. CAPTAIN KRÄTZ HERE. I SAW THE *WASP* HAD TALKED HER WAY IN AND FIGURED YOU MIGHT STILL BE ABOARD.

HOW ARE THE GIRLS, AND YOUR JUNIOR COMMUNICATIONS OFFICER?

THE GIRLS ARE FINE. LOOKS LIKE SOME WEDDINGS ARE IN A COUPLE OF THEIR FUTURES. GOOD MEN ALL. IT WILL BE A JOY TO MARRY THEM OFF. AND THE JUNIOR COMM WATCH STANDER PUT THIS CALL THROUGH. HER DAD WANTS HER ON SOUTH CONTINENT WITH HIM, BUT SHE'S IN NO HURRY. YOUR FILE SAYS YOU LIKE TO STAY CLEAR OF YOUR OLD MAN, TOO. GLAD MY GIRLS DON'T HAVE WHATEVER DISEASE YOU TWO GIRLS HAVE.

I LOVE TALKING FAMILY, CAPTAIN, BUT I DON'T THINK THAT'S WHY YOU CALLED.

NOPE, I FIGURED I BETTER WARN YOU. REAL SOON YOU'RE GOING TO BE ASKED TO DUMP YOUR REACTOR CORE AND OFF-LOAD ALL SHIP-STORED POWER TO THE STATION. THAT IN-CLUDES THE CAPACITORS FOR THE LASERS YOU DON'T HAVE.

"We're going to be asked to dump our reactor core before we dock," Kris said out loud.

"What?" was Captain Drago's reaction.

NELLY, GO PUBLIC WITH THIS CALL.

"Yes," Captain Krätz said. "Every ship tied up, including my *Surprise*, is cold reactor and empty capacitors. If I didn't know better, I'd think they didn't trust us."

"What could possibly make them think that?" Drago muttered.

At that moment, a harried man in a rumpled uniform appeared on-screen. Behind him stood a man in the impeccable black uniform of Greenfeld State Security. He had a machine pistol slung at his waist and looked all too eager to use it.

"As soon as you attach to the first dock tie-down, you must vent your reactor to space. Both of them. You still got an engine problem that just has to be worked on here."

"I told you I do." Drago tapped his commlink. "Engineering, prepare to vent all reactor contents to space. Be sure to do it away from the pier."

"You got it, boss."

The man disappeared from the screen.

"Thank you, Captain Krätz, for the warning," Kris said.

"I figured you'd like a bit of advance word. Your file says paranoia runs in your family."

"Understandable since someone does seem out to get us."

"I would know nothing of that."

"Speaking of that, you must be curious as to why I'm here."

"The thought did cross my mind," the captain said dryly.

"There is a plot afoot to kill Mr. Henry Peterwald."

"Do tell. There've been only four attempts this week. Three died in the act and one during interrogation. Mind you, none of that is in the papers. My security officer told me as a stern reminder that all of the restrictions on movement for my crew are indeed necessary."

"Four," Kris said, and glanced around the bridge. The clanking of the first-pier tie-down echoed through the hull. Some kind of hissing quickly joined it, and the lights flickered.

They were committed to Birridas. No turning back.

"Captain Krätz, were any of the assassins connected to either Xanadu or the Abdicator movement?"

"Good heavens, are those nuts still running around? But no, all were homegrown from Birridas. At least that's the story. Me, I suspect if they looked real hard at some of those entrails, they might lead back to the Palace. But dead men tell no tales."

"Xanadu does exist, and I've been there twice in the last month or so. It appears that a small tactical team of young enthusiasts has been sent from the Guides of the Abdicators to start a war. Our best guess is that it would involve killing your Peterwald."

"The Abdicators, ah . . ." There was a short pause as the captain consulted his own reference. "They were street-corner noisemakers. Never used terrorist tactics."

"Things have changed. The new and improved version does."

"Oh." Another long pause. "But how would killing Henry involve us in a war?"

"As I said, Captain. I've been to Xanadu twice in the last month or so. They are now here. I suspect that the whole business is intended to have Longknife fingerprints all over it."

The "Oh," this time let a lot of air out of the captain.

"Princess, I need to talk to my security officer pronto. Will you be available to talk later?"

"I've been told not to leave the *Wasp*. None of us."

"Right. You're under even tighter restrictions then we are. Give me a bit. I suspect State Security will want to talk to us. Oh, and I'm going to tell Ensign Victoria what you've just told me. We may have a direct line to the Palace if we need it."

"I think we will," Kris said.

The pier tie-downs echoed through the *Wasp* as each engaged. The sound was like a prison door slamming shut. Kris had been in some bad situations before. Never had she felt so vulnerable. Then came the demand to drain all ship's power to the station. She'd spent the last four years doing her best to stay out of reach of the Peterwald family.

Now she was totally in their power. Literally.

Kris's stomach was a sour void.

Then things got worse.

A half dozen men in State Security black showed up at the gangway and barged right across it. Four of them carried those nifty-looking machine pistols. At least they did have Captain Krätz with them.

And he had an ensign tagging along as aide.

From her conference room, where Kris watched the developments, she relaxed a little. She knew that ensign.

It got rather interesting when the Black Uniform Mafia ran into six Marines in full battle rattle on the quarterdeck. Rifles at port; bayonet's fixed.

Did a couple of those gun boys flinch?

Gunny stepped forward to greet them. "Do you have business on this ship, sir?"

"I am Colonel vin Martin to see the Longknife girl."

"You request an audience with Her Highness, Princess Kristine Longknife," Gunny corrected.

"May I remind you that you are in Greenfeld space, attached to a Greenfeld space station. We have no truck with princes."

Yet people talk freely of the Palace, Kris thought.

"I know where I am, Colonel," Gunny said with a gentle voice that rang solid steel. "May I point out that you are on board a Wardhaven warship bearing the great-granddaughter of King Raymond I of United Sentients."

The two men glared at each other. The colonel's glare was that of a dog, foaming at the mouth. Gunny's glare was more like the sun. *I'm here. Get used to it. And don't forget your SP 8,000 sunscreen.* The dog surrendered to the sun.

"Please advise this putative princess of yours that State Security requests and requires a meeting with her."

Gunny paused just long enough to give the impression he had received orders, then smiled. "You are granted an audience."

Kris glanced around her staff room. Nope, no throne in sight. And she was in the undress whites of a lieutenant. Getting the power flow going her way for this meeting would not be easy. She mashed her commlink. "Gunny, take the long way. I need time for prep." Without waiting for an answer, she changed. "Abby, I need my ribbons. Include the star burst of the Wounded Lion." Earth's highest honor ought to give any soldier pause to rethink with whom he's dealing.

"On my way," said her maid.

Kris glanced around. No way to make the table disappear. But . . . "Captain Drago, I want the chairs out of here. Chief, can you get these walls covered with deep space and stars. Oh, and lower the lights. Jack, I want you at my right hand. Can you get in dress red and blues."

"If Gunny includes a tour of the reactor," he said, already running."

"Make it faster," she called after him.

Captain Drago disappeared. Sailors got busy making chairs disappear. Abby appeared, and Kris stood to have the ribbons pinned on. A sailor made a grab for Kris's empty chair.

"No you don't. I stay seated," Kris growled.

Yep. Now if she just had enough time to get this dog and pony show set up, one obnoxious State Security colonel would find himself in a very interesting situation.

Jack returned, still buttoning his collar.

Captain Drago appeared . . . in the full-dress blues of a Wardhaven Navy captain. Kris glanced at his fruit salad. It showed the usual ribbons a good man would collect during the long peace. A couple of his tourist ribbons had V's for valor. Likely in combat. How had he managed that?

Then Kris remembered how she'd earned V's for her supposed tourist medals. Maybe the long peace hadn't been as peaceful as the history books claimed.

Leaving Kris to wonder if only blind people wrote histories.

"Reserve commission," Captain Drago said. "Inactive."

"Consider it activated for the next hour. We need to talk."

Striding in right behind Captain Drago came Colonel Cortez, in the dress red and black of Lorna Do.

"Reserve commission?" Kris asked.

"They didn't cancel it," he said evenly.

Which begged the question why the man had been beached in times like these. And why he hadn't been recalled.

Kris coughed. "We all need to talk. Really talk."

Penny was next in, now sporting dress whites and struggling with the choker collar. Jack lent her a helping hand. Even Abby was back. Where had she gotten Wardhaven dress blues?

They arrayed themselves on either side of Kris. Drago, Cortez, and Abby to her right. Jack and Penny to her left. At the door, Cara watched them, giggling softly.

"Child," Kris said severely, "go back to your room. Nelly, arrange a feed to her monitor."

"Yes, Kris," Nelly said.

"Yes, Auntie Kris," Cara said.

The kid exited to universal smiles from Kris's staff, so she didn't risk mutiny by chiding her. Kris did find herself relishing a strange addition to the mixture of feelings in her gut. She'd never been anyone's auntie before.

The measured tread of boots drew Kris's gaze to the far door of the room. The lights dimmed a bit more. The bulkheads and overhead now showed deep space and cold unwinking stars; it would be easy to succumb to vertigo.

Well done, Chief.

Six Marines in dress red and blues entered, M-6s at port arms, bayonets fixed. The black-uniformed colonel trailed them, his face a mask. So did his junior officer and four gun toters. One of them took one look around and swayed. Only a hand out to the shoulder of a statue-solid Marine kept him on his feet.

Captain Krätz followed up the rear, a bemused look on his face as he took in Kris's side of the room. Ensign Peterwald edged over to put her back against the wall and assumed a stiff parade rest. From where she stood, she could see everything, including the look on her captain's face and his body language.

Quick learner. Kris could only hope she stayed friendly.

From outside, Gunny's voice came clearly as he posted his six armored Marines at the door.

The colonel eyed Kris through narrow slits. Kris gave the colonel a wide-eyed look, as innocent as any she had ever managed . . . but said nothing.

The colonel finally broke eye contact with Kris to take in those around her. Kris couldn't tell who caused it, but his eyes widened and his nostrils flared.

Suddenly, Kris had a strong suspicion the colonel knew more about the people around her than she did. Kris caught the frown that caused before it made it to her face. Yes, she needed to talk to her crew. And she was getting tired of this colonel using her time to figure out things she wasn't in on.

"You wanted to see me, Colonel," Kris said, superior to junior.

The State Security man pulled his gaze away from someone and focused on Kris. "I am told that you have information about a plot against the life of First Citizen Smythe-Peterwald. If so, the state demands and requires that you provide it."

"I have already given all that I know to your Captain Krätz. If you have talked to him, you know as much as I do."

"I am required to hear it from the source's lips."

Kris considered making an issue of it but found she was running out of patience with a man who couldn't say a word without making it a demand. She quickly told him what she knew.

"That hardly constitutes quality intelligence," the colonel snapped. "It is no more than an allegation of rumors heard."

"You may take it as you please," Kris said. "But I assure you, if your First Citizen ends up suddenly dead in the next few days, your superiors may not take it that way."

The colonel swallowed. Hard. "Do you have a picture of this Lucifer fellow? The devil's own, he sounds like."

"The Abdicators do not believe in making representations of themselves," Kris said.

The colonel paused for only a moment before saying, "That was not their way when last they were heard from."

"Suicidal terrorism was not their way when last we heard from them, either," Kris said. And got a chip of a grin from Captain Krätz for quoting him.

Now it was the colonel's turn to frown. Kris suspected the prospect of going back to his bosses with nothing helpful to add to their pot of boiling paranoia did not excite him.

"There is one thing I can give you, Colonel."

"What might that be?"

"We have the boy's father aboard. I have no qualms about photographing a man. We have run it through a computer program to take the years off his face. Captain Drago?"

"Yes, Your Highness." He spoke into his commlink, and a short while later Sulwan Kann, in a Navy lieutenant's uniform, brought in a large envelope for the captain. He handed it to Kris. "As you requested."

Kris opened the envelope. There was an enlarged photo of Prometheus and a similar-size reworked photo. It looked amazingly like Lucifer, his son. Kris handed off the photos to Jack, who took them to the colonel.

"Colonel, I have personally met the young man you are hunting. That reworked photo is almost a perfect image of him."

"You have met the young madman?" A dozen indictments lurked behind those words, starting with high treason.

"He was a guide when I first visited his world. I did not see him the second time. His father says he had already left."

"Ah, yes, there is the matter of the father. You will turn him over to us for questioning." That wasn't quite an order. More like the assumption of someone who'd never been told no.

"No. He is on board in our care," Kris said, switching to the regal plural. "We are satisfied from our own questioning that he knows nothing more than what he has told us."

"You are in Peterwald space." Was that a slip, or was the fiction of Greenfeld so quickly overshadowed by the man?

"You are on a Wardhaven ship," Kris said, standing up to her full six feet and looking down a good two inches on the colonel. "And you will depart from it now."

Kris would not have believed that the Marines behind the State Security team could get stiffer, but there was a silent click in the air as they did. The young security captain broke his attention to glance around, worry breaking through his mask.

At the door, Gunny appeared, pistol now at high port.

The colonel held his ground for a moment, then seemed to shrink. "Your embassy will hear of this. I will go now, but I expect to return soon." *With a large army* hung unsaid.

The colonel did a smart about-face, and started to march out. Captain Krätz rested a hand on his shoulder as he went by. "I have had dealings with this woman before. I'll stay behind and see if I can't wangle her out of a trifle more."

"You can give her the spanking she deserves, but get that man," the colonel snapped, then continued his march out.

The others in State Security black were soon herded out. When the tread of Marine boots grew distant in the passageway, Kris relaxed. "Lights, Chief. It's too dark in here to think."

The lights went to full. The bulkheads gleamed gray again. And without an order given, chairs were hurriedly pushed in by sailors and Marines.

Kris's staff collapsed into the chairs and found themselves staring at each other. Kris had a very puzzled team . . . that now included a captain from her sworn enemy.

Oh, and his daughter.

Vicky settled into the chair at her captain's right hand. He'd taken the seat at the foot of the table, opposite Kris. "Have you really come here to save my dad's life?" Vicky asked.

"I don't see much choice in the matter. If your father is killed anytime soon, Lucifer and his team will paint my fingerprints all over the plot. Propagandists will demand I either stand a kangaroo trial here or war. Since I don't think King Ray would hand me over for a show trial, it looks like war."

"You don't sound all that sure about your king," Captain Krätz said, a knowing smile on his face.

Kris made a face. "Let's just say I don't want to find out. Grampa Ray has tossed me into a lot of messes, sink or swim. I'd prefer not to see how I could manage on Greenfeld."

"I wouldn't want to take my chances with what passed for a justice system back home, either," Vicky said. Then changed the subject. "How do we stop this devil boy from killing my dad?"

Captain Krätz was shaking his head. "I don't see that he has any chance of getting close to the First Citizen."

"I agree," Kris said.

"Now, hold it," Jack said, half out of his seat. "You dragged us out here to stop devil boy. I like her choice of words. But now you say he ain't likely to kill anyone. Kris!"

Kris just shrugged. Since Captain Krätz made no effort to talk, she explained. "Lucifer and his Xanadu team are fish out of water. They're hicks with hayseed in their hair. They can hardly open their mouths without getting arrested. No. There is no way they'll get close enough to Peterwald to kill him."

"And we're here because . . ." Jack said, sounding very tired.

"Because," Captain Krätz said, "they will be captured. Under interrogation, they will mention your Kris. If anyone kills Ensign Victoria's dad, the trail is set to lead straight back to Kris. Heads, they win. Tails, you lose."

Jack settled back into his chair, eyed the overhead, and muttered a long stream of curses.

Now it was Kris's turn to lean forward. "Who came up with the stupid idea of having Vicky's father go on safari on a half-pacified planet?" Kris asked.

It was Vicky who answered. "It could have been any number of factions. Dad prides himself on being 'The Mighty Hunter.' Show him something he hasn't killed, and he'll be off in a flash. When I heard Birridas was joining the Alliance, I would have bet Dad would be here hunting in no time."

Captain Krätz nodded along. "It was just that none of us thought he'd come before planetary defenses were in place. And the idea of not trusting the Navy to guard the planet. It's almost as if . . ." The captain could not finish that sentence.

"It's almost as if you were being set up for something," Captain Drago said. Then paused. "Wait one." Now his eyes fixed on the overhead as he listened to something. Then he stood. "Kris, I strongly suggest that we continue this conversation on the bridge. It seems matters are developing."

"What's happening?" came in a half dozen voices.

"It's quicker to see than to explain it," hung curtly in the air as Captain Drago rushed for the door.

Kris had had enough of stately pomp and pretensions; she sprinted right after him.

48

A breathless minute later, Kris's team arranged themselves in front of the main screen. A deadly serious Sulwan Kann explained what they were looking at.

"Three minutes ago, the FolkFestiva starliner *Dedicated Workers of Tourin* came through Jump Point Alpha. It did so at twenty thousand klicks an hour." That drew a low whistle from those qualified to know just how suicidal that was.

"Is that a problem?" Colonel Cortez asked.

"Only if you want to get where you're going," Captain Drago explained. "Jump points orbit two, three, six planets, and the influence of all of them affect the jump point, making them seem to wander aimlessly from the perspective of any one planet. A smart captain and navigator approach a jump carefully to make sure it hasn't moved. You approach it too fast, and you may end up at some planet halfway across the galaxy. If you've got a spin on your boat, it only gets worse."

Drago rubbed his chin thoughtfully. "Usually liners and expensive battleships tiptoe through a jump. Strange."

"And it's gotten stranger," Sulwan announced. "She's hit the accelerator—3.26 gees."

"No captain of a liner puts his passengers under that kind of acceleration," Captain Krätz said.

"So we assume that the *Workers of Tourin* is no longer under its captain's control," Colonel Cortez observed softly.

"Talk to me about the *Tourin*," Drago ordered.

Sulwan brought up the required specs.

"A million tons," Jack said. "Oh God."

"Five thousand passengers and crew." Penny's voice broke.

"How long before she gets here?" Kris asked, voice cold.

"Assuming the *Tourin* keeps accelerating, and does not flip and start decelerating," Sulwan said as the screen changed to reflect her words, "we've got seven hours, thirty-three minutes before it digs a big hole off the coast of South Continent."

"Where my dad's hunting," Vicky added.

"You'll have to get him out. There's time," Kris said.

"No," Krätz cut in. "There's a storm raging there. Think big, bad hurricane. It's got everything grounded."

Kris frowned. "Assassin's luck, or planned?"

Krätz shrugged. "It is the season for those things."

"So, seven and a half hours. How many ships can you get under way?" Kris asked, eyeing the Greenfeld captain.

Captain Krätz shook his head. "We told State Security that this dinky station's reactor would need a month to boil enough plasma to power up the fleet, but no. 'One of your ship's engineers might send his reactor critical and try to kill the First Citizen.' Every ship had to go cold steel. They are all a bunch of idiots," Krätz roared.

With effort, he recovered his temper. "And now it seems that some of them are traitors as well. We have been set up."

Captain Drago cleared his throat. "With all respect to the captain, there is one ship that can get under way."

"Who?" Captain Krätz demanded.

"Us," Captain Drago said, with a sly smile.

The Greenfeld captain frowned. Then his eyes grew wide for a moment before he growled, "You wouldn't do that?"

"The *Wasp* was rigged for that procedure last overhaul," Drago shot back. "We are an exploration ship. There was no way to foretell what our needs might be out beyond the Rim."

"That's insane. Worse, it's suicidal and mass murder."

"Not when properly done with modern power supplies."

Kris felt like she was watching a Ping-Pong match. Only she had no idea what it was that the two men were batting back and forth. "Would one of you mind," she shouted into the rapid fire of words, "telling the rest of us what you are talking about?"

For a moment longer, the two captains stood eyeing each other. Then Captain Krätz gave a curt wave at Captain Drago.

Drago, with a confident half bow, began. "Our four landers have antimatter cells. We can remove them and rig two of them to our auxiliary power supply generators. Those two will get the magnetic containment field up. Then we dump the other two into the main reactor and jump-start the fusion process," he said, proud as the calico cat that swallowed the Cheshire canary.

Kris eyed the only slightly controlled rage on the other captain's face. "Is your *Surprise* rigged with such capability?"

"Hell no," he shot back. "It would be a violation of Society of Humanity rules as well as Greenfeld regulations. For the last sixty years, since the old *Canopus* blew up herself and half the Borden station, it's been illegal. A hundred thousand died in one second."

Kris walked away from the two captains. One offered a solution . . . that might be suicide and murder. The other offered no solution . . . and demanded that this one not be tried. Kris found herself staring at a very pale Victoria Peterwald.

"Vicky, what do you think?"

"I don't know what to think, Your Highness."

"Talk to me, Vicky. I need to know something about what you're thinking."

"Okay, Kris," the young woman said, and took a deep breath. "I want to save my dad. Other people may hate him, but he's my dad. Maybe not the best one around, but he's all the dad I have. How do we do it?"

There it was. A plea from a younger Peterwald to save the elder. A plea made by a Peterwald to a Longknife. Capulet to Montague. *Do I accept it?* Kris asked herself.

Stupid question. Her head was in the same noose. Let that starship smash into South Continent, and there'd be rocks and wreckage all over the place. Not to mention certain gun-happy fellows in black uniforms oh so certain that Kris had caused it.

With a sigh, Kris winked at Vicky. *Watch and learn, my friend.* She whirled to face the captains.

"Captain Krätz, how long would it take one, just one of these ships hanging on to this station to get under way?"

"Twelve hours. Maybe more. This station is a piece of shoddy junk. We'd have to jump up the electric production to get the containment field of a ship up and running, then get a containment chute from the station's reactor to the ship. Most of the plasma would cool in the chute, so it would take a lot of plasma to get the reactor critical. Then you've got to grow the reaction mass, get your own electricity generators going." Krätz's voice trailed down into a whisper as he spoke. He finished shaking his head. "Some son of a bitch set us up."

"*So*, you are set up," Kris agreed. "Somewhere about two-thirds of the way into powering up one ship, her dad gets suddenly dead. Out of curiosity, what happens next? Does your ensign get promoted to First Citizen?"

Vicky's eyes got wide with that question. The captain studied the polished toes of his shoes. "I don't know. You know our attitude toward women." Now his gaze rose to take in his JO. "But I'd fight to my dying breath to protect you."

"I don't want your dying breath," Vicky snapped. "I want to save my dad."

The captain's shoulders slumped. "That I cannot do. No one in the fleet can do that."

"But someone in the Wardhaven fleet is willing to make a good solid try," Vicky growled low. "A Longknife is willing to risk her neck to save a Peterwald!"

"And maybe kill us all."

"You just told me that I'm not likely to outlive my dad for more that a couple of months. Strange, Captain, that is one thing we can agree on. Maybe someday I could tame the Palace with a whip and a gun and a gallows working overtime, but not now. Not today. We need to save my father."

Vicky opened her arms, pleading, "Captain, please help these people save him."

"And if they fail?"

"None of us will be any deader than we're likely to be this time next year."

For a long moment, Captain Krätz continued to shake his head. Then he turned to Kris. "Your Highness, what can I do to help?"

49

One did not often get permission to blow up a space station and the squadron of ships attached. Kris felt no sense of elation, since that was a prospect she hoped to avoid.

She turned to Drago. "Get this ship under way—ASAP."

"Aye, aye, ma'am. I have had men stripping the antimatter pods from the landers. They should be done soon."

"Two have been off-loaded, Captain," Sulwan reported.

"Have them plugged into the emergency generators," Captain Drago ordered.

"No," came from around Kris's neck. "The pods that will be fed into the reactors need to be carefully aligned and balanced for the dump," Nelly said. "That's your critical path. The auxiliary power is pretty much a standard rig."

"Captain?" Kris said, raising an eyebrow. Around her, quite a few eyebrows were bouncing off the overhead.

"Let's do it the lady's way," he ordered,

"Nelly, are there any scientists that can help you on this?" Kris asked her computer.

"A few; I've alerted them to get down to Engineering. There are several assumptions about the status of the antimatter that we will need to create if they are not already so."

"You go, gal," Kris said, then, confident that the technical was in the best putative hands available, she turned to Captain Krätz. "Certainly, we'll have to advise the port authorities that we are getting under way."

"Even a blind man would notice what we're attempting."

"When do we have to tell them?"

The captain mulled Kris's question for half a second. "Usually it's easier to ask forgiveness than permission."

"So I've observed," Kris agreed.

"However, I'm not sure that I'd apply that rule, what with all the security paranoids running around the station just now. Sudden moves could have very immediate and violent results."

"If you say so."

"Let me talk to my political officer," Krätz said, and tapped a few buttons on his wrist unit. "Sooner or later we'll have to bring them in on this." Nothing happened for a long moment, leaving the captain frowning at his wrist. "What call is he taking that is more important than mine?"

He was still frowning when a hurried voice came on. "Sorry, Captain, I have Lieutenant General Boyng on the line, sir. May I pass him to you, sir?" hardly sounded like a question.

Captain Krätz turned white as a sheet. Behind him, Vicky went up on tiptoes with glee. "Uncle Eddie. He'll help."

Those two reactions told Kris all she needed to know about this new man walking into her life.

"Put the captain's call on-screen," Kris ordered.

And found herself facing a thin-faced man whose appearance could make a hatchet look dull. His pristine black uniform was crisp, with more sharp edges than military law allowed. Kris went down his ribbons . . . they told her nothing. Greenfeld State Security's awards had nothing to do with the rest of their military.

Kris made a mental note to herself to save this call. Ten to one, this would be the first time Admiral Crossenshield got a look at his opposite number.

That, of course, assumed Kris got out of here.

There was no time like the present to start getting out of here. "General, I am Lieutenant Longknife, Princess of Wardhaven. I and my staff have been examining the behavior of the starliner *Dedicated Workers of Tourin*. It is our opinion that it is on a suicide dive into South Continent, intent on assassinating your First Citizen. It must be stopped."

Kris paused. She was getting no reaction from Hatchet Face. No reaction at all. You'd think that announcing a plot was afoot to kill someone's beloved boss would get a blink.

Not from this guy.

"Go on," he said.

Not on my dime, Kris thought. "What conclusions have you and your staff drawn from the behavior of this starliner?" *This is a conversation we're having. I talk. You talk. Didn't your mother teach you anything?*

The general finally did blink. "The liner's behavior is out of the usual. However, the drill presently going on in your ship is also unusual. This makes us wonder if you are not intent on some suicide mission." The words came out as cold as ice. Kris had met a few cold-blooded people. Now she faced an ice man.

"There are two faults in that logic, General."

"Would you care to enumerate my errors?"

Kris raised one finger, not giving in to the temptation to make it the middle one. "First, you know from all the attempts made on my life that there isn't a suicidal bone in my body. I very much like being alive and will fight to stay that way."

"So it would seem. However, things might change. High objectives might be worth a high price."

"Not in my book. Secondly, your First Citizen is down on South Continent. My blowing up this station would hardly ruffle the hair on his head."

"Yes, but you might be trading a queen for a queen."

Again the same cold calculations. Kris had had enough. "That does not even qualify as a jest, General. No offense, Vicky, but I am a full-fledged queen in this game the likes of your general and my admiral play. You are at best a pawn, maybe someday to be a queen, but you have a way to go."

"No offense taken," Vicky said. "Now, Uncle Eddie, are we going to sit here arguing who might be doing something while doing nothing for my dad? Are the rumors true that you'd just as soon see him dead? Is that why you sit here jabbering while time ticks away from the one ship that could save his life?"

Before, Kris had considered the general stiff as a board. Under Vicky's upbraiding, he became as solid as marble. "It was necessary for me to assure myself that a treacherous Longknife was not playing us for fools. They've done that often enough."

"That is why I'm aboard. I have satisfied myself that this ship can do this difficult evolution," Vicky shot back.

"Maybe you would like State Security's best troops to take over the ship and do what is necessary."

"Eddie, when I need your State Security hacks to gun down a few hundred unarmed peasants, I'll call for you. I need a ship sailed and a battle fought and won. Let's leave that to a crew that knows how to do it."

"Yes, Citizen Victoria," the general said, almost bowing. "May I send a security team to assure your safety?"

"If you wish, but make them few and see that they keep out of the way. Oh, and send us a different colonel. One that isn't the dullest in your collection."

"Yes, Citizen Victoria. If you will excuse me, I will see that these things are done."

"One more thing. This ship needs power. Have the station give it full access to electricity." She turned to her captain. "What about plasma?"

"That would take too long. Electricity will do."

"To hear is to obey," the general said, and rung off.

The silence on the bridge was broken only by the necessary sounds of a spaceship. Pumps pumped, fans spun. Here and there, a light blinked. No one spoke.

Captain Krätz was white as a sheet. Kris suspected that Vicky's next lesson would have to come from her. "Ah, you may have been a little hard on that general, Ensign."

Vicky pursed her full lips. "You think so? Always when he came around the house, he was so friendly. Almost fawning. A new toy when I was young. A fancy dress later. After he was gone, Dad would say things like 'two-faced.' That comment about shooting peasants, that was one of Dad's sayings."

"But did he ever say it to his face?" Kris asked.

Vicky thought for a moment, then looked embarrassed. "You're right. I don't remember his actually saying it to him."

"You might want to tell your dad when next you see him that that particular cat is out of the bag," Captain Krätz said.

"We're getting extra power from the station," Sulwan announced. "I'm sending it straight to Engineering."

"Well, he's carrying out his orders," Captain Drago said. "Now let's see how huge Princess Vicky's 'security team' is."

"I'm not a princess," Vicky snapped, "except I guess you have a point. My dad is acting like an emperor or something, and I guess that makes me a princess or something."

"Mostly, it makes you a target or something," Kris observed.

Five minutes later, a large squad of black security types double-timed up to the gangway. Gunny met them with an equal-size Marine team and invited them aboard.

"I know that colonel," Vicky said, as they watched the exchange. "He's got a head on his shoulders, and he uses it."

"Let's see how good he is," Kris said, and tapped her commlink. "Gunny, advise the new colonel that this ship will be doing three gees plus when we sortie to contact. High-gee stations will be limited by space on the bridge. If he wants, he may join Citizen Victoria on the bridge. You'll need to find space and stations for his squad."

In silence, they watched the exchange between Gunny and he colonel. The colonel turned to talk to his captain, who listened, saluted, shouted orders, and led the squad after Sergeant Bruce.

Gunny and the colonel watched them go, then boarded the *Wasp* together.

"That went smoothly enough," Vicky said.

"Captain Drago," Kris said, "we're going to need some high-gee stations on this bridge real soon now."

"I've got a chief working on that. What station will you take, Your Highness?"

"Weapons, Captain." Someone would be taking a couple of shots at that liner with its five thousand souls aboard. Fast shots as the *Tourin* and *Wasp* passed each other at millions of klicks an hour. That was not something Kris would delegate.

Kris turned toward the bridge hatch. "Sulwan, could you send the information on the *Tourin* to my Tac Room?"

"Yes, ma'am."

"Nelly, if you have any spare capacity, could you search for more data on the *Tourin*."

"Yes, ma'am," came back in a raw computer voice. Nelly was very busy.

"Let me check with my political officer," Captain Krätz said. "He may have information that has not been published."

He did, but he most certainly would not send it to a Wardhaven ship. Krätz tried reasoning with him. That didn't work. He was on the verge of losing his temper when Ensign Peterwald stepped forward and raised her commlink to her lips.

"This is Citizen Victoria Peterwald, daughter to the First Citizen," was hard enough to cut marble. "His life is in danger. Is it your intent to hinder the fight to save his life?"

"No, ma'am," came back in a stutter.

"Then get those plans and files over here, or I will personably come over there and see you shot."

"Yes, ma'am. The files are on the way."

Vicky released her captain's wrist. He retrieved his arm as if he wasn't sure it was still attached to him.

"I'm sorry, Captain," Vicky said. "I know that is not how you taught me to lead. However, that is what I learned at my dad's knee. I am just starting to learn that there is a time to do things your way . . . and a time to do things Dad's way."

"It's not an easy lesson," Kris said.

"No," Vicky said, seeming to look inside herself, note the particular set of her soul. "You are right, Kris. It is not at all easy. Was it like this for you?"

"I think you'll find it harder. I get the feeling there's a bigger gap between the way your dad does things and the Navy way and the way my father goes about his business and the Navy way."

"That's something I hope we can talk about."

"First we save your dad."

50

Kris's staff room, now changed by the situation into a Tac Room, was just the way they'd left it during the stampede to the bridge. A chair was overturned on the floor.

One wall showed a schematic of the *Dedicated Workers of Tourin*. The wall next to it was covered with opened files. The wall across from it showed . . . a spiderweb. Beside it was a series of files not found, and similar error messages.

At the table, Chief Beni was alternately cursing, pulling his hair out, and pounding on his own large unit, which he'd plugged into the table. He looked up as Kris came in. "What kind of junk is this we're getting from that Peterwald ship? Are they trying to bring down our main ship's computer?"

"They better not be," Vicky said, and rattled off a long string of letters, numbers, words, and even a whistle at the end.

The wall of spiderwebbing blinked black for a moment, then came up steady with a schematic of the *Tourin* not at all different from that on the opposite wall.

"Sorry," Vicky said. "It's all password encrypted. I didn't expect the files to get here so fast."

"You did threaten to shoot the man," Kris pointed out.

"Yes, but I still thought it would take more time to get the information together and over the net."

"I think State Security has a priority for 'it gets there now, or I get shot,' " Captain Krätz said.

Kris hoped he was joking, but wouldn't have taken the bet. The nod from Vicky looked far too *of course* for her to even consider that bet. For the first time in her life Kris could honestly think, *Thank God I was born a Longknife.*

How can the Peterwalds run an empire this way?

Are they running it, or is it running them? Killing them?

Point taken.

Kris focused on the *Tourin*. Where warships like the *Ty-phoon* were built small and slim and rounded to offer lasers less of a target, the *Tourin* was huge and built like a brick to contain more cabin space and, apparently, to give each premium cabin its own view out. Forward, the ship tapered deck by deck with the most expensive rooms having both views out and ahead. The bridge was at the very apex of the stepped pyramid.

"Do we target the bridge?" Kris asked, half to herself, half to those around her. Captain Drago had stayed on his own bridge to oversee the powering-up process. Still, Kris had one cruiser captain. He was shaking his head.

"I don't think the bridge will get you anything. There's a backup control room well aft, just before Engineering," Krätz said. On the schematic behind Kris, a space glowed red just forward of where she'd expect the power plant to begin. "These liners are intended to be easily converted to either troop transports, or, if big lasers are provided, ships able to stand against anything but a battleship."

"Might explain your security man's reluctance to provide this to us," Abby said.

Captain Krätz gently cleared his throat. "You do know, Your Highness, that your maid, now apparently Army officer, regularly publishes information about what you do?"

"Oh," Kris said, a puzzle piece falling into place. "Is that why that Security colonel was about to swallow his cud? He was meeting Abby face-to-face and couldn't figure out how to react to a spy being in our midst."

Abby, for her part, did a letter-perfect curtsy.

"You don't sound surprised," Krätz said.

"Abby, what's it worth to you not to have your cover blown?" Kris called cheerfully over her shoulder.

"Hey, not fair. You're supposed to be paying me for early copies of my reports and slightly modified ones that you can use for your paperwork." The maid sounded very unhappy.

"It's not me you need to bribe. Looks to me like you better buy this captain's silence."

"Me, too," Vicky called. "I always need a new dress."

"What bribe?" was a low growl coming from the door as the State Security colonel followed Gunny in.

"A bit of levity," Kris growled right back, "to lighten the

burden of figuring out how to damage a starliner with five thousand souls aboard."

"Why damage it?" the colonel said. "Just blow it up."

That brought a strained silence.

"Kris," Vicky said in a low voice, "that is how I feel too. It's my dad's life we're talking about."

"Your dad and a whole lot of people down on that planet," Kris agreed. "But it's not as easy as that. Has anyone calculated the kinetic power of one of our pulse lasers?" Normally Kris would have asked Nelly to do it, but the low hum in the back of Kris's head said that the old girl was fully occupied.

"I've got it," Penny said. "Entered it before that battle above Chance and never purged it."

Beside Kris, Vicky swallowed hard at the mention of the battle in which her brother died. She also threw Penny a hard glance, as if memorizing her face.

Penny looked back just as hard. "A lot of us fought at Chance, and my husband died stopping those battleships above Wardhaven."

Vicky started to open her mouth.

Kris cut her off. "Enough, girls. A lot of people are hurting from a lot of things that might have been better not done. Today, we have today's problems. Captain, can you tell us something about the thickness of the hide on this thing? The decks and strength girders."

"That is a state secret," the colonel pointed out.

"You can keep the secret and start looking for a new First Citizen, or you can tell us and maybe we can save his life. Your call. Or should I have Miss Victoria call Lieutenant General Boyng again?"

The colonel in black looked like he'd swallowed something bitter, but he nodded Captain Krätz's way. That Greenfeld officer ran off a list of numbers.

Penny fed them into her computer, then paused a moment before announcing, "Not good. We'll achieve complete burn through, one side to the other, using only twenty-five percent of the power of one of our four pulse lasers."

"So we can punch four or maybe sixteen holes in that can," Kris said. "Can we slice it in half? Quarters? Sixteenths?"

Penny eyed her wrist unit. "Half, definitely. Maybe into three chunks. Not four."

"And they would hit the planet in three places with one-third the power," Colonel Cortez said.

"No," Kris said at the same time Krätz did. Kris deferred to the Greenfeld captain.

"If we do anything to the engines as we pass, the ship stops accelerating. Its course assumes that it will keep its acceleration constant right up to collision. If we stop its acceleration, it will miss the planet entirely."

"Assuming they do not change its course," the security colonel snapped. "Just one hit in the right part of its power plant, and the containment field collapses. The ship and terrorists vanish, and we have no more problem."

"Kris . . ." Vicky said, not quite pleading.

"That is an option," Kris said slowly. "But it is my last option. I did not put on this uniform to kill five thousand people whose only crime was buying a ticket to ride or taking a job to pander to them. Am I understood, Colonel!"

Kris locked eyes with the man from State Security. He glared right back at her.

"My duty is to the state, and the First Citizen."

"And you know way too much about blowing up a ship for my liking and seem only too quick to do it."

"Enough, the two of you!" Vicky shouted. "If you don't want to hit the electric generators, what do you intend to hit?"

Kris ran her hands along the schematic on the wall. "The bridge, the living spaces have no value to us. The colonel is right, we need to hit the engineering area," she said, coming to rest there. "The question is how do we cripple and drive the ship hopelessly off course, so that it can't be put back on course," Kris glanced at the colonel. "But not blow it apart."

"The engines," Penny and Captain Krätz said together.

"Will someone turn the ship engine-on to me?" Kris asked, again not wanting to bother Nelly. For once her pet computer did not cut in with some snide remark about her being able to calculate pi and chew gum at the same time. Nelly was busy!

"I got it moving," Chief Beni said from where he still sat at the table, quietly observing the rest.

Kris found herself facing a three-quarters on view of the aft end of the *Tourin*. Four huge rocket motors glowed along the middle of the ship's end. Above and below them nestled three more equally huge bells. A short row of two topped the three.

Fourteen huge rocket motors pumped tons of hot plasma into space, so a million tons of human engineering could safely travel among the stars—normally.

Now it was a million tons of death for those aboard and those on the planet below. Unless Kris stopped it.

"Can the jets move?" Kris asked. "How do they steer?"

"Very carefully," Captain Krätz said dryly. "Assuming a speed of between .95 and 1.05 gees, there is a battery of steering jets circling the bow, amidships, and aft that make it as maneuverable as a ballet dancer . . . at 1 gee. At this speed, God only knows what they would do if you cut away three or four of the rocket motors. Nip three or four more, the thing will take off doing loops. They'll never get it back under control."

"How much time will we have to take our shot?" Kris asked.

"Somewhere between 1 and 1.5 seconds. Assume 1.25 as most likely," Chief Beni said.

The wall went blank, speckled by a few unblinking stars. Then one of them grew huge, filled the screen, and was gone. If anyone blinked, they didn't see a thing.

"Thank you, Chief, I expected something like that."

"But now you've seen it," he said. "By the way, the reason we don't know just how much time you'll be in range of the *Tourin* is because we aren't sure just what our acceleration will be."

"Captain Drago said 3.2 gees," Kris said. "Maybe more."

"Or maybe less. I called one of my buddies who has a buddy down in Engineering. Turns out they never tested this ship above 2.25 gees, Your Highness."

"Didn't we do 3 gees or so around Panda's moon?" Penny asked.

"Yeah," the chief agreed, "and the snipes sweated blood. We do it steady for three, four hours this time."

"Thanks for the clarification," Kris said . . . and meant it.

"So all is not so well in the vaunted Wardhaven Navy," the security colonel said with a smile.

"Whose ship is ready to split its guts to get under way and whose ships are tied up like beached whales?" Vicky shot back.

The colonel swallowed his smile.

"Chief, give me the broadside view, again." The wall changed. "Where are the main electrical generators?"

Captain Krätz eyed the other schematic, then indicated an

area forward of the engines. A bit farther forward were two huge areas that could only be the fusion reactors.

Kris put her finger on one. "I hit here, and what happens?"

"Nothing or everything," Krätz said.

Kris nodded along with him. "My shot could go through and do nothing but stir the plasma the wrong way. Or I could take out enough superconductors to let the plasma eat the ship."

"Everyone dies," Jack concluded.

"Farther aft, I hit the electrical generators and, again, everyone dies. Only if I hit the rocket engines do people live."

"But if you miss aft," Vicky pointed out, "my dad dies."

"Yes," Kris whispered softly.

"Could you slice the ship in half?" Colonel Cortez asked.

"Why?" Jack asked.

"Well, the other young lady mentioned a few moments ago that you might be able to cut it in half or thirds."

"Yes," Penny said. "Our lasers have the power for it."

"And the ship is a huge target, is it not?"

"It looks that way," Kris agreed.

"Where is the reaction mass carried?" the infantry colonel went on.

Captain Krätz eyed the other files for a moment, then said, "In huge tanks in the center of the ship." He stepped to Kris's schematic and ran his hands along the middle of the drawing. "From just where it starts to taper at the bow to where it starts to narrow at the stern."

"And what if you cut into those tanks? Where would the reaction mass go? Could the engines continue their huge acceleration if that reaction mass was bleeding out elsewhere than the reactors?"

"Captain Krätz, how much reaction mass would the *Tourin* have on board at this point in her voyage? How much is she gulping down to keep up this acceleration? Could we damage her enough to make this whole stunt impossible?"

The Greenfeld captain just shook his head.

"And assuming we unleashed the reaction mass into the ship, what would it do to the people on board?" Kris said.

"And if we did separate the forward half of the ship from the aft half," Penny pointed out, "the havoc as different parts of the ship lost power, the wrenching as the forward portion twisted away from the aft portion with its reactors still trying to push the ship. No, I'm sorry, it would be more merciful to grant these people a quick death. I have been on a wrecked ship."

Once again, the room fell silent.

Kris spread her arms to reach back for the engineering spaces and ran her fingers over the tiny target she and Nelly would be aiming for. "So this is it. The engines themselves."

"That or the containment field," the colonel said.

"We are Wardhaven Navy, not murderers."

"If your softheartedness causes our First Citizen to die, there will be a lot to talk about."

"Enough," Vicky half shouted. She walked in Kris's footsteps, running her hands along the large bulk of passenger area, and deep within it, the reaction mass to feed the reactor.

"It's a big, easy target. Are you sure it's not the best?"

"We don't know how much reaction mass is in it," Kris pointed out, raising a finger. "We'd have to use two of our lasers to burn through any try at cutting the ship in half. That would be chancy at the best of times." A second finger came up. "At the speed we'd be traveling, it's a huge gamble." A third finger joined the others. "We could punch lots of holes in the tanks, and they'd still have enough to complete their suicidal dive." All four fingers were up now. "Yes, Vicky, it would be the easiest to hit, but no, there is no good chance that we'd be hitting what we need to hit."

"Which brings us to Engineering," Vicky said. "I've never understood power plants. I've had to walk through several. They make a lot of noise and have huge things spinning around and a lot of places marked 'Do Not Enter.' I will have to trust that you are aiming at the right target."

"I tell you she is wrong," the security colonel snapped.

"Don't be tiresome, Colonel. It is the measures of State Security that have left my captain's ship a beached observer of this drama. Has someone chosen to take advantage of your brain-dead measures, or were State Security's orders an integral part of this plan? I wonder."

The colonel opened his mouth several times before "Of course not. You can't even think such things" finally got out.

"Oh, but I can, and I think my dad will, if he lives. Captain Krätz, may I have a word with you? In private."

The ensign led the captain into the passageway. The colonel made to follow.

At a nod from Kris, Gunny stepped on the colonel's polished toes. "Pardon me, sir," Gunny said, but by the time the colonel recovered, he found himself surrounded by an infantry colonel and a Marine captain. An Army lieutenant and a Navy lieutenant, too.

Kris looked at the schematics one more time. "I am finished here. Jack, I'll be on the bridge, setting up a shoot with Nelly as soon as she's available. Tell Ensign Peterwald that she is free to join me with her associates when she is done."

Kris passed the ensign and her captain in the passageway, their heads together. So that was what a palace coup looked like. Kris hoped it didn't come down to that. Vicky deserved a better chance at survival than she'd have today. Given three or four years, who knew what the woman could grow into.

Hopefully, someone who liked Longknifes better than most Peterwalds did.

51

"We've got the minimum containment field up. Prepare to release antimatter into Reactor A," Captain Drago said, as Kris entered the bridge. Silently, she slipped into a high-gee station that was in the usual place for weapons. Careful not to jiggle any elbows, she left the station cold and inert.

"Captain, we've got a steep drop in power from the station," Sulwan suddenly announced. "Containment is weakening."

"Hold the antimatter," the captain ordered.

Kris snapped her commlink and raised the station chief. "This is Princess Kristine. We were promised power. We are at a critical stage. Who cut it? They are criminals and enemies of the state. Do I need to talk to General Boyng?"

"No. No, ma'am, I swear it's just a glitch. We got a lot of ships making demands we aren't anywhere close to rated for it."

"Get us power," Kris demanded.

"Yes, ma'am," and the man was off-screen.

"Should I rely on our own auxiliary power?" Drago asked. "I wanted to save it to jump-start our second reactor. Get us out of here faster."

"Keep auxiliary ready to use antimatter, but see if we can get a start using station power the next time it comes up."

"Station power coming up to specs," Sulwan announced.

"Engineering ready to bleed antimatter into the reactor."

"Everything is ready," Nelly said in her normal voice.

"No questions?" Kris asked.

"I think we will rewrite the procedures on how to do this," Nelly said. "Nothing our boffins and I couldn't handle. But I'd hate to see anyone do it without all we have here."

"Nelly, we need to work on a firing solution when this is done."

"I figured we would. First things first. We have plasma. The containment is holding. We have enough plasma to start our own power generation. Yes!" The computer's cheer was echoed by several on the bridge and over the commlink.

"We have fusion," Captain Drago announced. "We are growing the plasma core. Thank God we are taking electricity directly from the core. Give me another five minutes, and I'll be ready to jump-start Reactor B. Sortie in fifteen minutes, Princess."

"What do you mean you're drawing power directly from the core?" Captain Krätz asked as he escorted his ensign onto the bridge. The colonel behind him had heard the question; he said nothing but seemed to want to look at everything at once.

"Something we can't talk about," one captain said to the other. "However, we do have plasma and should be under way in fifteen minutes." Drago tapped his commlink. "Set getting-under way details, minimum." Throughout the ship, came the noise of hands moving to stations.

"I understand we are going into another battle," announced Professor mFumbo, following Vicky's team onto the bridge.

"You want to get off?" Kris asked.

"If I wanted off this tub, I would have left before these mad scientists jump-started the reactor. No, I'm not leaving, but do we really have to be confined to bed?"

"Afraid so," Drago cut in. "Unless you like the idea of standing around at three times your own weight, maybe more, I'd suggest you get in bed. A nice soft one."

mFumbo scowled. "Could we at least see what's going on?"

"Won't be much to see, but I'll send you the picture," Drago said, and ordered his quartermaster to get the scientists off his neck. With quick efficiency, the *Wasp* prepared to get under way. Today, some things were different. Kris's station came up as a fire-control post. Vicky's high-gee station next to hers had all the readouts of Kris's. Just none of the active controls.

Captain Krätz settled into a high-gee couch next to Captain Drago's station. The State Security colonel was parked at the rear of the bridge, where he could see everything and touch nothing. He had two Marines behind him and Gunny in front.

Jack took position closer to Kris, where he could keep an eye on all of the strangers aboard. With a glint in his eye, he looked ready for anything.

Exactly thirty minutes from when Captain Drago said he could get the *Wasp* under way in a half hour, the pier tie-downs began to rattle backward, and the *Wasp* smartly backed away from the dock.

"Nelly, start an intercept clock," Kris ordered. A clock before her began to count down. The initial display was 3 HR 24 MIN 24.242 SEC, but it quickly changed.

52

FOᴦ the rest of Kris's life, she would know exactly when things began to go wrong. And like so many of the things that would go wrong, Kris made the decision herself.

It seemed like a very good idea at the time.

"Stand by for high gee in five minutes," Captain Drago announced as soon as the *Wasp* was away from the pier. "If you need more time, holler, but don't expect to get it," he finished.

Kris mashed her own commlink. "Professor mFumbo, can your scientists get their best sensors up and running? I want to know everything I can about that ship. If its reactors burp every five minutes, I want to know."

"We were expecting this call, Your Highness. Our people should have everything we have online well before our captain starts putting on weight. You can count on us."

"Thank you, Professor, I expected I could."

Beside Kris, Vicky had a strange look on her face. "Courtesy, huh. Does it work?"

"When you have the best people who can think for themselves, honey is a whole lot better than a baseball bat."

Which left Vicky with a thoughtful look.

"Captain Drago, do we gain anything by putting on more than 2.5 gees. I understand the *Wasp* was only tested up to there."

"That, sadly, is true. Sulwan, could you please calculate two intercept courses. One at 2.5, the other at 3.2."

Two lines appeared on the main screen, showing close encounters for both accelerations. "If we intercept and damage them closer to Birridas, we need to do more damage to their engines, but they have less time to repair them or correct course. Farther back, they have more time to effect repairs, but they are farther off course for a collision."

Kris studied the lines and the tables. While the distance was measured in millions of kilometers, it didn't really seem to matter all that much on the cosmic scale of things.

"Captain, it's your call, but pushing the *Wasp* above 2.5 gees doesn't seem to gain me anything."

The captain said, "2.5 it is." There might have been a hint of a sigh behind his words, but Kris was too busy with her next question to be sure.

"Captain, do we gain any advantage by being under acceleration when we actually make the flyby of the *Tourin*?"

"Help me follow your thinking, Your Highness."

"Our closing speed is going to be nothing short of breathtaking. We're going to have to track that ship while firing at close to maximum range. Any wobble could be the difference between hitting it and missing. Between hitting the aiming point and slashing the ship somewhere that could start catastrophic failure for the people aboard."

The captain was nodding before Kris was half-done. "Sulwan, can we go from 2.5 gee to zero acceleration?"

"I don't see any reason why not. Though I'd like to practice it at least once before we do it."

"How long would you need to make sure the ship was rock steady?" Kris asked the navigator.

"A minute, two to be on the safe side." Sulwan glanced at the screen with its expected tracks to flyby. "Three today."

"Sounds good to me," the captain said.

"One more thing," Kris said.

"You are just full of questions, Your Highness," the captain said, but his eyes were on his board, monitoring the *Wasp*'s departure from High Birridas at a full gee.

"Chief Beni said I'd have as much as 1.5 seconds at close encounter to shoot. The pulse lasers have a maximum range of forty thousand kilometers. Was he assuming that I'd be firing at them for eighty thousand klicks, both coming and going?"

"Yes," Nelly said. "With the *Wasp* slowing down on its approach, you may have as much as 1.76 seconds to fire."

"Captain Drago, how much can you swivel the laser mounts from dead ahead?" Kris asked.

"Hardly at all. Fifteen degrees to right or left. Battery 1 and 2 have an up thirty degrees. Battery 3 and 4 a down thirty. We can't rotate the batteries to follow the *Tourin*."

"Can we rotate ship?" Kris asked.

"Of course," came back immediately.

"How fast?"

All eyes turned to Sulwan. "Usually it takes a second or two. I hit the jets to get us going. When we get there, I hit the opposite jets to stop us."

"And if you use the jets the full time you're starting and stopping?" Kris asked.

"That's in the book under DON'T NORMALLY THINK ABOUT IT. You've only got so much fuel for the reaction jets."

"How much fuel do we have?"

"We're pretty much topped off. If we have to load more, it's a manual job."

"We could do it after the flyby," the captain said.

"Let's plan on it," Kris said.

"High gee in one minute," the quartermaster announced.

"Bridge crew, let's get cracking," Captain Drago said.

Kris turned back to her board. "Nelly, show me the stern rocket engines of the *Tourin*." They appeared on Kris's board.

"Now, assuming I fire two lasers at thirty thousand klicks from close encounter, what kind of an angle could I get on those jets?"

A red wash swept over the right side of the rocket engines, cutting the two outer ones off at their tops, the next three in their middles, and even taking a nip out of the four inners.

"That's optimum?" Kris said.

"Yes," Nelly said. "We would need all the luck in the world to pull that off." Beside Kris, Vicky raised an eyebrow.

"Nelly's been reading fiction for several years now. It makes her easier to talk to."

"Makes you easier to understand," the computer added.

"Assuming I fire two more lasers at thirty thousand klicks, or as soon as we can get the *Wasp* settled down after a flip, what kind of damage can I do to the left side?"

The red wash now took out most of that side.

"Assuming we have all the luck in the world," Vicky said.

"Assuming," Kris agreed.

"Is it always like this?" Vicky asked.

"Always like what?"

"Your planning. You start with one plan. Bounce it around among your team, get it better, then have some others look at it, and it keeps getting better."

Kris thought for a moment. "It was like this at Wardhaven."
Then Kris remembered her audience and cut off the longer explanation. "At Chance, your brother didn't give us a lot of time
to plan."

"Do you think he'd be alive if he had?" came across as an
honest question.

"I really don't know. I tried and tried to talk him down. He
had a captain with him, just like you do, but he was the commodore, and I understand Captain Slovo spent the first half of
the battle in the brig."

"Poor planning on my brother's part."

"And part of the reason you're an ensign."

"That's the story of my life, doing penance for my brother's
sins. What about on Eden, did you plan for that?"

"Not for any of the things you threw my way. Those were
run-and-shoot, shoot-and-run affairs."

"I didn't do any planning," Vicky said, shaking her head
thoughtfully. "Just hired whoever I could find available. Very
poor planning on my part."

"I hope you aren't thinking of having me plan your next as-
sassination attempt on me," Kris said, trying to make it into a
joke . . . but only half of one.

"No. I'm sorry, Kris. I'm not *ever* planning another attack on
you." But she left unsaid whom she might be planning for.

And Kris doubted Vicky's promise of peace between the two
of them would hold up in a court of law.

They were less than thirty minutes from intercept when a
boffin called up to the bridge.

"Are you aware the target is rotating?"

"No, we weren't," Kris said.

"Kind of hard to tell, but there's a dull part on the ship. We
clock it as coming by about every fifty-six seconds. That puppy
is making 3.2457 gees acceleration and rotating about every
minute. God help the passenger that tries to get up and walk."

"Send me your data," Kris said. "That may have an impact
on my targeting the lasers."

"It's on its way, Miss Longknife."

Vicky gave Kris a look. "Miss Longknife?"

"With the mad scientists, I can never tell what they're going to call me. My father cut back long-term research this budget, and half of them aren't talking to me at all."

"So it's not all crumpets and cream on Wardhaven."

"I never told you it was."

"I don't know if the *Tourin* is having trouble keeping up its acceleration," Nelly said, "or if your boffins are giving me better data, but it appears the acceleration is falling a bit."

"What about the rotation?" Kris asked.

"If I was a bunch of gomers," Captain Drago said, "flying a ship into a planet, I'd put on rotation. Right, Captain Krätz?"

"Yes, we should have expected it. By rotating the ship, they don't have to correct for any rocket engine that can't quite keep up the demanded thrust. Just as an arrow spins to balance any wobble in its flight."

"So now we don't know exactly which way is down for the stern when we hit it," Vicky said.

"I should have mentioned that," Kris said. "No battle plan survives contact with the enemy. That's what makes sure that all our planning doesn't make life boring for us."

Once again, the Peterwald heir looked lost in thought.

With a sigh, Kris said, "Let's see what our last ace can give us." She tapped her commlink.

"Mr. Prometheus, we think we've found your son."

The former official of Xanadu came up on Kris's display. Behind him, she could just make out cramped scientist's quarters. "Where do you think my son is?" the father pleaded.

"Diving a loaded starliner into a planet at about .03 the speed of light," Kris said. "When he hits, there'll be an explosion like a trillion tons of dynamite."

The man said something that might have been a prayer or a curse for an Abdicationist. It meant nothing to Kris. "What can I do?" he said.

"In half an hour, I'll try to shoot the engines out of the ship. Could you say something to him that would make him change his mind, slow his ship, turn away from the planet?"

"I will try."

Kris turned the man over to the comm chief on the *Wasp*, an old chief with kids of his own. The two hit it off. In five minutes, a message for Lucifer was on its way to the *Tourin*.

Fifteen minutes later, a reply came back. There was no question it was laced with curses. "You have thrown yourself against the Guides. You are no better than a nonbeliever. Your eyeballs should be boiled in blood with all the heretics."

"Should I pass this to his father?" the comm chief asked.

Kris shook her head. "The man's hurting enough. This won't help. If he asks, tell him we're still waiting."

At Kris's elbow, Vicky took a sip of water from her high-gee station before whispering, "So Longknifes do lie."

Kris rotated her shoulders, trying to make the padding just right for a body that suddenly weighed over 250 kilos. "Yeah, sometimes I'd rather lie to an old man than tell him the truth. Next time you hear tell of a Peterwald lie, see if it does as much good as my last one."

Vicky said nothing to that.

The clock on Kris's station counted down the last five minutes. The target ship was one of the brightest stars on the screen. Their encounter would be very soon.

53

"**Four** minutes to close encounter," the quartermaster said.

"Cut acceleration," the captain ordered.

Kris went from near three hundred kilos to weighing nothing.

Vicky grabbed for the burp bag, held it clamped to her mouth for a while, then put it aside, still looking green.

The State Security colonel filled his bag. Gunny handed him another and it was half-filled before he finished.

Kris took in normal life out of the corner of her eye. She concentrated on the reports from the *Wasp*'s inertial platform.

"We are steady," Sulwan reported.

"All hands," the captain announced, "where you are is where you will stay. Do not even think of moving." The inertial platform reported the *Wasp* steady to the tenth decimal place.

"Rotate Batteries 3 and 4 to minus thirty," Kris ordered. The lasers on the bottom of the *Wasp* angled themselves down as far as they could. "Rotate ship up thirty."

Now the *Wasp* herself nosed up 30 degrees, bringing the lower two batteries zero on to the approaching liner. When it came time to flip ship during the precious second fragments the *Tourin* was in range, the *Wasp* would only have to do 150 degrees.

The actual close encounter would happen too fast for human participation. Kris, Nelly, and Vicky had gone over and over the actual plans for that fleeting second. Those plans were laid into the computer . . . waiting.

When it came time to execute, only Nelly could do it fast enough. Nelly would fire the two lower batteries. Nelly would rotate the ship, using full power throughout the spin, as Sulwan had approved. Nelly would fire the top two lasers up the kilt of the departing liner.

Humans decided what to do, but Nelly would do it.

Except that Kris had a red button under her palm.

At the first sign that the plan had gone awry, Kris would mash the button. And Nelly would find she had no plans to execute. Probably, Nelly wouldn't remember she'd ever had a plan. With Nelly, you could never tell.

No question, Kris would remember that there had been a plan and that she had aborted it for some reason. Or had tried to abort it. Could something pass from her eye, to her brain to her hand to the red button in anything like the time they had?

She would find out soon enough.

The distance to the *Tourin* now counted down at a mad pace. The millions of klicks passed in reasonable time. When the count reached hundreds of thousands, the numbers raced. The last five hundred thousand klicks passed in a breath.

Kris quit breathing as the count passed a hundred thousand.

If Kris had to call it, Batteries 3 and 4 fired at a range of thirty-five to thirty thousand klicks.

Then the ship began to flip like a mad dervish.

She fought dizziness but refused to close her eyes.

The *Wasp* steadied for less than a heartbeat. Lasers 1 and 2 fired.

The *Tourin* raced on, seeming untouched by their efforts, unmarred by the lasers' caresses.

Kris's eyes widened at the thought of total failure.

A spark shot out from the liner. A split second later, the ship seemed to twist off its long axis.

Then, in the blink of an eye there was nothing left of the liner and five thousand human beings but glowing dust cooling through red and yellow into violets and blue.

"Holy God," someone whispered on the bridge.

Kris sat there.

"Well, I'm glad that's over with," came from the back of the bridge, no doubt the State Security colonel's opinion.

From around Kris's neck, a suddenly little girl's voice asked, "Kris, did I just kill five thousand people?"

What could Kris tell her computer?

"I'm sorry, Kris," Vicky said, reaching out to stroke Kris's elbow. "But it's not your fault. You did everything you could not to have this happen."

"Did I?" Kris said, then mashed her commlink. "Everyone who's been following this last evolution, save all your data. There will be an inquiry into it."

"Whose?" Vicky asked.

"Mine," Kris snapped. "Captain Drago, if you will, put one gee on this boat to help with saving data."

"Sulwan, one gee if you please."

Kris took on weight and stood. "Captain Drago. Captain Krätz, Jack." Kris looked around and found faces missing. She tapped her commlink. "Colonel Cortez, Penny, and Abby, please report to my Tac Room. Professor mFumbo, you come, too."

"Yes" and "As you wish" answered her commlink. "Why?" came on the bridge from Captain Drago.

"Because I am sick and tired of hearing that a Longknife did this or that or the other, all during the same supposed whatever. I'm tired of not knowing who did what to whom. This time, so help me God, I'm going to know just exactly what happened, and if Peterwald State Security wants to say one thing and Wardhaven intelligence patches together another story, at least I will know the truth. You understand me?"

It was Captain Krätz's turn to step forward and face the fire in Kris's eyes. "That assumes that, using the data we have, we can actually tell you what happened."

That took a little of the firestorm out of Kris's sails. But not much. "We have the best instrumentation of any ship in space, between what Captain Drago has pirated from whoever is his employer and whatever the boffins have ripped off from their universities. Maybe you can't tell me what I did and how it happened that five thousand lives were put to the torch. But I want you to face me, with your hands on the best information that these instruments can yield, and tell me that. You hear me."

"Yes, we hear you," Jack said, coming forward. "You've got a lot of people on this board you've set up. I understand the two captains. Maybe even the colonel. But me, Penny, and Abby?"

"You and Penny are trained criminal investigators. Abby's the board's secretary. That ought to make her job easier."

Jack didn't look like he liked what he'd heard. But he looked even less eager to argue with Kris at the moment.

"Now, if you will excuse me," Kris said, "I have to talk to a father who pleaded for me to save his son's life. Somewhere I've got to find the words to explain why I killed his boy."

"Kris, that's cruel," Jack cut in. "Don't do it."

"When somebody makes you prince, you can gainsay me," Kris shot back. "Until then, shut up."

The bridge crew stood aside as Kris marched out.

54

The silence from Nelly was suffocating as Kris strode the passageways of the *Wasp*, trying to locate Prometheus's stateroom. When Kris asked for the room assigned to him, Nelly told her, but she offered no directions, did none of the things that Kris had become used to getting from Nelly without asking.

Nelly's voice was normal, but clearly, she was deep in calculating something. Examining something. Deciding something.

That, or maybe the Nelly Kris had known was gone.

Then it got worse.

Kris found the room, but the door was locked.

No one answered when she called inside. Nothing. Nada. No noise. She flagged down a boffin to make sure it was the right room, that the stranger from Xanadu had indeed been assigned it. The scientist snagged two Marines, who started working on the door.

Was it an accident that Gunny arrived before the door gave way?

And Gunny's wide shoulders blocked Kris's view of the room.

"You don't need to go in there, ma'am. I know you seen dead and death enough. There's nothing pretty about a man who hanged himself."

Kris backed off, fighting the undignified urge to pound upon Gunny. She looked up at Gunny Brown's dark, lined face. "You think he could have hanged himself if I hadn't ordered one gee on the boat?" Kris asked, adding one more notch to her kills for today.

"Ma'am, a man who's made up his mind can be bare-ass naked and kill himself. You ever seen a man bite off his tongue and bleed out in zero gee. It ain't pretty."

Gunny put his arm around Kris's shoulder and turned her gently around. Kris had seen men do that to their grown sons and daughters. Father had never done that to her. "Now, Lieutenant, you done set yourself a real tough row to hoe. Why don't you go face that jury, as close as you can get to peers, and let them give you what truth they can about this day."

Kris started back.

KRIS, I CANNOT FIGURE IT OUT.

WHAT, NELLY?

WE DID EVERYTHING RIGHT, BUT WE KILLED ALL OF THOSE PEOPLE. I KILLED ALL OF THOSE PEOPLE.

IT'S WE, NELLY, YOU AND I. I TOLD YOU WHAT TO DO. YOU DID IT. YOU WERE ONLY FOLLOWING ORDERS.

YOU KNOW THAT IS NOT A VALID DEFENSE. AT LEAST NOT IF YOU LOSE.

I KNOW, NELLY, BUT YOU HAVE TO REALIZE, SOMETIMES, WHEN YOU DO EVERYTHING RIGHT, IT ALL GOES WRONG.

THAT DOES NOT COMPUTE. $A + B$ IS SUPPOSED TO EQUAL C, AND IF A AND B ARE GOOD, HOW CAN C BE BAD?

NELLY, I DON'T KNOW. IT DOESN'T SEEM RIGHT. IT ISN'T FAIR, BUT SOMETIMES, THAT IS JUST THE WAY IT IS. YOU DO EVERYTHING, WANTING THE BEST FOR EVERYONE, AND IT JUST BLOWS UP IN YOUR FACE.

THAT CANNOT BE RIGHT. I TRIED AND TRIED AND TRIED TO CALCULATE ALL OF THAT, AND IT JUST DOES NOT COME OUT. IS SOMETHING WRONG WITH ME OR MY CIRCUITS?

NO, NELLY. THERE IS NOTHING WRONG WITH YOU. PROBABLY NOTHING WRONG WITH ME. IT'S JUST SOMETHING WE HUMANS HAVE FOUND OUT.

NOW I THINK I UNDERSTAND SOMETHING I HAVE READ.

WHAT IS THAT?

SOMETIMES SHIT HAPPENS.

YES, NELLY, SOMETIMES, NO MATTER HOW HARD YOU TRY, IT DOES.

Kris found herself facing the passageway to her staff room. Down that hall, through that door, were the men and women she'd given the job of measuring her soul, her conscience.

And yet, now that she and Nelly had had this little talk, Kris didn't feel so in need of anyone else's approval. Somehow, in facing Nelly's first pangs of conscience, she had found her own measurement of right and wrong.

Did she really want to hear what these people had to say?

Unbidden, a question floated to the top of her mind. *What would Grampa Ray do?* Yes, what would King Raymond feel about the death of a few thousand people? It probably would cool the war someone was trying to start. That was good. The five thousand was sadly unavoidable.

Greenfeld State Security certainly agreed with him.

But that way lay madness and easy choices that would take Kris . . . Kris really didn't know or want to know where that would take her.

She had urged Grampa Ray to accept the kingship. Asked him to help her generation make it through the tough times ahead. He had said it was time for them to make their own mistakes.

Had he really been dodging the crown for another reason? Did he know how burned and blackened his own soul was? Had he chased the easy decisions as deep as he wanted to go and now hoped to retire to some quiet life that demanded nothing more from him than choosing to golf or sail today.

What had Kris done?

Kris had started the day just trying to save Vicky's dad's life and avoid a war. That had taken her to demanding to know why five thousand innocents should die for that one life.

Now she was wondering if her great-grandfather had his head on straight enough to rule 150 or so planets.

All Kris wanted to do was go to bed and pull a pillow over her head. Instead, she marched down the hall to face a panel of her chosen judges.

Kris slipped into the staff room and settled into the seat closest to the door. Heads turned as she came in, took her in and her choice of seating, and went back to talking over what they were studying. Maybe their conversation was lower. Maybe their backs were more turned to her. But she was left alone, a ghost at her own funeral.

But Kris was never one to do nothing. NELLY, HAVE YOU LOOKED AT THE VIDEOS FROM THE BOFFINS' TAKE?

NO, KRIS.

WHY NOT?

BECAUSE CHIEF BENI DOWNLOADED IT ALL TO A STANDALONE SYSTEM THAT HE HAS COMPLETE CONTROL OF. THAT SYSTEM IS WHAT EVERYONE THERE IS LOOKING AT.

So they didn't trust Kris, or Nelly, or both of them. They'd grabbed a copy of the data raw and unedited and were using it for their own study. Interesting. Would that hold up in a court? In a court like Vicky hinted Greenfeld had?

Well, girl, you wanted a full court. Why are you so surprised that the people you have around you know how to give you a full and honest court just like you asked for?

Kris folded her hand and wished Tommy had been in her life long enough to teach her how to pray. When she had gotten them into messes like this, praying seemed to help him feel better.

Jack glanced her way. "You said we'd have an hour to look this stuff over. You know, in any normal investigation, this would take a couple of months."

"Yes, but you only have an hour," Kris answered back.

"Any chance you could go talk some more with that fellow from Xanadu?" Colonel Cortez asked.

"Not much of one. He hanged himself."

"Oh, I'm sorry," the colonel said.

"So am I," Kris agreed.

The women and men at that end of the room continued their quiet discussion for a few more minutes, hunching over screens on the wall or flimsies that sailors or scientists rushed in to them.

Finally, Colonel Cortez stepped away from the screen, stretched, and said, "Those pictures pretty much settle it for me. What about you?" There were general nods from the others.

Colonel Cortez turned formally to Kris. "Lieutenant Long-knife, if you will take your seat." With an open hand, he directed her to the middle seat on the long side of the table. He himself took the same seat across from her. Captains Drago and Krätz sat on either side of him. Jack and Penny took the chairs at Drago's elbows. Abby sat at Krätz's side with a full court-recording suite in front of her.

Where had Abby gotten all that gear? Kris wondered, then answered her own question. *Of course, I've got a judge aboard for civil cases. She'd have a recording set.*

Kris had wanted the *Wasp* outfitted for every eventuality that might arise beyond the rim of human space. She'd brought a judge. She'd brought a court.

Just what all do I have aboard? Kris suspected she was about to find out.

Colonel Cortez cleared his throat. "By a strange quirk of fate, my date of rank is a week earlier than Captain Krätz's . . ."

"And lots earlier than mine," Drago put in.

"So I am presiding over this Court of Inquiry. While our findings have been expedited, it is the opinion of this court that more time would not result in a different decision . . . and would leave findings open to questions of data manipulation. I want that entered into the record as a challenge to anyone who attempts to reopen this matter and review our decision."

For an infantry officer, Cortez seems in full control of the global reality of the situation, Kris thought, but said nothing and schooled her face to an unremarkable mask.

"For the purpose of this investigation, the court has relied heavily on the Ultra High Density Optical Scanner of the scientific task force aboard the *Wasp,* as recorded by the Super High Speed Visual Spectrum Recorder. These were brought aboard by the scientists to record the fine details of stellar events."

Cortez paused and studied some handwritten notes in front of him. "Here I must ask a question of an unusual witness. Lieutenant Longknife, can your personal computer bear witness?"

"I believe so. Nelly, you understand that you must tell the truth as you see it, the whole truth, and nothing but the truth."

"I understand the oath, Kris. Colonel Cortez, I promise that I will do that."

Kris would not have been surprised if Nelly had called upon God to bear witness to her truthfulness, but the computer left it at that.

"Miss Nelly," Cortez said, "were you aware of the advanced scanner and visual recorder being on board and did you review any of their data during the close encounter with the liner *Tourin*?"

There was only a slight pause before Nelly spoke. "I have in storage the *Wasp*'s full inventory. As such, I know these items. They are listed by name with no further information about their capabilities. I have no information about their mounting or of any data they acquired. The *Wasp*'s central computer had no feed from them and, as such, I had access to no input from them. Put another way, sir, I knew these devices were aboard. I did not know they were active, and I saw nothing from them during the close encounter with the liner *Tourin*."

"Thank you, Miss Nelly," the colonel said. "That resolved

the only matter left unanswered for the board. Lieutenant Longknife, may I direct your attention to the wall behind you."

Kris turned in her chair. She found herself staring at a stern view of the *Tourin*. It filled the wall behind her in spectacular detail.

"This is photo 34,215 of the pictures provided to this court," Cortez said, and now Kris could spot that number up in the left-hand corner. Below it was a notation: RANGE, 20,412.

"The photos before this one show only the approaching ship or the blurred image of it as the *Wasp* flipped ship. This photo is the first one that interests the court. Lieutenant, could you describe in your own words what you see in it based upon your plan of attack to damage the liner while causing as little harm as possible to its passengers and crew."

Kris wanted to say, *Not fair. You've had an hour to look at this picture. And besides, you can't make me my own prosecutor.*

But the picture drew her. She stood, taking it in and knowing exactly what she was seeing.

The undamaged engines showed large white dots of plasma shooting from the huge mouths of rockets. It was easy to spot the two, no three engines that had been sliced off. Plasma shot out from the tiny holes at the end of the containment field. Two other engines showed a skew of white fire where the sides of the engines had been lopped off. Kris described that to the board.

"Is that the damage you had aimed for?" Captain Krätz asked.

"Basically, yes. I'd hoped to cut all five of them off like we did the first three, maybe nick the four inner ones a bit, but this was what we aimed for, and I think this falls within our desired results."

"Do you see anything else?" Captain Drago asked.

"I don't think so. Nelly, do you see anything?"

"It is hard to tell from a single picture, Kris, but note the occlusion of the stars to the right of the motors. The ship could be heeling over to the right. I would need further pictures to establish a trend."

"This is the next photos, 34,216," Cortez said. The range notation was 22,619. It showed the same damage to the engines. It was hard to tell if it showed more heel.

"And photo 34,219." Jumping ahead three pictures, and at a range of 29,239, it was still hard for Kris to decide if the ship was heeling or if it was just a function of camera angle.

"Nelly, did you have any visual on the *Tourin* during the close encounter?" Colonel Cortez asked.

"I was getting pictures at about half the pace of these, but the resolution was much worse. Does the court have one of the ship's visuals?"

"Yes we do," Cortez said. On the short wall facing Kris, a stern view of the liner appeared. The glare from the working engines showed as a single large dot.

"So you had no way to gauge the damage Pulse Lasers 3 and 4 had done," Captain Krätz said.

"That is correct, sir," Nelly said. "At that instant, I was operating on the assumption that our first two lasers had missed, and the only hope we had was the second two."

"Thank you, Nelly," Cortez said. "Lieutenant Longknife, did you have similar assumptions?"

"Colonel Cortez, I had no assumptions at the time. It was happening too fast for me to observe, review, or make a revision to anything I'd planned."

"That does not surprise me. Let's see the next picture." Photo 34,220 had a range notation of 31,445. Three more engines had been cut away from the left-hand lower engine grouping.

There was no evidence that Battery 1 had hit the *Tourin*.

"And the next picture," Cortez said.

The *Tourin* was tearing itself apart.

"Here we see that Battery 1 did not miss," Captain Drago took over the narrative, "but rather sliced through the damaged area left by Batteries 3 and 4. Meeting no resistance, it was free to penetrate into the power plant and even to the reactor area. The result is catastrophic."

"Yes," Kris whispered. At her neck, so did Nelly.

"I have personally gone over the records of repair and maintenance on the lasers. They were fully overhauled on Wardhaven before you called us to Eden. We bore sighted them after that overhaul. They were not just within specs but well within specs," the captain of the *Wasp* reported. Beside him, both the colonel and the Greenfeld captain nodded. "As proof of that, I give you the actual results of this shoot. Batteries 2 and 4 just about nailed their targets. Battery 3 was a bit high and to the left. Battery 1 was off a bit more high and to the left, but it hit its target at thirty thousand kilometers and passing at a speed nearly .03 of the speed of light."

Now it was Kris's turn to nod. "The equipment functioned better than anyone had a right to expect."

"So it would seem," Captain Krätz said. High praise from a Greenfeld skipper for a Wardhaven ship driver.

"Now one further matter," Colonel Cortez said. "Miss Nelly, I am going to send you the scientific team's pictures that are in evidence. Would you please overlay them and determine if the *Tourin* was indeed heeling to the right based on the unbalanced engine configuration."

For longer than Kris would have expected, Nelly was silent, then the large screen changed. "As you can see from the three stars that became occluded between the first and the sixth picture under consideration, the passenger area of the hull is indeed starting to roll to the right."

"Our analysis showed that," Colonel Cortez said, "but we were not able to calculate the impact that skid would have on the hull of the *Tourin*. Applying the spin data that the scientists found to the expected behavior of the reaction mass in its tanks, what would be the effect on the ship?"

"No one has ever calculated that on a ship at such a high level of acceleration and inertia," Nelly said.

"Yes, we know. Every computer aboard declined this problem as having too many variables to track and taking too long. Do you think you can do it, Miss Nelly?"

"Let me try."

Kris glanced at her watch, then tapped its options to stopwatch and started a clock running.

"Baffles," Nelly said. "Did the *Tourin* have any baffles in its fuel tanks to control splashing?"

"Yes," Captain Krätz said, "but they were all arranged to control slop fore and aft, not in any other direction."

"Oh," Nelly said. "That is not good."

"Not at this speed," Krätz agreed.

Nelly went back to gnawing on her modeling problem. Kris glanced around the room. Sometime during the last eternity, Vicky had come in and made herself small in a chair against the wall behind Abby. Vicky tossed her a look, as if expecting to be shooed away, but begging for a chance to stay.

Kris dredged up something like a smile, and Vicky settled back, relieved.

Kris's brain spun, hungry to force a conclusion from the data laid out before her but wanting to wait until everything was there. Her belly was a vacuum, threatening to swallow her up, spin her away to somewhere where she was nothing and no one.

Kris Longknife held on to herself with her fingertips and felt the blood begin to flow as her fingernails dug into the flesh of her hands, her fists were clinched so tightly.

With a deep breath, she forced herself to relax. Fists, arms, legs, belly. For a moment, she swayed, about to fall, but she tightened up just enough to keep herself on her feet.

How long can a computer take to solve a simple problem in hydraulics? Kris demanded.

It's not simple. It's never been done before, she snapped back at herself.

"This solution is not pretty," Nelly said, "but I think it conveys the general results." A schematic of the *Tourin* appeared on-screen. Fractions of seconds ticked off as the ship heeled. Then it seemed to right itself as the second set of jets was shot off. But the slow spin ground on, now adding a twist to a hull more and more out of alignment. Within the huge reaction tank, a tsunami formed, slamming itself first against one side of the tank, then another. Chunks of tank wall broke off. The tidal wave shot off needles of water that speared into the rest of the ship, taking down walls and girders.

For two, three seconds, the ship came apart until, finally, the crushing wave of reaction mass blew out the bottom of the tank, slammed into the reactor containment equipment, and let loose the plasma to devour the wreckage.

"Either way, the ship blows up," Kris said, her voice dead with exhaustion.

"I should have recalculated my assumptions," Nelly said, "once the scientists told us the ship was under spin."

"I didn't tell you to, and I didn't think of it," Kris said.

"None of us did," Captain Drago said.

"None of us wanted to admit what that meant," Vicky said.

"That any way it went, five thousand people were doomed."

"The only question was if my dad died," Vicky added.

"And we had a horrible, horrible war," Kris said.

Vicky walked over to stand beside Kris. "Once State Security let those hijackers board the ship, take it over, every solution involved deaths. Lots and lots of them."

"Don't let General Boyng hear you say that," Captain Krätz said. Vicky said nothing.

55

The *Wasp* returned to High Birridas at a gentle one gee. That allowed plenty of time for matters to develop on South Continent. A hurricane blew itself out. Several plots to kill Henry Smythe-Peterwald were uncovered. Some people sang under interrogation, leading to further arrests. Others died.

Kris wondered what leads died with them.

Vicky sent several coded messages to her father. She got several replies. Kris personally made sure all copies of those messages were wiped from the *Wasp*'s logs.

Call it professional courtesy, one princess to another.

Kris seemed to be getting along very well with the scion of the Peterwald family. Just how good was quickly put to the test.

No sooner had the last pier tie-down locked on to the *Wasp* than the State Security colonel demanded to see Kris on the bridge. See her with his entire detail backing him up.

"Ignore him," Vicky said.

The look on Captain Krätz's face did not agree.

"It's critical that you get in touch with your father," Kris said. "Captain Krätz, can you get a security detail up here from your ship?"

He tapped his commlink. Then shook his head. "I'm jammed."

"So are we," Captain Drago said, answering Kris's question before she asked it.

Kris reached for the Greenfeld ensign. "Vicky, if something happens to you, I won't have a chance. Jack," Kris said, turning to the Marine captain.

"Kris, I'm your security chief, not hers."

"But my safety lies with her. See that she gets back to the *Surprise*. I don't care if it takes Gunny and half the Marines, but get her home safe."

There was noise at the bridge hatch; Kris had just enough time to organize a bland face for herself . . . ignoring the near mutiny on several others . . . before the colonel in State Security black marched onto her bridge.

No, not marched; it was more a confident prance.

"Longknife, you will accompany me," he demanded.

Kris considered the prospects of bloody slaughter on her bridge, then dismissed them. They were pinned to the wharf. Breaking free unaided from pierside would be nearly impossible. Kris would not leave Marines and Navy on the pier so that she could escape.

Still, there was room for drama. Why not make him earn his pay? "And why should I accompany you?" Kris said.

"Shall we start with the murder of five thousand loyal citizens of the Greenfeld Alliance and destroying a million-ton liner."

An ensign began to open her mouth; a far from gentle nudge in the ribs from her captain shut her up. Vicky fumed.

The colonel ignored the ensign. Why did Kris suspect that was a mortal mistake?

"Your attitude intrigues us," Kris said regally. "It pleases us to go with you. May this ship depart in peace?"

"The sooner the better," the colonel said, playing into Kris's own hand.

She turned to Drago. "If I'm not back in three hours, go. Alert Wardhaven and both my grampas. General Trouble should enjoy this place."

"Your call, Your Highness, but maybe you better take this," he said, and handed Kris a large envelope.

"What's this?"

"The conclusion of the board, suitable for framing, and all the supporting documentation."

"It won't matter where I'm going," Kris was pretty sure. "We're stalling for time, right?"

Kris let State Security escort her from her ship. Along the hatchways, sailors and Marines were conspicuous by their absence.

The boffins turned out in hordes. Some who'd never talked to her said, "Hi." Others were three deep and slowed the colonel's progress to a crawl. The third time Kris spotted a dyed-in-the-wool member of the opposition party, it became clear to her what her brain trust was up to.

There was nothing high-tech here. They knew all the routes of the *Wasp*. The colonel didn't. No sooner had Kris said a tearful good-bye to one, than he would race for an end around and be waiting ahead of her to shout "Good luck" a minute later.

It took the colonel ten minutes to figure the ploy out. Then, in a loud voice, he told Kris, "If I see another one of these wellwishers for a second time, I'll have my corporal shoot him in the knee. A third time, and I'll shoot him in the head."

Professor mFumbo took the lead of the troupe, and they progressed to the gangway more quickly. Kris crossed the gangplank of the *Wasp* to calls of "See you soon," "Good luck," and "Mazel tov."

Free of the crowd, the colonel hustled Kris to the escalator to the station's main deck. Riding up, Kris looked back. Except for the two Marines at the *Wasp*'s gangway, the dock was empty.

That didn't prepare Kris for the main deck of the station. It was also vacant as far as the eye could see. Admittedly, the long vista was broken up by some station structure amidships; still, up and down and around the curve of the main deck, no one stood or moved.

On High Chance, Kris had been surprised to find herself alone. Here, with over a dozen ships in port, the vacancy was spooky. The security colonel seemed to sense that, too, and urged his men on. With heads swiveling to spot any threat from any direction, the men did.

What frightens men whom everyone was supposed to be scared of? Kris wondered, and marched head high and eyes straight ahead.

The amidships structure was their destination. The colonel piled his men into a large freight elevator, spoke one word into his commlink, and it rose. From her loss of weight, Kris estimated that they were about a quarter of the way to the center of the station when the elevator stopped.

The door slammed open, and the colonel found himself facing a brigadier general. "What took you so long?"

"The Longknife did everything she could to delay us."

"And you let her," the one-star sneered. Behind him, double the number of machine pistols stood at the ready. It would not

have surprised Kris if she'd been gunned down right there with
the others in the elevator. The bobbing Adam's apples around
her attested to the fear of her former escort.

Instead, the general waved Kris out of the elevator, the colonel to stay, and barked something that closed the door. Kris now
had a new escort, but at least her old one lived.

For now.

Without a word spoken, the larger team in State Security
black formed around Kris, and all of them marched off. Her file
must attribute true ferociousness to her if all this was felt needed
to get her from point A to point B. She considered taking a flying leap at the guard next to her, or maybe rolling on the floor,
foaming at the mouth. A quick glance at the men around her
showed the distinct lack of a sense of humor.

She marched along, "Not a lot of reporters," she remarked.

"You think this is Wardhaven," the brigadier snapped.

"That's where I was when last I was arrested."

"You will soon see we are different," he growled. "I would
say more efficient, but you might not find us as easy as *those*
people." Kris hadn't found "*those* people" all that much fun, but
she held her own counsel.

She and the State Security men put on quite a parade, to no
one's delight or even notice. Again the halls were notably empty.
They stopped outside a door that was unremarkable.

"Here you go, Longknife," the brigadier snapped, opening
the door for her.

Kris moved, quickly enough not to be shoved, slow enough
not to be mistaken for a threat, through the door. The general
followed her into an outer office, empty except for two guards at
an inner door.

"That is for you," the general said, but made no effort to lead
her. Kris carefully marched across the outer room to the door,
squaring her corners. At the door she paused for only a moment.
The one-star general cackled.

She opened the door and entered.

The room was unlit. Kris closed the door behind her, and it
went totally dark. Backing up to the door to keep her bearings,
Kris felt around the wall for a switch.

She found none.

"Lights on," she said.

And the lights came on to show her a rather large office furnished in dull shades of tan. Its focus was a heavy wooden desk with a comfortable leather chair behind it. The only other chair in the room was over against the wall with the door.

Kris flipped a mental coin, decided that she would most likely soon be talking to someone seated at that desk . . . and moved the chair to the side of the desk. She took a moment to take in the other furnishings, which were mostly noticeable by their absence: no bookcases, no books, no other seating, no place to organize an informal meeting.

There were several oil paintings. Mostly landscapes and sunsets, two featured ancient gibbets with corpses hanging on them and crows feasting. Kris refused to flinch at the tastes of her host but noted them.

A door opened, and Lieutenant General Boyng entered. "You are early," he growled.

"You are late," Kris said. She kept her words light but gave no ground.

"Generals are always on time. Lieutenants are early or late."

"I'll meet your three stars and raise you a princess," Kris said, wondering how long she could banter words with a man who probably considered a day lightly started if he hadn't sentenced a dozen men to death before breakfast.

Just don't choke on a word, she told herself, swallowing hard.

"We'll see how you banter with your betters when you're wearing a pain collar," the general said, and, pulling one from a drawer, tossed it onto his desk. "Put it on."

"I'd rather not. It's not the fashion on Wardhaven. So why should I?"

"Because I ordered you to."

"Our chains of command do go in somewhat divergent directions."

"Then maybe your Wardhaven sensibilities would be better served if I told you it's the perfect fashion statement for a mass murderer."

He pinned her with his eyes, challenged her to deny her guilt.

Maybe yesterday she would have accepted the punishment, but not today. She had been cleared by a court of her superiors. "Sorry, you have the wrong princess."

"Didn't your ship fire on the *Dedicated Workers of Tourin*?

Aren't you responsible for the work of your ship's weapons officer?" He smiled at that, sure of her entrapment.

"General, I *was* the gunnery officer."

"You personally killed those five thousand innocent people!"

Kris leaned on the desk to go eye to eye with the shorter man. "Yes, I did."

"Oh," he said, and settled into his comfortable chair. He eyed Kris as one cobra might another, one from another territory . . . maybe threatening his . . . maybe not.

"My field agents seem to have misjudged your stomach for killing."

Not likely, but this was no time to disabuse this man about her taste for blood. "Your field agents may have misjudged me in many ways. It would be interesting to see how much is correct in the file I keep hearing about."

That brought a laugh from the mouth of hell. "No, no. You are in my power. Not the other way around. And no, I have no intention of playing with you. Didn't your mother teach you not to play with your food?"

"No, my mother taught me not to eat people. They are much more fun to rule when free and sovereign."

"Words, words," he said, reaching into his desk and removing an ancient revolver from a drawer. "Put on the pain collar."

Without thought, Kris had put on a spider-silk body stocking that morning. Abby laid one out; Kris put it on. Just another day in the life of a princess. If the general shot her in the chest, he'd be surprised at the results.

Then again, if he shot her in the face, she'd be dead.

It was hard to tell exactly where he was aiming.

If Kris dropped for the floor, she might get facedown below the desk before he drilled her where she wasn't protected. No one had frisked her; her service automatic was still in easy reach.

Kris went through the options, options she could almost see mirrored in the general's eyes.

The phone rang.

56

"Put on the pain collar," the general demanded.

The phone rang again. There were two phones on the desk, one white, the other red. The red demanded attention.

"You need to answer your phone," Kris said, taking a seat in the available chair.

"Put on the pain collar, or I will kill you."

The words were harsh, demanding. Kris stared them down.

"Your master's leash demands attention."

"You could be dead before ever he says a word."

Kris knew that only too well. "If I am dead before you answer that phone, you will be dead before sunset."

"Are you so sure?"

"Why don't you answer the phone and find out?"

It had rung twice more while they debated their respective fates.

The general reached for his phone, pistol steady on Kris. She did not budge. Win or lose, that call would decide it.

Well, if she lost, she'd go down doing her best to kill this murderer. Her hand edged closer to where her automatic rode snugly at the small of her back.

"Yes," the general said.

"Yes, sir," he snapped immediately, and leapt to attention, gun still in his hand but no longer aimed at Kris.

"You are well, sir. Thank God, sir" was followed by a long pause as the general listened. "Yes, sir, the girl is safe with me. I was examining options for her final disposition."

So Kris was of interest to the old man. Now, was he thinking about the son she was supposed to have killed, the five thousand she'd just killed . . . or the fact she'd saved his life?

"Yes, sir. It will be so, sir. Long life, sir," the general said rapidly, then slowly put the phone in its receiver.

"You are a very lucky girl," he said.

"Those who survive have to be," Kris said, standing up.

"You are free to go. Your ship may leave as soon as you return to it." The voice was stripped of emotion, like a skeleton stripped of flesh.

"And how will I find my way back to my ship?"

"However you may. Greenfeld is not so populous that we can detail escorts to every girl with pretensions to importance."

Kris was about to turn her back on the general when he reached out. "I'll trouble you for that automatic you were edging for a few moments ago."

Kris shook her head curtly. No way would she face this station unarmed. "You can tell your thugs to be careful. I'm no easy takedown."

"I'll tell my men what I choose to," the general said, but he kept his pistol arm at his side. Kris turned, caught the general's reflection in one of his paintings, and strode to the door. His gun arm stayed down, and Kris did no drop and roll and recover with automatic in hand as she had mapped out in her mind.

At the door, she turned. The general did not look like he had so much as twitched a muscle. "See you around," Kris called.

"I doubt it," he said.

Kris was through the door in a blink and slammed it behind her. The two guards actually jumped at the noise, or at her presence. She doubted many people who went in that door came out again under their own power.

"Bye, guys, it's been a great time," Kris said, and covered the distance to the outer door before they recovered.

She slammed that door, too. Which left her a lot of balled-up anger in her gut and no more doors to slam. The temptation to gallop for the freight elevator was strong, but Kris denied it. As she expected, when she got there, the thing had no visible controls. NELLY, CAN YOU CALL IT?

KRIS, I AM SO JAMMED. ROCK SOLID AND TOTALLY JAMMED.

I GUESS WE KNOW NOW WHERE IT'S BEEN COMING FROM.

YOU THINK SO, MAYBE, JUST A LITTLE BIT was pure sarcasm, unusual from a computer, all too familiar from Nelly.

ANY IDEA WHERE WE ARE?

KRIS, I DO NOT HAVE A CLUE EVEN. WE ARE SO ON OUR OWN, LIKE TOTALLY.

YOU'VE BEEN SPENDING TOO MUCH TIME WITH THAT GIRL.

HOW I WISH I WAS WITH HER NOW.

A freight elevator usually meant there'd be a passenger one not too far away. Kris started walking in the direction she hoped was forward. She found nothing. But a couple of guys were following her, using the next hallway of the station.

On both sides. Kris kept going.

At the next cross point, the two guys on her left were heading to cut her off. Kris started to put on extra speed . . . then came to a complete halt.

As the two fellows passed one door, it opened and two sailors with billy clubs stepped quietly out behind them and very efficiently put them down. A chief stepped out behind the two left standing and signaled to Kris. "This way, Your Highness."

"And why should I go with you?" Kris said, already moving their way.

"Because Captain Krätz sent us. He has some wedding pictures he wants to show you. It's quite a scandal. His second girl married first.

"None of the captain's girls would ever do anything scandalous," Kris sniffed.

"Unlike you, huh?"

"Do we know each other that well?" Kris asked as she came even with the chief. He did look familiar.

"You gave me a tour of your defenses on Chance, remember? The ones that even our little commodore saw would be a bad idea to take on." The chief led Kris into a gray-painted work area with pipes and conduits. He pointed at a ladder.

"Up or down?" Kris asked.

"Down."

Kris began descending; he followed. The sailors stayed behind. "I thought you were the flagship's senior chief."

"I was, but after that incident, the commodore didn't much like my puss. Captain Slovo shipped me over to the *Surprise*."

"Sorry about Captain Slovo," Kris said.

"A lot of good men disappeared with him. Sure would like to know who made it happen," the chief growled.

Kris wondered if the chief shared her own opinion about

that, but kept the thought to herself and kept going down the ladder. After quite a while, there was no more down.

Two sailors with automatic rifles guarded a platform that seemed to rest on the outer shell of the station.

"Time to see how fast you can trot," the chief said, joining her and pointing at a catwalk that stretched into the distance. To the right and left, it curved up.

Kris started trotting.

And kept on trotting for a very long time. There were cross catwalks, but the chief said nothing, and Kris just kept trotting. It would have been nice to stand up, but even a short man would have had to bend at the waist in this crawl space.

Finally, they came to a crosswalk with two armed sailors. "Go right," the chief called. Kris gave the sailors a smile and did the ninety-degree right turn called for.

"Isn't there a slidewalk we could take?" Kris asked, her back aching.

"You want to shoot it out with security types?" the chief shot back.

"So that's the choice, run like rats in the walls or shoot."

"Seems that way at the moment." He started to say something else, apparently thought better of it, and trotted on. "Wait until that long, tall back of yours has my kind of miles on it. Then you can complain."

"I thought sailors had a right to complain," Kris quipped.

"That don't extend to junior officers, now does it?"

Kris shut up and trotted.

After a left turn at a cross marked by two Greenfeld Marines, they came to a platform with six Marines and sailors guarding it. They helped Kris climb a short ladder . . . which brought her to the main deck promenade. Kris stood, straightened her uniform, turned . . . and found herself facing the escalator down to a pier that was crawling with armed sailors and Marines. Kris couldn't figure out what they were doing, but they seemed to know because there was nothing purposeless in their movements.

The chief escorted Kris down to the first deck of the pier, then across the guarded gangway, saluting the flag and requesting permission to come aboard. Kris also boarded in the traditional manner, and followed the ensign that the JOOD assigned to show her to the wardroom.

A very busy wardroom.

Schematics of the station covered two walls. Maps of the planet below filled in the other two. A captain and his ensign studied them for a moment more after Kris entered, then, with a word, the walls went blank.

"Keeping secrets?" Kris asked.

"What are Greenfeld internal matters are ours," Vicky said. "Let them stay that way for now. I'm sure your Admiral Crossenshield will give you a badly garbled and totally wrong assessment of this situation. It may take him a few days to jump to the wrong conclusions, but, no doubt, he will find his pole vault somewhere. How do we stay alive with such bunglers?"

"I think I've given you a pretty up-front and honest sample of how I do it over the last few days," Kris said evenly.

"So you have," Vicky said. "But you can't tell me that my dad getting you out of old Eddie's maw wasn't a big help."

"You've talked to your dad?"

"Yeah, the Navy has a landline down the beanstalk that State Security doesn't know about. Dad says thank you. He says he'll rethink his attitude toward you Longknifes."

"Can I take that to the bank?" Kris asked.

"Probably not. We'd best get you out of here fast."

"Am I going to do more catwalk dancing?" Kris asked.

Krätz allowed a very small smile at Kris's joke. "You can return to the *Wasp* the way we got to the *Surprise*. Your longboat is in our Number 2 lander bay."

Vicky insisted on doing the honors. But the walk turned out to be mostly quiet. At least until they got to the longboat's hatch. "I'm glad I didn't kill you on Eden," Vicky said.

"So am I," Kris agreed.

"I'm really sorry I brought your great-grandmother into the thing. I've never known my grandmothers. Hardly knew my mother before Dad broke up with her."

"It hasn't been an easy life for either one of us."

"Ever had a real friend?" Vicky asked. "A bosom buddy?"

"Oh, you would have to bring those two up, wouldn't you?"

"These?" Vicky said, glancing down at what with the effort of a fast walk behind them could only be described as heaving bosoms. "They get in the way when I'm running. They're two big pains in the back. You don't know how lucky you are to have gotten off lightly."

"And, of course, the boys just never notice your problems," Kris jabbed.

"You have no idea," Vicky began.

"The troubles I've got," Kris finished.

Vicky laughed for a moment, then swallowed hard and glanced off into the unmeasured distance. "You don't, do you?"

"Mine are different," Kris agreed.

Vicky opened her arms, Kris went into an honest hug. "I hope someday we can get together when no one's life is on the line. Someday when we can just talk girl talk."

"It would be nice," Kris agreed. "I'm not sure I've ever done that."

"Me neither. But all the books make it sound so nice."

Kris hated breaking from the hug. It was the only equal hug she could remember. But worry was gnawing at the corners of Vicky's eyes, and Kris suspected she needed to get the *Wasp* out and away before all hell broke loose.

"I *will* see you," she said.

"Looking forward to it," Vicky said,

And they went their separate ways: Kris into the launch, which sealed hatches the second she was aboard; and Vicky to whomever the internal affairs of Greenfeld were killing at the moment.

"Hang on," the pilot of the longboat hollered, not even giving Kris a moment to sit down and buckle in.

57

The trip to the *Wasp* was made at one gee with plenty of zigging and zagging to throw off any of the station's lasers that might have been brought up and calibrated in the last few days.

None fired.

Kris wasn't out of the longboat before the *Wasp* was backing down the pier. The clanking of tie-downs coming off warned Kris not to let go of her handhold on the boat. Only after Captain Drago announced the ship under way at one gee did she risk trotting across the hangar bay's space.

Once Kris was on the bridge, Penny grabbed her for a hug. "We were so worried."

Abby was next. "I wasn't. Everyone knows you can't get rid of a Longknife." But the hug was tight.

Jack looked like he'd love to hug her, too, but limited his greetings to "Glad to have you back aboard."

Even Professor mFumbo was there, only his welcome was more what Kris would have expected. "Now can we do some real science?"

"Didn't we come here to get out their Jump Point Gamma?" Kris asked Sulwan.

"That's the rumor I picked up, long ago and far away."

"Well, Captain Drago, how long will it take us to set a course for Jump Point Gamma?"

"That course is locked in."

"Then make it so, my good captain. I could use some nice boring scientific discoveries for a change."

Only Kris's inner ear told her the ship was changing its course. Blinking that discomfort away, Kris wondered how many days she could go without anyone trying to kill her.

NELLY, START A COUNTER. LET'S SEE HOW LONG IT IS BE-
FORE SOMEONE TAKES A POTSHOT AT ME.

KRIS, I AM NOT SURE I CAN COUNT THAT LOW.

About the Author

Mike Shepherd grew up Navy. It taught him early about change and the chain of command. He's worked as a bartender and cabdriver, personnel adviser and labor negotiator. Now retired from building databases about the endangered critters of the Northwest, he's looking forward to some fun reading and writing.

Mike lives in Vancouver, Washington, with his wife, Ellen, and her mother. He enjoys reading, writing, dreaming, watching grandchildren for story ideas, and upgrading his computer—all are never-ending pursuits.

His website is www.mikeshepherd.org, or you may reach him at Mike_Shepherd@comcast.net.

For my older brother, Lee, and
my younger sister, Laurie.
I've never been between two nicer people.

PROLOGUE

The sudden appearance of the foreign proteins was the molecular equivalent of the Black Plague. It was a death sentence with no chance of reprieve, and Cedric Harring had no idea of the drama about to happen inside him.

In sharp contrast, the individual cells of Cedric Harring's body knew exactly what disastrous consequences awaited them. The mysterious new proteins that swept into their midst and through their membranes were overwhelming, and the small amounts of enzymes capable of dealing with the newcomers were totally inadequate. Within Cedric's pituitary gland, the deadly new proteins were able to bind themselves to the repressors that covered the genes for the death hormone. From that moment, with the fatal genes exposed, the outcome was inevitable. The death hormone began to be synthetized in unprecedented amounts. Entering the bloodstream, the hormone coursed out into Cedric's body. No cell was immune. The end was only a matter of time. Cedric Harring was about to disintegrate into his stellar elements.

11

1.

The pain was like a white-hot knife starting somewhere in his chest and quickly radiating upward in blinding paroxysms to paralyze his jaw and left arm. Instantly Cedric felt the terror of the mortal fear of death. Cedric Harring had never felt anything like it.

By reflex he gripped the steering wheel of his car more tightly and somehow managed to stay in control of the weaving vehicle as he gasped for breath. He'd just entered Storrow Drive from Berkeley Street in downtown Boston, and had accelerated westward, merging with the maddening Boston traffic. The images of the road swam before him and then receded, as if they existed at the end of a long tunnel.

By sheer strength of will, Cedric resisted the darkness that threatened to engulf him. Gradually, the scene brightened. He was still alive. Instead of pulling over, instinct told him his only chance was to get to a hospital as fast as possible. By lucky coincidence the Good Health Plan Clinic was not too far off. Hold on, he told himself.

Along with the pain came a drenching sweat that started on Cedric's forehead but soon spread to the rest of his body. Sweat stung his eyes, but he dared not loosen his grip on the steering wheel to wipe it away. He exited the highway onto the Fenway, a parklike complex in Boston, as the pain returned, squeezing his chest like a cinch of steel wire. Ahead cars were slowing for a traffic light. He couldn't stop. There was no time. Leaning forward, he depressed the horn and shot through the intersection. Cars went by, missing him by inches. He could see the faces of the startled and enraged drivers. He was now on Park Drive with the Back Bay Fens and the scruffy victory gardens on his left. The pain was constant now, strong and overpowering. He could hardly breathe.

The hospital was ahead on the right, on the previous site of a Sears building. Only a little further. Please. . . . A large white sign with a red arrow and red letters that said EMERGENCY loomed above.

Cedric managed to drive directly up to the emergency room platform, braking belatedly and crashing into the concrete abutment. He slumped forward, hitting the horn and gasping for breath.

The first person to reach his car was the security guard. He yanked open the door and after a glance at Cedric's frightening pallor yelled for help. Cedric barely choked out the words, "Chest pain." The head nurse, Hilary Barton, appeared and called for a gurney. By the time the nurses and the security man

had Cedric out of the car, one of the emergency room residents had appeared and helped maneuver him onto the stretcher. His name was Emil Frank and he'd been a resident for only four months. A few years previously he would have been called an intern. He too noticed Cedric's cream-colored skin and profuse perspiration.

"Diaphoresis," he said with authority. "Probably a heart attack."

Hilary rolled her eyes. Of course it was a heart attack. She rushed the patient inside, ignoring Dr. Frank, who'd plugged his stethoscope into his ears and was trying to listen to Cedric's heart.

As soon as they reached the treatment room, Hilary ordered oxygen, IV fluids and electrocardiographic monitoring, attaching the three main EKG leads herself. As soon as Emil had the IV going, she suggested to him that he order 4 mg. of morphine to be given IV immediately.

As the pain receded a little, Cedric's mind cleared. Even though no one had told him, he knew he'd had a heart attack. He also knew he'd come very close to dying. Even now, staring at the oxygen mask, the IV, and the EKG machine as it spewed paper out onto the floor, Cedric had never felt so vulnerable in his life.

"We're going to move you to the coronary care unit," Hilary said. "Everything is going to be okay." She patted Cedric's hand. He tried to smile. "We've called your wife. She's on her way."

15

The coronary intensive care unit was similar to the emergency room as far as Cedric was concerned—and just as frightening. It was filled with esoteric, ultramodern electronic technology. He could hear his heartbeat being echoed by a mechanical beep, and when he turned his head he could see a phosphorescent blip trace across a round TV screen.

Although the machines were frightening, it was a source of some reassurance to know all that technology was there. Even more reassuring was the fact that his own doctor, who had been paged shortly after Cedric's arrival, had just come into the ICU.

Cedric had been a patient of Dr. Jason Howard's for five years. He had begun going when his employers, the Boston National Bank, insisted that senior executives have yearly physicals. When Dr. Howard suddenly sold his private practice several years previously and joined the staff of the Good Health Plan (GHP), Cedric had dutifully followed. The move required changing his health plan from Blue Cross to the prepaid variety, but it was Dr. Howard that had attracted him, not GHP, and Cedric had let Dr. Howard know it in no uncertain terms.

"How are you doing?" Jason asked, grasping Cedric's arm but paying more attention to the EKG screen.

"Not . . . great," Cedric rasped. It took several breaths to get out the two words.

"I want you to try to relax."

Cedric closed his eyes. *Relax! What a joke.*

"Do you have a lot of pain?"

Cedric nodded. Tears were running down his cheeks.

"Another dose of morphine," Jason ordered.

Within minutes of the second dose, the pain became more tolerable. Dr. Howard was talking with the resident, making sure all the appropriate blood samples had been drawn and asking for some kind of catheter. Cedric watched him, reassured just seeing Howard's handsome, hawklike profile and sensing the man's confidence and authority. Best of all, he could feel Dr. Howard's compassion. Dr. Howard cared.

"We have to do a little procedure," Jason was saying. "We want to insert a Swan-Ganz catheter so we can see what's going on inside. We'll use a local anesthesia so it won't hurt, okay?"

Cedric nodded. As far as he was concerned, Dr. Howard had carte blanche to do whatever he felt was necessary. Cedric appreciated Dr. Howard's approach. He never talked down to his patients—even when Cedric had had his physical three weeks ago and Howard had lectured him about his high-cholesterol diet, his two-pack-a-day cigarette habit, and his lack of exercise. *If only I'd listened*, Cedric thought. But despite Dr. Howard's doomsday approach to Cedric's lifestyle, the doctor had admitted that the tests were okay. His cholesterol was not too high, and his electrocardiogram had been fine. Reassured, Cedric put off attempts to stop smoking and start exercising.

Then, less than a week after his physical, Cedric

felt as if he were coming down with the flu. But that had been only the beginning. His digestive system began acting up, and he suffered terrible arthritis. Even his eyesight seemed to deteriorate. He remembered telling his wife it was as though he had aged thirty years. He had all the symptoms his father had endured during his final months in the nursing home. Sometimes when he caught an unexpected glimpse of his reflection, it was as if he were staring at the old man's ghost.

Despite the morphine, Cedric felt a sudden stab of white-hot, crushing pain. He felt himself receding into a tunnel as he had in the car. He could still see Dr. Howard, but the doctor was far away, and his voice was fading. Then the tunnel started to fill with water. Cedric choked and tried to swim to the surface. His arms frantically grappled the air.

Later, Cedric regained consciousness for a few moments of agony. As he struggled back to awareness, he felt intermittent pressure on his chest, and something in his throat. Someone was kneeling beside him, crushing his chest with his hands. Cedric started to cry out when there was an explosion in his chest and darkness descended like a lead blanket.

Death had always been Dr. Jason Howard's enemy. As a resident at Massachusetts General, he'd carried that belief to the extreme, never giving up on a cardiac arrest until a superior ordered him to stop. Now he refused to believe that the fifty-six-year-

old man whom he'd examined only three weeks earlier and had declared generally healthy was about to die. It was a personal affront.

Glancing up at the monitor, which still showed normal EKG activity, Jason touched Cedric's neck. He could feel no pulse. "Let me have a cardiac needle," he demanded. "And someone get a blood pressure." A large cardiac needle was thrust into his hand as he palpated Cedric's chest to locate the ridge on the sternum.

"No blood pressure," reported Philip Barnes, an anesthesiologist who had responded to the code call that automatically went out when Cedric arrested. He'd placed an endotracheal tube into Cedric's trachea and was ventilating him with oxygen by compressing the Ambu bag.

To Jason, the diagnosis was obvious: cardiac rupture. With the EKG still being recorded, yet no pumping action of the heart, a situation of electromechanical dissociation prevailed. It could mean only one thing. The portion of Cedric's heart that had been deprived of its blood supply had split open like a squashed grape. To prove this horrendous diagnosis, Jason plunged the cardiac needle into Cedric's chest, piercing the heart's pericardial covering. When he drew back on the plunger, the syringe filled with blood. There was no doubt. Cedric's heart had burst open inside his chest.

"Let's get him to surgery," Jason shouted, grabbing the end of the bed. Philip rolled his eyes at

Judith Reinhart, the coronary care head nurse. They both knew it was futile. At best they might get Cedric on the heart-lung machine, but what then?

Philip stopped ventilating the patient. But instead of helping to push the bed, he walked over to Jason and gently put an arm on his shoulder, restraining him. "It's got to be cardiac rupture. You know it. I know it. We've lost this one, Jason."

Jason made a motion to protest, but Philip tightened his hold. Jason glanced at Cedric's ivory-colored face. He knew Philip was right. As much as he hated to admit it, the patient was lost.

"You're right," he said, and reluctantly let Philip and Judith lead him from the unit, leaving the other nurses to prepare the body.

As they walked over to the central desk, Jason admitted that Cedric was the third patient to die just weeks after having a clean physical. The first had been another heart attack, the other a massive stroke. "Maybe I should think about changing professions," Jason said half seriously. "Even my inpatients have been doing poorly."

"Just bad luck," Philip said, giving Jason a playful poke in the shoulder. "We all have our bad times. It'll get better."

"Yeah, sure," Jason said.

Philip left to return to surgery.

Jason found an empty chair and sat down heavily. He knew he'd have to get ready to face Cedric's wife, who would be arriving at the hospital at any mo-

ment. He felt drained. "You'd think by now I'd have gotten a little more accustomed to death," he said aloud.

"The fact that you don't is what makes you a good doctor," said Judith, attending to the paperwork associated with a death.

Jason accepted the compliment, but he knew his attitude toward death went far beyond the profession. Just two years ago death had destroyed all that Jason held dear. He could still remember the sound of the phone at quarter past midnight on a dark November night. He'd fallen asleep in the den trying to catch up on his journals. He thought it would be his wife, Danielle, calling from Children's Hospital, saying she'd be delayed. She was a pediatrician and had been called back to the hospital that evening to attend to a preemie in respiratory distress. But it had been the turnpike police. They called to say that a semi coming from Albany with a load of aluminum siding had jumped the central divider and rammed into his wife's car head-on. She had never had a chance.

Jason could still remember the trooper's voice, as if it had been yesterday. First there'd been shock and disbelief, followed by anger. Then his own terrible guilt. If only he'd gone with Danielle as he sometimes had, and read at Countway Medical Library. Or if only he'd insisted she sleep at the hospital.

A few months later he'd sold the house that was haunted by Danielle's presence and his private prac-

tice and the office he'd shared with her. That was
when he had joined the Good Health Plan. He'd done
everything Patrick Quillan, a psychiatrist friend,
had suggested he do. But the pain was still there,
and the anger, too.

"Excuse me, Dr. Howard?"

Jason looked up into the broad face of Kay Ramn,
the unit secretary.

"Mrs. Harring is in the waiting room," Kay said.
"I told her you'd be out to talk with her."

"Oh, God," Jason said, rubbing his eyes. Speaking
to the relatives after a patient died was difficult for
any doctor, but since Danielle's death, Jason felt the
families' pain as if it were his own.

Across from the coronary care unit was a small
sitting room with outdated magazines, vinyl chairs
and plastic plants. Mrs. Harring was staring out the
window that faced north toward Fenway Park and
the Charles River. She was a slight woman with hair
that had been allowed to go naturally gray. When
Jason entered, she turned and looked at him with
red-rimmed, terrified eyes.

"I'm Dr. Howard," Jason said, motioning for her
to sit. She did, but on the very edge of the chair.

"So it is bad . . ." she began. Her voice trailed off.

"I'm afraid it is very bad," Jason said. "Mr. Harring has passed away. We did all we could. At least
he didn't suffer." Jason hated himself for voicing
those expected lies. He knew Cedric had suffered.
He'd seen the mortal fear in his face. Death was al-

ways a struggle, rarely the peaceful ebbing of life portrayed in film.

The color drained from Mrs. Harring's face, and for a moment Jason thought she would faint. Finally, she said, "I can't believe it."

Jason nodded. "I know." And know he did.

"It's not right," she said. She looked at Jason defiantly, her face reddening. "I mean, you just gave him a clean bill of health. You gave him all those tests and they were normal! Why didn't you find something? *You might have prevented this.*"

Jason recognized the anger, the familiar precursor to grief. He felt great compassion for her. "I didn't exactly give him a clean bill of health," he said gently. "His lab studies were satisfactory, but I warned him as I always did about his smoking and diet. And I reminded him that his father had died of a heart attack. All these factors put him in a high-risk category despite his lab values."

"But his father was seventy-four when he died. Cedric is only fifty-six! What's the point of a physical if my husband dies just three weeks later?"

"I'm sorry," Jason said softly. "Our predictive abilities are limited. We know that. We can only do the best we can."

Mrs. Harring sighed, letting her breath out. Her narrow shoulders sagged forward. Jason could see the anger fading. In its place came the crushing sadness. When she spoke, her voice was shaking. "I know you do the best you can. I'm sorry."

Jason leaned forward and put his hand on her shoulder. She felt delicate under her thin silk dress. "I know how hard this is for you."

"Can I see him?" she asked through her tears.

"Of course." Jason got to his feet and offered her a hand.

"Did you know Cedric had made an appointment to see you?" Mrs. Harring said as they walked into the corridor. She wiped her eyes with a tissue she'd taken from her purse.

"No, I didn't," Jason admitted.

"Next week. It was the first available appointment. He wasn't feeling well."

Jason felt the uncomfortable stirring of defensive concern. Although he was certain no malpractice had been committed, that was no guarantee against a suit.

"Did he complain of chest pain when he called?" Jason asked. He stopped Mrs. Harring in front of the CCU door.

"No, no. Just a lot of unrelated symptoms. Mostly exhaustion."

Jason breathed a sigh of relief.

"His joints ached," Mrs. Harring continued. "And his eyes were bothering him. He was having trouble driving at night."

Trouble driving at night? Although such a symptom did not relate to a heart attack, it rang some kind of a bell in Jason's mind.

"And his skin got very dry. And he had lost a great deal of hair—"

"Hair naturally replaces itself," Jason said mechanically. It was obvious that this litany of nonspecific complaints had nothing to do with the man's massive heart attack. He pushed open the heavy door to the unit and motioned Mrs. Harring to follow him. He guided her into the appropriate cubicle.

Cedric had been covered with a clean white sheet. Mrs. Harring put her thin, bony hand on her husband's head.

"Would you like to see his face?" Jason asked.

Mrs. Harring nodded, tears reappearing and streaming down her face. Jason folded back the sheet and stepped back.

"Oh, God!" she cried. "He looks like his father did before he died!" She turned away and murmured, "I didn't realize how death aged a person."

It doesn't usually, Jason thought. Now that he wasn't concentrating on Cedric's heart, he noticed the changes in his face. His hair had thinned. And his eyes appeared to have receded deep into their orbits, giving the dead man's face a hollow, gaunt look, a far cry from the appearance Jason remembered when he'd done Cedric's physical three weeks earlier. Jason replaced the sheet and led Mrs. Harring back to the small sitting room. He sat her back down and took a seat across from her.

"I know it's not a good time to bring this up," he said, "but we would like permission to examine your husband's body. Maybe we can learn something that will help someone in the future."

"I suppose if it could help others . . ." Mrs. Harring bit her lip. It was hard for her to think, much less make a decision.

"It will. And we really appreciate your generosity. If you'd just wait here, I'll have someone bring out the forms."

"All right," Mrs. Harring said, with resignation.

"I'm sorry," Jason told her again. "Please call me if there is anything I can do."

Jason found Judith and told her that Mrs. Harring had agreed to an autopsy.

"We called the medical examiner's office and spoke to a Dr. Danforth. She said they want the case," Judith told him.

"Well, make sure they send us all the results." Jason hesitated. "Did you notice anything odd about Mr. Harring? I mean, did he appear unusually old for a man of fifty-six?"

"I didn't notice," Judith said, hurrying away. In a unit with eleven patients, she was already involved in another crisis.

Jason knew that Cedric's emergency was putting him behind schedule, but Cedric's unexpected death continued to disturb him. Making up his mind, he called Dr. Danforth, who had a deep resonant voice, and convinced her to let the postmortem be done in house, saying death was due to a long family history of heart disease and that he wanted to compare the heart pathology with the stress EKGs that had been done. The medical examiner graciously released the case.

*   *   *

Before leaving the unit, Jason used the opportunity to check another of his patients who was not doing well.

Sixty-one-year-old Brian Lennox was another heart attack victim. He had been admitted three days previously, and although he'd done well initially, his course had taken a sudden turn for the worse. That morning when Jason had made rounds he had planned to move Lennox from CCU, but the man was in the early throes of congestive heart failure. It was an acute disappointment for Jason, since Brian Lennox had to be added to the list of Jason's inpatients who had recently gone sour. Instead of transferring the patient, Jason had instituted aggressive treatment for the heart failure.

Any hope of a rapid return by Mr. Lennox to his previous state was dashed when Jason saw him. He was sitting up, breathing rapidly and shallowly in an oxygen mask. His face had an evil grayness that Jason had learned to fear. A nurse attending him straightened up from adjusting the IV.

"How are things going?" Jason asked, forcing a smile. But he didn't have to ask. Lennox lifted a limp hand. He couldn't talk. All his attention was directed toward his breathing efforts.

The nurse pulled Jason from the cubicle into the center of the room. Her name tag said Miss Levay, RN. "Nothing seems to be working," she said, concernedly. "The pulmonary wedge pressure has gone up despite everything. He's had the diuretic, the

hydralazine and the nitroprusside. I don't know what to do."

Jason glanced over Miss Levay's shoulder into the room. Mr. Lennox was breathing like a miniature locomotive. Jason didn't have any ideas save for a transplant, and of course, that was out of the question. The man was a heavy smoker and undoubtedly had emphysema as well as heart trouble. But Mr. Lennox should have responded to the medication. The only thing Jason could imagine was the area of the heart involved with the heart attack was extending.

"Let's get a cardiology consult stat," Jason said. "Maybe they'll be able to see if the coronary vessels are more involved. It's the only thing I can think of. Maybe he's a candidate for bypass."

"Well at least it's something," said Miss Levay. Without hesitation, she went to the central desk to call.

Jason returned to the cubicle to dispense some compassion to Brian Lennox. He wished he had more to give but the diuretic was supposed to reduce fluid while the hydralazine and nitroprusside were supposed to reduce pre-load and after-load on the heart. All of this was geared to lower the effort the heart had to expend to pump the blood. This would allow the heart to heal after the insult of the heart attack. But it wasn't working. Lennox was slipping downhill despite all the efforts and all the technology. His eyes now had a sunken, glazed appearance.

Jason put his hand on Brian's forehead and pushed the hair back from his perspiring brow. To Jason's surprise, some of the hair came out in his hand. Momentarily confused, Jason stared at it, then he carefully pulled on a few other strands. They came out as well with almost no resistance. Checking the pillow behind Brian's head, Jason noticed more hair. Not an enormous amount but more than he would suspect. It made him wonder if any of the medications he'd ordered had hair loss as a potential side effect. He made a mental note to look that up in the evening. Obviously hair loss was not a major concern at the time. But it reminded him of Mrs. Harring's comment. Curious!

After leaving word that he should be called after the cardiology consult on Brian Lennox and after one more masochistic glance at the sheet-wrapped corpse of Cedric Harring, Jason left the coronary care unit and took the elevator down to the second floor, which connected the hospital with the outpatient building. The GHP Medical Center was the impressive central facility of the large prepaid health plan. It incorporated a four-hundred-bed hospital with an ambulatory surgery center, separate outpatient department, a small research wing, and a floor of administrative offices. The main building, originally designed as a Sears office building, had an art deco flair. It had been gutted and totally renovated to incorporate the hospital and the administrative offices. The outpatient and research building was new, but it had been built to match the old struc-

ture, with the same careful details. It was built on pillars over a parking lot. Jason's office was on the third floor, along with the rest of the department of internal medicine.

There were sixteen internists at the GHP Center. Most were specialists, though a few like Jason maintained a generalized practice. Jason had always felt that the whole panoply of human illness interested him, not just specific organs or systems.

The doctors' offices were spread around the perimeter, with a central desk surrounded by a waiting area with comfortable seating. Examining rooms were clustered between the offices. At one end were small treatment rooms. There was a pool of support personnel who were supposed to rotate positions, but in actual fact the nurses and secretaries tended to work for one or another of the doctors. Such a situation promoted efficiency since there could be some adaptation to each doctor's eccentricities. A nurse by the name of Sally Baunan and a secretary by the name of Claudia Mockelberg had aligned themselves with Jason. He got along well with both women, but particularly Claudia, who took an almost motherly interest in Jason's well-being. She had lost her only son in Vietnam and contended that Jason looked just like him despite the age difference.

Both women saw Jason coming and followed him to his office. Sally had an armload of charts of waiting patients. She was the compulsive one, and

Jason's absence had disturbed her carefully planned routine. She was eager to "get the show on the road," but Claudia restrained her and sent her out of the room.

"Was it as bad as you look?" Claudia asked.

"Is it that obvious?" Jason said as he washed his hands at the sink in the corner of the room.

She nodded. "You look like you've been run over by an emotional train."

"Cedric Harring died," he said. "Do you remember him?"

"Vaguely," Claudia admitted. "After you got called to the emergency room, I pulled his chart. It's on your desk."

Jason glanced down and saw it. Claudia's efficiency was sometimes unnerving.

"Why don't you sit down for a few moments," Claudia suggested. More than anyone else at GHP, Claudia knew Jason's reaction to death. She was one of only two people at the Center in whom Jason had confided about his wife's fatal accident.

"We must be really behind schedule," Jason said. "Sally will get her nose bent out of shape."

"Oh, screw Sally." Claudia came around Jason's desk and pushed him gently into the seat. "Sally can hold her water for a few minutes."

Jason smiled in spite of himself. Leaning forward, he fingered Cedric Harring's chart. "Do you remember last month the two others who died just after their physicals?"

31

"Briggs and Connoly," Claudia said without hesitation.

"How about pulling their charts? I don't like this trend."

"Only if you promise me you're not going to let yourself"—Claudia paused, struggling for a word—"get into a dither over this. People die. Unfortunately it happens. It's the nature of the business. You understand? Why don't you just have a cup of coffee."

"The charts," Jason repeated.

"Okay, okay," Claudia said, going out.

Jason opened Cedric Harring's chart, glancing through the history and physical. Except for his unhealthy living habits, there was nothing remarkable. Turning to the EKG and the stress EKG, Jason scanned the tracing, looking for some sign of the impending disaster. Even armed as he was with hindsight, he could find nothing.

Claudia came back and opened the door without knocking. Jason could hear Sally whine, "Claudia . . ." but Claudia shut the door on her and came over to Jason's desk. She plopped down Briggs's and Connoly's charts in front of him.

"The natives are getting restless," she said, then left.

Jason opened the two charts. Briggs had died of a massive heart attack probably similar to Harring's. Autopsy had shown extensive occlusion of all of the coronary vessels despite the EKG done during his